Praise for Luan Goldie

'A beautiful novel. It was a real pleasure to read'
Jing-Jing Lee, *How We Disappeared*

'A compelling novel . . . The exquisite eye for
detail and delicate turn of phrase will linger
long after you've raced through the pages'
Guardian

'A warm, confident writer with the lightest of touches'
Observer

'Masterfully written – it had me completely
gripped from the very first page'
Beth O'Leary, *Sunday Times* **bestselling
author of** *The Flatshare*

'A stunning debut that heralds a new
and exciting voice in fiction'
Mike Gayle, *All The Lonely People*

'Flawlessly portrayed . . . A riveting read'
Candis

'Pacey and powerful'
Mail on Sunday

'The type of story that will stay with you
long after you've read the last page'
Closer

'Gripping from the get-go . . . Goldie's talent for writing
with pace and creating flawed characters you really grow to
care about, makes it all the more affecting . . . important'
Newcastle Evening Chronicle

'A beautiful story about family, relationships and love'
Prima

Luan Goldie is a primary school teacher from East London. Her debut novel *Nightingale Point* was longlisted for the Women's Prize for Fiction and the RSL Ondaatje Prize. She has written several short stories and is the winner of the Costa Short Story Award 2017 for her short story 'Two Steak Bakes and Two Chelsea Buns'. She was also shortlisted for the London Short Story Prize in 2018 and the *Grazia*/Orange First Chapter competition in 2012. In 2019 she was shortlisted for the h100 awards in the Publishing and Writing category. Her short stories have appeared in *HELLO!* magazine, *Sunday Express* and *The Good Journal*.

Also by Luan Goldie

Homecoming
Nightingale Point

London Borough of Tower Hamlets

THESE STREETS

LUAN GOLDIE

ONE PLACE. MANY STORIES

HQ
An imprint of HarperCollins*Publishers* Ltd
1 London Bridge Street
London SE1 9GF

www.harpercollins.co.uk

HarperCollins*Publishers*
1st Floor, Watermarque Building, Ringsend Road
Dublin 4, Ireland

This edition 2022

1
First published in Great Britain by
HQ, an imprint of HarperCollins*Publishers* Ltd 2022

ISBN: HB: 978-0-00-841967-7
TPB: 978-0-00-841965-3

MIX
Paper from
responsible sources
FSC™ C007454

For Auntie Elaine, Auntie Lorna and Auntie Irene

Chapter One

Jessica

'He's sent you a message. Wants to meet up.'

'Which one?' Jess leans over her daughter's shoulders and peeks at the screen. 'Oh, that one. Wants to meet? What, in real life?'

'Obviously,' Haze says, 'that's how it works, Mum.'

Jess feels slightly put out by how comfortable her eighteen-year-old is swiping for men online. 'How often do you do this? I hope you're not meeting anyone in real life from this website.'

Haze laughs, that kind of pitying chuckle she emits when Jess does or says something embarrassing.

'Course not. This site is for old people.' Haze wriggles her fingers then starts tapping her thumbs quickly across the screen. She's having too much fun with this.

'Stop it,' Jess says. 'I don't really want to meet a man, not in real life.'

'Yes, you do. You're always talking about wanting to meet men.'

'For fun, yes, not for—' Jess stops as her daughter scrunches up her nose. 'What I mean is I'm not interested in having a relationship.'

'Are you familiar with the term TMI? Anyway, I'm going to reset what you're looking for as some of the guys in your age bracket look primeval. You're way out of their league. Ooh, how about this one? He's a hard swipe right.'

'Stop. That's the third one you've done that to. I don't want them to think I'm easy.'

'You *are* easy. And they can't see if you like other people. I think it's time you met someone decent, someone who wants to buy you flowers and take you on mini-breaks. Enough of these divorced losers you keep meeting down the pub.'

Jess, offended by the truth, pulls herself up and snaps, 'As much as I'd like a romantic mini-break I don't have time for it, not between working six days a week, looking after you two, plus Pa, and running this place.' She stops and glances around the mess of the front room, the piles of washing not yet put away, the Hoover intentionally plugged in yet unused, and the magazines she said she'd clear. Some days all she does is domestic work, yet the place is constant chaos. 'Enough of this now.' She takes the phone and looks for a way to delete her profile, but someone catches her eye. Now *this* is a good-looking guy and with fifteen photos, doesn't he know it. Jess sinks back onto the sofa and enjoys the images of the kind-eyed man hanging off the monkey bars at his local park gym.

Haze takes the phone away. 'No. Just no. Your taste is horrible. Plus, he has four kids. That's four pieces of baggage to carry.'

'Most men my age are going to have children.'

'Yeah, and you need to avoid those men.'

'Why? I have children.'

'Jacob and I don't count as baggage. We'd enhance anyone's life.'

Jess laughs. 'You're full of it, Haze. How long have you been home anyway? I thought I asked you to do a bit of tidying.'

'I've been at college,' she pulls her laptop from the coffee table and hits a key, the page going straight to a paused YouTube video of Dua Lipa.

'What time does college finish?'

'Oh, you know, early.'

'How early?' Jess wonders, not for the first time, what her daughter's routine consists of. How can someone so high-achieving study so little and attend so few lessons? It's a complete mystery. For all Jess knows, Haze could be spending every day walking around Westfield eating pretzels. College is simply a word, some mythical place she claims to visit every so often. It's the same with her part-time job at Boost Juice. There's no hard evidence Haze does either of these things in real life.

'It's Friday,' Haze says.

'So?'

'Friday is sports day. There are never lessons in the afternoon.'

'In that case, shouldn't you be playing sport?'

'Don't be silly, Mum,' she laughs. 'Oh yeah, Dad asked you to call him.'

Jess groans. She'd already spoken to Steadman this week, or rather he talked to her. Endless ramblings about his new keep-fit regime and the camping trip he was planning to take Jacob on. Though he'd have more chance getting Jess into a tent than his son. Just then, Jacob comes down the stairs wearing a pink frilled apron over his school uniform and a pair of goggles on his head. He sits in his armchair and pulls a book and a Mars bar out from the side of the cushions.

'What are you reading, sweetheart?' Jess asks.

'*52 Times Britain was a Bellend*,' he says deadpan.

'Oh, that's nice. Is it for school?'

Haze laughs. 'It's definitely not a schoolbook. Though, at least it sounds educational.'

'I don't want my mind to be trapped within the National Curriculum,' Jacob says before putting half the chocolate bar in his mouth.

Jess makes a mental note to have a read of the book later. She adds it to the list of things she's got to do this evening, such as make dinner, hoover, empty the washing machine and call Pa to check he's consumed something other than Guinness and chicken wings today. Then, there's another, longer list, of all the things she's got to do at work tomorrow. Jess loves her job as a Community Theatre Outreach worker, but the end of April is always hell. She's got school workshops to plan, risk assessments to complete, funding bids to read and of course there's all that other moon-on-a-stick stuff her boss demands, which frankly isn't likely to happen unless she manages to add another five hours to each day.

She grabs her work iPad from her bag and composes a few emails, timing them to go out during working hours. There's so much to do all the time. Her mobile pings with a direct match from the dating website.

'Why are you groaning?' Haze asks.

'Because I'm drowning in admin. Here, help me out, delete my profile off this thing.'

Haze takes the phone and sighs. 'Mum, it's a Friday night and you're stuck inside doing risk assessments on an under-eighteens' production of *Oklahoma!*. Wouldn't you rather be getting into something slinky and heading out for a night on the town with this guy?' Haze holds the phone up, displaying a heavy-lidded man biting on his finger seductively.

Jess cackles then hides her face. 'Okay, enough now.'

'What's funny?' Jacob asks.

'Nothing, sweetheart.' Jess's knees click as she stands, then her elbows crick as she stretches above her head and lets out a yawn. 'Night on the town,' she laughs, 'if I can manage to stay up for Graham Norton it'll be an achievement.'

'You're still hot, you should be out there.'

'Err,' Jacob says, 'don't say Mum's hot.'

Jess prickles, as she knows she's still got it. She regularly gets honked at while walking home and gets chatted up down the Red Lion after work by men. Sure, some of them are questionable middle-aged men who have never kept a girlfriend longer than two months, but still. Plus, there's a young guy, can be no more than twenty-five, who covers the box office on weekends and he's always offering her *coffee*. Yeah, she's definitely still got it.

'I'm telling you, Mum, all you need is a good-fitting bra and off you go.'

Jess hoists her bra straps up. 'Good bras are expensive.'

'Look, they're always on display, so *invest* in the display.'

'Stop talking about bras,' Jacob shouts. 'I don't talk about pants around you guys, do I?' He shakes his fists in the air and cries, 'Is nothing sacred anymore?'

Jess laughs. 'Right, I'm going for a shower. One of you two start cooking, please.'

Jess stays in the shower till the water cools, which isn't long given the house's antique boiler. She heads into her bedroom and starts kicking clothes, both clean and dirty, into a pile to sort out tomorrow after work, or possibly on Sunday, if she has any energy left. As she moves to close the curtains she spots Mustafa, her landlord, strutting, because he is a man who struts, across the road. Then the doorbell goes downstairs. Shit. There are only two things Mustafa, who tries to keep a 'professional distance' from Jess, ever pops over for. The first and most unlikely is to pretend to fix something; among Jess's recent complaints have been a leaking tap, a stubborn patch of damp in the bathroom and of course the boiler. Though it's more likely he's here to bring up a rent increase. Every year it comes around, another fifty or so quid whacked on in return for what? It's not as if the place is getting any better. 'But the area,' he always says, 'it's on the up.' As if having more places to buy sourdough bread has any impact on Jess's living standards. This is the third time this week he's tried to get hold of her.

She cracks the bedroom door and tries to listen in, though it's too muffled and the screams of the baby in the house next door cut out everything anyway. Her phone's ringing. It's Steadman. Again. 'Oh, for fuck's—' She answers: 'Hi.'

'Hey, babe.'

'Steadman, I've had a manic day at work, can't talk long, okay.'

'Cool, cool. Me too. Real tired. Been on a run this afternoon. I did eleven minutes non-stop. That's a personal best. I didn't think my body could do it. I surprised myself. You know what they say: mind over matter.'

'I really can't chat right now. What is it?'

'Hazel's coming over to see me tomorrow, but Jacob won't commit. Can you have a word with him?'

'Jacob's thirteen. I can't tell him how to spend his weekends anymore.'

'I've sent him loads of suggestions of things we could do together. He's moaned about it all.'

'What kinds of things did you suggest?' Jess tightens her towel and looks outside again at Mustafa as he struts back across the road, stopping at the beautiful electric-blue Maserati he bought last year. He licks a finger and rubs at a spot on the hood.

'I've suggested cricket, tennis, swimming, even bowling – and that's not a real sport. I know he's not interested in football, so I don't go there anymore.'

'What about something non-sporty?' she asks, wondering if this is one of those calls where she can put him on loudspeaker until he wears himself out.

'Like darts?'

'Suggest something he enjoys. Like um, well, he's really getting into British history at the moment.'

'Okaaay.' Steadman sounds dubious.

'And of course horror – maybe you could go and see a film together. Though I don't know how much we should be encouraging him to watch that kind of stuff. Look, can we talk another time? I'm just out the shower and need to get dressed.'

'Oh. Are you naked?'

'Bye, Steadman.' She hangs up and begins her skincare routine from tip to toe, using several different cleansers, lotions, toners and stretch-mark creams before pulling on some round-the-house clothes and wrapping her hair into a scarf.

Downstairs, no one is cooking and the pile of laundry has collapsed onto the floor.

'What did Mustafa want?'

'He asked if you could pop over when you have a minute,' Haze says. 'I told him you would go after you made dinner.'

'Who says I'm making dinner?'

'Mum,' Haze pleads, 'we've got to eat. I would cook but I'm exhausted. I had back-to-back lessons all morning.'

'Just the morning?' Jess snorts. 'I wish I only worked in the mornings.'

'I also had a meeting with my tutor through lunch, so didn't even get to stop and eat. And then I had to trek all the way to Plaistow to pick up a book I ordered online, which turned out to be the wrong one.'

'I'm *also* tired,' Jess says, feeling the Friday-evening slump hit her. 'I *also* worked through lunch.'

Haze does a very theatrical yawn and opens a bottle of garishly coloured nail polish. 'Do you think this colour looks too Halloweeny?'

So that's it, Haze is just going to ignore her.

'Errr,' Jacob says as he pulls his goggles off, 'look at your nasty toes. What you putting them on the table for?'

'Because it's almost sandal season,' Haze replies.

Jacob puts his book down and shuffles onto the sofa with his sister. 'Will you do my nails too?'

Should he really be going to school with orange nails? 'Jacob,' Jess starts, but Haze shoots her a look. 'It's fine, Mum. It's not the nineties anymore. Loads of boys wear nail polish.'

Jess sighs and heads to the front door. 'Start cooking,' she yells once more as she slips her feet into Haze's Adidas sliders. Mustafa's being quite persistent; she might as well rip off this plaster and get it over with. She crosses the street, resisting the urge to stroke the Maserati as she passes, and rings the bell.

'Jess.' It's as if he was waiting by the door. 'I've been trying to catch up with you all week.'

'Has it really been a week? Sorry, I've been busy.'

'We need to talk. Come in.'

In the twelve years Mustafa has been Jess's landlord and neighbour she's only ever been in his place twice. Once when she first came to get the keys and a second time when she locked herself out during a storm. She had perched on his

sofa, awkwardly trying to breastfeed Jacob while simultaneously praying Haze wouldn't break anything in the pristine
living room.

'Ooh,' he says, 'we're a no-shoes house.'

'Oh. Of course.'

'There're slippers, if you want?' he says, nodding to a wicker
basket filled with fresh white pairs.

She declines and pads through in her bare feet. The living
room hasn't changed much: all white walls, glittery ornaments
and cream carpets. Jess had made a joke back then about
having kids and cream carpets, and Mustafa corrected her by
saying they weren't cream but 'cascading white'.

'Shall I ask Inayah to get you a tea or coffee?' he asks.

Again, she declines, not wanting to make this visit any
longer than it needs to be. Plus, it always makes her awkward
to see Inayah, as Jess is convinced she knew that her and
Mustafa once had a bike-shed kiss back in school.

'There's no easy way to say this,' he starts.

Really? Because she hasn't even sat down yet.

He opens his mouth and closes his eyes. Here it comes. A
£75 rent hike . . . £100 . . . £200 . . .

'I'm selling up.'

'What?'

He nods.

'Selling? You're leaving?'

He exhales dramatically and flicks his eyes open. 'Yeah, I'm
done. We're offski.' He sits down on one of the white sofas and
gestures for her to do the same. 'The Upton Park house too.'

'Oh.' He was always alluding to the Upton Park house as

if it were his family's second home, the same way one of the theatre directors once said for Christmas he was going back to 'the Barbados house'.

'And,' he takes another breath, 'yours.'

'What?' Something shifts beneath her.

'All three. I'm selling all three.'

What is he talking about? This isn't what he was meant to talk to her about.

'You saw what happened to the house down the road. Went in a day, and I heard for well over the asking price.' She remembers it. The leaflets coming through the door from the estate agency warning, *Do not be alarmed! This Saturday you will see many people on your road. They are desperate for properties in this area.* Though they've been desperate ever since the Olympics were announced, since the Westfield shopping centre opened, since Newham became the last place you could buy a family house in London without having to sell your first-born.

But all that was irrelevant, because Kenmure Street was proper Stratford. Full of people who dropped their Hs, washed their doorsteps and rented property off boys they went to school with.

'Why are you selling? Surely, it's better for you to keep rent coming in?'

'This place is worth over half a million,' he says, straight-faced. 'I had it valued last month. Crazy when you think how much I paid for it pre-2012. It was pocket change, Jess, pure pocket change.'

She lets out a laugh, a dry, hacking sort of laugh. 'Half a million?' He's talking rubbish.

'I know, world's gone mad,' he says. 'People are really dropping big bucks to live here, in Stratford.'

But her place definitely isn't worth half a million. It's hard to imagine it being worth anything to anyone other than her family. Even when Mustafa first rented it out to her, it was like she was doing him a favour by living in it. She sort of assumed she'd stay there forever.

'I want to get yours valued ASAP. I'm not sure what kind of price we're looking at for it. It's not really in tip-top shape, is it? Bit run-down. Would it be all right if I got in to do a bit of smartening up? Lick of paint, cut the grass back, quick window wash, that sort of thing.'

Why is he still talking? This can't be happening.

'Next week all right with you?'

'Next week? No. I'm still trying to process what you're telling me. What it all means.'

'Jess, we've spoken about this before.'

'Have we?' She tries to recall him bringing this up during one of their brief chats on the street over the years. Her mind is too muddled to think straight.

'Yeah, I've been saying I'm looking to leave London for ages.'

'We all say that "leaving London" shit. I didn't think you would be one to do it.' Her voice is so much louder and angrier than it sounded in her head.

Mustafa looks down at his hands, at his perfectly manicured nails. This is embarrassing now. Jess, sitting here barefoot in joggers, in his perfect home, shouting her mouth off and about to cry.

'Sorry, girl, you're a great tenant, you really are. Especially when I think of how much trouble the Upton Park house gives me. I don't want to judge, but it's a house for a family and when I pop by it's filled to the rafters with men. Builders – you know the type.'

She wipes her nose with the back of her hand.

'I've always looked out for you,' his voice softens, 'and I've let you pay well below market rate for years.'

Is this true? She doesn't even have a rough idea of what the standard rent on a three-bedroom place would be around here. She's heard the young people at work moaning about their rent, though she's sure they all live around Hackney in converted bagel factories with concierge services and on-site gyms.

'We've never really done the contract thing either, have we?' Mustafa asks.

When she originally moved in, her contract was for twelve months; then it ended and they never bothered doing another one. She's lost count of the times someone has told her how risky it was, how she would have no rights if Mustafa wanted her out. She's never worried. Until now.

'I need time.' Her voice is strained by a rising lump of dread in her throat.

'Course. I'm not telling you to move out tomorrow, am I? I looked into it and the standard would be one month's notice.'

'A month? I wouldn't even be able to pair up my shoes in that time.' The lump comes out as a sob.

'Okay, okay, maybe longer. Once we get it cleaned up, then valued, then sold, two months maybe. Three even. It's what, end of April now, so sometime in June. Though if I'm honest, it's easier for me to sell if,' he contorts his face into something he probably thinks conveys apology, 'you guys aren't still living there.'

'No. I wouldn't want to risk putting off any potential buyers with my family.'

He gets up and hands her a tissue box, which is studded with diamanté. She wipes her face as she pictures herself and the kids standing out on the corner while strangers traipse through their home calling out prices for it.

'I'm sorry,' Mustafa says.

It's a little uncomfortable, because even though they've known each other since they were eleven, she's never cried in front of him.

'I really didn't think you'd be this upset. You're always moaning about the place: this needs fixing, that needs replacing.'

'It's home.' She looks around his beautiful, perfect living room. He has everything. Why would anyone leave this? 'Where are you going anyway?'

'Surrey, for the grammar schools.'

'What's wrong with our school? Your son has done great there, as you're always telling me.'

'Yeah, but that kid's a legend, he'd do well anywhere. And all this academy stuff is fake. Just cause they send a few kids off to Cambridge, it doesn't mean it's a good school.'

'Haze is tipped to go to Oxford actually,' Jess corrects, because it's important people get it right.

'Oxford, of course. You have told me that before.'

Yes, she has. So why does he keep dismissing it? 'And

you know she's getting a scholarship too? They want her that much.'

Mustafa nods quickly, almost dismissively. 'Still, though,' he says, 'she's in the minority.'

'You and I both went through St Margaret's when it was at its roughest and we came out all right.'

'Not like that for everyone though, is it?'

She shifts in her seat, on edge, because she knows what he means. He's talking about Dominic. It's so rare that Mustafa ever mentions her brother, she sometimes forgets he knew him.

'St Margaret's has been great for us,' she says defensively. 'Haze loved it there, she absolutely excelled. And Jacob, well, he's also starting to . . .' she pauses and tries to think of the most appropriate word: 'settle.'

'It's different for your two. Hazel was every teacher's pet, and Jacob . . .' he trails off.

'Jacob what?' Though Jess knows what's coming.

Mustafa reddens.

'Go on then,' Jess goads, 'exactly why is it different for Jacob?'

'I just meant that he's not academic.'

'How do you know Jacob's not academic?'

'I just thought with his . . .' Mustafa lifts a finger to his ear and twirls it.

'Deafness,' she fills in. 'You can say it, don't worry, it's not catching. And it doesn't stop him being academic. It doesn't stop him from anything. The school *is* great and it's been great for him.'

15

Mustafa lifts his shoulders. 'We all want different things.'

Yes, she thinks; there's so much she wants, for herself, for her kids. But right now, it feels like she's not likely to get any of them. She sinks her head into her hands, and is it her imagination or does the carpet smell like lilies? Of course, Mustafa would have perfumed carpets, because his life is practically perfect in every bloody way.

'I've got four boys, Jess. I can't have them growing up round here. You saw what happened last week? That kid was only sixteen.'

'It's always like this after a stabbing. Everyone panics and feels vulnerable for a bit, then the police tape comes down and we get on with life. Anyway, it was a gang thing. Those types of killings aren't random.'

'You tell that to his parents.'

Jess pictures the boy's poor family at a graveside and feels shame. Has she really become this desensitised to youth violence?

Mustafa looks down. 'It's changing round here. Can't you see it?'

'Yeah, of course I can. When we were teenagers, we had nothing. It was marshes and factories. *Now* there's Westfield and a velodrome and an Olympic pool and an airport and—'

'Mass brawls at the bus station, stabbings every week, and the homeless. Jess, come on. Before, you'd only see a few in the park, now they're all over the place, in tents along the main road, walking shoeless in the park, shooting up outside Wilko's. I don't want my kids growing up seeing that.'

'Why? You're making me homeless. Right now. Do you realise that's exactly what you're doing?'

'No, it's not,' he snaps at her. 'You're not going to end up in a tent with your kids, are you?'

She cowers back, again embarrassed. Is she being over-dramatic? 'I thought you liked it here.'

'I do. I love it here, it's home. But it's not good enough for my family.'

He walks her to the door. 'I'm sorry it's turned out this way.'

She nods and sulks off; what else is there to say? She's too angry to be buddy with him right now, to try and 'understand' his position.

'Jess,' he calls after her. She turns and the sun glints off the electric blue of the car hood. 'There is a solution if you don't want to move.'

'Really, and what's that?'

'You could buy it off me.'

She laughs and continues across the street, back to her home of twelve years, which no longer feels like it.

Chapter Two

Ben

At first Ben thought Skype was a miracle. He had banged on to anyone who would listen about how amazing it was, how it meant that he could keep in touch with his daughter despite her being almost 2,000 miles away. But that was before. Before their daily call was relegated to weekly and before Olivia turned six and instead of going to her birthday party, he got a video call.

The calls are also used by Shanice, his ex-wife, to clarify details. The last one being that he wasn't really welcome to 'hop on a flight to Spain' anytime he liked, to visit. So now, almost two months after his daughter has left the country, Skype has fully lost its appeal. And as much as he looks forward to his calls with Olivia, he's also come to dread the depression that sinks in after. The sense of disconnect that derives from not being able to feel the insane amount of heat her little body radiates as she tells one of her long, confusing stories.

Olivia blows a kiss at the screen, coming so close her lips blur. It's too cute. 'Hello, Daddy.'

'Hey, Squid, how are you?'

Again, the screen distorts as she butts her nose against the camera. 'Can you see me?'

'Yeah. Sit back a little.'

Shanice cuts in, ordering Olivia to sit on the chair properly. She probably puts out the most uncomfortable stool so Olivia gets restless quickly. Also, Ben's not the type to time it, but he swears the calls have been getting progressively shorter.

'Daddy, is that your new house?'

He lifts the laptop and shows her around the small open-plan living-room-kitchen. 'Yeah. You like it?'

'The walls look like porridge.'

'I noticed.'

'Where are the toys?'

'Don't worry, by the time you come to stay with me this place will be filled with toys.' The summer holidays, it's so far away. Though this was the agreement he made with his ex, that Olivia be given a good chunk of time to fully settle into her new life abroad without disruption. *Disruption* being the way Shanice had taken to describing Ben.

'Where's Harold?'

Ben angles the laptop towards his feet, getting a slumbering Harold in shot. 'He misses you.'

'Hello, Prime Minister,' she waves. Olivia has no clue what Prime Minister means yet loves the fact Harold is named after one. 'I miss him too. Mummy says I can get a new dog if I want, but I said no. I only want Harold.'

'Ah, that's sweet.' For the first few weeks after Olivia left,

Ben had sent a stream of Harold photos. Harold with a paw on the remote control, Harold eating a pizza crust he found in the street, Harold attempting to bury a rubber glove in the local park. Then Shanice told him to stop, that it was too upsetting for Olivia to be reminded so often of the pet she left behind.

'Daddy, I need to show you something. You're going to be very excited when you seeee it,' she sings.

'What is it?' He doesn't want her to go anywhere, to get anything. She hops down from her stool. 'No,' he starts as she takes off, her gangly legs running out of shot. And this is the other thing he hates about Skype, that Olivia's not quite old enough to get it, so most of their conversations end up like this, with him trying to keep her in front of the camera, to stop her wandering off mid-conversation to fetch some toy or snack, or to go and poop for fifteen minutes.

Shanice rarely comes on the call. She mostly sets it up and leaves them to it, out of sight, though definitely not out of mind. He knows she's in the room, listening, rolling her eyes or pulling one of her many practised to perfection condescending faces. Why can't she come on the call and fill in the blanks for him? Reassure him that Olivia will be back soon and, by the way, here's how she's been getting on at her new school, with her new friends, with speaking a new language, without you. Of course, she wouldn't do that, not for him.

He stares at the screen, empty of his daughter yet filled with his ex-wife's upgraded life. Her dream kitchen; a breakfast bar, copper pots, an American-style fridge plastered with photos of her, Olivia and Gerald. She's rubbing it in his face that she still has a family, while he has what? Skype?

Harold stands, walks in a little circle and sits back down on Ben's feet.

'Daddy, are you ready?' A big blonde doll fills the screen. It sings, its voice box so close to the mic it distorts. Olivia joins in, and her voice is possibly the only thing Ben doesn't love about her with every ounce of his being.

'That's so nice,' he says, and it plays again. Together, they had watched both *Frozen* films hundreds of times, not to mention all the spin-offs and the ice show, a day out that cost more than West Ham tickets, though worth every penny to see the pure happiness on Olivia's face.

'*Into the Unknownnn*,' she sings. 'I'll play it for you one more time, okay?'

'No, Squid. Why don't you show me your—'

Again, she presses the thing against the camera and he spends another two minutes not looking at his daughter's lovely little face, her fast-changing face, but a creepy plastic doll with eyes spaced too far apart.

'Daddy, I've got to go now. My lunch is ready. We're having Pinocchio.'

'Pinocchio?'

Then a voice from behind says, 'Gnocchi' and Gerald, all sixteen stone of him, steps into shot. It's still so hard to believe that Shanice, who used to criticise Ben for not being fashionable or muscular, would leave him for a khaki-wearing, overweight pastry chef from Plymouth. Gerald registers the laptop and Ben's reaction before quickly stepping away.

'Gnocchio,' Olivia says, giving Gerald her normal everyday smile. Far from the light-up smile she gives Ben. 'Elsa, say bye to Daddy.' The blonde doll hits the camera, its big eye the last thing Ben sees before the video blinks off.

'Right then, that's done.' He looks around his flat. Four days in and he's still not settled. Maybe he never will be. Maybe this is what the 'home' of a single, divorced, middle-aged man is meant to look like. Soulless, bare and kind of porridge-coloured. If he's honest he's not sure what's missing from it. All his stuff is here and he has tried to make it homely. He even bought a picture frame and got some photos printed from his phone to go in it. All of Olivia.

Ben leans down to pat Harold's side. 'Mate, what's going on? You've never smelt worse.' He checks the weather through the window of the Juliette balcony. The estate agent was so pleased with herself when she listed the balcony as one of the flat's merits. He had to look it up to discover it meant a fake balcony. 'Time for a walk?' he tries. Harold flaps one big brown ear but moves little else.

The park below the balcony is mostly full of parents with their kids on bikes and scooters. There are also teenagers everywhere taking part in various phone-related activities: posing, watching, scrolling. Then there are the drunks, who Ben found out yesterday are referred to locally as Fight Club. They gather around the war memorial, sharing Pringles and White Lightning. Families. Teens. Drunks. Ben doesn't fit into any of these boxes. What are single men meant to do on Saturday mornings anyway?

Moving back to East London seemed like the perfect tonic following his breakdown last year, and Ben was certain the city where he grew up would offer him endless entertainment and distraction to stop anything like that from happening again. Plus, his straight-talking mum was close by, should he feel down again. Though he doesn't see himself as that needy anymore. Those feelings are behind him. He's looking forward. Forward to his newly single life, including his new job in maintenance for Travelodge hotels, which came with a great package and a fire warden jacket.

He rattles the lead at the front door and waits for Harold to half-heartedly pad out, resigned to the inevitable prospect of another walk.

'Don't look at me like that, it's a nice park.' Ben clips the lead on. 'I know the other dogs are not the type of crowd you'd usually mix with. It's good to make new friends.' Harold trots down the stairs behind Ben. 'We can't judge other dogs because their owners name them things like Chainz, Bowie or Baby Shark.' Ben stops outside to pick up some empty Budweiser bottles at the foot of a tree. There are new ones almost every day. At least they're not smashed this time.

'*Bună dimineața,*' a voice calls from outside the house on the other side of the street.

'Morning,' Ben calls back. Despite the man's long jet-black hair, he looks old.

'*Dzień dobry,*' the man says. 'Polish? Romanian?'

'Sorry?' Ben asks as he crosses over.

The man looks confused. 'Czech?' He squints behind thick-rimmed glasses.

'Am I Czech? No.'

'Oh,' the man laughs, 'you're English?'

Ben's never been good with people's accents, but this man

definitely has one, so he hazards a guess. 'Are you, umm, Polish?'

'Pfff. Not travelled much, have you, son? I'm *German*,' he says, accentuating his accent. 'Though I've lived on this street for a hundred years so I'm pretty much a cockney. Welcome. Where are you from?'

'Originally, here. But I've lived in Essex for the last twenty-odd years.'

'Extraordinary. The last time a British white person moved onto this street was October 1989.'

Ben knows there's something about his particular blond hair, blue-eyed brand of whiteness that often attracts racist rhetoric. 'Happy to add to the mix,' he says, keen to shut it down. 'It's one of the greatest things about London, the diversity.'

'Tell me about it,' the man says. 'When I married my first wife, in 1971, we couldn't walk down these streets without a comment.'

'Because you're German?'

'No,' he hoots, 'because she was black. By 1977, with the second wife, things were easier, but we don't talk about *her*,' he laughs, leaning over to punch Ben lightly on the arm. 'Ah, can you hear something? It's my phone ringing.'

'Oh, okay, see you around.'

'No,' the man says, holding up a finger, 'don't go anywhere yet, I haven't told you what days the bins get collected.' He disappears into his house, leaving Ben standing on the other side of the wall. Sometimes Ben wonders how much of his life he's spent chatting with elderly neighbours. It was one of the things Shanice used to complain about. 'It's like they see you coming,' she'd said once, as if being sociable was the equivalent of being robbed.

'I couldn't find it,' the man says as he comes back out. 'It was probably those people from Help the Aged, they're always calling me. Wolf,' he says, sticking his hand out.

'Ben.'

'And who's this mutt?'

'This is Harold.'

Harold, who's hardly moved all morning, makes a bunch of quick strides into Wolf's lowering arms.

'Strong name for an animal.'

'I can't believe he's letting you pet him like this.'

'Why not? Beagles are friendly.'

'Not this one. He's usually quite bad-tempered. What's going on? Do you have bacon in your pocket?'

'Animals love me, it's a gift. How's the flat? You settled in?'

Ben nods. 'I guess so. Wasn't much to settle.'

'No. Because you hardly had any shtuff.' The way he says *stuff* makes Ben smile. 'I saw you. One van, was that really all?'

'People are always saying you realise how much you own when you move. I found the opposite.'

'Have you met the woman who lives in the flat below yours yet?'

'No. There are so many people in and out of that place.'

'Exactly. But it's just one woman who lives there, a sexy one. Have you seen her?' Wolf grips his chest. 'Watching her clack up and down this street is the highlight of my day.

She's like a young Hedy Lamarr. Though I think maybe she's a woman of *abilities*.'

Ben laughs then catches himself.

'Where were you off to before I intercepted you?'

'Taking this one for a walk.'

Harold bites at a thread hanging from Wolf's sleeve. 'Really? He looks like he's ready for a nap.'

'He's thirteen. He always looks that way.'

'I feel the same way about walking in Stratford Park. I'd much rather go to the pub, oh yes I would,' he baby-talks as Harold jumps up and down, 'would you like to come too? Would you like to have a shandy with Wolf and the boys?'

That's what's missing from Ben's life. The pub. And the boys. Not that he ever had 'boys', just a few colleagues and the odd dad from the school gates.

Wolf grabs onto the wall as he stands back up. 'So, it's Tuesday for the rubbish and every second Friday for the recycling. Don't put glass in your recycling though, it blows their tiny minds.'

'Right, got it. Thanks. And where can I get a good take-away around here?'

'There's a chicken shop every ten metres, what more do you want?'

'Yeah. I'm not a huge fan. There used to be a great Moroccan place.'

'Why would you ever pay for Moroccan food? Anyone can make couscous. I have a cookbook actually, hold on.'

He steps back inside and Ben calls after him, 'Oh no, really, don't bother.'

'It's no bother at all.' Wolf scans a wall of book spines in the hallway, beckons Ben in and hands him a large hardback cookbook with a brown cover falling off.

'Secrets of the *Turkish* Diet,' Ben reads.

'It's all very samey,' Wolf says. 'You can keep that. I'm having a clear-out. Let's see what else I can palm off on you today.'

Harold pulls at the lead as he makes a break closer to Wolf. 'It's fine, come in, come in.'

'Big reader then?'

Wolf takes in the books as if surprised to see them, 'Oh, these. Yes, this is the section I'm trying to sort out.'

'Section? There's more?'

'A couple more, yes. Are you a reader?'

Ben blows out a breath. 'If they make something into a film, I'm interested, other than that—'

'Philistine,' Wolf says. 'Though I don't read fiction. Fiction is for films. These are all fact. What is it you do for work?'

'I'm in maintenance, I work for Travelodge.'

'I once spent a very exciting night in an Ipswich Travelodge with a lady whose name I cannot recall. What do you know about shelving? I'm thinking of getting these replaced.'

'Er,' Ben pushes the underside of one of the bowing book-shelves, 'I've never seen MDF hold so much weight.'

'And radiators. Any knowledge in that department? I've been looking at hiring someone to come and bleed mine. That's a nasty little phrase, isn't it?'

'I could do that for you. It's a ten-minute job.'

'Good. I can pay you in food, since you don't cook,' he laughs. 'Which reminds me, hold on a minute.'

Again he disappears.

Ben turns the book over in his hands and wonders how to get away. In between the books is a framed photo of a young woman in a striped tie and navy blazer, being handed a certificate. The picture isn't the sharpest, though it's clearly a St Margaret's uniform and the older woman in the photo is Mrs Anderson, a teacher so disengaged she once began an English lesson by telling those who didn't want to learn to shut their books and lay their heads on the tables.

'You're not allergic to nuts, are you, son?' Wolf asks as he returns, this time holding a bowl covered in tinfoil.

Ben flinches away from the photo. Even the uniform makes him freeze up inside, he hated that school so much.

'I once gave nuts to the child next door and you'd think I'd given him a toke on a crack pipe the way the mum reacted.' He pauses to pull his trousers up and adjust the belt round his skinny waist. 'That's my Jess,' he nods towards the photo, 'there she is getting her attendance award. Can you imagine how bad a school is when you get a prize for simply showing up. Though this was a long time ago. It's one of these fancy academies now, outstanding and inclusive. My grandson tells me they no longer launch chairs at teachers during hymn practice.'

Throwing a chair at a teacher was among the tamer pursuits happening back when Ben was at the school.

'Apple kuchen.'

'Sorry?' Ben asks.

Wolf nods to the bowl in his hands. 'It's cake and I made too much. See it as a house-warming gift.'

'Thanks.' Again Ben looks up at the shelf, this time noticing a certificate, for attendance, and the name Jessica Bakker.

'Your surname's Bakker?'

Wolf turns his nose up and repeats it with an accent.

Dominic's surname was definitely Bakker. But German? He wasn't German. Ben's sure of it. Though how many mixed-race kids called Bakker could there have been at St Margaret's? 'You have any other kids?' Ben asks.

Wolf shakes his shoulders, like he just got a shiver and says, 'No, just my Jess.'

One kid. So it's a coincidence then.

'Right, son, the pub is calling. Adieu, adieu,' he says, stroking Harold.

Ben steps back out onto the street and wanders across to the park.

Dominic Bakker.

Ben feels like he spent a whole year of his life thinking of nothing other than him. Then he left Newham and never thought of Bakker again. He always knew there was a risk coming back here, that it would be impossible to live in the same area and not run into someone who knew him from back then or had some vague recollection of what happened. It was all so long ago. What does it matter if Dominic Bakker is some distant nephew of the friendly old man who lives across the road? It doesn't matter. It doesn't matter at all.

Chapter Three

Jess

Even in her most boring days of early motherhood, Jess would never have dreamed of paying £10 to watch her kids roll around on the floor to a Michael Rosen poem at the local theatre. Not that she could have afforded to do that anyway. Yet, following a recent appraisal with her boss, Brainstorming Norman, Jess had agreed that a Baby and Me Music and Movement Group was exactly the type of event she should be running as part of her community outreach work.

'Busy today,' Precious says, walking over. Walking being a generous way to describe the movement of the most pregnant woman Jess has ever seen.

'I know, apparently someone put it in the Yummy Newham Mummies WhatsApp group.'

'If I ever join that group, you can kill me.'

'How are you doing?' Jess asks, putting both hands on her friend's stomach.

'I've got haemorrhoids.'

'Oh,' Jess recoils. 'Still, not long left. Soon enough you'll be back here for Music and Movement.'

Precious scrunches up her nose as she takes in the crowd of mums entering the auditorium. 'Actually, I see myself as being more of a Tchaikovsky for Toddlers kind of parent.'

'I can't believe how popular this class is. When Norman suggested it, I laughed.'

'Middle-class people love this sort of stuff,' Precious says.

'Yeah, I guess so. I didn't realise there were so many of them around here.'

Jess checks the addresses on the mailing list sign-up sheet. Yep, the women are mostly local. When did things change so much? She hadn't even noticed it happening. Sure, there was a difference in the types of cafes that had started opening in the area, an increase in white wooden-slat blinds on the houses and, as Pa was always pointing out, a larger selection of alternative milks in the supermarkets. Jess thought of these as good things, though now, looking at the women, she feels a slight twinge of . . . What is it, resentment? Are *they* the reason she's having to move? Is her family, each of them born and bred within this postcode, having to move on to make space for families with more money?

Another two mums come in, pushing their brightly coloured pushchairs. One baby eats a mini rice cake and the other chews on a bamboo toothbrush.

'Good morning, ladies,' Jess says. 'Are you here for Music and Movement?' She spends some time answering their questions and complimenting their babies before they walk off.

Precious laughs. 'Why do they all sound the same?'

'Who?'

'These middle-class mums. You notice how not one of them has an East London accent?'

'You're being really judgemental. Would you be able to tell I'm from East London based on my accent?'

Again Precious laughs.

'Fine. Don't answer that.'

Precious takes a half packet of Maryland cookies from her pocket. 'How's the house search going?'

'It's not. I haven't started looking yet.'

'How long have you got?'

Jess stuffs a cookie in her mouth and crunches with great effort. 'Who knows? I mean, is he really going to sell it?'

'A three-bedroom with a garden, walking distance from the station? Yes, he's definitely going to sell it. Probably to one of these chicks,' Precious says, pointing to the auditorium.

'Two of the bedrooms have mould, the garden is mostly thorns and cat shit, and what counts as walking distance anyway? Because, depending on the shoes, it's a bus ride for me.'

'Jess, you might need to accept this is happening.'

'Hmm.' Jess opens her emails and scrolls through the hundreds of things she has to action today. There's no time to stress about housing.

'Has he had it valued yet?' Precious asks.

'Oh, he keeps talking about that. He was over last night, poking around. Says someone will come next week.'

'Next week? That's quick. I really think you need to start looking.'

'Oh look, there's an email from Brainstorming Norman. Did you get it too? He's cancelled all training sessions.'

'Jess?'

'Sorry.' She puts the iPad down.

'How much do you pay for that palace anyway?'

'Grand a month.'

'A thousand pounds? Your landlord lets you pay a thousand? What have you been doing? Getting changed with the curtains open?'

'It's a fair price.'

'It's robbery. You've literally been robbing him for years.'

'We went to school together. I think he fancied me back then, though not now. Now he only has eyes for his car, he's always stroking it, which is weird because I regularly see him pat his wife on the head. Why have they cancelled all the training courses?'

'Because God is good.'

'I was quite looking forward to it.' Jess loves a training day, a chance to zone out in front of some expert's PowerPoint presentation. 'I need to get hold of Norman to ask when they're hiring your replacement.'

'You know full well they're not going to do that. They're simply going to merge our roles while I drag out my maternity leave for as long as possible. And Jess, when they do that, you need to ask for more money. It's not fair the way you keep taking on so much and not getting paid for it.'

'Hmm.'

'Have you ever asked for a pay rise before?'

'I've never needed to. They should know what I'm worth.'

'They don't, and nor do they care. All they know is you love this place with all your heart. You'd probably work here for free, wouldn't you?'

Jess smiles because it's true. Volunteering at The Anstey was one of the first things she did when Haze started nursery. She knew no one was falling over themselves to hire a twenty-year-old with a handful of bad GCSEs and a baby. So, three times a week she came here to answer the phones, serve the coffee and help the performers get changed backstage. It was more than a year later when they offered her a paid position, a fifteen-hour, minimum-wage contract. That moment remains a career highlight.

Jess bites her bottom lip. She really could do with a proper sit-down meeting with Norman. One where she comes out of it with more money rather than simply more work.

'Jess?' Precious asks. 'Do you want me to help you?'

'With asking for more money?'

'Yes. And with the house search.'

'Oh, that. I was sort of planning to ignore it and hope it goes away.'

'Grand a month,' Precious says, shaking her head. 'You're in for a big dose of reality.'

Jess has never quite got the hang of alerts, so between the tube station and Pa's place she feels her phone ping continuously with all the property bulletins Precious signed her up for. They had sat in the staff-room together at lunch, going through Zoopla, an endless sorting of lowest to highest price, miles from tube station, prevalence of knife crime, etc. All that searching, getting more and more depressed with each reset of the tabs, only to find she couldn't afford anything other than an ex-council flat on Canvey Island with a toilet behind a curtain in the kitchen.

It all reminds her of those horrible few months her and Steadman spent looking for their first place together. They were both young, broke and too unqualified to do anything. Plus, she was pregnant. It was terrifying, trudging around grotty flats, trying to imagine herself as a new mum on one of the area's notorious estates, bumping a pram up four flights of stairs. However, the worst part of it was how everyone expected her to accept it. Like because she made the choice to have children young, she should have been happy to lower her standards. Her brother, Dominic, had enjoyed taunting her about becoming 'one of those girls'. She didn't even have to ask what he meant; it was obvious he had written her off as someone who would never achieve anything more than having babies. As if his achievements – two convictions by the time he was twenty – were so enviable. It hurt. Though, of course Jess doesn't feel this anymore because she's come through it and managed to not only raise two amazing children but also build a career for herself.

Ping. Ping. Ping.

She stops and looks at the property alerts, wondering how necessary a living room really is. Maybe now that Haze and Jacob are older, they would be happy to go without a communal family space, to eat on their laps and watch TV on their phones. She's already accepted that a garden is out of the question, as are windows that look out onto things other than brick walls. Of course, she's not told the kids any of this. When she returned from Mustafa's the other evening, she simply feigned a headache and slipped into bed, leaving them to eat toast for dinner and watch Netflix downstairs.

Pa opens the front door and immediately launches into a tirade about potholes. She's not sure when he started doing this, cutting out basic greetings and going directly into one of his rants. It's an annoying habit, one that tires her out before she's even through the door.

'And the worst thing is,' he says, the smell of beer on his breath, 'you have to report them online. Through an apt, can you believe?'

'You mean the app? The Newham app. It's very good.'

'Why can't you tell the lady at the desk anymore? Why can't you tell her to apt it?'

They reach the kitchen, which is fuggy with the smell of cinnamon and apple.

'Not sure, Pa. I'll do it for you later.' Though she won't. He doesn't even drive, why does he give a crap about potholes? 'Are the kids here yet?'

He waves a hand. 'I sent them to Lidl. They were talking too much and I couldn't hear the radio.'

The hot-pink Hello Kitty stereo is blasting Kisstory. Jess turns it down and opens the fridge, glad to see it full of fresh vegetables and fruit, which will hopefully be eaten rather than left to rot. 'You've been shopping. Good. And what are you making for dinner? Do you need any help with it?'

'I made two trays of apple kuchen. I had to use up the flour. It goes funny when it rains.'

This has become another habit of his, baking twenty portions of cake for no reason, then forgetting to make an actual meal.

'Did you have lunch at the pub?' she asks, suspecting this is where he's spent most of the day.

'No, because I don't understand the menu anymore. Hand-cut chips. What are they on about? What were they using to cut them before?' he shouts, throwing his arms up in the air. 'I went to the cinema, then popped into Millennium Fried Chicken on the way home.'

'You had chicken and chips? Again? You shouldn't be eating like that.'

He waves her away, like she's worrying too much, like he's not about to turn eighty.

'I'm going to make eggs for dinner,' he says, lifting a frying pan before putting it back down and sitting across from her. 'I'll put some cucumber on the side. Jacob does eat cucumber, doesn't he? I know he has some conspiracy theories about fresh produce.'

'You're drunk,' she says.

'No. I'm tipsy.' He glares at her over his glasses, 'Jessica, *Liebling*?'

'Yes?' Why is he staring at her like this? Does he know? Already? Has he somehow, through his large network of gossips, found out Mustafa is selling up and she's about to move into a mobile home off the A13?

He reaches across the table and gestures for her hand.

'I know you're very busy with work, so I really appreciate you and the kids coming over to eat with me.'

Jess nods and tries to smile, though surely Pa knows how little joy she takes coming here and eating his hugely fattening meals several times a week. But she sucks it up because she's all he has now. Her and the kids.

The front door opens and the kids come in. Haze starts emptying shopping, mostly junk food, from her rucksack, while Jacob unrolls a pair of dungarees with high-visibility stripes. 'Check this out,' he says. 'These were only £9.99.'

'You should have seen what he *didn't* buy,' Haze says. 'Lidl is so random. I can't wait till I'm deep pocketed enough to shop exclusively at Waitrose.'

'Hazel, could you help me?' Pa asks. 'There's a song I like. I heard it on the radio. Do that thing on your phone to find it. It goes like this . . .' Pa hums off tune until Haze starts to join in with lyrics. 'Yes, I love that song too,' she says. 'Check out Opa, getting into K-pop.'

'Can you turn it down?' Jacob moans. 'I hate K-pop. Like, why do they have to put so many people in one group? It's confusing.'

'You hate K-pop yet you watched a Blackpink video seventy times one weekend?' Haze says.

'I like learning the dance routines,' he snaps back.

Music has never been something Jacob has been able to enjoy, yet he does love to dance. 'You're a great dancer, hun.'

'Mum,' Haze laughs, 'he's not really looking at the choreography.'

'Shut up, Haze,' he shouts. 'Unless you want me to put on my dungarees and dance all over you.'

Haze turns the stereo off and starts tapping on the table. 'Come on then. Show us what you've got.'

'Nah,' Jacob says, 'you're not ready for it.' He yawns and looks down at his phone, where some people wearing Scream masks dance.

Jess hates herself for it but she can't help asking that classic mum question: 'How was school today?'

'Good.'

'Good.'

She looks again at the screen and asks, 'Is that Blackpink?'

'Oh my God, Mum, no,' he says, shrugging her away. 'I'm going to the garden where I can scroll in peace.'

Pa starts making the food, baked beans and an omelette of some kind, while Haze butters half a loaf of bread and sings along with the radio, declaring, 'Oh, this is so old,' to songs Jess is sure only came out very recently. Pa asks Haze about her studies and she responds to him in broken German, over-emphasising the accent she's learned mostly from an app on her phone. It's funny how Haze has always been so keen to learn the language, the very opposite of Jess and Dominic, who would answer back in English and get embarrassed when Pa would speak their home language in public. But then everything about her family now is opposite to the family she had growing up.

A song comes on the radio that causes Haze to do a series of jerky robot-like dance moves that Pa tries to mimic, immediately breaking into a sweat. Jacob looks through the back-door window and doubles over laughing. And this is another reason

Jess spends time here: it's not always guilt-driven, sometimes it's fun and even healing to witness laughter in a place that for so long was a battleground.

The front door goes. 'I'll get it,' Jess says. As she moves through the hallway, the letterbox goes again. 'Coming,' she shouts. On the other side a man, tall and broad, with skin the colour of powder, colours along his cheeks. Her mind races quickly: who is he? Who is he? She recognises his face, but can't think from where.

'Sorry,' he says, stepping back and dropping his head. 'I tried the doorbell but—'

'It's not worked in years,' she says.

'Right. Of course. Um. I came by to drop this back in for Wolf.' He hands her a pink ceramic bowl.

She holds it up as if waiting for an explanation.

'He gave me some cake. I don't know why he put it in that bowl though. Maybe he couldn't find any tubs or the right size lid or—'

'Sorry, do we know each other?'

He reddens.

Shit. Is he someone she once kissed on a park bench? 'You look familiar.' His face, his voice, she's not sure from where or when. Definitely a long time ago. 'Are you Daniel Thorpe's brother?'

'No.' He looks crestfallen, like he expects her to remember him from somewhere else, as if she's taking up valuable mental space holding onto everyman's face and name.

'Sorry, my memory is terrible, I'm always getting people mixed up.'

'It's okay. I think I have one of those faces,' he says. 'I'm Ben. I moved into number fourteen this week, across the road, not the downstairs flat but the upstairs—'

'And he made you cake? Is that really something that happens outside of television? That someone welcomes a person to the area with cake?'

'Yeah, it's a pretty friendly street, the guy at number twenty already offered me some smack and the woman at number twelve, the one with the face tattoos, she threatened to slash my tyres if I parked in her spot again so, hmm . . .' He stops and rubs at his jaw before looking up at her again. She doesn't think she's ever seen eyes this pale before. So unusual. 'Anyway,' he says, taking a step further back as if to leave, 'tell Wolf I enjoyed it and if he's home tomorrow morning I can do his radiators – not that it's cold, but if he wants me to, I can, yeah, okay.'

'You sure you want me to tell him you enjoyed this?' she says, holding up the bowl. 'Cause that will then give him the green light to send you food parcels at least seven times a week.'

'Sounds great.'

'You think it's great until you realise he puts half a tub of margarine in everything.' She looks down at her own belly. Ben looks too, his light eyes passing over her then stopping on the ground. 'Where have you moved from?' she asks, suddenly aware of how much she wants to keep him here, keep him talking.

'Romford.'

'Wow. I'm not sure if you've moved up in the world or down.'

'Me neither. Sorry, I didn't mean that. Stratford's great.

I love the whole Olympic legacy thing. Super Saturday and all that.'

She laughs. 'You're so familiar, it's going to bug me.'

'Actually, I grew up around here. Left when I was sixteen. So it's possible that you might recognise me from, I don't know,' he rubs at the back of his head, 'hanging outside McDonald's, or drinking Hooch in West Ham Park. Not in a drunk, homeless person sort of way, I didn't mean that, um, I was a normal teenager.'

'Did you go to school around here?'

'Er, yeah, for a bit. The school doesn't exist anymore I've been told, it's now—'

Haze shouts from inside, snapping Jess out of it. 'Sorry, that's my daughter.'

'Course. I'll let you go.' He lifts his hand. 'Nice to meet you.'

'You too.'

She watches him cross over to the other side, wondering if she should have invited him in.

'Mum?' Haze calls again.

'What?' she asks, still slightly distracted as she goes back into the kitchen. Jacob is back inside and the radio is off.

'Have you heard Opa's absurd plan to go on *The Great British Bake Off*?'

'Oh, was that Ben?' Pa says, nodding at the empty dish.

'Yeah. Who is he?'

'Ben,' he answers simply.

'Yes, you've said. But *who* is Ben? Why do I recognise him?'

'*Liebling*, I don't know why you recognise half the men in London, and nor do I want to.'

Jess tuts at him.

'He's moved in across the road, above the hooker.'

'Please,' Haze shouts, 'don't say hooker.'

'I don't mean it in a bad way. She's well within her rights to make her money any way she wants. Jacob, have I shown you any Hedy Lamarr films yet?' Pa closes his eyes and kisses the air.

'Who is Ben?' Jess, feeling the conversation is running away, repeats.

'He lives at number fourteen,' Pa says. 'Remember when that place was a whole house? The Robertsons lived there for decades – I hated them, they used to breed ferrets. I heard some Chinese person bought it last year and changed it into two flats. They don't even have real kitchens, just a sink and a hob, like that YMCA I once stayed in near Oxford Street.'

Jacob gasps. 'Is YMCA a real place?'

Jess gives up and checks her blinking phone. She opens an email titled 'perfect property', yet when she clicks through it's an illegal-looking structure above a shisha lounge in Barking, and to add insult to injury, it's over budget. Then underneath that is an email from Mustafa with one line: 'valuation booked for Saturday 3 May'. Next Saturday.

Precious had said Jess needed a dose of reality; well, there's no doubt that's what she's getting today. It's hitting hard now.

This is really happening.

They're really going to have to move. To pack up their lives and start again someplace else.

Pa's still talking. 'They're doing the same to the houses up the road. Buy them, shrink them, sell them.'

Sell them? Why is everyone selling everything? This is too much. Everything feels too much. Impossible even. Completely impossible. Jess removes herself from the table, stands at the sink and closes her eyes. She grips the taps and tries to remember the mindful breathwork she learned during one of Norman's staff well-being meetings. It's not working. Nothing is bloody working.

'Jess?' Pa says. 'What's wrong?'

'Nothing,' she blurts, 'nothing at all.' She loosens her grip on the taps and digs her nails into her palms before reaching for a cup from the drying rack. It's money that's scaring her. Her ends just about meet each month, but sometimes they marginally miss each other – and thank God for credit cards when that happens. She's not the best with money and admittedly does like to treat herself and the kids. Though why not? She works hard, sometimes six days a week. She deserves the occasional Fenty lipstick or pair of square-toed boots. Shit. She's actually going to be homeless. On the streets. Living in a tent, with her two kids and seventy pairs of shoes.

'Jess,' Pa says, 'are you crying?'

'No,' she answers, because she didn't think she *was* crying until the tears started running down her face. 'I'm okay. Really. Ignore me.'

'*Liebling*,' he whispers, 'are you pregnant?'

'What?' She turns towards his genuinely questioning face. Haze laughs and they all turn to look at her. 'Sorry,' she says, covering her mouth.

'Are you?' asks Jacob, wide-eyed and panicked. 'Because I really don't want that. I don't think I'm middle-child material.'

'Of course she's not pregnant,' Haze says, pushing Jacob lightly on the shoulder. 'You're not pregnant, are you?' she confirms.

'Because if you are pregnant,' Pa says, 'I'll need to make sure I cook these eggs thoroughly. You'll need to stop drinking too.'

'Pa, I'm thirty-seven,' she shouts.

'So? Women have babies well into their fifties now. Look at Naomi Campbell.'

'Who's Naomi Campbell?' Jacob asks.

Why won't they all shut up and listen? Or at least stop for long enough to allow her to gather her thoughts.

'I'm. Not. Pregnant. Why would you even think that?'

'Because,' Pa says, 'the crying, the mood swings . . .' he shrugs his arms in her direction and adds, 'the weight.'

'The weight?' Jess runs her hands down her front and wonders if she really has put on weight. 'I'm a little stressed because, well,' she wipes her face again and tries to stand tall. Is there any way out of this now? Is there any point? 'Mustafa is leaving London.'

'Why would anyone leave London?' Pa asks.

'Apparently it was always his plan and he's, well, he's decided to sell his house. Houses. Including ours.'

There's a gasp.

'Yeah. He told me last Friday. And the valuation thing is happening next week. All a bit quick. It's okay, though. I've begun looking for something new.'

'Mum, this is crazy. Why didn't you tell us this before?'

'I'm sorry, hun, I didn't want to tell you until I sorted out somewhere new. Which I almost have.' Her voice catches as quickly as the lie comes out.

'Why is Mustafa moving?' Jacob asks. 'Their place is so nice. They even have one of those pop-up pools in the garden.'

'How do you know that?' Haze asks.

'I saw it on TikTok.'

'Of course they have a pool,' Jess says, her voice choking between a laugh and a lump. 'They have everything: a sports car, leather sofas, cascading white walls. Yet it isn't enough. They want something else. Something better. Because they're so much bloody better.'

'Hazel,' Pa says, 'could you take your brother to watch TV in the other room for a bit?'

'Why? I'm old enough to be involved in this conversation.'

'Please, give us a minute,' he says, firmer this time.

Haze slams the chair against the dining table and huffs, sliding the door shut behind herself and Jacob.

Jess gathers herself, unsure if Pa is going to hit her with enragement or empathy.

'When?' he asks.

'He wants to get it cleaned up and valued really quickly.'

'House buying takes time. Sometimes months. It's not like you see on Phil and Kirstie, in the pub one minute and knocking through a wall the next.'

Jess nods. He's right. It could take months. Even a year. Though the issue remains. 'I've looked online at places and I'm shitting it. I had no clue how expensive things were around here. I can just about afford my place now, and that's with my wages, child benefit and the money Steadman gives me each month.'

'Can't you get Mustafa to change his mind? Use your powers of persuasion. That rich little creep has always held a torch for you.'

'No, Pa. Are you listening to me? He's selling. This is happening. The thing that worries me most is how I'll be able to pay any more than I already do.'

He takes off his glasses and rubs his eyes. 'I can help you.'

'No. I know you've worked out your pension and it's all accounted for—'

'I'm not talking about my pension.' He puts his glasses back on but doesn't look at her. 'I'm talking about my trip money.'

It takes her a few seconds to realise what he's talking about, then it dawns on her. 'Your Hollywood money? Gosh, Pa, I hadn't realised there was any left.'

'There's . . .' he tips his head to the side, 'a little. I've been saving and selling things.'

Pa was always saving money, obsessed with getting enough to take a trip to Hollywood and join a series of Golden Age themed coach tours for seniors. The trip was meant to have happened years ago. But on the eve of him finally booking it, Dominic turned up on the doorstep. There was so much talk of change: a woman who'd made him reassess his life, a warehouse packing job that gave him the satisfaction of earning an honest pound, and the severing of negative influences. As if it was the world that had made him behave the way he did, rather than something deep and unstoppable within him. Pa ate it all up, believing his son was reformed. Two months later Dominic was gone and so was most of Pa's money.

This is the first time in years Jess has heard him mention the trip again.

'I had no idea you were saving. That you still wanted to go.'

He laughs through his nose, ungenuine. 'It's fun to imagine, but I'm not really going to go to Hollywood. What a crazy thought. Old man like me, flying all that way to traipse around film locations. No.'

Jess puts her hand on his. 'Pa, if you've been able to save that money again, then you should go. It's your dream.'

'The Hollywood I want to see doesn't exist anymore. It's all yoga and silicone and Kardashians now.'

'It was yoga and silicone eight years ago and you still wanted to go, what's cha—'

He slaps the table with both palms, his signal to close down the conversation. 'You need money, I have money. End of.'

'No, it's not *end of*. You're almost eighty. This might be your last chance. Don't worry about me: I can sort this out myself.' She takes out her phone again and opens Zoopla. 'See, plenty of houses. I'm on it.'

'Hmm,' he says.

'Pa.' Again she takes his hand. 'If I get stuck, like really, really stuck, I promise I'll tell you. Though I'd have to be completely desperate to take that money from you.'

Chapter Four

Ben

May

Mum holds her cigarette in one hand, a spicy Mexican bean wrap in the other and alternates between the two. 'Another day, another picnic.'

'Do you like it?' Ben asks. 'You said you were getting fed up with sandwiches. That's why I went for the wrap. It's still part of the meal deal and you get a—'

'Yep. It's fine, love.' She rewraps it and tucks it in her weird handbag, the one that doesn't really look like a bag at all, more like a doll's house with a zip. 'I'll have the rest for dinner. Save me cooking.'

'That's why I said we should have dinner together sometimes. At least then we're both not having to cook for one. I hate cooking for one.'

'Dinner? We're already having lunch together. This is what, the third time I've seen you this week?'

'We've a lot to catch up on. We've hardly seen each other

over the years. I was always too busy with Shanice's family, I know that. The number of weekends I spent fishing with her dad or repainting her mum's craft room. I'm going to make it up to you.'

'There's no need. It's been lovely spending all this time with you recently,' Mum says between drags. 'In fact, I was thinking, now that we see each other in *real life*, you don't have to keep calling me on a Monday anymore.'

'Our Monday call? We've been doing that for years, since I first moved away, since I was sixteen.'

'Exactly.'

He can so clearly remember the way his eyes stung the first time he called his mum as he sat on the bottom step of Dad's unfamiliar house. He missed her but also felt so guilty for everything. Not only was he a pathetic son who never played sports or had girlfriends or excelled at anything, he was also a coward.

'I speak to your sister twice a month and sometimes that's too often,' Mum laughs.

Is she implying that he needs to start calling his sister too? Because he tried that once and found they had nothing to say to each other, the conversation dying after seven minutes. Never could two siblings have less in common.

'No point in you calling me when I see you all the time.' She stubs her cigarette out on the bench, which is pretty antisocial.

'It's not all the time.' He looks at her and she lowers her eyes, the lids caked in shimmery pink powder. 'Ben,' she says, 'have you managed to make any friends yet?'

'Friends? What is this, my first day at big school? I'm busy working. I don't have time to start hanging out with people.'

'Though you have time to hang out with me, don't you? Often.'

'Often? Hardly. Why'd you keep saying things like this? It's almost like you expected me to move back and not want to spend time with you.'

'I expected you to take a bit more advantage of being back in London. You came home to build a new life for yourself.'

'I know that.'

'Are you doing it? Or are you hiding behind me?'

He deflates a little. 'That's harsh.'

'I don't want you to get unwell again, Ben.'

Unwell. She always uses this word. Why can't she say breakdown? That's what it was. There's no shame in it. Ben sits forward and looks at the cracked paving slabs beneath the bench and the chewing gum in splodges across it. Why do people do it? No one will ever be able to get that off. He knows because he's tried.

'I'm not saying that I don't love having you around – it's great having you back here, living so . . .' she stalls, 'so close. It's more that I'm running out of things to say to you.'

'I thought they were companionable silences.' He'd even come to enjoy them. In fact, sitting on a park bench with Mum, swapping theories about the parakeets while sharing a packet of pistachios, was one of the highlights of his week. It made him feel calm and less alone than he'd felt in months. It made him feel that by moving back here, he had done the right thing.

'Aren't there any nice people at work you could go to lunch with?'

'Hmm, yeah, nice people who spend their entire lunch hour rubbing talk of their happy families in my face.'

'You'll never make friends if you don't put in the effort, Ben. It's really important that you put in the effort. That you show people what a great guy you are.' She reapplies her purple lipstick. Purple. It makes her look cold and kind of dead. 'I need to be heading back now.'

'Already?'

'I've got to set up the farm role-play in the nursery. And it's going to bucket down. I don't want my make-up running.'

'But—' he starts, then stops. Does he really want to open up this topic with her? It's too late; she stares him down, knowing there's something on his mind. 'What?'

'Nothing. Not really. Though, well, do you remember if Dominic Bakker had a sister?' He doesn't look at her but senses the tension as she shifts next to him.

'Where the hell is this coming from?'

'I, um, this is a funny story . . .' He turns back to her and smiles, the way he learned sometimes softened the blow before he landed it. 'I met this really nice old guy on my street and we got chatting and I, er,' Ben pauses, 'I think he might be related to Dominic Bakker.'

'You've only been back two minutes. How are you already digging up the past?'

'I'm not. I could be wrong. I'm sure I'm wrong.' He rubs at the back of his head. 'Anyway, his name's Wolf, the old guy, he's German and he has a daughter who went to St Margaret's. She's convinced she recognises me. Though she's a few years younger. And she's, er, well, she's mixed race. And her surname's Bakker.'

'I can't believe this. What is she then? His sister? His cousin? What?'

'I don't know. That's what I'm saying. Wolf told me he doesn't have a son, only one daughter. I'm not about to start asking after nieces and nephews. That would be weird.'

'I'd put money on Dominic Bakker being at Her Majesty's Pleasure. Or perhaps he's dead.'

Why did she have to say it? It's the thing Ben's been actively trying to push from his mind. Not because the idea of Dominic dead or in prison is tragic, but because when he thinks of these two scenarios, he feels kind of relieved.

'He was always a wrong 'un,' Mum says. 'I don't think I knew he was German either. That explains plenty, if you ask me. Why you making friends with old men anyway?'

'I'm not. No, actually, I am. Well, we got chatting and I've been doing a bit of DIY for him this last week.'

'And he just so happens to be a Bakker.'

'What are you trying to say? That I sought him out? Like I came back here looking for a link—'

'You always idolised Dominic Bakker.'

'How can you say that?'

'Because it's true. That's how it started. You wanted to be his friend. But people like him don't have friends. They have victims.'

Ben groans. This was a mistake, bringing this up with her. 'Did you say you have something for me to post out to Olivia for you?'

'We've finished talking about this then?'

'What else do you want me to say?'

Mum tuts and slowly pulls up a carrier bag. 'You were the one who brought him up. Here you go, few royal glossies. I know Oli loves her princesses.'

Ben pulls a magazine from the bag. '*Kate and Meg at War Again,*' he reads. 'I think she's too young for this.'

'Stop fussing. She can look at the photos.' She pecks him on the cheek and stands.

'Should I call you tonight?'

'No, I'm going to an Ann Summers party.'

'Of course you are. Okay, tomorrow?'

'Possibly,' she says. 'I'll let you know, and Ben?'

'Yes, Mum?'

'This ain't Essex. Be careful who you make friends with round here, okay?'

He watches her saunter off, and feels a fog descending. He had used his mum as the justification for moving back here. It was easy telling everyone his reasons for moving were to look after his ageing mum. He'd even somewhat convinced himself of it. Especially when he'd listen to her on the phone complaining about how hard she found it to order things online and put the duvet inside the duvet cover. Though the real reason for moving was never really about Mum, it was about escaping the reminders of his failed family life and the circle of people he'd thought of as friends. When he had begun telling them all he was leaving, they acted surprised, though he could see they were secretly relieved. The bottom line was he was now a single man in a world filled with play dates and birthday parties.

A little kid in a Jordan T-shirt toddles over and sits on the bench next to him. 'Hello,' she says.

'Cool T-shirt.'

'Thanks.' She leans in closer, inspecting the magazines. 'Hey, that's the Duchess of Cambridge.'

'Good spot. Are you a big fan?'

The mum comes and frowns slightly at the pile of magazines in Ben's lap. 'My daughter,' he explains, 'she likes the royal family.'

The woman gives him a tight smile and beckons her kid away. And now he's become one of those weird middle-aged men who sit on park benches trying to strike up conversations with small children about the monarchy.

He gets up and heads back to his van, chucking the magazines on the passenger seat and checking his phone. He's already been warned that Friday afternoons are generally quiet. Some of his colleagues had spoken of clocking off early and going to the pub, they'd even invited him along. Though it felt kind of empty, like they were only asking to be polite and didn't really want him there. He gets the sense they, especially the women, have become wary of him since finding out his 'situation'. They're probably wondering why a man's wife and child would leave him and move to another country. Was he philandering? Abusive? Possessive? If someone would ask him outright, he could set the record straight, tell them all, 'She left me because I'm boring. She left me because when she thought of another forty years with me, she cried with weariness.'

*

55

The traffic crawls along Green Street, with cars, buses and Deliveroo drivers all fighting for road space. Even though the Boleyn Ground has gone, replaced with some soulless housing development, the rest of the area seems completely unchanged by time. Ben still loves looking at the swatch of shops selling sparkly saris, wedding clothes, yellow gold, eggless cakes, dishes, pots and pans. As a kid, Green Street was a happy place for him. It meant a West Ham game with his uncles and a giant samosa from a neon-lit cafe on the way home.

As the rain starts, people lose patience. Someone honks their horn, then others join in and before long everyone's beeping and swearing and trying to cut in, and no one's moving anywhere fast. Except the pedestrians; crowds of them squeeze between the stalled traffic, pushing children, dragging shopping, eating KFC.

When Ben eventually makes it back to Stratford, he considers calling it a day and heading home to sit alone in the flat. Then he spots her: Jessica Bakker. She's standing at the crossing, holding a couple of bags and a few big storage tubs. Weird, not only because he was just talking about her, but he'd also been thinking of her. In fact, ever since he first saw her last week, she's crossed his mind more than a few times.

Her dress flies up at the knees as the wind takes hold and she tries to flatten it down with one hand while simultaneously holding an umbrella and her shopping. How the hell did he not notice her at school? It doesn't make sense. She doesn't look that much younger than him; their paths must have crossed at some point.

A car honks behind him and he moves on, watching Jessica

shrink in his rear-view mirror. He loops the van around and reasons that if she's still standing there, he'll beep his horn or wave, or simply take it as an opportunity to stare at her again like the weirdo he is. When he gets back round, she's moved further up the road, her umbrella pulled low as she totters through puddles in high shoes. He watches her for a few seconds, then cuts off and pulls in slowly; he doesn't want to make it look like he's pouncing on her or anything.

The rain hits him as he winds down the window. 'Jessica?'

She looks up and there's that blankness he knows too well. 'Ben,' he says. 'I live across the road from your dad.'

'Number fourteen? Hi. Fuck,' she shouts as the umbrella turns itself inside out.

'Can I give you a lift?'

'Which way are you going?'

Your way, he thinks, wherever it is, I'll happily make that detour.

'I'm not far, up by the library?'

'Yeah, I'm going that way.'

'Lifesaver,' she shouts, tossing the umbrella on the ground.

He's already out of the door, sliding open the back and taking her bags. 'You can chuck that stuff on the floor,' he says as she climbs in the passenger side.

The smell of her perfume fills the front and he's suddenly aware of the van smelling like Harold.

'Royalist?' she asks.

'Huh? Oh, the magazines,' he feels himself blush like he's embarrassed, as if he's an actual royalist. 'They're not mine.'

'I'm sure,' she says, smiling.

'They're for—' She's staring at him, and he instinctively touches the side of his face.

'You've got some lipstick on your cheek.'

'Oh,' he looks in the mirror and wipes away the purple print. 'My mum.'

'Purple? Brave colour.'

'Yeah, she's kind of' – he makes an effort to sit straighter in his seat – 'eccentric.'

'Eccentric parent? I couldn't possibly relate.'

They drive on, and he wishes for each traffic light to flick red, for every pedestrian to need the crossing, to get stuck behind a rubbish truck, anything to buy time while he thinks of what to say. He glances over to see if she's as uncomfortable as him and she smiles back. 'You said you grew up around here?' she asks.

'Yeah.'

'Which school did you go to?'

'St Margaret's.'

'No way,' her face lights up.

This is it; this is how easy it's going to be to ask her about Dominic Bakker.

'So we did go to the same school. I knew I recognised you. I'm guessing we weren't in the same year though?'

He shifts in his seat and decides to have a stab at a joke. 'Are you assuming I'm older than you?' She laughs, thankfully, and Ben says, 'I'm forty-one.'

'Okay, then you would have been a few years above me.' She clears her throat and flicks through one of the magazines. 'Urgh, Kate Middleton. How does she get her hair that shiny?' She slaps the magazine closed. 'See, look what these magazines do to a person. Two pages in and I'm already filled with self-loathing.' She pulls down the sun visor and rubs away the smudgy black liner around her eyes in the mirror. He's going to crash the van if he doesn't stop looking at her.

'My dad tells me you helped him with a bit of DIY at the weekend.'

'Yeah, I, er, I tried to secure the bookshelves so they wouldn't collapse.'

'I heard you did more than that.'

It almost sounds suggestive. It's her low, gravelly voice. He could listen to her all day.

'Hmm, yeah, a few table legs needed tightening. The fridge was making a weird noise too, though I'm not actually qualified to deal with that. I only went in to bleed the radiators.'

'That sounds about right,' she laughs. 'I hope he's paying you?'

'In cake and biscuits.'

'That'll pay your rent.'

'And books. Though I've not got around to reading most of them. Or any of them.'

'He used to give me a reading list for my birthday. I'm on the left here.'

Already. 'Oh, okay.' He pulls in, feeling down, like he missed some great opportunity to talk to her, to roll out all the sparkling conversation starters he regularly practised in his head. He stops the van and turns off the engine.

It's a pretty shabby street, even by Stratford's standards, with untidy front yards and overflowing wheelie bins. Ben's still surprised by the level of poverty around here. It's something you don't notice when you're young and grow up somewhere. It's only when you go away and come back that things like single-glazed windows held with duct tape and uncollected rubbish on street corners stand out to you. Though Jessica's street also has that other thing typical of poor areas: flashy cars. It's the same on his own street; young guys stepping out of their parents' house and into a brand-new motor. Here there's a sparkling blue Maserati parked out front. 'Nice car,' Ben says, then the van rolls forward an inch. Jessica gasps and he jumps to put the handbrake on.

'Shit. So sorry.' He keeps his hand tightly on it, scared another blunder will cause him to roll them both straight into forty grand's worth of car. He can't look at her, he's so embarrassed, but she's laughing.

'I used to do that all the time,' she says. 'Even my driving instructor told me to give up.'

'Sorry. I have never done that before. Never. I'm a very good driver. I've been driving since I was sixteen. Passed first time,' he rattles on, and she keeps laughing. 'I wasn't trying to roll my van into your car.'

'As if that's my car.'

'Or your neighbour's car?'

'It's my landlord's car. He lives across the road.'

Ben looks at what must be her house, the one with the broken wardrobe outside on the grass. Ben grew up in tidy houses, places where you'd put a cup down and it was washed, dried and put away before you could get a refill. He'd love to see Jessica's house. He wonders if it's packed like Wolf's, with books and clutter.

'We're having a clear-out,' she says as if having read his mind. 'My landlord wants to sell the property. At least he *thinks* he wants to sell. He's having the place valued tomorrow morning, is expecting some huge million-pound windfall when really he should be grateful to keep rent coming in and have good tenants that don't try to rip out the copper piping.'

'Yeah,' Ben agrees, slightly surprised at how open she is.

'I don't even think it will sell. The market, you know?' she turns to him and he nods, completely unsure of *the market*.

She leans her head on the seatback and makes no move to thank him for the lift, to say goodbye, to get out of the van. 'My kids are so stressed about it all. I've tried making out like it's no big deal, like it won't sell and, even if it does, we'll find somewhere else. Though my son, he's starting to get anxious, and my daughter, well, she always wants everything to be so perfect.'

Ben looks again at the house, at the touches of effort and personality: a hanging basket filled with petunias, large golden front door numbers, a BLM poster in an upstairs window. 'Shouldn't you be trying to make it *less* attractive if you want to stay?'

'Gosh, you're right. I should punch some holes in the wall, sew a herring in the curtains, that type of thing? I have so much stuff to get rid of. It's overwhelming.'

'Your dad also has a lot of stuff.'

'I'm not as bad as him. No one's as bad as him. Though I think he's getting better at getting rid of stuff.'

'Probably because he's slowly passing it all over to me.'

They catch each other's eyes and Ben feels stumped as to

what to say next. He's not looked at another woman this way since Shanice and it makes him feel a little off-kilter.

'Sorry,' Jessica says, 'I'm sure you have places to be.'

'No, I—' Ben stops as the front door opens and a teenage girl in shorts and a vest stands in the doorway. She sticks a hand out, then shakes the rain from her fingers.

'And there she is,' Jessica says, 'my darling girl.'

When Wolf had banged on about his high-achieving grand-daughter, Ben pictured a young version of Jessica, perhaps wearing glasses, though the two don't actually look related. The girl is tiny, short and stick thin, and even from here Ben can see she's got on a ton of heavy make-up. She flicks her long poker-straight hair and shouts something to whoever's inside the house.

'Right, I better go.' Jessica opens the door and he follows, going round the back to remove her shopping.

He wishes he was a different sort of guy, one capable of using this moment to ask her for her number. Is that how it goes now? It was how it worked when he was last single and drunk enough to start talking to Shanice. Though, come to think of it, it was probably her who asked for his number. She always did the asking; he always did the submitting.

Jessica has all her stuff now; she stops in front of him and smiles. 'Thank you so much for the lift.'

'I, er. It's okay. It's—'

'I'll tell Pa he owes you another cake.'

'Okay.' Is that all he can manage? This is his moment. His chance. 'Bye,' he calls awkwardly as she heads to her house.

Chapter Five

Jess

Jess nurses her coffee and watches Haze, who is watching Jacob, who is watching the toaster. He hits the stop button; the bread pops up and he tuts several times like a disapproving old lady. 'Won't do,' he says, 'simply won't do.'

'Jacob?' Haze slaps the counter to get his attention. 'Answer me.'

'What?' he says, briefly looking up at her.

'Are you coming to Dad's?'

'I told you. I'm thinking about it.' He whirls his fingers either side of his head. 'Thinking takes time and consumption of complex carbohydrates.'

'If you don't want to come, you can just say no.'

Jacob clicks a finger. 'Then I say no.'

Haze folds her arms and looks at Jess. 'Mum? Aren't you going to say something?'

With great effort, Jess shakes her head. Usually, she would jump in and try to sort things out. But they're growing up

63

and need to be able to work out their own problems. Also, it's interesting to see how Jacob is increasingly trying to stand up to his sister, to disagree with her and tell her no. Jess thinks of how her own older brother would dictate things to her growing up, telling her who she could and couldn't talk to. It was especially bad when she started at the same secondary school as him, when he would shout her down for sitting with the younger sister of one of his enemies or liking a teacher who once had him suspended. There were always so many rules to follow. Rules that Jess blindly abided by, especially if they meant keeping on the right side of Dom.

The toast pops again and Jacob checks the level of darkness carefully, then puts it back down.

'You're being unreasonable,' Haze says. 'Why can't you come for lunch? Dad's putting on a proper lamb roast and you've got absolutely nothing else to do today.'

'I have. I've got *relaxing* to do today.'

'You've been relaxing all week. Mum, please, time to get involved.'

It's only half past nine but Jess has found when you get up at five a.m. to panic-search properties the morning tends to drag and your kids tend to grate. Since Mustafa got the valuation figure of his dreams, Jess has done nothing but panic and search. So far, she's seen three houses, two flats and something that was neither, though to its credit, did have four walls. All of them were unsuitable, either too boxy, too dreggy, or too perilous. How can it be so impossible? How can there be so little available within her small, yet perfectly reasonable, budget? Weirdly, despite not even being on her radar, she has a viewing later on for a three-bedroom flat in the East Village, the development based in the former athletes' village.

'Mum?' Haze snaps.

Jess downs the rest of the coffee, closes her eyes and dreams of five minutes where no one squeals 'mum' at her.

'Perfect,' Jacob says when his toast pops for the third and final time.

'Sweetheart, your dad would really appreciate you going over today. He's not seen you in weeks.'

Jacob licks the Marmite knife. 'Look, stop bullying me.'

'We're not bullying you,' Jess says. It's been a while since he accused them of this, of 'ganging up' on him. It's only because they both have his best interests at heart, and having a good, healthy relationship with Steadman falls under that.

'I don't want to go out today. I want to stay home and watch TV.'

'You can watch TV at Dad's,' Haze says through gritted teeth. 'In fact, Dad has Sky. Remember when you said having Sky was one of your last unfulfilled dreams?'

'Yeah, but he's going to push me into watching something I don't want to watch, like a football match or a golf game or *Star Wars* or, or—' Jacob stops to munch his toast and Jess thanks God he didn't bring up *Black Panther*. Steadman just about accepted his son wasn't fussed about sports and girls, but falling asleep during *Black Panther* crossed some sort of line for him, some point of no return.

Jess reboils the kettle and makes another cup, adding two teaspoons of granules this time.

'He never lets me watch what I want. Mum, are you going?'

'To your dad's place?' she asks in horror. 'Why would I?'

'That's a great idea,' Haze says.

'I don't have time to hang out with Steadman. I've got to clean this place up. Mustafa is coming in to take photos later.' The dreaded photo shoot, another step closer to their home being put up for sale. Mustafa has said he's keen for it to 'go live' in the next few days. It makes Jess feel ill. 'I'm seeing a flat later. Haze, do you want to come along after your dad's?'

'First of all, this place couldn't be any tidier, like I didn't even know you were meant to be able to see through the oven door. And second of all, after the last place you showed me, I'm not looking at any more flats.' Haze returns her gaze to Jacob and begins to poke him in the shoulder repeatedly. He ignores her at first then snaps, 'I'll go to Dad's if Mum comes too.'

Jess laughs. 'I told you, I'm really busy today.'

'Mummm,' Haze says, 'come. Don't make me guilt-trip you about how much we need to see our parents successfully co-parent us.'

'I really don't want to—'

'I'm only going if Mum goes,' Jacob says.

It's then Haze widens her eyes and pouts. 'Pleassse.'

Jess has to weigh up what's more important. Helping her daughter be the bridge in the relationship between Jacob and his dad, or being able to eat lunch without her ex leering at her. 'Urgh, okay then,' Jess says. 'I'll come for a bit. But you need to make an effort, Jacob. I don't want to be stuck making small talk with him. You two need to communicate.'

'Yeah,' Haze agrees, putting her arm around Jess, 'communicate and bond. Our parents won't be with us forever. We've got to treasure them while they're still here.'

Jess removes Haze's arm. 'What a lovely thought.'

'You know what I mean. Let me go and ring Dad now,' she says, taking her call into the garden.

'It'll be nice for me to see your dad's new place,' Jess says to Jacob.

He scrunches up his nose. 'I've already been and, spoiler alert, it's not nice.'

Jess feels herself smile, then straightens her face and says, 'Well, interior design has never been your dad's strongest skill.'

'That's because Dad has no skills. He just has like—' Jacob stops and puts another piece of bread in the toaster.

'Has what?'

'I don't know. He's just Dad.'

'He is trying, you know.'

'Yeah, trying with Haze,' he mumbles. 'Trying with you.'

'That's not true.'

'No. Because he doesn't have to *try* with Haze.'

This comes up often, the fact he feels his sister doesn't really have to try at anything, that everything about her, from her achievements to her popularity, comes from a place of effortlessness. Which is, annoyingly, not 100 per cent untrue.

'Look,' Jess says, taking the liberty of putting a hand on Jacob's shoulder. 'Relationships take work. You really think I don't have to put effort in with Opa?' The word effort is actually an understatement. 'Parents and their children don't always get along automatically.'

'Okay,' Jacob nods. 'I'll try.'

Haze knocks on the window and shouts, 'Dad is super happy you're coming to his place.'

And Jess isn't sure if this is meant for her or Jacob.

Haze holds her finger on the doorbell, while Jess stands back with Jacob, looking over the third-floor balcony.

'Coming,' Steadman shouts from within, probably as he runs around the flat, chucking the mess out of sight. 'Baby girl,' he shouts as he finally opens the door, 'where's the fire?'

'We just couldn't wait a second longer to see you.'

He kisses his teeth and gathers her up for a hug.

'Dad, please,' she says, pulling away, 'what is this outfit?'

'It's from Sports Direct. Karrimor, proper nice stuff.' He smooths down his teeny-weeny shorts and vest combo, which is, in Jess's opinion, a bit too much flesh for this time of the day.

'My Young King.' Steadman doesn't hug Jacob, but instead holds out his fist to spud him, which Jacob reciprocates awkwardly.

'Looking good, girl,' he says to Jess, and she makes sure she keeps a wide berth in case he tries to hug *her*. 'Hmm, you smell good too.' Apparently, not wide enough.

'Why are you dressed like this?' she asks. 'We did say noon.'

He tips his head to the side and the smile is a mixture of pride and a weird sort of coyness. 'I'm getting in shape.'

'Oh yeah, you said.'

'I'm looking to reach my full physical potential this summer.'

'Really.'

'I'm going to look like Jason Momoa in a few months.'

Jess cackles, 'Good luck with that.' They walk through to the living room, which smells beautifully of roast lamb, but the look of the place leaves a lot to be desired. In the centre of the room is a mid-size pool table and a home gym covered in drying washing, mostly T-shirts, though some boxers too. There's a paper tablecloth and a salt and pepper shaker on the table and it's pulled close to the sofa, which makes Jess wonder if Steadman sits here at night, eating dinner for one off a kids' pool table. It's too depressing.

'Right, let's get our drink on,' he says as the kids slouch down on the sofa and get their phones out. 'Young King, I'm going to fix you up with a protein shake, get those muscles popping for the summer.'

Jacob doesn't even look up.

Jess follows Steadman through. The kitchen's cleaner than she would have predicted, yet still grim. Steadman taps at the glass tank of his gecko. 'Do you think Lil J looks a weird colour today?'

'I don't know. What colour is it meant to be? And I'm not drinking a protein shake. Do you have coffee?'

'Come and look.' He beckons her closer. 'Lil J?'

She had told him ages ago how it was weird that he named his reptiles after his actual children, though he claimed it was in 'homage' to them, as if they were long-dead rappers he admired.

'My baby's looking peaky today,' Steadman coos. 'Are you hungry? Is that it?'

A dusty smell slinks out as he opens a tub of locusts. They're mostly dead, except for the odd one, which scrambles over the others as it tries to escape. He empties a few in, slides the glass door shut and looks Jess over. 'It's nice to see you. I never thought you would ever make it over here.'

'No, well, I was never planning to.'

He puffs and puts on the kettle, which Jess can see from the monitor is empty. They stand facing each other while it dry boils.

'Steadman,' she whispers, 'talk to him.'

'About what?'

'Ask him what he's been up to this week.'

'I hate asking him that, he always says something weird. Last time I asked him he told me he'd been crying while watching videos of animals being rescued. Is that normal?'

'Probably not. But he enjoys it, so what's the harm?'

'I try, Jess. I really try.'

'Maybe don't try so hard then.'

'I even tried texting him. Long messages, pouring my heart out, and you know what I got back?'

Jess raises her eyebrows, wondering why anyone in their right mind would text Jacob.

'*Cool*,' he says in a perfect imitation of Jacob's voice.

'What do you want from him? He's a happy geek who doesn't want to have deep and meaningfuls with his dad. Don't be offended that he doesn't want to hang out with you.'

'He hangs out with you.'

'No. I don't have time to *hang out*. I'm busy. I'm working. It's a miracle I've got two days off this week and here I am, spending one of them with you. Don't you feel privileged?'

Steadman begins to make a drink with scoops of something labelled EXTREME HENCH.

'Anyway,' Jess says, 'if Jacob is telling you he's *cool* and he's busy watching animal rescue videos then ask him about animal rescue videos. Or ask him about the liquid clock.'

'The what?' Steadman makes a face.

'Him and Cameron are entering it for this year's Science Fair.'

'Which one's Cameron again? Is he the other deaf kid?'

'They're all deaf kids.'

Steadman had been happy that Jacob was able to go to a mainstream school, though he also seemed a little put out that his son's social circle was largely made up of the other kids from St Margaret's Additional Needs Unit.

'Ask him about the Science Fair. They really want to win. The prize is a quadcopter.'

'Liquid clock? Quadcopter? Isn't there something more normal I could talk to him about?'

'I've given you a tip, use it.'

Jacob comes in. 'Can I take Lil J out for a selfie?'

'Sure. Course.'

'I need the loo,' Jess says, keen to leave them alone. 'Does your bathroom reach basic hygiene levels?'

Steadman kisses his teeth and waves her off.

The windows in the bathroom are open yet it still smells like mould. There's no mirror, and one greyish towel, troublingly damp at this time of the day, hangs over the side of the bath because there are no hooks. On the window ledge a bottle of shower gel sits, faded green, clearly topped up with water. She hovers over the toilet seat then picks a toilet roll from the pile of empty cardboard tubes on the floor. It's not as if their own home is so pristine, but this place is another level. He really is a man that needs someone to look after him.

She goes back into the living room, shaking her wet hands. Steadman's standing in front of his stereo, the kids back out on the balcony.

'I was going to put the wrestling on,' he says.

'Wrestling? On the radio? Why would anyone listen to wrestling?'

'To hear the atmosphere.' He turns on crowd noises and offers her a tall plastic cup of a weird-coloured liquid with pink flecks. 'Or what music do they like? Drill? Trap? Ed Sheeran? I don't have a clue.'

Jess turns it down. 'Let's try and keep the background noise to a minimum.' Why does she still have to remind him of these things?

'I forgot. Sorry. So, fill me in, what's this about you viewing properties? Mustafa's selling up?'

Jess tuts. 'Haze told you?'

'Course she did. When were you going to tell me?' He slides his arms into a lilac resistance band.

'I didn't think it would happen. A part of me still thinks it won't.'

'Probably not. We all say that stuff about leaving London,' Steadman grunts, 'no one ever does though. How much did he say he's selling it for?'

'What does it matter?'

72

'I'm sure Mustafa would give you a discount if you asked *nicely*,' he says, struggling to separate his arms.

'Come on, Steadman. This is serious. This isn't school anymore. He's not going to give me his house because he once fancied me.'

'I always wondered if anything ever happened between you two.' He removes the band and looks closely at it. 'I don't think these things stretch in the heat.'

She takes the band off him and manages to separate her arms about an inch more than him before handing it back.

'Kenmure Street's a bit rough anyway. You could buy it off him for cheap, I reckon.'

'With what?' she laughs.

'You've been at your job for years; you must have some money hidden away in an account somewhere. I remember when you all moved into that place.' He makes the face he always makes when recalling the break-up of the family. 'Then, the first time I had to *visit* my kids.'

'Can we not talk about this right now?'

Steadman groans a little as he pulls. 'You been in that house years. You should have just got a council place.'

'I'm not entitled to one.'

'Because you make too much money. That's why you should never work more than sixteen hours a week.' Steadman throws the band onto the sofa and rubs his shoulders.

'Thanks for the career advice.'

She gets on well enough with Steadman, in very small doses, but she's about to lose patience with him. Why are the kids not in here too? They've done this before: invite her over to see Steadman then leave her to it while they hang out in another room.

'I don't know why you're stressing,' he says. 'You need to welcome change into your life. Change is good. It helps us grow. Look at me' – he gestures down to his offensive activewear – 'last week I couldn't run to the post box and now I can make it all the way to the corner shop. Babe, you look stressed.'

'I'm not stressed.'

'You are. I can see it in how your head creases up.'

Jess rubs her forehead and attempts to relax her face.

'Here's my boy,' he says as Jacob comes back in the room with the gecko on his arm. 'Tell me about this science exhibit you're entering?'

'It's a school thing.'

'Sounds like a big deal.'

Jacob shrugs. 'I guess. There are five schools entering this year. Bigger than last time.'

'Five schools, eh? I bet there will be plenty girls there too,' Steadman laughs and Jess cringes. Why is he doing this?

Jacob takes the gecko, places it in his hair and takes a selfie.

'You got a girlfriend at the moment?' Steadman asks.

'No, Dad. I don't like girls.'

'Oh.' Steadman takes a step back. 'So, uh, what you're saying is . . .' he looks at Jess for help, as if his son is about to come out, right here, while a gecko crawls through his afro.

'I don't think anyone in this family understands how busy I am,' Jacob says. 'I've got so much stuff to do all the time. I don't have time for girls.'

'No,' Steadman says. 'So what is it you're busy doing at the moment?'

'You know, regular cool stuff.'

'Cool,' Steadman says.

Jess feels the moment stretch on for too long to be comfortable. 'Right, Steadman, I think the lamb should almost be done. Shall we crack on?'

Lunch passes uneventfully. No one mentions *Black Panther* and no one cries. Though Steadman does try to put his hand on Jess's lower back a few times. Then before two, she wanders over to East Village, passing Celebration Avenue, Prize Walk, Anthem Way and Cheering Lane. Gosh, they really ran with the theme when mapping this place out. Jess watched these blocks go up in the run-up to the 2012 Games and then again as they were transformed into homes. There was something about the way the marketing boasted of 'luxury living' that didn't really scream 'family friendly' to her. Pa had said it was indicative of the times, that whole communities would be built where children weren't welcome. Though as Jess is walking to the right block, she does spot a small playground, with one harassed dad chasing around a toddler gone rogue.

The estate agent, an elfin-looking girl called Narsatina, waves Jess over to the intercom door. 'I know the last place I showed you wasn't quite right,' she admits as she rummages in a sandwich bag full of keys.

'Hmm, you could say that.' Jess checks her reflection as they step into the lift.

'There's not a lot in your budget,' the estate agent says.

'No, so I've been told.' Repeatedly, as in, every time she

talks to one of these people. 'Is there any wiggle room on the rent for this place?'

'There's quite a high demand for these apartments.'

'How much more does a flat have to cost before it gets to be called an apartment?' Jess laughs, but Narsatina, who on close inspection could quite possibly be under eighteen, says without irony, 'It's down to the build quality.'

The lift doors open and they walk through a brightly lit corridor. Inside the flat – no, the apartment – is all white walls and grey laminate flooring.

'Technically, this place is a three-bedroom.'

'What do you mean *technically*?'

Narsatina gestures into a pokey little box. 'Here's the first bedroom.'

'No,' Jess laughs, 'it's a cupboard.'

'It's perfect for a little kiddie.'

'Or a pet rabbit. Is this really allowed to be called a bedroom?'

'It has a window,' she replies plainly.

The beanbags, Jess thinks, if Jacob had this room there would be no floor space for the three beanbags allocated to each of his friends when they come over to game. It's okay, she would just need to allow them to play in the living room instead.

Growing up, Jess always had the box room; it never bothered her. Even when Dominic left and Pa suggested she move into his room for more space, she didn't see the point. She had stood in the doorway of his room trying to picture herself in there, where her bed and posters would go. Even with his things gone, she was convinced the room still held a little of his smell, the fresh chemically scent of his hair wax combined with a faint undertone of the spliffs he used to smoke in bed. That space would always be Dominic's, Jess could never fill it. The same way she could never, despite the time she put into her relationship with Pa, fill the gap having an estranged child left.

'The master's a good size,' Narsatina says.

It is. There's also a balcony, built-in mirrored wardrobes and an en suite. An en suite. It doesn't get much further from the mould-covered bathroom on Kenmure Street than this. 'Wow. So this is what you're paying for.'

'How old are your children?'

'Thirteen and eighteen.'

'Ah, teenagers. They're probably never home, are they?'

Jess smiles and thinks of how her children spend most of their time sat on the sofa next to her, making a mess and talking through every programme she wants to watch. Maybe this is why she doesn't spend much time worrying about the things people tell her you ought to be worried about when you have teenagers.

Narsatina jangles her bag of keys and asks. 'What do you think?'

What *does* she think? While this flat is great, financially it would stretch her a bit too thinly and she doesn't want that. She wants to have money to enjoy her life, to even entertain the idea of a little holiday next summer when Haze finishes her A levels. 'It's a lovely flat. Expensive though.'

'Course. Remember, we're also seeing those two flats on the Dockers Estate tomorrow. They're ex-council but in good shape.'

The Dockers Estate was where people went when they wanted to dump a stolen car.

As they walk out, Jess feels a tug. She looks around again, at the way the residents have put planters on their balconies and rubbish in the bins provided rather than the floor. It's a big step up from Kenmure Street and that's the important thing: that they keep stepping up and making progress. The last thing Jess needs right now is to go backwards, back to the kind of crappy flats she used to live in when her and Steadman first tried to stand on their own feet.

'The area's really nice,' Narsatina says. 'Do you know it?'

'I grew up here. My son goes to St Margaret's and my daughter, well she'll be off to the University of Oxford to study Law after college, so she can have the cupboard room.' Jess talks more about the kids and the woman smiles blankly; this wasn't going to be like her relationship with Mustafa. No one would be over fixing a broken tap on a Sunday evening or dropping by with halwa on Eid. This would be a purely professional set-up, with boundaries and a contract and a deposit. Shit, a deposit. 'How much would I need to put down to secure it?'

'One month's rent. Very reasonable. Look, if I'm honest, we want this one to go quickly, so I'm sure we could work something out.'

Okay, that's still a lot of money. A lot more than Jess has to hand right now. Though there are probably a few obvious savings that could be made, small things she can cut out that would add up to huge amounts over the year, like instead of having her eyebrows threaded by a professional, she can ask Haze to pluck them. And instead of impulse shopping in Sainsbury's every few days she can start planning meals and going to Asda. She saw a family do this for a TV show and they ended up saving enough for a trip to Florida. It will be good for the kids too, especially Haze, who's about to go off into the world on her own, to learn how to budget.

'There's also an annual service charge on these flats, it's about eight hundred and fifty,' the agent says.

'Eight hundred and fifty pounds? For what?'

'The grounds.'

'Ah, of course. The hedges.'

'It's a secure building too, it has a 24-hour concierge service.'

'A guy who takes in Amazon packages?' Jess laughs, to which Narsatina pulls a tight little smile.

'Sorry, of course, a concierge does so much more.'

Still, £850. But it's what the kids deserve, a new start, somewhere people take pride in their homes, somewhere aspirational.

On the way back, Jess checks her work emails. There's no reply from Norman about hiring a replacement for Precious, though there is an email to all staff informing them that the board of directors will be visiting the venue on Monday. Such a rare occurrence.

Jess calls Precious. 'Hey. You at work?'

'Unfortunately, yes.'

'Is everything okay? I'm just reading this serious-sounding email about the board of directors coming in next week. We only ever see them at the Christmas meal. What's happening?'

'I don't know what you're talking about.'

'Don't you check your emails?'

Precious sighs. 'No. I'm too pregnant to check emails. Isn't it enough that I showed up here at all today?'

Jess laughs for a moment then stops, 'Is Norman in today? How does he seem?'

'Like a man who hugely regrets his life choices. So, no different from usual.'

'You're sure?'

'Yes,' Precious says, her voice heavy with boredom.

'I'm paranoid. I keep hearing about all these venues losing their funding and—'

'This place opened during a global financial crisis and it's run at a loss every year since. It's a community theatre – as long as it's serving the local community, then it's successful.'

'Hmm.' Jess can't help but notice how the sound of birdsong stops as she crosses the border of East Village back into normal Stratford. 'Have you heard the rumour about The Melody closing down? It only just hired an outreach team and now they're all being made redundant.'

Precious tuts. 'Do we seem like the kind of people lucky enough to get redundancy right now? Anyway, you've been here yonks, redundancy would sort you right out.'

'Don't say that. Redundancy would be terrible.'

'Stop stressing. I'll see you Monday, all right.'

Would not having a job work out better? Maybe then she could do as Steadman said and get a council place. Then she wouldn't have to stress about high monthly rents and service charges. No. She's getting carried away. It'll be fine. It always is.

Chapter Six

Ben

Ben hovers over the Skype icon, at the offline symbol for Shanice. The call is now seventeen minutes late and Shanice hasn't even bothered sending him a message to say why. He said he wouldn't chase her if she was running late, that he would be 'online anyway' all evening, as if this was something he regularly did. He doesn't get it when people complain about losing so much time to social media or falling down wiki holes. He's got a Facebook account, though when he logs in it's just a bunch of people he doesn't really like, moaning about Muslims or joking about growing up British. He reads a few news sites, checks the weather in Tenerife and googles Hedy Lamarr. That took all of twenty minutes. Now what? Is Skype definitely working? Yeah, and it's late. He messages Shanice.

Still online. Looking forward to seeing Olivia.

He descales his coffee machine, keeping one eye on the screen and occasionally muttering, 'Come on, ring,' under his breath.

Maybe he should have called her instead. He sits at the laptop again. Harold climbs on his lap and Ben pulls up YouTube videos of Labradors falling into ponds and Shih Tzus springing through hula-hoops. Harold makes a weird little noise, somewhere between a whine and a bark, to show he's excited.

A message from Shanice comes through:

Popping out. Back soon.

He planned his whole evening around this call. How can she change things last minute? It's so typical of her, so thoughtless. He picks up his phone.

'Didn't I just say back soon?' Shanice hollers. It sounds like she's in a wind tunnel.

'I've been waiting here—'

'Ben, we're busy, we're on the be—' Her words get lost.

'I can't hear you. Shanice, I can't hear you.' Then he does hear her, her screeching laugh against bellows of wind. 'Shanice?' he presses the handset against his ear. Is that Olivia laughing too? Both of them, having the time of their lives without him.

'Call you later,' she shouts, then hangs up.

He rests his head on the table and closes his eyes, sinking into the darkness and silence. Here he is, here he is again. Harold brushes at his leg and makes a slight whimper before padding off into the hallway, leaving Ben alone in the room.

Alone. The same as he was back in Essex. Rattling around in the house without his family. Why did he think it would feel so different here? That because he was in a different setting, he wouldn't miss his life.

Harold's nails click against the lino in the hall. Ben never usually allows them to get this long. He's being neglectful. Useless. Pointless. Then the barking starts. Ben pulls his arms around his ears, he doesn't want to deal with this, he just wants to stay here, in the dark and go to sleep.

The barks get louder and louder until they can't be ignored.

'What?' Ben asks, going out to the hallway. 'What is it?'

Harold bounces up at the back of the front door in an attempt to reach his lead. This damn dog who never wants to get out when it's time to walk, sometimes knows when Ben is the one who needs to get out.

'Okay. We'll go. Not like I have to sit in online anymore.'

They come out of the flat and Ben stops to photograph and report a particularly creative pile of fly-tipping by the park gates. A mattress, flanked by two old PC screens and a manual for Windows 95. As they do a loop of the park, Ben calms down and the darkness gradually seeps away. He *did* need to get out. He'd spent most of the day inside at work, upgrading every lightbulb across fifty rooms. It had given him a headache, going up and down the ladder, creaking his neck at ninety degrees while Rick, who Ben's been asked to train, went on and on about his Ironman training.

Shanice messages.

beach windy. will txt when home

Why is she doing this? Doesn't she realise how important these calls are to him?

He types her a message.

What time will you be home?

The message goes unread.

He pictures the two of them braced against the wind, Shanice stressing about her hair going frizzy and Olivia laughing her head off, the rotation of squealing and farting she gets into when too worked up. In one way, it's comforting to think of what they're doing, that they're happy and having fun, but it's also so painful, because he's not part of it. And Gerald, is he there too? Is he the one blocking them from the wind, adding his laughter to theirs?

Harold begins to yap like crazy as a pair of power-walking elderly women in salwar kameez and New Balance trainers catch his attention.

'I love beagles,' one of the women says, stepping forward.

The woman's friend says something in their language then adds, 'Small dog. Yap, yap, yap.'

'Yeah, he can be quite vocal,' Ben says, tightening his grip as Harold bounces forward, still snapping at the lady. 'I think it's your scarf.' He nods to the flowing pink and yellow material over the woman's shoulder. 'He wants to play with it.'

'Naughty dog,' the woman says as she tucks away the tail end and lowers onto her haunches to stroke him. 'Ah, he must make you very happy.'

'Yeah, he does. He's a good dog.'

The woman stands up and smiles at Ben before resuming her speed-walking, arms swinging, mouth going a hundred miles an hour. That's it then, the extent of Ben's social interaction for the day. He cuts out of the park, then as he crosses the street, he hears Wolf.

'Hey, Benny Boy.'

Ben waves back, a little too pleased to see him. Is he really so desperate for company?

'How did you like those Chelsea buns from yesterday?'

'I loved them. Thanks.'

'Come over?'

'Can't.' Ben nods down to Harold.

'Bring him. I have dog food.'

What else is there to do apart from sit and stare at his four potato-coloured walls and feel sad?

As he enters Wolf's place, he's hit by heat. The hallway radiator is searing.

'You want dinner?' Wolf asks, flicking his hair, most of which is pulled back in a ponytail today.

'Oh, no thanks. I've got food at home.' Moussaka for one, what an absolute treat. Ben discreetly swipes the heating knob down to twenty as he enters the kitchen. The place is really messy today, books fanned with post-it notes are sprawled across the table alongside rusty baking tins, jelly moulds and a large bowl of plastic fruit. 'What's going on? Are you having another clear-out?'

'Yes, it's endless.'

'Was it you who fly-tipped by the park?'

'Smart arse,' Wolf laughs. 'What a mess though. Let's see

how long it takes those pricks from Newham Council to come and clean it up.' He shuffles over to the fridge and pulls out a plate, peels away some tinfoil and dangles a piece of bacon above Harold.

'He can't eat that.'

'Nonsense. Look at his little face lighting up. He'd love some bacon.'

'I'm sure he would, but he can't eat it.'

Wolf shrugs and gives Harold a slice of bread instead. 'Now, your neighbour, I need an ally on my theory.'

'The woman downstairs?'

'Yes, there's men in and out all hours. The odd woman too.'

'She might just like a good time.'

'We all like good times. What I want to know is, is she being paid for having hers?'

Ben's still new to the street, so while it's true the woman does seem to have a lot of visitors, mostly male, he's trying to be a good neighbour and not jump in, assuming people are sex workers when they're probably just sociable.

'You do like cheese, don't you?' Wolf asks.

'Really, I can't stay. I've got a call with my daughter later.'

The oven clock he fixed last week is wrong again. He gets up to sort it. 'How can you stand this? And that drives me mad too,' Ben says, nodding out into the tiny garden at the shards of fence scattered across the grass.

'It's the left side, neighbour's problem.'

'No, right side is neighbour's problem. Left side is *your* problem. I told you it was going to blow down. Do you want me to get some panels from B&Q for you?'

Wolf waves a hand. 'I like the broken fence; it adds to the general chaos of living here. Here, help me box this stuff up.'

There's something intriguing about Wolf's house. Each time Ben's here he spots another shelf of books, a brown framed map of a country that no longer exists, a bit of furniture piled with interesting crap. It's grubby though and when it doesn't smell of baking or cooking, it smells like cheap coffee and something earthy and mulchy.

'You want any of this?' Wolf asks, indicating down to the table.

'I'm not really one for the whole fake fruit thing.'

'Pah, take something. It will jazz your place up.' Wolf pulls out a lobster-shaped jelly mould. 'No? It's all for the charity shop then. And this is the box I'm keeping; I need to get myself down to an auction house.'

'You really think this stuff is worth anything?' Ben asks, looking at the junk in the box marked *Antiques Roadshow*.

'Yes, I do, and every penny earned brings me closer to my dream of sitting in a red booth with a beautiful broad, eating a steak at Musso and Frank's.'

'I don't get it. Why are you putting on that accent?'

'It's my dream, son. To go to Hollywood and live out my Bogart fantasies.' He hangs a bunch of plastic grapes over Harold's head. 'I've always wanted to go. Ever since I was a boy, I've been completely enraptured by it.'

Ben pictures Wolf in holiday mode wearing sunglasses and a bumbag. It makes him smile. 'Sounds great.'

'Yes. Yes,' he says, as if trying to convince himself.

'Is this something you've already booked?'

'Ah, not yet. No.'

'You seem unsure.'

'Do I? Perhaps it's my age. I had a nightmare recently about dying on a Virgin Atlantic flight. What a way to go. How did I get so old? I was meant to do this trip years ago, then it all went tits up financially.'

'You made a bad investment?' Ben teases.

'Family troubles – don't ask. I think once I book the flights, that's it, I'll be sure. Until then, it's a little scary, the idea of travelling so far away.' Harold finally bats down the grapes then sits on them and closes his eyes. Wolf laughs. 'I love this mutt, he's the dog version of me.'

On the table is a booklet, a diary, left open on a date from last week and a record of everything Wolf had to eat that day, followed by some numbers at the end. Ben knows what this means but why hasn't Wolf, who has already shared his glasses prescription and blood type, mentioned it? Ben picks up the book, being sure to close it. 'I'm assuming you don't want this going to the charity shop?'

Wolf snatches it up and stuffs it in a drawer, saying nothing. They continue packing until the table is clear. Ben can't deal with the silence, the tension, it's so obvious there's an issue here, a sensitive subject. He stops and looks at Wolf. It's not Ben's place to know or ask anything.

'I'm still getting used to it myself,' Wolf says finally.

Ben shrugs his shoulders, as if unclear.

'Used to this diagnosis.'

'It's a new thing then? When did you find out?'

'Last month. I'd been pissing for Britain but you've got to

88

be at death's door before you get a doctor's appointment round here.' Wolf tuts and turns away. 'The doctor is making me do this. You think I want to keep a diary like a little love-struck girl? It's only a touch of diabetes.'

'A *touch* of diabetes?'

'Yes, and it's very inconvenient at this point in my life. I've only just decided to let myself go and now I have to start watching what I eat again.'

'Have you told anyone? Your daughter?'

'Pah,' he says, waving a hand.

'Unbelievable. You've got to tell people. It's not a death sentence.'

Wolf grumps.

'My granddad had Type 2 diabetes. I get it.'

'If you're going to tell me he died from some horrible condition linked to it, I don't want to hear it.'

'No, he didn't die from it. He died from being ninety-two.'

They both start laughing. Wolf takes off his glasses and pinches the top of his nose.

'He was a stubborn old fart as well,' Ben says.

'Old fart? I don't want to be an old man. I still feel young. Like I'm just getting started and now I have to get ready to die.'

'Bit dramatic.'

'What do you know? You're about twenty-three.'

'I'm forty-one, Wolf.'

Ben's phone buzzes with a message from Shanice.

Busy now. Will b back 2 late. Tlk another time.

He hates the way she texts. The way she shortens some words and spells others out.

'What's wrong?' Wolf asks. 'Why is your face so long?'

'My ex cancelled my call with Olivia. They're too busy for me.'

Busy now. It's become an increasingly common excuse. A photo follows, one of Olivia, her tongue blue from eating bubblegum ice cream, her face bronze and freckled from the sun. Ben knows he should be happy to see this, but it hurts.

'Isn't she a toddler? What could she be busy with?'

'Olivia is six. She doesn't want to spend her time talking to me through a computer screen. The last time we talked she couldn't sit still, kept looking away like there was somewhere else she had to be.' He laughs a little, because even though it hurts, it was kind of cute, the way she made her excuses to get off the call, telling him that while she loved him *the most* she also wanted to go and play with her Sylvanian Families. 'I knew I would miss her. I didn't know it would feel like this though.' He feels the darkness descend again, and leans his head into hands.

'Ah son, I'm sorry.'

When Ben had tucked her in bed at night, right before they moved away, she told him how she was going to live with him when she was a 'big girl' so they could read *The Princess Diaries* every night forever. And as much as he hated those princess books, a part of him loved the idea.

'Divorces are painful. The first part is the worst, you feel like your whole life's been smashed up, and it has. It gets better though. Trust me, I'm mad enough to have done it twice.'

'I should go.'

'Why? To sit in your flat and sulk about how much you miss your ex?'

'It's not her I miss. We weren't the best together. It's the whole thing I miss: being a family. I can't believe—' He stops. This isn't the place to start sinking, he needs to go home.

'She'll always be your little girl,' Wolf says. 'Nothing changes that, not divorce, not distance, not the years.'

'It's easy for you to say, you got to bring up your kid.'

Wolf winces.

'Sorry, I shouldn't have said that. I'm not up for being social right now. I really should go.'

'No, no. I'm not offended. I understand. You said she's coming to stay with you soon?'

'Yeah, in the summer holidays. It's still ages away.'

'Keep yourself busy and it'll fly by. You need a distraction. A bit of fun. What are you into?'

'In terms of?'

'Women. What's your type?'

Ben laughs, it's awkward on so many levels. His own father never spoke to him about women. In fact, his own father, so stoic and practical, probably spoke to him less in a week than Wolf does in a day. Even now Wolf is talking, going on about some woman he met while browsing the olive counter in the local international supermarket. 'Let's cheer you up, son,' he says, pulling two bottles of beer from the fridge. 'Here you go, cheers. Now tell me what you like, Ben. You like big girls? I love them curvy.'

*

By the fifth beer it's less of a conversation and more of a monologue as Wolf seeks to help Ben improve his love life.

'What you need is a woman who'll appreciate what you
have. You think I'm a catch on paper?' Wolf says, expanding
his arms, 'I'm a skinny old man with a funny accent, and
guess what? They keep coming.'

'What happened to your second wife anyway? Is she buried
under your patio? Is that why it's so uneven?'

Wolf mimics Ben's drunken laugh and says to Harold, 'Oh,
he thinks he's a funny drunk?'

'Tell me what happened. Why did you split up?' Ben can
hear himself slur. He looks down at Harold, fidgeting with
a burst tennis ball by the radiator.

'She got fed up. Had enough. She wanted to restart her life.
Be someone different.' Wolf turns the bottle around. 'And she
thought I drank too much.'

'Oh.' Ben presses the balls of his hands into his eyes in an
effort to stop his head spinning. 'And did you?'

Wolf turns out his bottom lip as if considering the facts
before answering. 'Probably.'

'And now?'

'No, oh no no no. This is rare,' he says, lifting the bottle.
'I gave up drinking heavily when Claire left. I had kids to
raise.'

'Kids?'

Wolf looks over at Harold and smiles. 'Your daddy is shit-
faced. I think you need to get him home to bed.'

*

Ben gets in the flat and it's true he is drunker than he's been in years but there are definitely two things that don't make sense to him. One, why Wolf was barely tipsy, and two, why he said *kids*, plural, he definitely did.

Ben opens the laptop, quits Skype and does what he swore he wouldn't when his mum suggested it. What he knows other people do all the time. He types Dominic Bakker in online. He hits return and closes his eyes, feeling his head spin. When he looks back at the screen, there's nothing. Not an account, not a news article, no trace at all. Even Ben has links to his Facebook and a local newspaper article about sliding-door wardrobes he has no idea how to get rid of.

Kids. Wolf definitely said it, then brushed it off like it was Ben who misheard, which, given that it took him three tries to get his key in the door, may have been the case. Of course, Dominic Bakker exists, he just isn't anything to do with Wolf. He wasn't German. And he didn't have a younger sister, because there's no way Jessica Bakker, the most perfect woman Ben has ever met, could be related to such a monster.

Ben types *her* name in, praying not to be met with another void.

Thankfully, there she is: a Facebook account full of photos of her in brightly coloured leggings at workout classes in the park and red lipstick on nights out. He genuinely can't decide which photos he likes more. Suddenly all the mystery about what people do online disappears as he loses about half an hour drunkenly looking at photos of Jessica Bakker and reading her profile. He wishes he could tear himself away and stop being a creep but there's something about her.

Maybe he should take a chance and send her a friend request. No, that would be weird. But then he wants to take chances. That was always the thing Shanice said he never did. His lack of spontaneity used to drive her crazy.

He's already met Jessica twice now. Would it be that weird to request her virtual friendship? He thinks of Wolf asking him about his type. Ben didn't think he had a type. Though, if he did it would be Jessica. Curvy, beautiful, with a slightly chaotic edge about her. Quick to laugh. Fun-loving. Yes, it's time to change his life. He hits the button to send a friend request and sits back. Done. See? Easy.

He feeds Harold, reads the latest issue of the *Newham Mag* cover to cover and then waters the tiny plants his mum dropped off yesterday; succulents, she called them, but it's difficult to get the water into the silly little pots without spilling it all over the place.

Jessica was definitely online when he sent the request, yet there's no progress on the virtual friendship. 'Hmm. Do you think I've been too forward?' he asks Harold, who makes a little humming noise before crouching down to watch a moth on the other side of the Juliette balcony. Ben goes over to open the doors, and hears voices from below. A couple walk hand in hand through the park, despite the fact darkness is falling and it's almost witching hour for Fight Club. The couple stop under a tree and lean into each other. Maybe they're love-struck teenagers with strict parents and nowhere else to go, or more likely she's a wife bored by her husband and he's a sexy pastry chef looking for new adventures. Ben slams the balcony doors shut and sits back in front of his laptop. 'I hate

Facebook. Why do we do it to ourselves? Nothing good ever came from seeing your uncle Bob's political views.'

From downstairs he hears laughter, then silence. Everyone's getting it on in some way or another tonight. Everyone except him. Sitting in alone. His phone goes, a message from Mum.

Are you watching Casualty? Fantastic episode tonight.

He blows a raspberry and looks again at Jessica. Beautiful, sexy, accomplished, confident Jessica. She's probably looking at his friend request, baffled, with no idea who he is. Then, something changes and just like that he becomes friends with Jessica Bakker.

Chapter Seven

Jess

June

Dockers Estate was a dump, and Jess was done living in dumps. So no good-sized bedrooms, newly fitted kitchen or garden space could compensate for the group of teens smoking in the playground, the burst nappies by the bins or the scrawl of *flat 29 for a good time* on the lift door. When she turned those flats down, both Steadman and Pa accused her of being a snob and thinking she was too good to live on an estate, but they didn't get it. Because they couldn't put themselves in the shoes of a beautiful teenage girl coming home after dark, or a geeky kid with a disability passing a group of older boys. The bottom line was, there was no way Jess was taking her kids to live in that kind of environment. Plus, the pressure was on. The photos of her home had already gone live, followed by what Mustafa called a 'flurry of interest' from potential buyers. All this without them even seeing the place in real life. Then, the final push was a call from Narsatina, the confirmation that the flat in the Olympic Village, the one Jess had fallen in love with before talking herself out of, was still available and that the landlord was willing to offer a 'slight reduction' in the rent if the new tenant could move within the next two weeks. It was meant to be.

'Congratulations,' Narsatina says as Jess wedges a copy of the signed tenancy agreement into her handbag.

'Thanks.' It's official, Victory House is theirs. Jess is delighted with it, slightly anxious about the cost and also, more urgently, running late for work. As she walks quickly through the streets and back into the centre of Stratford, she slightly regrets the gold high-heeled cork sandals she put on this morning, though they went with the new dress, which was also flashy. It was a day to celebrate, after all: finally a new home, a new start. The sun cracks through, as the weather report promised it would, and while Jess waits at the crossing she finds herself embarrassingly aware of checking out the driver of every passing white van. There are so many white vans. She's never noticed this before. Though this morning, none of them are Ben's. A young guy, blasting Ghetts from a blue Escort, slows to honk his horn at her. She tucks her hair behind her ears and feigns embarrassment.

When she arrives round the back of the theatre Precious is standing by the smokers' entrance, engaged in some sort of leg stretch.

'Precious? What are you doing out here?'

'Having a fag. What does it look like?' Precious lifts her left foot and jiggles it about. 'I've got restless legs. You look nice. Showing off your waist. I remember when I used to have a waist.'

'I'm telling you, it's the stress of last month, it's knocked pounds off me. I've been honked at twice already this morning. Here, wiggle your toes like this.'

'You got your papers signed for the flat then?' Precious asks.

Jess smiles and nods.

'I'm happy for you. I think you'll enjoy living somewhere less ghetto.'

'Shut up,' she laughs. 'How long have we got before this meeting anyway?'

'About five minutes.'

Jess bites her bottom lip.

'Stop stressing,' Precious says. 'You know it won't be you.'

It had been three weeks since the board of directors had visited The Anstey. It was odd, they had spent a short time touring the facilities and avoiding eye contact with staff before disappearing into Norman's office for the whole afternoon. Everyone had been tense since then, waiting for 'news'. Redundancies were expected, especially as no one could call them the leanest of teams. Of course, Jess wasn't in the firing line, because her work in community outreach was one of the key reasons The Anstey kept getting funding year after year, funding that propped up all its other money-losing ventures.

'I think they're going to announce Norman's leaving,' Precious says. 'How much do you think he gets paid anyway? I don't have a clue what he does all day.'

'Me neither. Still sad though.'

'Getting rid of Norman would probably be the same as cutting me plus all the cafe staff.'

They continue to speculate as they walk through to the auditorium, where some of the staff are already waiting. The house lights are up, though Jess notices how many have blown. There used to be a team of technicians and now there's just Phil, an old roadie approaching retirement who spends most of his time swearing at the interns. Jess never sits in the auditorium, there's never a need to, though being here now she notices how sticky the floors are, how mucky the maroon seats have become. This is what happens when the cleaners' hours get cut. Last week, customers had complained about there being no toilet roll in the toilets and it fell on Jess to top them up and chuck some bleach down the loos while she was there.

Norman walks in and takes a seat, alone, in the front row.

'What's he doing?' Jess whispers. 'I thought he was taking the meeting?'

Then the board of directors enter. They line up in front of the stage in their black and grey suits, like some obscure am-dram collective, and one indicates for Norman to join them.

'Look at Norman,' Jess whispers. 'He looks like he's been crying. Oh my God. Something awful is about to happen. I can feel it.'

Norman steps forward and claps to get everyone's attention, as if every pair of eyes in the house isn't already on him, every breath held.

'Good morning, folks. Thank you all for making it here today.'

'As if we had a choice,' Precious mumbles. But Jess is no longer in the mood to snipe.

'This last year here,' he begins, 'has been one of the greatest of my career. I've never worked with a team so committed and dedicated to the world of theatre, and of course to their community.'

Precious makes a winding motion with her index fingers.

'But all journeys, even the most beautiful ones, must come to an end. And it is with great regret that I must tell you all that this season will be our last.'

There's a gasp from the seats and Jess notices she's been pressing her jaws together, clenching her fists.

Norman raises his hands, facing his palms out towards the seats. 'Please, please,' he tries, his voice breaking. '*Oh! What a Lovely War* will be our final youth production, and what a fine show it has been.' He tries to inject a smile, as if this makes it all okay. 'I will personally talk to each of you about the redundancy process. I'm sorry. So very, very sorry.' He breaks down and one of the directors takes his place, picking up where he left off with a timetable about what happens next. Though Jess hears none of it.

Jess and Precious had sat in the Lime Tree cafe for hours after the announcement, nursing coffees and trying to work out how long their redundancy packages would last. Despite being at The Anstey her whole working life, Jess's payout wouldn't be great. Her first year there was voluntary, followed by years of low-paid, part-time contracts, and she had only been running the outreach programme for the last two years.

After Precious had waddled home to begin what she described as her new life of 'eating cookies and watching *Loose Women*', Jess had one more coffee alone and then cried in the toilets.

She now stands on the Broadway, the contract for Victory House heavy in her bag. Shit, she thinks, shit, shit, shit. It's too early to go home, so she kills twenty minutes outside the tube station, watching a group of young men in expensive tracksuits perform Christian rap. When it's done, she takes their leaflet and promises to attend their church.

What now? She half considers joining the hordes of people marching up the steps to Westfield. Though what would she do there, besides gaze at things she has absolutely no business purchasing now she no longer has an income? The idea of that is so completely terrifying she pushes it from her mind.

The clouds begin to thicken and she doesn't have a jacket. Then, as the rain falls, she regrets wearing such a light-coloured dress with such a dark-coloured bra. Sod's law, she thinks, this wasn't even forecast. The buses are too busy and the drivers take one look at the crowd at the stop before waving a hand and driving on. So, despite the rain, her exposed bra and her beautiful, yet painful shoes, Jess walks home.

Home is full of signs that her offspring are back before her: every appliance seems to be on, there's a strong smell of burnt toast and the *Hamilton* soundtrack plays loudly. Jess unlaces the gold straps from her ankles and throws the heels onto the shoe pile. They've left blisters on her toes and imprints around her ankles. She rubs at the dirt on her feet and pulls on some bed slippers sitting by the door in an attempt to bring her temperature back up.

The coat-rack is full of puffas, denim jackets, sports bags and dripping umbrellas. She should sort it out, and usually she would, it's a little game she likes to play with herself, seeing how many chores she can identify and complete within the first ten minutes of getting home. In the living room she steps over the £120 Adidas jacket she bought for Haze, lying on the floor. It's the same jacket Haze said she would die without. *Die*, she actually used that word. Yet now it's been abandoned in the corner of the room and covered in dust.

Jess sinks onto the sofa and closes her eyes while 'My Shot' rattles through to its big finale. The room is silent for a few seconds, she counts them, 1, 2, 3, 4. Then the song starts up again, this time with Haze's piercing voice over the top.

'Haze.' Jess's shouts disappear into the noise. 'Hazel Bakker Glen,' she screams.

The music stops and moments later Haze thumps down the stairs in that particular way she has, which makes it sound as if she's a fifteen-stone man rather than a five-foot-four girl. 'Mum?' she huffs. 'I didn't know you were home already.'

Half of Haze's hair lies straight and shiny over one shoulder, while the other half, still un-straightened, is tied up in a fluffy bunch.

'That,' says Jess, pointing to the ceiling, 'is exactly what the neighbours have been bitching about.'

'It helps me concentrate.'

'How? How can it be possible that you study with that on?'

'Are you saying I can't play music in the daytime?'

'I'm saying you don't need to play it so loudly.'

'It wasn't loud.' Haze sits on the arm of the chair then slides herself down beside Jess, squashing her legs. 'Did you get the keys?'

'No. Today was about signing the papers.' Signing the papers and feeling like she was on top of the world seems like something that happened a lifetime ago.

Haze cocks her head to the side and narrows her eyes in an expression she's picked up from her dad. 'What's wrong? Have you been crying?'

'No.' Jess pats at the skin around her eyes. 'I got caught in the rain.'

'You look a bit rough.'

'Thanks.'

'Sorry. The dress looks good on you though. I'm hoping you didn't wear it with those fluffy socks? And I know flashing the goods is like your thing, but maybe a white bra would look classier.'

'Ha ha.'

'Did you go to the post office for me? You said you'd do my Boohoo returns.'

'Oh. I forgot. It's still sitting in the hallway.'

Jess wouldn't usually run around doing these types of errands but she had felt so guilty the other night, watching Haze repackaging the clothes she'd treated herself to. Jess knew her daughter wanted a new dress for some upcoming party but the reality of uni costs, on a partial scholarship, was starting to sink in. The least Jess could do was take the package to the post office for her.

'And did you manage to get the paint for my room?' Haze asks, pushing it a little.

Strictly speaking, they weren't allowed to decorate Victory House, but agreeing to a makeover was the only way Jess could calm Haze down after she saw the measurements of her room.

'When would I have had the chance to do that?' Jess resolves to get up, though she's not sure what for. What is she meant to do if she doesn't have to go to work tomorrow? They said she was welcome to come in, that she was free to use 'the facilities' as she wished, as if she would clock in each morning of the four-week consultation process to use the free high-speed internet.

She wriggles away from Haze and goes into the kitchen, looking into the washing machine and finding it still filled with the load of bedding and towels she put in before work. 'Could you not have hung this stuff up?'

'How was I meant to know there was a wash in there?' Haze asks defensively.

'Because you watched me pile it in this morning.'

Haze storms over as if to help, and pulls one item from the drum. 'I can't believe you put this in the machine. It's meant to be handwashed.' She shakes a purple skirt out. 'It's wrecked. I might as well bin it. I can't believe you chucked it in with a bunch of towels.'

'Haze, I've had a really, really long day.' Too long to stand in this kitchen, with its laundry to be sorted and washing-up to be done and dinner to be cooked.

'It's only half four.'

'Really? Cause it feels about two a.m. I'm exhausted and—' Jess closes her eyes and rubs her own shoulders. 'I had a bit of a bad day at work.'

'You, bad day?' Haze leans against the fridge. 'That's rarer than you coming home early. Are you working this weekend?'

'No.'

'Wow, you're going to be at home?'

'What's that meant to mean?'

'Nothing, Mum.'

She stares at her daughter, her bratty, ungrateful daughter, who has no concept of how hard Jess works. 'I need to work, Haze.' It hurts to say this because it's like she's saying it for herself. She *does* need to work. There's no alternative to that, yet Haze says it like it's such a bad thing. 'You're eighteen. You should be able to organise yourself. To do your own washing, post your own parcels and make your own food. I'm not your PA.'

Haze's face changes. 'No, but you *are* my mum. And I do need help right now.'

'You're off to university next year. Who's going to look after you then?'

'The same person who looks after me now,' she snaps, 'myself.'

'What?'

Haze storms out of the kitchen and up the stairs.

Chapter Eight

Ben

There used to be a delivery driver who would sit outside Ben's old flat. Every lunchtime this guy would consume a baguette and Ribena while sat alone in his van. Ben, who would come home from work to quickly walk Harold, always thought it was the most depressing thing. Yet, here Ben is, sitting alone in his van, about to eat two meal deals after Mum said she was having a 'working lunch'. As if that was something nursery teachers did.

He parks outside his flat, where someone's dumped three empty bottles of Budweiser and a burst carrier bag of potato peelings. Across the road, Wolf's front door is open, yet he's nowhere to be seen. Ben crosses over, then notices the key in the lock.

'Wolf?' he shouts into the hallway. A part of Ben's mind flashes to an image of Wolf spread across the kitchen floor, passed out or, worse, knocked out. 'You here?'

He pulls out the keys and steps inside. In the kitchen the

Hello Kitty stereo blasts Sugababes, then he hears the old man in the garden, chatting and laughing to a neighbour over the pieces of broken fence. Ben considers backtracking, literally, and pretending like it never happened but Wolf spots him. 'Ben,' he shouts, gripping his chest.

'Sorry.'

'You scared me.'

'Sorry. Your front door is wide open and you left your key in. I thought something had happened to you.'

'Lizzie, thank you for this, talk later,' he calls to the woman. He winks at Ben as he comes inside the kitchen, taking the keys and putting them in the pocket of his chinos. 'My neighbour,' he says, raking his fingers through his loose hair, which looks extra dark and shiny today. 'Lovely, isn't she? A little young for me, though recently single. Would you be interested?'

'No. Thank you.'

'She's going to fix that fence.'

'I said I'd do it.'

'You've already done enough. Let her take care of it. Good you popped by.'

'I didn't. Your door was—'

'I haven't seen you this week. Remember I'm away this weekend? Did I tell you?'

'Oh yeah. Is this the German chess club thing?'

'Yes, two days by the coast and the weather is looking fine,' he says while doing a little dance. 'I dropped my ring down the sink last night. I think it's stuck in the U-bar.'

'The U-bend?'

'Exactly, I knew you would know.' He pats Ben on the chest. 'Usually, I wouldn't care, but the women in Kent tend to be a bit randy and a wedding ring always helps to deter them. Can you fish it out for me?'

'I, er, I don't have my tools.'

'Go and fetch them. Bring Harold too. I'll make lunch.'

'Actually, I've already got lunch.' Ben holds up his meal deals.

'You have company?'

'No. I bought one for my mum, but she couldn't make it. Here.'

Wolf takes the packages. 'Ah, spicy Mexican bean wrap. A man after my own heart. Though you can't eat this cold. Go and get your tools. I'll get the panini machine out.'

How can he say no? He walks over to his flat, getting Harold, and then to the van to get his tools, wondering if he should tell Wolf outright that he 'knew' Dominic. He's almost worked out how to say, 'By the way, I think you had a son who made my life so unbearable I had to move school and area. Is he dead? Is that why you haven't brought him up?'

'So, how are you?' Wolf asks as Ben returns. 'How's the work going?'

'Okay. Busy. I wanted to ask you something—'

'*Kleiner hundi*,' Wolf says, his attention on Harold, who does his little sideways jump to get close enough to lick Wolf's hand. The room begins to smell of oil and burnt cheese. 'I went to one of those trendy cafes with Haze once,' Wolf says, waving a hand over the machine. 'I had a halloumi and chicken panini, delicious, but £7.50. Then I thought, why am I paying so much to eat what I could make at home?'

Ben opens the cupboard under the sink and starts removing all kinds of crap from it. He's not done a U-bend in years, plumbing being his weakest area.

'Come and drink your tea before you do that,' Wolf says.

Ben washes his hands and sits at the table. It seems like an awkward moment to blurt out anything about Dominic. He needs to ease into it somehow, to get Wolf back onto the topic of parenting.

'How's Jessica doing?'

Wolf widens his eyes. 'My Jessica?'

'Yeah.' Immediately Ben wishes he could take it back. In any given visit he asks Wolf about twenty questions that get little to no relevant response, so why does he appear so completely engaged with this question? Could it be that she's told Wolf about the friend request? Ben cringes, wishing he'd never done it. What must she think of him? Some random neighbour of her dad's, wanting to virtually befriend her.

'I didn't realise you knew Jess,' Wolf says.

'I don't. Not really.' Ben busies himself inspecting the jars in the centre of the table. 'I've only met her a few times. She was moving house?' he adds, making great attempts to sound vague.

'She told you that? Hmm. Yes, her landlord, the little creep, is selling the place from under her feet. Three hundred and sixty-two thousand for an ex-council place in Stratford. Can you believe that? It's a scandal. He should have to split the profit with the local authority.'

This sets Wolf off on a political rant that jumps from Thatcher to Grenfell to street homelessness. Ben loves politics but can't stand people ranting about them, and when it comes to housing, he's not sure where he stands. His parents both bought their council houses back in the eighties. Even the flat he's in right now is ex-council.

'I've put myself off lunch now,' Wolf says, exhausted. He turns to Harold and makes a kissing noise with his lips.

'Has she found somewhere else?'

'Yes, some pricey shoebox in what used to be the Olympic Village. She's moving next weekend – thank God I'm away for that. It's all been a bit of a rush job and I can't imagine she's even packed. And you should see Jess's place, packed to the roofers with shtuff.'

'Hmm.' Ben glances around the room.

'Don't judge me,' Wolf says, waving the spatula. 'I'm in the middle of a major clear-out.'

'So, uh, is Jessica single?'

Wolf wide-eyes Ben as if in shock.

'No, what I meant was, if she's on a single income, it must have been hard to find a place round here. I know I struggled to find my one-bed and . . .' Ben stops talking when he notices Wolf grinning. 'What?'

'She'd have you for breakfast. *Mittagszeit*,' he calls to Harold, throwing him a piece of cheese.

'I didn't say—'

'You didn't have to. You think I can't spot a *predator* when it's sat at my table?'

'Predator? No, Wolf, I didn't—'

Wolf pats Ben on the shoulder. 'I'm only messing with you.'

The front door opens and someone trudges into the hallway,

causing Harold to stand up, his ears pricked, before bounding away and barking.

'It's probably the Hermes guy,' Wolf says. 'He often pops in to use the toilet. Calm down, little one. Oh, it's you,' he says as Jessica's daughter comes into the kitchen. 'I didn't realise you were coming over.'

'Yeah, I finished early. I really don't want this dog ripping my tights.'

'Sorry,' Ben pulls Harold away and Wolf chucks another bit of cheese to placate him.

'This is Hazel,' Wolf says as he slides the wraps, now slightly charred, onto plates. 'My granddaughter. This is Ben from number fourteen.'

'Hi,' she says, not even looking at him. 'I've had the worst day. You know that grant I was telling you about, the top-up one? I didn't realise you had to be like an asylum seeker in order to be eligible for it. What a shitshow.' She starts opening and closing the cupboards. 'They bang on about diversity, yet I'm not in the running because I'm not quite poor enough.' She points to one of the wraps, 'Can I eat this?'

'Yes,' Wolf says. 'I'm going to make some cheese toasties too.'

'Anyway, I need to find something else quick, because I already spent that money in my head and I'm battling for shifts with the others at Boost right now and— did this dog just fart?'

'Sorry,' Ben says, again trying to pull Harold away.

'I like your hair by the way, Opa. Very Harry Styles.'

Wolf shakes his waves out with a flourish. 'Is that the rapper? Because yes, that's exactly the look I was going for.'

'Anyway,' Hazel continues, 'I'm already eligible for the Crankstart Scholarship – remember I told you about that? It's not enough though, there needs to be something else or I'll have to take a year out to work first.'

While looking on Jessica's Facebook page, Ben had discovered that Hazel wasn't some overachieving outlier, she was one of a bigger group, a new kind of alumni that left St Margaret's primed for elite universities and the kind of careers that people around here didn't even consider, never mind do, back in Ben's day.

She finally sits at the table, then carefully unrolls the wrap, rearranges the contents and makes a zigzag of sriracha sauce across it. 'You were here the other day, weren't you?' she asks, fixing her cat eyes on Ben.

'Ben's a kind of DIY renaissance man,' Wolf says. 'He's going to fix the U-bar for me.'

'Useful,' she says. 'And this is your dog?'

'Yep.' Ben heads back to the sink, feeling a little uncomfortable in the gaze of this girl because, while he's failed to see echoes of Dominic in Wolf, a minute in Hazel's company is already taking him back to being a teenager.

'Where's your mother?' Wolf asks.

'She's outside. Jacob's trying to save all the snails on the street.'

Outside. Shit. Jessica is coming in too. It's what Ben's waited on, wished for, though now it's about to happen he's not sure he's ready for it. It feels too awkward somehow. Like he shouldn't really be here, sitting on the floor of her father's kitchen, pretending to fix stuff. U-bend. U-bend. How hard can it be?

'Another panini, son.' Wolf puts a plate with a pale cheese toastie beside Ben's feet.

Ben slides under the sink as Jessica walks into the kitchen. Her hair is wet and tied up high on her head, her face damp and flushed. She looks completely distracted and doesn't even notice him. A teenage boy trails in behind.

'Whoa, Mum, you look weather-beaten,' Hazel says.

'It's raining,' she snaps. 'I hate this time of year. You're tricked into thinking it's summer yet it's rain, rain, bloody rain.'

'If you like rain,' the boy says in a game-show host voice, 'you'll love England.'

'Oh, Pa, your hair.'

'You like?'

'I wouldn't go out in the pouring rain with it,' Jessica laughs. 'Whose dog is this? Ah, hi,' she says, spotting Ben.

'My ring fell down the plughole. Ben's getting it out for me.' Wolf sends Ben a wink across the kitchen.

'Hi,' he says, possibly smiling too much. 'Harold, get down. Sorry. He likes new people.'

'Your dog's called Harold?' Jessica asks, smiling back. She really does have a great smile and she's beaming it right at him.

'Yeah, um, as in Wilson.'

Hazel laughs, 'Love that.'

Harold calms as the teenage boy scratches him behind the ears. 'Ah Mum, look how friendly dogs are. Why have we never had one? And they don't eat their babies like those creepy little gerbils we used to have.'

Ben slides his phone from his pocket and googles how to remove a U-bend, while casting quick glances over at Jessica as she goes about the kitchen speaking with Wolf in German. He's heard Wolf speak it before on the phone and sometimes, especially if you catch him after he's been in the pub all afternoon, his accent is so strong it sounds as if he's speaking it anyway. But Ben's finding hearing Jessica speak another language weirdly cute.

'What are you doing?' Hazel asks him.

'I'm, er, loosening the pipe.'

She looks behind herself to her mum, then back at Ben and makes an amused face. Is he *that* obvious?

'It's not a hard job,' Ben says. 'I'll be out of the way in a couple of minutes.'

Hazel laughs and calls behind her, 'Jacob, you like fixing things, don't you? Maybe you can help Opa's *plumber*.'

The boy comes over and crouches down by Ben.

'Hi,' Ben says. 'I'm not actually a plumber.'

'What?' the boy kneels lower, cocking his head to one side to reveal a hearing aid or something. It looks like a little machine stuck on the side of his head. Wolf's always going on about his grandson, why did he never mention the kid is deaf?

Ben comes out from under the sink, overwhelmed by trying to think of what to say and how to say it, without sounding like one of those Brits on holiday. 'Hello. I'm Ben. I'm fixing the sink,' he says, making sure to articulate each word.

'You can speak normally,' Hazel calls from the table. 'He's wearing a cochlear, he can hear you.'

Ben doesn't know what a cochlear is but knows he's messed up somewhere. 'Right,' he says, turning to look face on at the boy. 'Sorry.'

'It's okay,' he shrugs. 'How old is your dog?'

'Thirteen, so pretty old for a beagle.'

'I've wanted a dog my whole life, but Mum says I can't be trusted to walk myself never mind walk a dog. The thing is, she still sees me as a kid rather than the young man I am.' He pulls a spanner from the toolbox, inserts his finger in one end and swings it around. 'I'm the science lab monitor this term; do you know what that means?'

'Er, you get to wear a lab coat?'

'Bingo. And I'm in charge of everything. Glassware. Bunsen burners. Chemicals.' He lays one hand on his chest, the other still spinning the spanner. 'When it comes to responsibilities, it doesn't get bigger than that.'

Ben grabs the spanner from his hand. 'I don't think we'll be needing that one.'

'Me neither. Let's use a hammer instead. How much money do you make as a plumber?'

Ben laughs. He can hear Jessica and Wolf in the hallway, shouting.

'Sounds tense out there. Should I leave?'

'No,' Hazel says, not looking up from her phone. 'That's how they sound when they talk to each other. You don't have a clue what you're doing, do you?'

Harold rests his paws on the boy's crossed legs, looking at Ben as if joining in with the judgement.

'Typical man,' Hazel says. 'If you didn't know how to do it, you could have said so. If more men owned up to their shortcomings, then the world wouldn't be the colossal bin fire it is today.'

Jacob opens and shuts his mouth like a fish as she speaks. She starts rattling on about Jacinda Ardern, Tsai Ing-wen and Michelle Bachelet, explaining each one to him as if he's an idiot. Ben's used to being treated like a monkey with toolbox, though not usually by someone so young. He nods along with her monologue, hoping she'll report his interest back to her mum. Should he tell her he's a feminist too? At least Shanice said he was, she used to call him one after he'd done something pedestrian like tell her she looked beautiful without make-up or sew a button back onto Olivia's coat.

Jessica returns with Wolf falling two steps behind. 'Pa. *Aufhören*,' then in English, loudly, 'I don't want to hear it.'

'I should go,' Ben says to Jacob, who's again rummaging through the toolbox, taking things out one at a time and lining them up along the cracked lino. 'How did you become a plumber anyway?' he asks. 'I love water. I'm quite interested in becoming a pump operator or a tunnel engineer.'

'I'm not really a plumber, not specifically anyway. I do lots of things.'

'Ah, a hustler?' Jacob says, nodding approvingly.

Wolf shouts, 'Let's try the phone book. Hazel, can you get me the Yellow Pages, please?'

'The what?'

'I need a phone number.'

'Of a real plumber?' Hazel says, smiling at Ben. 'Yeah, I think so.'

'The Van Man cancelled,' Jessica says. 'We're meant to move next weekend. How can he do this to me?'

'*Liebling*, he's so cheap he can do anything he likes.'

'I knew this would happen, Mum. Why didn't you go for a real moving company? Like actual professionals?'

'Because I couldn't afford it.'

Ben scolds himself for enjoying how hot she looks when stressed, before saying, 'I can help. Sorry, I didn't mean to eavesdrop but I—'

'Am in fact not a real plumber?' Hazel chips in.

'Yes,' Wolf says, lighting up, 'Ben can help, he has a van.'

'I have a van,' Ben repeats.

'Oh, no, no.' Jessica laughs then stalls.

Was it the roll-back that's put her off? Does she really think he can't drive?

'I couldn't put you out like that. It's more than a few shopping bags this time. It's my *whole* house.'

'I can do a few trips,' he says, remembering how he fit his entire life in the van here just over a month ago.

'Thanks, but it's a lot of work.'

'He's not busy, Jess,' Wolf says. 'No offence, son.'

'Pa, it's not all going to fit. Don't be silly.'

'I could get a bigger van,' he tries.

'It's really kind of you to offer, but—'

'You have no choice,' Wolf says between them. 'Take his number.'

Ben nervously gets out his phone and Jessica hands him

hers. 'Your number?' she purrs. Ben feels his cheeks warm as he taps it in, his stupid sweaty fingers making him enter one too many digits. He deletes and tries again.

Jessica laughs, 'Do you know how to do it?'

'Yeah, I'm checking I put it in right.'

Wolf turns around, block of cheese in hand and says, 'He's still learning how to spell his name.'

'Pa, stop it,' she says, sniffing. 'Something's burning.'

The kitchen fills with smoke as Wolf lifts the grill lid and everyone starts to cough.

'Noodles, anyone?' Jacob says.

It's decided the noodle bar is the best place for lunch, as it's cheap and allows dogs in. Ben doesn't mention how much he can't stomach noodles. It wasn't always this way. Chinese food used to be one of his weekend treats until a case of food poisoning from some king prawn chow mein.

Jacob studies the big flappy laminated menu. 'Hmm, I didn't know they did sweet and sour duck. Is duck red meat or poultry? Because I try to eat red meat only on Mondays, Wednesdays and Thursdays.'

'Oh, I do love sweet and sour pork,' Wolf says.

'I bet you do, with your sweet tooth,' Ben mumbles.

Wolf briefly raises his middle finger at Ben over the menu before anyone else can see.

'I don't like when people make meat and I can still see what animal it was,' Jacob says, 'like roast chicken.' He shivers and puts down the menu. 'I think I'll go for sweet and sour chicken. I'll share with Harold.' He holds his hand close enough for it to be licked several times. 'Ben, what are you going to eat?'

Ben looks for the plainest meal on the menu, something without fish or spice, and ideally something without harmful bacteria. 'Er, not sure.'

Jessica checks her phone constantly and gazes out of the window. She's definitely got stuff on her mind, just like the last time he saw her. Maybe this is a bit weird, him being here, eating out with her family. It happened so quickly; Wolf practically dragged him along, and the son couldn't keep his hands off Harold.

'Hazel, can you call over the girl and ask if she'll make me some scrambled eggs?'

'Opa, seriously, it's a noodle bar.'

'They have eggs,' he says, tapping the menu, 'I don't think it'll be a problem.'

Further along the table a couple is served two steaming bowls of chow mein. Ben looks away and covers his nose.

Jacob grabs his stomach and whimpers, 'Can we get some prawn crackers to start, please? I'm going to die of consumption here.'

'Yeah,' Hazel agrees. 'I need to be home and at my books in the next ninety minutes to make up my study hours for this week.'

'You mean you want to get home to watch Netflix,' Jacob says as he flaps the menu, wafting the smell of noodles Ben's way. 'Stop pretending you do homework.'

Ben stands up, 'Let me get the waitress.'

As he waits by the counter, he looks back at the table to see

Wolf and the daughter leaning in and whispering. Wolf then tips his head backwards and laughs before looking over at Ben. What was that about? They're definitely talking about him, though he's not sure in what way. He goes back to the table, followed by the waitress and two bowls of prawn crackers. Jacob cheers.

'Benny Boy,' Wolf says, 'what's your opinion on scrambled tofu?'

'Um, I'm not sure I have one.'

'Do you follow Animal Rescue online?' Jacob asks. And this is pretty much how things continue, with Ben's head swinging left to right as Wolf and Jacob talk his ear off in turn. Wolf running through the top ten films from the post-war era Ben can watch this weekend, and Jacob explaining, in very lengthy detail, why badgers are in decline and what we can do about it. Ben does as Hazel told him to and speaks normally with Jacob, though he notices how focused the boy is when listening.

'What exactly did you lose down the sink, Pa?' Jessica asks.

Wolf rubs the papery thin skin of his fingers. 'My decoy wedding band.'

Someone's phone rings and Jessica jumps from the table to answer it; Ben catches the way her voice changes as she greets whoever is on the other end before she goes to a corner of the restaurant to talk. Maybe she already has a man. She tucks her hair behind her ears and rubs a hand over her neck. She *definitely* must have a man. Some perfect, rich, confident guy who's obsessed with her.

'So, Man with Van,' Hazel says, 'are you married?'

'No. Not anymore.' It sounds so flippant.

'Okay, sorry about that. Kids?' she fires back.

'Yeah. I have a daughter. She just turned six.'

'A daughter?'

As the food arrives Ben takes out his phone and pulls up some photos of Olivia. 'Look at this one, she loves dressing up. Cute. And this is her with Harold, he looks a bit fearful here. Olivia's hugs can be sort of aggressive. And this is Olivia at her graduation from Reception class. I love how they made them wear little mortar boards and gowns. So funny.'

'Sweet,' Hazel says, though she's not even looking.

Ben's food – he went for egg fried rice and a side of broccoli – doesn't look so bad, though he could do without seeing Wolf's big bowl of noodles. Jessica is still away from the table, preoccupied on her phone, so he tries to carry on talking to Hazel. 'I heard you're going to Oxford?' he says.

'You and the rest of the world.'

'It's a big deal. Congratulations. What are you going to study?'

'Law. Though I've still got over a year of college left.'

'Law? Wow. I would never have guessed.'

She sits back and folds her arms. 'Why not?' she casts her eyes up and down him. Ben recoils a little and wishes he had sat further away from her. 'Is it because I'm a female? Or because I'm black maybe?'

'Er, no, course not.'

'Is it because I don't sound—'

'Give the boy a break,' Wolf laughs.

'I really didn't mean it that way. I think it's amazing.

I never made it to university, but I'd love for my Olivia to go. Though I better start saving now.'

'Good idea,' Hazel says. 'The last thing you'd want is for your child to have to work thirty hours a week making up Kinky Kale smoothies to pay her own fees.'

Jessica comes back to the table.

'Everything okay?' Wolf asks.

'Yes, just a . . .' she smiles and throws her hair back, 'a call, you know. Oh look, the food's here.'

'Are you packed?' Wolf asks Jacob.

'The packing is not really an issue for me, as it's mostly *her* stuff anyway,' he says, tipping his head towards Hazel. 'Dresses. Bags. Coats.'

'Coats? I don't have that many coats.'

'I did tell you to get rid of some stuff,' Jessica says.

'I got rid of loads. What about all your stuff? Your mountains of high heels and books. And all those CDs.'

'I still play them,' Jessica says, laughing a little, obviously trying to lighten the mood. 'Anyway, I don't need to justify my belongings to you. Ben, you're my age, do you still have CDs?'

'Er, um, not since 2003.'

Hazel gasps and everyone turns to look at her.

'What is it? What's wrong?' Jessica asks.

She holds her phone closer to her face as she reads.

'Haze?' Jessica tries.

'Why didn't you tell us The Anstey is closing down?'

The Anstey? The place Jessica works. Ben always slows when he drives past, picturing her inside, sitting in a red velvet theatre seat and bossing people around. Of course, he doesn't have a clue what she really does there.

Jessica takes the phone and reads for a moment before putting it face down on the table and smiling, though the smile seems kind of forced now.

'What the hell, Mum? Why didn't you tell us?'

'Well. Yes. It's true. Kind of true. The theatre, it's . . . it's going to make some changes.'

'That article doesn't say changes, it says shutting for good.'

'What's shutting?' Jacob asks. 'I missed that. Can someone say it again?'

'The theatre,' Hazel and Wolf say in unison.

Shit. This is awkward.

'You lost your job?'

'No. I haven't lost my job, Pa. There's going to be a bit of restructuring.'

'You still have a job?'

'I'm in a four-week consultation process. So technically, I'm still employed.'

'Why didn't we know about this?' Hazel moans.

Jessica snaps her chopsticks to separate them. 'It was only announced internally at the start of last week and everything was up in the air and we had this whole moving house thing to focus on first and so.' She stops and looks up at the faces surrounding her, then dips her head again, concentrating on her food while the table waits. Ben feels so sorry for her, burning under everyone's gaze like this. 'So yes,' she says quietly, 'they're closing the theatre . . .' her voice breaks. 'I've been made redundant. We all have.'

There's a groan from the kids and Jessica seems to shrink with it before looking up once more, plastering a smile on her face and adding, 'But the good news is, there's going to be outreach work, going into schools, children's centres, prisons, that sort of thing.'

'Prisons?' Jacob says. 'I don't want you to work in a prison.'

'It'll be fine, don't worry.' She jabs the sticks into a piece of prawn toast and laughs into the silence hanging over the table. 'There's even talk of doing this all online, so I wouldn't even have to leave the house. It's great news really. Absofuckinglutely great.'

Ben wishes he knew her better, that it was his place to put his hand on her knee under the table and let her know she wasn't alone.

'Step outside with me, *Liebling*.'

'Really, Pa? It's not a big deal, let's all eat our lovely noodles and—'

'Jessica!' he erupts, and they leave.

'Erm,' Ben says, looking around for help. 'Let me ask if we can get this to take away.'

'Good idea,' Hazel says. 'Jacob, are you all right?'

He stares down at his food, forehead slightly furrowed. Poor kid. Ben gets up and does the bill. This reminds him of the countless times they would be out in public and Shanice would snap at him or kick off too loudly and poor Olivia would just be there watching like it was normal. Because for them, especially towards the end of the marriage, it had become normal.

'First the house, now the job,' Jacob says as Ben arrives

back at the table. Harold clambers up onto the bench and lays his head down on Jacob's lap. Ben butts Jacob's shoulder with his own. 'It'll be all right. People get made redundant all the time. It's happened to me twice already. You get a payoff and then find another job. It's not the end of the world.' He looks at Hazel for help.

'Seriously, Jacob. Stop worrying.'

Hazel reaches across to push his chin up with her finger and then signs something that causes him to wipe his eyes. It's the first time Ben has seen anyone use sign language with Jacob, and he takes it as something private between the two of them.

Outside the restaurant Wolf is turning red, visibly shaking.

'Whoa, Opa is really kicking off though. This is embarrassing, everyone's staring. Jacob, I don't think we can eat here again.'

By the time they get out, Wolf is storming off down the street, while Jessica leans against a wall, looking completely deflated.

'I'll take your dad home,' Ben says to her.

'God, I'm so sorry. This is really uncomfortable.'

'No problem, really.'

'I'm sure a *drink* will calm him down.'

There's something in the way she says it that puts Ben on edge. Of course, he's noticed Wolf drinks, though it seemed to be casually more than problematically. But then, what does Ben know about Wolf really?

Jacob looks sad and Ben taps him on the shoulder to get his attention. 'The next time you're over at your, um, Opa's, let me know and we'll take Harold out, okay?'

The boy nods and reaches down his hand for Harold to give a goodbye lick.

Jessica and her daughter are now arguing as well, the girl standing with her arms folded tightly and head snapping back and forth. Maybe the Bakkers are one of those families who have lots of drama. Ben's definitely not looking to be around people who shout and bawl at each other all the time. Though for Jessica, he'd probably put up with it.

Chapter Nine

Jess

It had been one of those nights when Jess wasn't sure if she had fallen asleep at all. An hour drifting off followed by two hours of stress and worry. Not the best start to a long weekend. It would be great to pull the covers over her head and go back to sleep, but the sun is already blazing and the sound of Haze singing songs from *Chicago* is pretty difficult to ignore. Plus, when Jess checks her phone, it's already half ten. Shit. There's also a message from Ben:

> Happy moving weekend. I hope you got all your shoes paired and packed.

Jess had been mortified after what happened at the noodle bar, though he'd texted her later that evening to confirm he was still up for helping her move the following weekend. There had been a few texts over the last week too, innocuous stuff checking the time of move and yesterday one asking if Jacob wanted to walk the dog. Ben seemed very sweet, too good to be true even, and Jess wished he hadn't seen her during her worst moments. When she was looking like a drowned rat on the high street or stressed out by her imploding family. Where was he a few months ago when she was down the Red Lion, looking polished and hoping to hook up with someone nice? *Nice*. She's never really liked a guy she would describe as nice before. Hot? Yes. Exciting, electrifying, mysterious, arsehole? Definitely yes. But nice? This is something very different from what she's used to.

He was so nice that he was going to meet her at the flat later to have a look at some wood rot. She had discovered it yesterday when she popped by to measure up and couldn't be arsed making a big deal out of it, especially as a little part of her still felt so lucky to be able to secure this dream place that she didn't want to rock the boat.

Downstairs the board games and photo albums have been boxed, the picture frames and clock taken down and stacked neatly against the wall. The fridge is the only thing that looks normal, still covered in magnets and random bits of paper.

The kitchen smells eggy, yet there's no evidence of cooking. Jacob is in the garden, sitting in the shade doing a jigsaw, while Haze lies on a towel in a tiny pink army-print bikini.

'Morning. Gosh, it's warm out here.'

'Yeah, Mum,' Jacob says, 'you need to get out here before it starts raining again.'

'I'd love to, though we sort of have other things to do today. Anyone fancy some breakfast? I was thinking of making pancakes.'

'There's no eggs left,' Jacob says, lifting a mug with a fork in it. 'I had scrambled egg. I did it in the microwave.'

'And I finished the milk,' Haze says, not even looking up from her book. 'I don't really feel like pancakes anyway. I'd rather have something fresh. Do we have any pineapple?'

'I'll just pull one from my arse,' Jess says under her breath.

It's going to be a long weekend. Long and painful. Things have been tense between her and Haze over the last week. Jess hadn't meant to keep her job loss a secret, she simply wasn't ready to tell Haze what happened that first day she came home after getting the news. Then Jess had spent the next few days busying herself with house things and meeting with Norman about freelance outreach work. It was bad luck that Haze found out online before Jess had a chance to tell her.

She removes flapping pieces of paper from under the fridge magnets: the Royal Mail *Sorry We Missed You* cards, school letters detailing log-ins for Jacob's lunch-money account, and post-it notes of things Jess mustn't forget from months ago. She stalls on a photo of the three of them, taken on the log flume at Thorpe Park last year. Whose idea had it been to go there? It cost a fortune and took hours to get home, but in this, they look joyful. Jess and Haze are leaned into each other screaming, while Jacob's little face pokes through his tightly pulled hood, all teeth and squinted eyes. Jess slides the photo down the side of one of the boxes and leaves the magnets on the fridge, a job for later, for when she's feeling stronger.

Haze comes in, pushing her sunglasses up into her loose hair. Her face is free of make-up, making her look about twelve.

'How is he this morning?' Jess asks.

'Okay,' she shrugs. 'He had a good time at Opa's last night and he loves Man with Van's dog.'

'Ben. His name is Ben.'

Haze rolls her eyes. 'Whatever.'

Jess finds some crackers in the cupboard and a scraping of peanut butter left in a jar.

Haze sighs. 'I still can't believe we're moving.'

It's like a big, dark cloud. 'Me neither,' Jess says, then catches herself. 'Though we shouldn't look at it as a sad thing. It's a good thing, it's progress.'

'Really? How'd you work that one out?'

'Because we're going somewhere better and that's all I've wanted to come from this: that you two get to grow up somewhere better.'

Haze scoffs. 'We're still going to be in Newham, not like we're moving up that much in the world. And you're saying this like you engineered it all to happen.'

Jess smarts a little. Where is this coming from?

'You always do this,' Haze says, staring down at the fridge door. 'You always make out like you're doing things for our sake.'

'I am,' Jess says, because how can Haze even question this? 'Everything I do is for you and Jacob.'

'Like losing our home and your job within the space of a month?'

It's such a cutting take on things. As if Jess planned for everything to fall apart at the same time. 'You need to be on my side, Haze, because I can't do it all. Sometimes a ball is going to drop and when it does, I don't need you to make me feel bad about it. You're almost a grown woman. Help out.' She turns away, hoping it landed correctly, that Haze can feel how hurtful her accusation was.

'Now I'm a woman?' she snaps. 'Even though you're constantly treating me like I'm too young to know anything.'

Jess turns back, surprised at Haze's outburst.

'You didn't tell me for days about Mustafa selling, then you kept the fact you're unemployed from me, going off to work all week like there was nothing wrong. And now, you're telling me I'm a woman who should be helping.'

'Where is this all coming from? Why are you so angry with me?'

'Because I'm fed up of being on the back foot. Of always being one step behind everyone else.'

'Behind who? Who's everyone else?'

'Forget it. You don't understand.'

'No, I don't, that's why you need to tell me. Haze? Talk to me.'

'You wouldn't get it. Because you've never wanted more than what you already have. You've never wanted better than this.' She throws her arms up and Jess isn't fully sure what her daughter is trying to indicate.

'This life,' Haze says, 'here, in this house, this area – your job, even. It's always been enough for you.'

There's so much bitterness in what she says, how she says it. Jess feels deflated, so completely flat. 'Well, I'm sorry,' she says. 'I'm sorry it's not enough for you.'

'Forget it.'

Jacob steps over the threshold into the kitchen. 'Do I need to wear sunblock?'

'Yes,' they both fire back at him.

Haze busies herself moving things around, though Jess can tell from the set of her shoulders she would have kept going with her outburst had Jacob not interrupted.

'Why? It's so confusing. They tell black people to go in the sun and get vitamin D but then they say if you do that too much, you're going to get skin cancer.' Jacob sounds frantic, jumping back and forth between the full sun and shade. 'Don't you think that's a bit weird? Like the message is one thing then it's another? Like they're trying to *confuse* us on purpose.'

The doorbell goes.

'It's Mustafa,' Jacob says. 'Do you think they're going to take the pool with them when they move? I bet it's difficult to pack.'

'I'll handle this.' Haze pulls on a T-shirt and heads to the door.

'Stop,' Jess whispers as she catches sight of Haze's arse sticking out the bottom of her T-shirt. 'You're half-naked.'

But she doesn't listen because Haze isn't programmed to listen.

'She does it on purpose,' Jacob says. 'The half-naked thing, she knows it makes people act stupid.'

Jess almost feels sorry for Mustafa, standing on the other side of the door, trying to avert his eyes. 'I wanted to check everything's okay?'

'Check we're really going, you mean? Don't worry,' Haze says. 'You're lucky, we're decent people. We could have refused, you know, asked you to put the notice in writing. Technically we could still change our minds and stay.'

'Jess,' he calls over Haze's shoulder. 'Can we have a chat?'

'Why didn't you advertise it as a buy-to-let with live-in tenants?' Haze asks.

'Jess?' he calls again.

'Haze, please,' Jess says. 'Go inside.'

Haze stomps away from the door.

'I'm sorry about her,' Jess says. 'This is putting a bit of a strain on us all.'

Mustafa nods.

'Why didn't you do that, though? Say you already had tenants, good ones.'

'Even if I did, the first thing any landlord would have done is whack your rent right up in line with the market rate. You've been lucky with me.'

'Lucky?' she laughs. It's as if he thinks the rent she paid each month was some small gesture, rather than the majority of their household income.

'Yes, Jess. Lucky. You've paid mates rates on this house for years.' She sulks back, a small part of her knowing he's right, that she has been privileged, even if it's not felt that way.

He leans on the doorframe and she can smell his aftershave; he always smells so good. 'Also, I noticed you didn't pay this month's rent.'

'No. You can use my deposit instead.'

'What deposit? You never paid a deposit.'

She laughs. 'Everyone pays a deposit.'

'No, really. Don't you remember?'

'You let me live here without a deposit?'

'Yeah.'

'Why?' she shouts, though she knows why, it was because back then he fancied her. She even remembers the conversation, how she flirted her way into this place with no references or deposit. How she completely took advantage. Shit. 'I can't believe you let me live here all this time without paying a deposit.'

'I felt sorry for you,' he says. 'You were on your own with the kids, and because we knew each other from school, I trusted you.' He takes a step away and makes a sort of humming noise. 'This is awkward,' he mumbles.

Yeah, awkward for Jess.

He pushes his hair back and squeezes his eyes shut. 'Could you send me this last month's rent, please?'

'I don't have it,' she says, still feeling bruised at how he really saw her back then. All this time she had thought he liked her, when really he had pitied her, this struggling single mum. 'I have so many costs right now.'

'Me too.'

How can he even look her in the face and say this? She laughs at the situation, laughs because it's that or crying.

'I know you think I'm rolling in it, but I support six of us—' he stops. 'Look, you don't have to get it to me today or anything, I know you must be busy packing up. Though, ideally, sooner than later.'

She's already cut into her savings to cover the deposit and service charge for the new place. How on earth is she meant to find another month's rent?

'Okay?' he asks her, as if she has a choice.

'Yes, yes, okay. I'll sort it.'

He takes another step back and nods before crossing over to his side.

Jess mentally shuffles her money around. The cost of moving is a pressure, and now this. Shit. This is hard. This is really, really hard.

There's always Pa's money, that would sort everything out. But no, she already decided she can't accept it. It had been great to hear him talk about the trip again after all this time. He used to tell anyone who would listen about the things he planned on seeing, the landmarks he fantasised about visiting. He had been obsessed for years and saving meticulously. Then, after Dominic came back needing money, Pa chucked away his travel brochures and never spoke of it again. Until now. So no, there's no way Jess can accept his money. No matter how desperate she is. Mustafa can wait till something else comes up.

In the kitchen Haze leans against the counter, eating a banana and mimicking Mustafa, '*I wanted to check everything's okay*. Dickhead.'

'Stop it, Haze.'

'Why?'

'He's been good to us. He's been fair.'

'Then whose fault is this?'

'I'm going to Tesco's,' Jess says, overwhelmed by the need to get out of the house. 'I can grab some bits for a fruit salad? Make us all something nice to celebrate our last weekend here.' Yes, fruit salad. Perfect. A great idea, something to put everyone back in a good mood.

'Not that bothered anymore,' Haze says. 'I just had a banana. A plain, old boring banana.' She takes a magnet from the fridge, 'Windsor Castle? That was like three years ago. Why have we kept this? Bin.'

The magnet makes a clanging sound as she launches it into the metal bin. 'And who went to Paris and brought us back this lousy fridge magnet? Bin.'

'I was going to do that later,' Jess says.

'No time like the present. Jacob made this one, I'm sure he doesn't want to keep it.'

Jess jumps forward, grabbing the little clay model from Haze's grip. '*I* want to keep it. It's mine, he made it for me.'

'You're keeping a lot of stuff.'

'So?' Jess snaps.

'So are we really going to drag all these magnets to our new place? The apartment has a fitted kitchen; the fridge has a wooden door on it.'

'I'll keep them in a shoebox or something.'

'I can't believe how you've been nagging me to get rid of things, yet you're sentimental about everything. Why can't you let go?'

'Because these things make up our lives. Your childhoods.' Her voice breaks and she bites her lip. It's far too early to have felt this many fucking emotions already.

Haze looks at her for a moment then cuts away, back to the fridge, where she takes off the last two magnets, one of Mickey Mouse as an angel and the other of Elmo wearing a Santa hat. 'We're not children anymore. I'm almost a woman, remember?'

How can she be so cold? So completely free of sentiment for what is pretty much the only home she's ever known. Or perhaps it's all an act, her way of coping. 'I'm going to go over to the new place,' Jess says. 'Do you want to join me?' Please say yes, please let's sort this out.

Jacob comes in, interrupting the moment Jess was trying to build. 'I had to abandon the jigsaw; the pieces are swelling in the heat. So hot. This is what I love about England. Rain, sun, rain, sun, snow, rain, sun.' He shakes his head. 'You never know what you're going to get.' He flops down on the sofa, which looks sad and bare without the cushions. 'What? Why are you two staring at me like that?'

'No reason, hun.'

'Oh boy,' Jacob says, 'I've been so busy I haven't even put on the TV today. Aren't you both tired too? Someone wanna take a break with me?' He switches on Netflix and Haze walks over to join him, leaving Jess alone in the kitchen to her sad breakfast of crackers and coffee. She wishes she could restart the morning, the month, the year even. She fills a bucket with cleaning products and puts on a little lipstick to make herself feel better.

'I'm going now,' she shouts over the TV.

Jacob pauses whatever they're watching and they both look up at her.

'Why are you so done up to clean the flat?' Haze asks.

'I'm not.'

'You do know Man with Van fancies you?'

'No, he doesn't,' Jess says, untying her hair and fluffing it up.

Jacob wide-eyes his sister and asks, 'How do you know that?'

'Opa told me. Man with Van was asking if she was single. As if she'd be interested in him.'

'Why are you being so horrible?' Jess snaps.

'Yeah, why are you being so horrible?' Jacob repeats. 'I like Ben. He's cool.'

Haze laughs. 'No, he's not. He's boring.'

'Haze, stop it.'

'It's true. Anyway, you don't really like him, do you? You're just using him because he's useful, he has a van and knows how to fix stuff.'

Jess smarts. It's a spiteful thing to say. 'That's unfair. And also untrue.' Because as useful as Ben is, there's definitely something else there. Jess wants to get to know him. She likes him. Why is Haze being difficult about it? 'What happened to you wanting me to meet someone?' she asks. 'Remember when you were signing me up to dating websites?'

'That was for fun. Back when things were different.'

'So, what now, I don't deserve a little fun?'

Jacob stands from the sofa and says, 'This conversation is not for me,' before going out into the garden.

Haze spreads into the space left behind and puts the TV back on to signal the end of the conversation.

'If you really don't like him,' Jess starts, but stops when Haze laughs. 'What?'

'It's not about if I like him or not. It's your life, Mum, you make your own choices. And if you think now, with everything else that's going on, is a good time to add some recently divorced local handyman to the mix, then go for it.'

Before she leaves the house, Jess takes a piece of damp kitchen roll and rubs her lipstick off.

Chapter Ten

Ben

'Jessica?' Ben pushes the front door open and steps into the oversized hallway, which smells overwhelmingly of bleach. He's never been so excited to look at wood rot before. Hopefully there's a lot of it.

'In here,' she calls.

He follows her voice through to a small boxy white room. Her hair is wrapped in a yellow scarf that matches her Marigolds, and she's got on a skimpy T-shirt and brightly coloured leggings. It's the same look Shanice used to sport when she first started seeing Gerald behind Ben's back. Back when 'going to box fit' really meant 'going to have it off with a pastry chef'.

'Hi,' Jessica purrs.

'Hi. Uh, you left the front door open.'

'Did I?'

'I know it's very fancy round here, but it's still Stratford.'

Should he mention that last week he also found Wolf's

front door wide open with the key left in? It had worried him, making him wonder if Wolf had a touch of dementia, though now it seems like they're just a very trusting family.

'Will this be your bedroom?' Is it creepy he asked that? That he's a tiny bit excited to be in Jessica Bakker's bedroom?

'This box? You're kidding. This will be my daughter's room. She's being so difficult at the moment. Packed up a few pots and pans this morning and thinks she's now got the green light to sit on her arse for the rest of the day.' Jessica sighs from somewhere deep and says quietly, 'I don't know what's going on with her at the moment.'

Ben tries to think of something comforting to say, but what does he know about teenage girls? Instead he goes with, 'She's very impressive. Oxford, whoa.'

'Yes, she's brilliant. But it doesn't stop her from being a pain in the arse.'

'Jacob's great too,' he adds. 'He's a big character.'

Jessica smiles before reaching in the cupboard. 'Uh-huh, that he is.'

Ben half wants to let her know how much research he's since done into cochlear implants. He doesn't want Jessica to think he's still the same ignorant person from last week who panicked on noticing the boy was different. But before he can speak, she says, 'And let me say it again, I am so sorry you had to witness all that drama.'

'Don't worry about it. It's nothing. Really.'

Jessica stares ahead and he thinks of how often she seems distracted. In the van that day she had closed her eyes and drifted off, then again, while they sat in the noodle bar, Wolf had twice tapped her shoulder to get her attention, to bring her back into the conversation. She must have so much on her mind.

'Are you okay?'

She looks up at him and smiles, 'Yeah. Course. Lot on, that's all. You're good for doing this, Ben. For giving up your weekend to help me. I really appreciate it.'

'It's no problem.' He flicks the light switch then realises there's no bulb. The door handle is also loose. There are probably a hundred small jobs he could do around here for her, enough to fill all weekend, every weekend.

Why is he thinking like this? Getting ahead of himself. 'Nice place,' he says. 'Good view.'

Jessica is sidetracked again, this time staring fixedly at the cloth in her hand. Then she peers into the wardrobe and her eyes follow something along the wall.

'What's wrong?'

'I keep seeing these little beetles,' she trails off, grabs a spray bottle and directs a jet at the wall. 'That's the third one I've seen. They're in the other room too. I don't know what they are. I'll need to get some bug killer. There,' she says as Ben steps closer. 'There's another one.'

'Bedbugs,' Ben says as he spots the round, dark-red creature.

'Don't be silly,' she laughs. 'They're not bedbugs. You can't *see* bedbugs.'

'Yes, you can. Shit. That's a bedbug,' he backs away from the wardrobe.

'Ben?' She stares again at the creature. 'These are big.

Bedbugs are tiny, microscopic things that live in pillows and old dirty mattresses.'

'That's not true. Oh no,' he itches his head, wondering if he leant on anything since he came in. He shivers, conflicted by how much he wants to stay here and reassure Jessica, versus how desperate he is to get out.

'Can you really see bedbugs?' she asks.

'Yes.'

'And what do they look like?'

'Round, rust-coloured things. Those,' he says, spotting another making its way up the wardrobe. 'Sorry, I need to get out of here.'

'No. I'm sure they live in beds.' She creeps near the base of the bed. 'And there are no mattresses here. They removed them all. Ben? Ben, wait.'

He heads outside and stamps his feet.

Jessica pulls off her rubber gloves and he swears he spots something crawling on one so takes them from her hands and chucks them to the ground. 'You can't move into this place,' he says.

'I'll call pest control. They can come and spray it down or whatever it is they do.'

He shakes his head. 'No. Seriously, don't do it. When I worked for the council, a children's home got infested and it took months to eradicate them. It would have been less work to burn the building down and start again. When exactly did the last tenants move out?'

'I don't know.'

'Doesn't it make you itch?' he asks, scratching at his hair.

'I'm moving tomorrow. I'm already packed.'

'I know, I know. Oh no, is that one of them?' he leans closer towards her white T-shirt where a dark-coloured dot moves.

'What? Get it off.'

'Shit, it is.' He leans closer and tries to flick it but chickens out.

'Ben. Help!'

'I'm trying. Stop moving.' This time he flattens his hand to swipe it off.

'Ow,' she says.

'Um, sorry, it was a bit of fluff. Sorry, sorry for hitting you.'

'Aren't you being a bit dramatic?' She takes her phone out. 'Bedbugs, bedbugs, let me look this up.'

While she's checking he inspects his body for infestation.

'Okay, you're right,' she says finally. 'This is a problem.'

'Course, I'm right.'

'I can't move in there, can I?'

'No.' He shakes his head. 'Cut your losses and find something else. You won't lose any money on this – the deposit or whatever you've already paid, they'll need to give it all back.'

She puts her hands on her face and mumbles something.

'What did you say?'

'Shit,' she says. 'I said shit. Shit. Shit.' She walks to the end of the balcony and sits by the lift. 'Is this safe? Sitting here? Or will they walk themselves up to me? I can't believe this. I can't believe all this shit keeps happening to me. I need to call the kids. The letting agent. Mustafa. Oh, this is a lot. It's really a lot.'

Desperately he wants to scoop her up and hold her. Even if she is crawling with bugs.

She holds her phone in her hand, Hazel's photo brought up. 'I don't know who to tell first. I don't know what to tell them. I can't,' she cries, red-eyed as tears begin to fall. 'I can't tell them right now. I need a Plan B first, then I'll tell them. Don't you think? Oh my God, what's my Plan B?' She sniffs and wipes her eyes.

He crouches down opposite her. 'I can drive you home?'

'Home?' she sounds horrified.

'Or to your dad's?'

'And say if I take the bugs there? It would be impossible to even spot them in that place, never mind get rid of them.'

'You're right.'

She's sobbing now. It's horrible.

'Jessica?'

'Sorry,' she looks up.

'Come to mine. You can take a minute there to think what to do next.'

'But I can't, because I'm probably covered in bedbugs.'

'It's okay, I'll hose you down first.'

They take off their shoes at the door. She's stopped crying and pulls off her socks once she gets in. Harold pads over, still slow from sleep though excited to see Jessica again.

She reaches down to pat him then stops. 'Oh no, say I give him the bugs. Are they like fleas? They probably love fur, don't they? No, Harold, get down.' She twists and scratches at the back of her neck. 'I feel like I'm covered in them. I know I'm not, that I'm being irrational. Do you have something I could change into?'

He nods and fetches her a T-shirt and pair of joggers. This day is really not turning out how he expected it to.

'You feel better?' he asks when she comes out of the bathroom.

She nods and pulls at the drawstring on the joggers.

'Do you want me to wash your stuff? Or, er, I can drive you back—'

'I'm not ready,' she sulks over to the sofa. 'I need a strong drink.'

'Okay,' Ben says. She looks so at home here. Weird. Even he doesn't look at home here.

'Oh, you're lovely, such soulful eyes,' she says, stroking Harold's ears as he climbs up close to her. 'The smell though.'

'I'm sorry. He can't help it.'

'It's awful,' she laughs.

'Do you want me to lift him off you?'

'No, it's okay, I think it was a one-off.'

'Don't be so sure about that. Your dad's been feeding him all kinds of stuff he's not meant to have.'

'Jacob is obsessed with getting a dog. There's no way. Not after what happened with the fish. And the salamander. And the gerbils. Oh God, I'm still traumatised by those bloody gerbils. You'd think a kid who loves animals as much as Jacob does would be better at keeping them alive. How old is Harold?'

'Thirteen. He was mine then Olivia's, now mine again.'

'Olivia? Is that your . . . ?'

'Yeah, my little girl.'

'I didn't know. Pa never said.'

So she really was in her own world at the noodle bar, she'd

pretty much missed that whole conversation. Also, it never occurred to him that he would need to explicitly tell someone he was a dad, rather than them simply knowing from passing him on the school run or seeing him eat a plate of discarded nuggets and chips at the local trampoline park.

Ben passes her the nearest photo.

'So cute. She doesn't look like you at all.'

'Thanks.'

'I didn't mean it like that.'

Olivia is a beautiful girl. People were always commenting on it. It made Ben cringe sometimes, how people would say it like they were shocked he'd managed to produce someone so perfect. Though sometimes, he was shocked too.

'She's six.'

'I love that age. Hazel was perfect at six. Not that she isn't darling now.'

Ben hopes his expression doesn't give away how much of a struggle he found Hazel when he met her. She has this arrogance about her, an air of being too good to spend time talking to anyone who doesn't have something for her.

'I'm guessing Olivia doesn't live here? With you?'

'What gave that away?'

'The tidiness. Does she live close by?'

'Tenerife,' he says quickly, keen not to get into it right now. 'You sure you're okay with him lying on you like this?'

Jessica strokes Harold's chin. He opens one eye and shoots Ben a smug look.

'He's making me feel calm,' she says. 'Now if you could just put something alcoholic in my free hand.'

The only drink he has is the bottle of sake his mum gave him as a welcome-back present, clearly a regift. 'I don't actually have anything to offer you. I've got coffee, good coffee, or . . .'

'No, I wasn't joking, I really do need alcohol.'

Me too, he thinks, pouring them each a small glass of sake. 'Why Tenerife?'

'My ex, well, she met someone else and he's a chef. He got a really good opportunity at a hotel out there, so they, they, uh' – he adds another inch to his glass – 'left.'

'I'm sorry. That's so shit.'

Ben scoffs a little, no one ever says that. 'You're right,' he says.

'When did you split up with your ex?'

'We separated about a year ago, but the divorce, that took time to come through.'

'And she already met someone new and moved abroad with them? Sorry. I'm prying.'

'No, it's fine. To be honest, there was some crossover. For the first few months I mostly had Olivia with me. Then, Tenerife happened and um, well, it's not ideal.' He hands her the glass then stalls, noticing how small his sofa is, it would be far too intimate to sit next to her on it, so he sits on the coffee table opposite.

'Why didn't you move there too?'

'And follow them?' he laughs.

'No, I didn't mean that. But you moved here?'

'When it comes to Newham versus Tenerife, there really is no contest.' They smile at each other and knock their glasses.

'My ex didn't want me out there. It's her fresh start. It still all needs some working out. As much as I want to see Olivia, I don't want her being bounced back and forth. Neither of us do. I've not seen her in months.'

'It's quite a distance. You really didn't consider building a life there too?'

'No. I don't think I could face being that close to my ex's new life. Seeing her with the man she's decided to be with, the man who's bringing up my daughter.' There's got to be another way to tell this story, one that doesn't make Ben feel as if he's reaching in and clawing out his own heart. 'Also, my mum's getting older. She retires next year and I didn't want her here alone.' Even worse, he thinks. Not because his mum is, as he thought, ageing, lonely and in need of him, but because she's perfectly fine and he's now moved all this way only to struggle to get any time with her. Like Stratford itself, his mum has emerged into some shiny new reality that doesn't include him.

'You must miss Olivia. I can't imagine. You've already lived here a while though, right?'

'Yeah.' He follows her eyes around the room, nervous at what she's about to say.

'No offence, it's very bare.'

'Still? I put up pictures. I've got plants. My mum gave me cushions. What else do I need?'

Jessica takes the tassels in her hands. 'I noticed, they're very nice. I was admiring your selection of scented candles too,' she laughs.

Originally, he thought he would drop the candles off at

the charity shop but one evening after cooking he lit one and found he quite liked it. Does his flat smell like Cinnamon Christmas to her? That's so embarrassing.

'I love that your mum gives you cushions.'

'I think she's trying to emasculate me.'

Jessica laughs again and this time he takes the credit for it.

She's right. It's so bare, so unlived-in. 'I thought I had a lot of stuff. Our place was always so full of clutter. I think it was mostly Olivia's.'

'Yeah, kids are really good at accumulating. I was shocked when we started packing.' Her phone rings and she groans.

'You're not going to answer—'

'No.'

Ben can't even bear to hear an alarm go off on television. 'It might be one of your kids. Do you want me to—'

'No,' she says again, downing her drink in one. 'Is this sake? You know you're meant to warm it up first?' She lays her head on the back of the sofa, and he has to look away from her neck.

The phone keeps going. She really is going to let it ring out. It's excruciating. When it finally stops the room feels extra silent.

'So, um,' he clears his throat. 'Let me know what you want to do. If you need me to drive you somewhere or—' He stops and glances at her, her eyes are shut. Is he stressing her out more? Should he shut up? 'Or if you . . . sorry, I don't want to worry you. I want to— Sorry.'

She opens her eyes and tilts her head at him. 'No wonder you never stayed at St Margaret's. You're so wholesome.'

The mention of the school bursts his bubble.

'Everyone I met there was an arsehole. Though, I'm meeting you as an adult. You were probably an arsehole as a teenage boy too.'

'Maybe,' he says, 'probably.'

She laughs a little, so it surprises him when she stops and says, 'I hated it there.'

'Me too.'

It's definitely the first time she's really looked at him, because it's too intense, like she's going to see something he's been trying to hide from her.

'Did you do A levels there too?' she asks.

'No. I left right before GSCEs. I did them at another school.'

'How come?'

He wonders which part to tell her. It all seems equally bad. 'The school wasn't for me. I found it hard to . . .' he's aware of how important it is to make this next part as ambiguous as possible, 'do well there.'

'Academically?'

'No, not that. It was a tough school.'

'It was like a supply chain to prison. The only way I got through my last two years there was by distracting myself with boy after boy.'

Ben's eyes flick up and she flippantly says, 'Don't judge me. I still did okay. Though for someone like my brother, that place sent him right off course.'

'Your brother?'

'Yeah.'

Ben looks down at her bare feet and red toenails. Of

course, he knew this, even though Wolf explicitly said he only had one child.

'You didn't know I had a brother, did you?'

'I, um, can't remember Wolf talking about—'

'Don't cover for him. I'm well aware of how he picks and chooses which parts of his life to share.'

As much as Ben wants Jessica to explain why Wolf denies his son, he also knows there's probably no version of the story worth hearing. At least not now.

Jessica is still staring at him.

'I'm guessing he told you about my mum, that she walked out on him, on all of us? It wasn't easy for him, bringing us both up alone. Especially as my brother was always quite difficult.'

'Were you young? When she left.'

'I was ten, Dominic was fifteen.'

'It must have been hard for Wolf, raising two kids alone, especially with no extended family around. He mentioned that you never go back to Germany, that no one there has ever really been involved with—'

'Ben, I know you think he's great, but he's a complicated man. We try now, I mean, I really do because I have no relationship with my mum or brother, and that'll never change. Pa's my only family and the kids love him. My mum left for a good reason.' She breaks eye contact and pushes her hair behind her ear. 'And the family back in Germany don't speak to him for a hundred good reasons.'

Harold stands, stretches out his back and treads over to the balcony, pressing his nose against the window.

'I don't know why we're talking about this,' Jessica says. There's this kind of resigned look on her face, almost like when someone's given up, when the energy isn't there anymore. 'The day's been stressful enough without me rattling the skeletons in the family closet.' Her glass is empty.

'You want another one? I can heat it up for you this time? Or is it disgusting? I can pop out and get your something else.'

'Yeah, a bottle of Italian sparkling rosé,' she says drily.

'Really?' he stands up. 'Okay.'

'Ben, I'm kidding.' Then a small smile makes its way onto her face. 'This is fine.'

He stares at her for a moment. She's so hard to work out. One minute completely full of despair and the next it's almost like she's flirting with him. No, that's what he *wants* to believe.

'Your brother,' he says as he heads back over into the kitchen. 'I'm guessing he went to St Margaret's as well. He must have been in my year.'

Jessica looks over and bites her lip. 'Shit. Yeah. You're the same age. His name's Dominic.'

'Dominic?' Ben repeats, noting how Jessica used the present tense. 'And where is he now? Does he live around here still?'

She pulls her knees closer. 'Not quite. It's a long story.'

Chapter Eleven

Jess

A pregnant teenager stands smoking outside the housing office. Her phone rings, she answers it and shouts, 'Stop calling me, you're not the dad.'

'Did that really just happen?' Haze asks.

Jess unthreads her arm from Haze's. 'You don't have to come in with me,' she says for the tenth time this morning. 'We might have a long wait and I don't want you to be late getting back to college.'

'It's fine, Mum. Besides, I don't think I'll go in later.'

'Should you really be bunking off?' Jess asks as they walk inside.

'It's not bunking off if you've already completed the work. My tutor knows I'm ahead.'

They find two seats in the waiting room amongst all the other needy people. Jess looks at everyone and tries not to judge. Though who is she kidding, all she can do is judge. She had a turn of bad luck to get here, to have to come to the local council for housing; what happened to everyone else? To the woman sitting a few seats up who Jess overhears telling a friend, 'It's got to have a garden or I'm not going', or the man sitting across from her on his £700 Galaxy phone? Jess scolds herself because she's being exactly what Steadman accused her of, judgemental and stuck up. *Too good for a council place,* he loved spouting that line to her, even though it's not that, it's more that she shouldn't need this kind of help. Because she's not this kind of single mum. Never has been.

Haze laughs at something on her phone. 'Look what Jacob posted this morning.' She shows a photo of him and his friend Cameron standing cross-armed and poker-faced outside a room marked 'Science Lab'. The caption on the post reads, 'Where the magic happens.'

'Bless them,' Jess says.

'You know, the last time Cameron came over he tried brushing his hand against my bum?'

'He did not. He's only fourteen.'

'A fourteen-year-old sex pest. Who's our meeting with?'

'Tim.'

'Tim? Bit informal.'

Jess hopes Tim is the kind of man with a warm heart and access to well-priced property. She also hopes he'll reveal a raft of places the council owns across the borough, places hidden from young professional couples on double incomes capable of paying extortionate rents. Though this isn't what happened in the housing documentary she watched last night. In it, a working-class couple with a baby had gone to the council for help, only to be sent packing hundreds of miles away, all the way to Scunthorpe. Jess had called Precious in a state after watching and Precious told her watching documentaries while house-hunting was the equivalent of watching *One Born Every Minute* while pregnant. A bad idea.

'Do you want me to double-check the paperwork?' Haze asks, as if concerned Jess has misspelt something. 'Why have you filled this out saying you're employed?'

'Shh,' Jess says, looking over her shoulder, 'because for the next eight working days I am still *technically* employed by The Anstey. Also, by the time we move again I'll definitely be in work.'

Jess is waiting to hear back following her second interview for a programming assistant role at a toy museum in west London. It's a dead cert. They loved her, laughed along with all her jokes and even seemed to agree that, while she was academically unqualified for the role, education wasn't everything.

'You've got to be honest, Mum. And surely if they know you're not working then they can help you more.'

Urgh. *Help you more.* Like Jess is so needy. Though it is true that as time ticks by she's getting more and more desperate, as is Mustafa, whose buyer is now threatening to pull out due to the delay. In the first few days after the Victory House flat fell through it was hard to know whether to start unpacking for the sake of normality and sanity, or if having their whole lives still boxed would send some kind of message to the universe that they were ready to move. 'I'm not bothered,' Jacob had said after wearing the same *Play Hard or Go Home* T-shirt for three days in a row. 'I could live like this forever.' It made Jess's heart ache because him sitting there, with his back against the boxes of everything he owned, did make him look like one of Stratford's rough sleepers.

Twenty minutes past their appointment time they're called over to meet Tim, a balding baby-faced man wearing a tie with pictures of cats doing yoga on it. Before Jess has a chance to turn on the charm, he's already bypassed the small talk and is down to business.

'Ms Bakker, you're currently not in a council property?'

'I rent privately. Have done for years. Though my landlord is selling and I can't afford to buy it. I can't afford to rent privately again either – some of the rents I'm coming across are ludicrous. Have you seen?' she laughs. 'Surely no one can afford them, especially someone with dependants.'

'Well, you're working, that's a good thing.' He stops and reads off the screen, 'Community outreach.'

Jess senses Haze perk up beside her at the little white lie. 'Yes,' she smiles, ready for some recognition, something to show him that she's not like the others he probably deals with here, she's employed, she's earning, she's middle class aspiring. 'I work for a theatre; I've been there for a long time. It's a great job, really great.' Is she laying it on too thick? No, there's nothing to lose here. 'And my current landlord would give me a very good reference. Like I say, I have spent time searching the private market, but if you could help me find somewhere with a more sensible price that would be really helpful.'

He looks up and nods blankly as if waiting for her to stop

talking. 'I can't help you find a place on the private market, I'm not a letting agent.'

'Oh no,' Jess laughs and, despite the man's rudeness, beams her best smile across the desk. 'I didn't mean that. Of course not. I meant—'

'Your daughter?' he asks, turning to face Haze. 'You're eighteen. You're at university?'

'Not yet. I'm still at college.'

Jess leans on the desk, 'She's going to the University of Oxford after college.' Tim clearly didn't hear her properly because he comes back with, 'You'll be leaving home?'

'Yeah,' Haze says. 'But this is ages away, and it's obviously only term time. You can't like fully live there. You still need a home. Right?' she asks, turning to Jess.

'Of course, hun. You'll always have a room at home with me.'

Tim cuts in: 'I'm afraid that you're not really a priority case for the council, as you're not technically homeless. Also, in your salary bracket you're already receiving everything you're entitled to – child benefit, tax credits. Yes. You're in quite a good position.'

Jess ignores the burn of Haze's eyes on her.

'What I would advise you to do, if you're having difficulties finding housing in the private sector, is to wait until your landlord starts the process to evict you.'

'He's kind of done that already.'

Tim glances up at her. 'And you're still there?'

'Yes. Because we have nowhere else to go.'

'What type of tenancy agreement do you have with him?'

'I don't.'

Tim sighs. 'Nothing at all?'

'No. He was a friend. Sort of. But now he needs us out and we have nowhere else to go.'

'If you stay put, he'll need to begin court proceedings against you. I know it sounds dramatic, but the only way the council is going to help you is if you're officially homeless.'

Jess leans on the desk, causing Tim to flinch back a fraction – rightly so because either she misheard or he just made a completely ridiculous suggestion. 'Homeless?'

They've all been guilty of throwing around the word *homeless* recently, though not in a serious way, certainly not in an official way, because what they were talking about was the inconvenient idea of being homeless, as in the transition from one home to another. However, what Tim is talking about is real homelessness. Like on the street, with a bundle of cardboard and a dog on a string.

'Once you really have nowhere else to go,' he continues, 'the council has to help you.'

Of course, they don't have somewhere to go. 'My landlord has given me lots of notice,' Jess says. 'It's not like he changed the locks while I was out. He's being fair. I can't imagine putting him in a position where he'll have to take me to court. Plus, he's already accepted an offer on the place and now we're the ones holding up the chain. No. This is ridiculous.' She moves back in her seat, satisfied she's made her point. 'What else can we do?'

Tim waits a beat, as if to ensure Jess has finished saying her piece. 'This is my recommendation, Ms Bakker.'

She looks at Haze, in need of an ally to laugh this off with, this meaningless, over-the-top, dramatic proposal. 'No. This is silly. There's no way we would do this.'

Haze turns back to Tim and says, 'If we *did* do it,' she casts a quick cautious glance at Jess, 'who would be liable for the fees? For the courts, lawyers and all that – it costs money.'

'Your landlord would be liable, though these things rarely get to that stage.'

'Let me get this straight,' Haze says. 'If we refused to move out, our landlord wouldn't end up out of pocket? It's more for show, like, part of the paperwork trail? Would any of us even have to attend court?'

'Haze, why are you asking all this?'

'Isn't it worth knowing?'

'No, it's a good point,' Tim says. 'You would attend court, with your landlord. The bailiffs would serve you notice and—'

'Bailiffs?' Jess blurts. 'No, no, we're not going through that.' She gathers her bag. 'Thanks for your help. It's been really informative.'

'Mum?'

Unbelievable. She knew the council would be no help. What a waste of time coming here. She stands up, feeling slightly dramatic and also annoyed at how she's no wiser than when she first arrived.

'Mum, what are we doing? We should listen to that guy. We should take Mustafa to court.'

It's not worth the energy to stop and explain to Haze all the things wrong, immoral and unnecessary about going through with such an act. Once outside, Jess glances around for the swearing, smoking pregnant teenage girl, though thankfully she's gone.

'Let Mustafa hire a lawyer, he can afford it,' Haze rants. 'We can stay till we're removed. I know, we can contact those women – you know, those single mums who campaigned against social cleansing? Remember that? Cause this is kind of the same thing, part of a wider problem.'

Jess recalls how proud she felt watching a group of women with their East London accents and babies on hips, publicly shaming the council for failing to look after local people. So why does she now feel a shred of shame at sharing their predicament?

Haze has her phone out. 'What were they called again? I'm sure I've seen them on Twitter.'

'Haze, please stop. That group deals with serious issues. Homeless families. Young mums practically thrown out on the streets.'

'Yeah, like us.'

'No—' Jess starts then stops herself because what she's really thinking is, I'm not like them, our situation isn't that bad.

'Found them,' Haze says. 'I'm sure they'd love to hear about our greedy landlord.'

'I know you don't like Mustafa, but he's been good to us. He's kept the rent low all these years, so low that I had no clue what the market rate was. Haze, what are you doing?' Jess pulls the phone down. 'Stop it. It's over, he's moving on. We need to move on too.'

Haze's face falls and she looks young, not immature or childish, just young and in need of someone to look after her.

'I'm sorry but it's not *our* house.'

'It is. It's our home.'

'Yes, it *has* been our home. Not anymore. It's his house and he wants it back.'

Haze looks completely beaten, like something inside her has been shattered. This must be what it feels like when your kids find out Santa isn't real. Jess never had that moment with either Haze or Jacob; they simply went along with the whole carrot and cookie charade for years because it was fun. Or was it because Jess went out of her way to keep it going so she would never have to see the look of disappointment on their faces? So she would never have to feel the guilt that comes when you can't keep up the facade of the world being wonderful.

Her phone rings. 'I need to get this. It's a withheld number, it's probably about the job.' She steps to the side and answers.

'Morning, Ms Bakker, it's Bill from Swish Estates. I've found something lovely for you. It's a three-bed. Cosy size. Mature garden. Brand-new kitchen. Can I show it to you later today?'

'Where is this one?'

'Little bit further than you wanted, in Dagenham, but it's really—'

'That's too far. I told you already: I need something within good distance of the school. My son has needs, he can only travel so far.'

Jess registers the quick flick of shock on Haze's face and her guilt kicks in instantly. Never before has she used Jacob's disability as a way of getting anything.

Bill from Swish laughs nervously. 'Like I say, the kitchen *is* brand new.'

'Okay, can you send me the link, please? I can't talk now, I'm at work.' She hangs up and plasters on a smile for Haze. 'See, the hunt goes on. I'll find somewhere. I'm going at it harder this time. And perhaps it's time to be less picky.'

'Less picky? I've seen some of the places you've looked at.'

'Okay, some of them haven't been great. Though when I start this new job, I'll have so much more money to play with.'

'You're putting a lot on getting this job,' Haze snaps.

It's so hard with her at the moment. As much as she wants to be treated like an adult, whenever she's given a taste of real adult life it's like she falls to pieces and starts acting like a spoilt kid again.

'I looked too,' Haze says. 'I've seen how much places are. Do you really have fifteen hundred a month? Two thousand a month?'

Put like this, so plainly, it hurts because the answer is no, Jess doesn't have that kind of money. Even when she *was* working. Actually, how does anyone have that kind of money each month for rent alone?

'It'll be okay. We've been unlucky so far. This next place could be the one. We could be moved in by the end of the month and won't have to deal with any of this anymore, not with the council and taking Mustafa to court and . . .' she trails off. This is it, she's thrown all the conviction she has at it, and now Haze has to accept it and believe that everything will work out. The same way Jess, at twenty-two, used to accept everything would work out despite having a two-year-old and a boyfriend who was shaping up to have ambition for nothing other than seeing Arsenal win the league.

'People lose everything,' Haze says.

'That's not going to happen to us. We're not in that position.'

'Mum, I'm scared about this. And Jacob, well, he's—'

'Jacob's going to be okay as long as he's not given any reason to panic.'

It was the one thing they could agree on: that Jacob be kept in the dark about as much of this as possible.

'I saw this documentary,' Haze says, 'where this woman lost her job, then her private rent got too expensive and she ended up homeless. Having to live in a shelter with tons of other families.'

Jess hopes they weren't both covertly watching the same depressing piece of TV. The saddest part of which wasn't when the mum explained how far her money went in the way of paying bills and buying food, but when the teenage son was shown taking his posters down from the wall and trying to roll them so they wouldn't get creased during the move. It had felt like a sharp hit in the chest.

'That's TV, Haze. They make it sensational on purpose, they find the worst stories, the disabled widower, the single mother of ten, the asylum-seeking doctor who now works in a chicken shop to make ends meet. It's not us.'

'And single mums,' Haze says, her voice wobbling. 'Single mums who work. Women who have good jobs and then one thing changes and everything falls apart.'

Jess swallows. 'We're different.'

'How? What makes us different?'

She can't answer that, she just knows they are. She's never needed help from the government before. She should never have allowed Haze to come today. Suddenly, a thought hits her.

'You didn't watch that show with Jacob, did you?'

Haze's eyes widen. 'Of course not. Mum, those other people didn't make the choice to be homeless. They didn't want to use food banks and drink UHT milk. They didn't want to move to Scunthorpe.'

'You need to stop. We're not going to be homeless. We're not going to need food banks and we're not moving to bloody Scunthorpe. We're at a bump in the road and it might mean that money will be tight for a bit, and that's fine. We can manage.' Jess is struck by how pretty her daughter manages to look while crying, little twinkly tears and eyeliner still in place. 'We can manage if we – and I mean all three of us – watch our spending.'

'Spending?'

'Yes. Spending. You know that thing you do in Westfield every weekend? As well as the takeaways, the eating out, the Boohoo packages – you said you'd stop, but I see them, Haze, they're still arriving. All that sort of stuff needs to stop.'

Haze's expression can only be described as 'terrified'. Jess takes her by the shoulders and gives her a little shake in an attempt to be playful. As much as she sees Haze wanting and trying to grow up, she's definitely not there yet. She's still so young and, really, she shouldn't have to deal with any of this stuff. No teenager should. 'We're going to be okay, we're always okay, aren't we?'

'Yeah, I guess so.' Haze sounds doubtful.

'No, not guess so. Come here.' Jess pulls her in for a hug, the kind of hug they both give Jacob all the time, yet rarely give each other. 'It'll be fine. Don't worry.'

They pull apart as Haze's phone pings. 'Sorry, it's Sarah. We're meeting for lunch.'

'No more Nando's, Haze.'

'I'm one chilli away from a free half chicken.'

'Okay, then make this the last time. Not forever, just till we get sorted. Or till you graduate and get a good enough job to sort us all out. Okay?'

'Okay.' Haze doesn't look up from her phone.

'I'm sorry this is happening. I really am. I know the timing is terrible, especially with college and—'

I'm going to wait over the other side of the road for pick-up.'

'Pick-up?'

'My Uber.'

Jess knows it's not a real thing to feel your blood boil, but in this instance it's the only way to describe how she feels. She presses her jaws together and forces a smile. 'You ordered a cab?'

Haze looks at her, the sadness slightly turning to embarrassment. 'I'm late and it's about five minutes in a cab as opposed to a twenty-minute walk.'

'Get a bus.'

'No. They don't go close enough to her flat and I hate walking around West Ham, it's full of crackheads.'

'Get her to meet you at the restaurant,' Jess spits, her tolerance evaporating.

Haze starts to cry again. Waterworks on cue. 'It's my money, if I want to spend it on chicken and cabs, I will. I earn it, I'm careful with it.'

'What's that supposed to mean?'

'Well, where is it? Your money? Even Dad thinks you should have more than you do.'

'Your dad doesn't know what he's talking about. Because all he does is pay a lump sum once a month. He has no idea how to divvy it up and make ends meet. Did he really say that? How dare he.'

Haze checks her phone again. 'I have to go.'

'No, you can't throw that at me and expect to get away with it. If you're old enough to hear about the council, you're old enough to know how much your dad truly contributes.'

Haze looks at the Prius across the road, and sends Jess an apologetic look. 'I have a five-star rating. Sorry.'

'Fine. Go.'

As she lets herself in, Pa walks into the hallway. He startles slightly and pulls the straps of his towelling robe. 'Jessica?'

'Why aren't you dressed yet? There's not a woman here, is there?'

'No. Why, do I look delighted?' He rubs his eyes and pushes straggles of hair from his face. 'I was out last night.'

'With who?' She follows him through to the kitchen.

'I can't remember who was there at the end. I *am* allowed to have a few drinks with friends.'

You think he would be used to the after-effects of alcohol by now, but no, his face looks grey and withered. He takes the milk from the fridge, sniffs it and recoils. 'Is Ben's van outside?'

'I didn't notice.' She lies, because of course she looked for it, reasoning that if it was parked, she would buzz his doorbell. After her morning so far it would have been the perfect tonic to sit in his little flat, talking and feeling that even though everything was beyond shit, it was also somehow salvageable. Because that was the thing about Ben, he made her feel like everything would work out.

Pa groans and rubs at the dark bags under his eyes.

'You really look terrible,' she says.

'Full of charm today, aren't you?' He makes two black coffees and places them on the table. 'I didn't know you were coming over.' As he sits across from her, he bites into an apple. Jess has never, in her life, seen her father consume a whole apple. Apple cake, apple sauce, apple martini, yes, but a raw piece of fruit?

'What's going on, Pa?'

'Breakfast,' he mumbles.

She laughs. 'Fresh fruit?'

'I'm trying to look after my health.'

'Maybe cut out binge-drinking first.'

'I didn't binge-drink last night. As if I could,' he says, wistfully. 'I used to be able to drink for days and feel fine. It's incredible really, how I've got this far with so few ailments.'

'It's bloody miraculous.'

'I have Type 2 diabetes,' Pa says almost proudly.

'What?'

He sips his coffee and winces.

'Since when?'

'April.'

'Pa? Oh my God. Diabetes.'

'See, this is why I didn't want to tell you. I've been handling it. I have a very nice nurse and there's a hotline you can call if you need a chat. It's not as bad as everyone thinks it is. Oh, stop it.' He tears off a piece of kitchen roll and hands it to her.

Jess wipes her eyes as she pictures Pa injecting himself with insulin. 'You've been giving yourself injections since April? Gosh.'

'Type 2, Jess, it's a different thing. Not a big deal. No injections.'

'Oh,' she says, unsure if a 'different' thing means a 'less serious' thing. 'Why didn't you tell me straight away? I could have come to your appointments with you. This is a huge deal, Pa.'

'It's not huge. It's inconvenient is what it is. Having diarrhoea for weeks from all this medicine is probably the worst part of it.'

He's been dealing with this all alone because Jess has been too wrapped up in her own problems to notice. It makes her feel even worse.

'*Liebling*, calm down.'

'No,' she sobs. 'How can I? Everything's going wrong. And I'm sorry. I'm sorry that I've not been here for you, that my head's been too full of other things, of estate agents and viewings and properties and—'

'Oh no,' he says, 'today was your meeting with the council. I didn't even ask you how it went.'

She squeezes her eyes shut.

'That bad? Though I'm not surprised. You know how many times I've had to talk to those imbeciles about the potholes? Why can't they come and fill them in? It will take five minutes. Jess, it's going to be okay.'

'Okay,' she repeats, stirring her disgusting too-black and too-sweet coffee. 'It's just a lot, you know. The job, the house, now you.'

'I'm fine. Your bag is ringing.'

Her heart skips as it flashes with an unknown number. It used to be a signal to ignore, some recorded message assuming she'd recently been in a car crash or fallen over at work, but now an unknown number could mean the offer of a perfect job or a property within her price range. A range that, given she now owes Mustafa almost two months' rent, has shrunk.

'Answer it,' he says.

'I can't, Pa. I'm too upset.'

He tuts and she knows he's right. 'Hello?' she answers, her voice muffled from crying.

'Ms Bakker, it's Ellen calling from ArtHub Jobs.'

'Hi.' Jess crosses the fingers on one hand.

'Got a bit of bad news, I'm afraid: the toy museum won't be taking your application further.'

Jess feels her stomach drop. No.

'They liked you, thought you were great, very personable,

and of course your experience was exactly what they were looking for.'

'But?'

'I did discuss with you before how competitive it is for these jobs. Especially with you not having a degree.'

'A degree? What the hell does that matter if I can do the job?'

'I know, it's silly really. They said they'll keep you on file though. Sorry for this, I know it's not the news you wanted to hear.'

'No.'

'I'll call you as soon as anything else comes up, all right?'

Jess squeezes her temples as she hangs up. Having that job would have sorted out so many problems. She was so sure of it too. She hadn't considered what would happen if she didn't get it. 'I didn't get the job I went for. Could this day get any worse?'

Pa shakes his head. 'I have to ask, are you being picky? Holding out for the dream job?'

'I can't believe you said that.' And just like that, Jess's feelings towards him go from being compassionate and worried to pissed off and angry. 'As if I can afford to be picky right now?'

'Then why is this all taking so long? It's the same with finding a new house. You're not going to find the perfect property; you may need to think about settling a little.'

Images of brown bathtubs, wood rot, bedbugs and metal-grilled windows fill her head.

'If your budget is modest, stop looking for a palace,' Pa adds.

'Have you seen how much places go for around here? And I don't mean council rents, I mean privately?' She takes her phone and opens the site she believes she's spent more time on than any other ever. 'Go on, see for yourself.'

'It's fine. You've told me already. I know it's expensive.'

'No, you don't get it. You think I'm exaggerating. You think I'm being picky. Here. Look. You have no idea what I'm up against.' She pushes it across the table until he takes it, putting on his glasses and scrolling through. 'Nineteen hundred pounds,' he says, 'a month?'

'Yes,' she replies, exasperated.

'You have nearly two grand a month to spend on rent? No wonder the theatre went bust – it was probably overpaying you.'

'Of course I don't have that kind of money,' Jess says. 'That's the problem.'

'This is a desirable area. People are falling over themselves to live here. So where does that leave me? Where am *I* meant to go to make space for them?' she shouts.

Pa rises from his chair and puts his arms around her. A sob escapes. The last time he hugged her . . . she can't remember. It would have been years ago. It only adds to her emotion, to her complete loss of control. She can smell alcohol on him. Should he be drinking with this diagnosis? Is he allowed sugar? There's so much she doesn't know and has to find out. Why is he comforting her when he's the one dealing with bad news? She taps his arms until he removes them. 'I'm fine,' she says. 'Fine.'

'Jess, please, take the money I offered.'

'I can't do that, Pa.'

'Why not? It's there.'

'I can't.'

'Why not?'

'Because then I'm just as bad as him,' she cries. 'And I don't want to be like him. I want to be better, I want to stand on my own two feet. Look, I'm not going to steal your dream to sort out my own shit, okay? So please, stop offering me that money.'

'You'll never be like him,' Pa says, his voice stern. 'Never.' He sits back on the other side of the table. The two of them wait in silence, as if a solution will present itself. Then, after a few moments, Pa says, 'Come home.'

He can't really be suggesting what she thinks he is. She scoffs.

'Jess?'

'Pa, I haven't lived here since I was eighteen.' She laughs at the very idea of it. 'I appreciate the offer, I really do, but . . .' But what? She's not insane?

'Not forever – I can see the fear in your eyes. Come home temporarily, until you find work, clear some debt, pile up some savings.'

It was never far from her mind that she would be the sole carer for Pa as he aged. Is this how it will start? That she'll move in with him temporarily and end up seeing how much help he really needs in the house? 'Are you finding it hard to live alone? Is the diabetes too much to handle?'

'Why are you asking me this?'

'Well, why are you asking me to move in?'

'Because you've nowhere else to go,' he says, his tone sharp.

The silence is heavy and Jess feels confused as to where they go next.

'I love living alone,' Pa says, calmer now. 'But I would also love to have my family here.'

'We wouldn't all fit.'

'You can move into your old room and the children can share the spare room.'

'What *spare* room?' Then, seeing Pa's face before he turns away, she says, 'Ah.'

The spare room is what used to be Dominic's room. He used to kick the bedroom door shut with his foot as she passed by. She never even really saw the inside of that room until he moved out.

'I can't, Pa. Thank you, but I can't.'

He leans back in his chair. 'I thought you would like the idea of lying under your Boyzone posters again. And the spare room,' he stops to straighten his glasses, 'it's big. It's empty,' he adds, as if needing to clarify that nothing of Dominic remains there.

Jess shifts in her seat. It always surprises her how often the subject of Dominic seems to bubble under their conversations, how so many problems and issues roll back to him.

'It's just a bedroom, Jess,' Pa says, clearly thinking along the same lines.

'You've lived alone for years now. Having us all here, it would do your head in. It's a terrible idea. A really, really terrible idea.'

'Hmm.'

Though on paper it makes sense. She needs help, he needs help. She needs space, he has space. This is what families are for. Jess tips her head to the side and looks at Pa, like really looks at him. He smiles at her and rubs his eyes. 'Jess?'

'Okay,' she says slowly, her voice a little resigned and perhaps already a little regretful. 'You're right. We *should* all move in here for a bit.'

Chapter Twelve

Ben

July

When Ben first started working at Travelodge, an overzealous HR lady called Sandy talked him into joining the 'birthday club'. From what he could tell it was basically a pyramid-type scheme where everyone paid £10 every few months so that when it was their birthday, they got a present.

'We weren't quite sure what to get you,' Ben's boss Harry says, handing him a card and a beautifully wrapped bundle.

'You didn't have to get me anything,' Ben replies, even though he had essentially paid for this gift.

'Happy birthday, mate.'

Ben notices the office girls looking at him blankly and whispering to each other. They're probably wondering who he is. To be honest, when he looks in his card and sees the names Cheryl, Sarah, Vicky and Vic, he feels the same way.

'Thanks, everyone. Really kind of you.'

'Open your present now,' Harry says, a little too eagerly.

Inside is a three-pack of socks with little beagle heads on them and a £5 voucher for Pets at Home.

He thanks everyone again and reiterates the offer of cake in the staff-room: a vanilla tray-bake he'd picked up from Asda on the way in, as he assumed it was the done thing. Most people grab a slice and shuffle back to their stations, and Ben passes the morning by removing two rats from an air-conditioning unit, repainting a bathroom and, most excitingly of all, taking a rug someone threw up on to the dump. He repeatedly checks his phone for a message from Shanice and finds none, but Mum has asked him to come by the nursery at lunchtime.

Lunch with Mum, that's a nice idea.

He parks near the nursery and sends Shanice a message.

Would love to chat to Olivia later before I head out for my birthday.

He reads it back. It doesn't even give her a chance to pretend like she remembered. Also, it sets him up with having to fabricate an outing, which he knows he won't be able to do. He deletes and types:

Hey. Hope you are well? I might be out later, but free to chat to Olivia whenever.

There it is, vague enough.

Mum knocks on the window of the van and he holds up a finger while he carefully chooses the right emoji to end the message on.

177

'Hello, birthday boy,' Mum says, handing him a Marks & Spencer bag.

'Thanks.'

'Forty-two. Good grief, what does that make me? Oh, you got presents,' she says, nodding towards the package in the van window.

'It's from my work friends.' It feels good to say *friends*. 'Socks.'

'You can never have enough,' she says, casting a quick look down to the bag she gave him. He squeezes it and concludes that yes, it's definitely more socks.

'Don't make that face,' she says, checking her watch. 'Really. You're too old to be getting presents from me anyway. Forty-two, how'd I end up with such an old kid already? Your card's in there too. Any plans for the rest of the day?'

'Work.'

'And after work? Going out with your friends, are you?'

The way his face falls lets her know that this isn't something likely to happen.

'No, guess not,' she says flatly, as if saddened Ben failed to arrange a meal out at TGI Friday's.

'Forty-two, not a big deal, is it?' he tries.

'Nah, course not,' she agrees, though her own birthday is celebrated each year with a rowdy trip to Blackpool with 'the girlies', a scary group of women in their sixties who pride themselves on acting like horny, feral teenagers.

'All right, love, enjoy it, whatever you do.'

'You're already going back?'

'I only wanted to pass on your card. We've got some firemen

coming to visit the kids. I need to get back and prepare myself.'
She leans in and kisses him on the cheek before tottering back
into her building.

Ben thought it would have taken a bit longer with her today,
that maybe they would have gone for lunch or at least stopped to
share a bit of cake. He gets in the van and opens the card, which
has a smiley gorgonzola on the front and text that says, 'Don't
be blue about getting old'. The printed message inside reads,
'You're mature'. Underneath she's written 'Best wishes, Mum'.

That's the celebrations done then, Ben thinks as he eats the
last two portions of cake while sitting at the steering wheel.
Might as well head home to get Harold out for a walk; he
was up whining for most of the night.

As Ben drives into Stratford, he spots partially deflated
balloons flapping around the entrance of The Anstey Theatre
and a large tarpaulin outside that reads 'Save our theatre' and
'Stop slashing the arts'. At the noodle bar Jessica had gone on
about opportunities for outreach work, a way to keep doing
her job despite the closure, though when it was the two of
them last week at his flat, she had confided that this work
seemed all too unreliable to live off and she was struggling
to find anything permanent.

Still no call from Shanice. Maybe there's some post at his
place. On her birthday he always made an effort from the
start, jewellery, proper flowers from a florist, a particular bag
she wanted, a heartfelt message in a card. When Olivia was
tiny, he had stuck one of her chubby feet in poster paint to
make a card, it was so cute. Why can't he remember any of
his cards from Shanice?

Only when he's walking in the park with Harold does Shanice ring him back. Finally. 'Hey.'

'Hi, Ben. What's wrong?'

'Wrong? Nothing.'

'So why did you need to speak?'

'I didn't need to speak. I just fancied a chat with Olivia. Is she there?'

Shanice tuts. 'She's watching TV. We said Monday, Wednesday and Sunday evenings. I'd like to keep it that way, structured. Then we all know where we're at.'

No, *she* had said Monday, Wednesday and Sunday evenings, and he had agreed.

'It's disruptive when you message out of the blue and expect us to drop everything to talk to you.' She doesn't sound mean, like normal, she sounds more tired.

'I wasn't asking you to drop everything. I'm sorry. Are you okay? You don't sound good.'

'Yep. Fine,' she says shortly, then off to the side, 'Oli, your dad's on the phone, quickly come and say hi.'

She *has* forgotten.

'Daddy.'

'Squidalicious, what are you watching?'

'*Sugar Rush*. What are you doing?'

'I'm in the park walking Harold, he's had a bit of a bad stomach recently.'

'Maybe he ate too many carrots again and needs to poo.'

'Yeah. You're probably right.'

'Did you know I've got a wobbly tooth?'

'Another one? No. I didn't.'

'Mummy forgot to tell you. Maybe because she's not well. She's been in bed. Sleeping.'

It hurts to think of Olivia alone while Shanice sleeps off whatever bug she's caught. Even the mildest of colds would leave her incapacitated and Ben taking full charge of the house. 'Don't worry, I'm sure she'll feel better tomorrow. You can always call me if you want someone to talk to,' he adds.

'It's okay. Gerald is here. I can talk to him.'

Kick a man when he's down. Though there's a tiny part of Ben that is grateful to hear Gerald is there, keeping Olivia company.

'I saw Nanny today, she says hi.'

'They're going to say who won the cake challenge now. Hold on.'

The phone rustles and then there's silence. 'Olivia? Olivia?' It cuts off.

When he tries to call back no one answers and the text message he sends goes undelivered. Ben storms around the park, fed up. It doesn't help that everyone else looks so unusually cheerful. A smiling mum pushes a double buggy filled with gurgling babies, a few of the Fight Club share energy drinks and laugh raucously, and even the park keeper is smiling, singing 'her name was Rio' while sweeping up crisp packets and chicken bones.

'Harold!' Jacob runs over and squats down to let Harold lick his face.

'Hey, what are you doing here? Shouldn't you be in school? Are you bunking off? Because I'm not sure that's a good idea. I mean, if you were, I would probably have to tell someone.'

Jacob springs back up. 'What did you say?'

'Oh, never mind.'

Jacob frowns. 'I hate when people do that.'

'Do what?'

'Say, "oh, never mind" when I miss something they've said.'

'Sorry. I was just asking if you're bunking off school.'

Jacob feigns insult, 'Do you really think I'm that sort of person? No, I value my education, Ben. Mum's right there.'

Ben turns to see Jessica finishing off something on her phone and walking towards him. 'Oh, hey lovely,' she calls. His breath catches then she stops to stroke Harold. 'Are you actually walking today?' she baby-talks to Harold, who rubs himself against her silky-looking leggings. 'Hi, Ben.'

'Hi.'

'I read recently that beagles need ninety minutes of walking and running a day,' Jacob says. 'That must really cut into your social life.'

'Um, yeah, I guess so.'

'So, can I?' Jacob wiggles his fingers in the direction of the lead. 'You can trust me. I'm responsible.'

Jessica smiles at Ben encouragingly as if keen to be alone with him. He hands the lead over.

'Don't go far,' she calls after Jacob. 'I'm glad I bumped into you. What's wrong, you okay?'

'Constipation,' Ben says. 'Uh, not me, Harold.'

'Oh,' Jessica laughs. 'Poor thing.'

'Yeah, he's been crying all night.'

Though the way Harold bounces after Jacob makes Ben

look like he's making it up. 'He's the same with your dad, you know? He loves your family.'

'Then he's a very bad judge of character.'

'Everything okay? Why no school?'

'Jacob had a dentist appointment earlier and now we're just heading to Pa's to check out how much stuff we're going to have to dump before moving.'

'It's really happening then?' It's obvious that Jessica and Wolf don't have the best relationship, so the idea of them living together is insane. Still, when Jessica had first mentioned it to Ben, he knew to keep his opinions to himself.

'Yeah, it's time. My landlord, he's been great, but I can't let this drag on any longer. And the places I'm seeing are all in such a bad state. I can't do it to the kids.'

The more time he spends with her, the more he's coming to recognise the ways in which she dresses up bad news, how she smiles through it.

'I could always help you, if you've found somewhere you like but it needs work.'

'Stop doing that.'

'Doing what?'

'Offering to fix every problem.'

'Not *every* problem. I won't be able to help you if you move in with Wolf.'

She laughs and punches him lightly on the arm. 'And there was me thinking I'd found the perfect man.'

Ben blushes and reminds himself that Jessica *is* flirtatious. There's no way she's looking at him like that, like a potential . . . well, he's not even sure. A potential boyfriend? Partner?

'I never dreamed I would move back home. But you know, Pa has all this space, so . . .' she trails off.

'You don't sound like you've fully warmed to the idea.'

'Would you want to live with him? Don't answer that. You're like your dog, a bad judge of character.'

They walk on. Ben feels for her, this entire situation must be so stressful.

'He's going to drive me nuts, isn't he?' Jessica asks.

Ben recalls the way Jessica's jaw had tightened with each of Wolf's jibes at the restaurant. 'You can always escape across to mine, if you ever need a break.'

'You're doing it again.'

They stop walking. 'What? What am I doing?' Apart from staring at her for too long?

'Being a white knight.'

Is this something he should be doing more or less of, 'Er, so, should I ask you about your job search?'

'Bloody hell, no. Looking for work is so time-consuming. When I lost my job, I thought I'd have tons of time, but instead I seem to spend every minute filling out application forms online and wondering if I'm proficient in Excel. Sorry, am I power-walking? I do that when I get stressed. Distract me.'

Is she being suggestive? Because it definitely sounds that way. 'Hmm,' he stalls.

'How's your work going?'

He wants to tell her about the pushy HR woman and the birthday club, though is embarrassed to bring up his own birthday. 'It's okay. Not too busy. I've got an afternoon of flower-bed work lined up, all very exciting. I'm hoping it'll rain to add to the experience.'

Jacob is now heading out of the park gate, with Harold tottering along beside him.

'Sorry, you're working, aren't you? Why are you letting me take up all your time, chatting your ear off?'

'It's fine,' he says, 'I always take a long lunch to come home to walk Harold.'

'Really? Well, as of yesterday I'm officially unemployed, a real lady of leisure now. So if you ever want to meet for lunch I'll be around.'

'Lunch?'

His reaction causes her to backtrack. 'I just meant like, if you had the time.'

This is it; she's actually asking *him* out. 'Yeah,' Ben says, 'I'd really like that.' Though he no longer has her attention because she's staring up ahead. Ben looks too, to where Jacob and Harold are paused by Ben's van.

'He's doing the biggest dump I've ever seen,' Jacob shouts.

Jessica laughs as Ben gets out his bags to clear it up. 'So he wasn't constipated, he was just being an arsehole. Harold, why here?'

'Harold is my favourite animal ever,' Jacob says quite seriously. 'Do you need a dog sitter for him? I would accept minimum wage. Oh, is it your birthday?'

Ben follows Jacob's eyes to the van window where the card from Mum has slipped down the front of the glass. He scratches at the back of his head. 'Yeah, kind of.'

'It's *kind of* your birthday?' Jessica asks. 'Why didn't you say something?'

'It's not a big deal.'

'Birthdays are a huge deal. We go big for birthdays. And you're a summer baby. We're all January, which is a bit grim.'

'All of you? Expensive month.'

'Tell me about it.'

Jacob leans against the van and folds his arms. 'What's the plan for tonight then?' he asks. 'Go-karting? Drinking? Hitting the clubs? Few games at the casino?'

'Casino?' Ben laughs. 'No, at my age, birthdays are like . . . no one cares.'

'You're not celebrating?' Jessica says, looking genuinely put out by it.

Who would Ben even invite if he did want to celebrate his birthday? His mum's social calendar seems to be booked up weeks in advance and he doesn't know anyone at work well enough yet. 'I'm not bothered. I'll probably just watch a film at home, get a takeaway.'

'You sure?' Jessica and Jacob look at each other then back at Ben before saying, 'Oh,' in unison. They think he's sad. That's it. This is embarrassing.

'Actually, I better start making my way back to work.'

'Of course,' Jessica says, stepping back. 'We also need to get home to, you know, pack some more boxes. Well, happy birthday, Ben. Whatever you end up doing.'

When he finally gets home that evening, he has a long shower and half a mug of sake, which is definitely better warm. Being alone on your birthday isn't that bad. He's got a money-off voucher for the local pizza place and there's a three-hour documentary on 9/11 he's been meaning to watch.

The buzzer goes and when he heads downstairs to open it, it's Jessica.

'Now, I know you said you didn't want to celebrate, but I'm sorry. I couldn't help it.' She holds up a large Sainsbury's bag.

'What's that?'

'I did your weekly food shop for you. What do you think it is? We're going to barbecue.'

'You have a barbecue in that bag?'

'Yeah.' She digs in and pulls out a disposable barbecue tray. 'It's from Poundland.'

Ben takes the tray from her. 'Aren't these things responsible for a lot of carbon monoxide deaths?'

'You're more likely to die from my cooking. I even have dog biscuits.'

'Oh, he's asleep.'

Her face falls, 'That's a shame, because it was him I really wanted to see.'

'Oh,' Ben looks behind himself, up the stairs, wondering if he should wake up Harold for another walk.

'Don't be silly,' Jessica laughs. 'Get your sun hat on. Let's go.'

'It's almost seven p.m., you really want to barbecue?'

'Why, were you off to bed already? Come on, Ben.'

They're barely through the park gates when confronted with a couple necking on a bench. Ben looks away, as he always does when faced with such lively public displays of affection, while

Jessica glares at them before leaning into Ben and whispering, quite loudly, 'Look at those two, proper going for it.'

He hears himself say, 'Young love.' As if he's turned into someone's grandma.

'I give it a week. I'm never in the park at this time, I didn't realise it's where all the horny teens hang out. Look, there's more.' They pass another couple, sitting close enough to kiss, though not quite getting there.

Jessica walks past them and onto a patch of grass by the flower beds near the fence. She throws down a blanket and starts unwrapping the mini barbecue.

'You want me to do it?' he asks.

She holds a hand up in front of him. 'Stop.' She lights the tray and unpacks the rest of the shopping. Sausages, bag salad, buns and half a bottle of own-brand ketchup. 'Also,' she pulls out a bottle of rosé cava, 'ta-dah.'

'Sparkling rosé, my favourite,' he smiles.

'Don't be macho about it, it's really nice and was on special offer. And for dessert,' she raises two tinfoil-covered bananas. 'They're filled with chocolate.'

'Hmm, uh. I don't eat chocolate,' he says apologetically.

Her jaw drops. 'What do you mean, you don't eat chocolate? I thought you were a normal guy?'

'It gives me really bad reflux.'

'Well, that's sexy,' she laughs.

'Sorry,' he looks away, wondering if it's too late to present himself as a different kind of man to her. He's starting to believe that she likes him, though nowhere near as much as he likes her. 'Thanks for doing this.'

'It's my way of saying thank you, for helping me out after Bug Gate.'

'You didn't have to thank me. Actually, I wanted to ask you—' he stops. Can he do this? 'I wanted to ask *you* out. I've wanted to for a while.'

'Finally,' she says, turning her full glare on him.

He lets out a dry sort of laugh and has to look away to regain his composure.

'I was beginning to wonder if I'd read things wrong,' she says. 'Why are you only asking me now?'

'You had a lot going on.'

'I still do, to be fair.'

'Yeah, I know. I'm sorry, this is probably a bad time to ask you, especially when—'

'No,' she says, 'it's a perfect time to ask me.'

One of the drunks stumbles from the flower garden on the other side of the path, turns to a tree and leans one arm against it to balance himself. This is not how Ben wanted to do things. 'Would you be interested though? In going out with me, somewhere nice, a place where—'

'Tramps aren't pissing a few feet from where you're eating?'

'Exactly,' he laughs, turning back to her and seeing for the first time that maybe she's nervous too. Wolf had made comments about Jessica having more than a few men in and out of her life, though Ben got the impression there had been nothing serious since her relationship with the kids' dad.

She pulls her shoulders to her ears briefly and smiles.

'I'd love to take you out on a date,' he says, then exhales, relieved he got the words out. 'However people do that these days. Because I don't know. Because I don't think I remember.'

'It's not that hard. You book a restaurant, you tell me when, I put on a dress I'm too old to wear and meet you there.'

'I haven't done this in so—'

'You need to get over this, Ben. You either like me or you don't.'

He's losing her before it's even begun, and why? Because he's still got that internal monologue telling him he's not good enough, that he's boring, that no woman will have the time for him. She's right, he needs to get over it. He wants to get over it. 'Jessica,' he shuffles along the blanket, trying not to be awkward, and takes her by the chin. 'I definitely like you.' Then from somewhere within him the confidence comes to kiss Jessica Bakker.

Chapter Thirteen

Jess

Steadman drinks the whole pint of water in one go, not even stopping to take a breath. 'Thanks,' he says, handing back the empty glass. 'I could do with a snack as well, you know?'

'Oh really?' Jess raises an eyebrow at him. What does he think this is?

'You're really going to look at me like that?'

'You're *really* expecting me to hop in the kitchen and whip you up a ploughman's?'

'It's the least you could do,' he kicks a box into the front garden. His moving skills are shabby, he's slapdash, careless and has constantly complained about what a bad choice of moving day this is, but he was also free and had a driver's licence.

In the house the children are also half-heartedly kicking boxes along the floor. Haze with both hands on her phone while shuffling along a box marked *fragile* with her shins.

'Haze, sweetheart?'

'Yeah?' She tucks the phone in her back pocket and Jess marvels at how anything can fit there, especially as it looks like Haze's arse just about fits in the jeans. 'Careful with that, please. By the way, your dad's hungry. He's being really kind in offering to help us so last minute. Maybe one of you could run to Greggs and get him something?'

Jacob, in a perfect mimic of her, raises an eyebrow.

'Sure, have you got money?' Haze asks.

Jess finds a couple of coins in her purse and hands them over. 'Be quick though. I want this done before midday.'

'What's with her mood?' Steadman asks as Haze saunters off past him.

Jess waits till Haze is out of earshot then says, 'Oh, you've finally noticed, have you? She's been a nightmare. I can do no right by her at the moment. Has she said anything to you?'

'Nah. She's probably stressed out with all that studying. She needs to get out and have some fun. I knew this course was a bad idea.'

'This course? Her A levels, you mean? The ones that will lead her to the university of—'

'Oxford. Yes, Jess, I know. Everyone knows. Don't you think it's a bit much? When was all this Oxford stuff decided anyway? Just because she's smart it doesn't mean she has to go to some stuck-up university. She should be out there trying to find out what she really wants from life, not running up debt to read books and write essays.'

'We're not talking about this today.' It's hot, so very, very hot, and Jess's patience doesn't stretch far enough to have this argument with him again, so instead she focuses on loading more boxes and bags into the van.

'You think he'll come over to say bye?' Steadman asks, nodding across the road.

'No, he's out. Thankfully.' She's glad Mustafa isn't home; he made a big scene this morning of leaving with the boys 'for the day' so he wouldn't have to watch her go. Having Steadman here would have only made it worse in a way; she always used to feel a little embarrassed by Steadman, her uncivilised partner who worked in retail, got the bus to work and never earned any money. Plus, she'll never forget the one word Mustafa said after he met Steadman for the first time: 'Really?' As if he knew, even then, that she was punching well below her weight and that really, she should have been with someone like him instead.

Haze returns and hands her dad a baguette. 'Here you go. I'll keep the change.'

'Thanks, princess.' He sits on the wall. 'Did Mustafa say anything to you this morning?'

Jess sits next to him. 'He said bye.'

'How long you been here now?'

'Twelve years.'

Steadman laughs. 'Twelve years. That's a long time for a guy to figure out a girl ain't interested in him. Twelve years to get over it.'

'It's not funny. And I think Mustafa is very happy with his wife.'

'The one he once patted on her head?' Steadman wipes his mouth with the back of his hand and shouts inside for someone to bring him another glass of water. She finds the way he eats kind of endearing, a little ravenous, like Jacob but also picky like Hazel, pulling out slightly wilted salad leaves and rearranging the chicken pieces before each bite. 'How comes I've been roped into this anyway? Was your new man not free today or something?'

'New man? Who told you I had a new man?'

'Who'd you think?'

'Well, Haze is wrong. There's no new man. It was a guy on Pa's street who happened to have a van and was free the last time we attempted to move.' Jess feels instantly bad, not for lying to Steadman, but for downplaying Ben.

'Were you paying him?' Steadman asks between bites.

'No, it was a favour.'

'A favour? What kind of person is going to spend a day moving a hundred boxes of shoes as a favour? Haze told me he likes you. That you met up in the park the other evening,' he makes air quotes and adds, 'to *walk his dog.*'

'What would she know?'

Steadman shrugs and laughs.

'And there was no walking the dog,' Jess adds, which only makes him laugh more.

'You're not going to tell me then?'

'There's nothing to tell you.' It's funny because ever since meeting Ben, Jess has been desperate to talk to someone about him. Over the years she's fancied a few guys, but there was something different about this one and she's not quite sure what it is. 'I don't want to talk to you about other men.'

'I don't want to hear about other *men*. Though I can tell you like this one.'

194

'How?' How has she given that away so quickly?

'Because I know you. Is this a serious thing?' Steadman asks.

Is it? Jessica's not sure. She definitely fancies Ben, and whereas before she thought he was way too passive and introvert for her, she's starting to understand that he's actually quietly confident, a trait she finds interesting.

'Your silence says a lot.'

Jess stands from the wall. 'Does it? Oh, I don't know. He's different from the type of guys I usually go for.'

'You know what I always say, change is good. Different is good. So, tell me. He's different. How? Don't make that face. I tell you things about other women all the time.' Even when she'd rather not know.

She takes a breath. 'It's a bit complicated. I mean, my life is a mess right now. And as much as I'd love a really good distraction—'

'Stop.'

'What?'

'I don't need to know about your sex life.'

'I wasn't going to tell you. Because I don't have one at the moment. Because he's a complete gentleman.' She says it like it's a compliment, though really, this is a big part of the issue. There's taking it slow and then there's Ben.

'Maybe he's weighed up how much he likes you with how much he wants an easy life.'

'Shut up. He's shy, that's all. Recently divorced too, and I'm not sure if he's fully over what happened or if he's still stuck on his ex. I don't know.' Surely that's the reason why

Ben's yet to set their date in stone. They've been messaging lots over the last few nights and each time she hints at meeting up, it's like he pulls back. It's confusing. They had this great kiss, the kind of kiss that even though you're in public and sitting awkwardly and possibly on the cusp of having your bag nicked, you don't care because the kiss is that good. Yet, it was *only* a kiss. And after that, they packed their stuff, put the rubbish in the bin and walked back, the whole time Jess assuming he would invite her up. Then there was nothing, an awkward kind of formal goodbye on the pavement and that was it.

Haze comes out carrying a blue Ikea bag filled with cushions. 'As busy as you two look out here, could someone come in and help us move the fridge?'

'I'm not carrying a fridge,' Steadman says. 'White goods stay with the property.'

'We have to,' Jacob cries. 'Opa's fridge smells like something has died in it.'

'No,' Steadman says.

The kids sulk off back into the house to gather the last few bits, while Steadman and Jess try to make more space in the van.

'How did you meet this shy guy anyway?' Steadman asks. 'He's old, right?'

'No. Why would you think that?'

'Haze said he's a friend of Wolf's. All Wolf's friends are old.'

'He's our age – well, a few years older. In fact, he went to St Margaret's.'

'Oh no. It's not someone I know, is it. What's his name?'

'Ben Braveheart.'

Steadman slaps his head with his palm.

'You don't know him. Or do you?' A little flare of anxiety goes up. One of the things she likes about Ben is the way he seems so unconnected to anything. He's not from the third sector, or one of those local guys everyone's been around already. And she knows this is hypocritical, but she likes how his only *baggage* is neatly packed away in another country.

'Braveheart, shit. I know that name. What year was he in?'

Jess bites her lip and admits, 'Dominic's.'

'Was he a friend of Dominic's?'

'No. Of course not.'

'You sure?'

'He's not the type of person to have hung out with Dom. Trust me. I don't think he's aware of him at all.'

Steadman narrows his eyes in that way when he's desperate to say something else, but Jess doesn't want to hear it. She busies herself in the back of the van until she can take it no more. 'I'm assuming he left the school before everything happened with Dom.'

Steadman nods. 'Yeah. Probably. Or he would have—'

'Made a run for it?' She doesn't mean to make light of the past, but Steadman was there, he knows what she went through, how Dom and his actions affected her life. 'Is that what you were going to say?'

'No, Jess, that's not what I was going to say because, as wild as your brother was, I don't think it would put a guy off seeing you.'

'Thanks. That's a really weird compliment.'

'I just think if he knew Dom it would have come up in conversation by now. Though, I do know that name, cause it's an unusual name. Braveheart. I'm sure of it. I'll ask around for you.'

She doesn't want her ex-partner asking around for her, trying to get some gossip on Ben and his past. She likes that he doesn't seem to have one.

Jacob comes out wearing a hat shaped like a chicken.

'Hey, my Young King,' Steadman tries, making a great attempt to ignore the headwear.

'Haze thinks this shouldn't have made the cut even though I wear it all the time,' he says to Jess, deadpan. She can see Steadman struggling, unsure of whether to laugh or be worried.

'You can take it if you swear to wear it at least three times in the coming week,' Jess says.

He thinks it over before lifting a thumb and saying, 'It's a jellied eel,' in a bad cockney accent.

'We done then?' Steadman shuts the doors of the van and puts an arm around Jacob. 'You wanna ride over with me?'

Jacob looks back at the house and Jess can see his awkwardness. She knows he'd rather sit and squirm through an awkward drive with his dad than turn him down to his face.

'Steadman, is it okay if you go ahead and we walk over together? I think it would be nice for the kids to say goodbye to the house.'

Haze packs away Steadman's abandoned glass into one of the last bags and squeezes it into the passenger seat before closing the door. Steadman takes the cue and for want of something better to do squeezes the top of Jacob's chicken hat. 'Okay, squad,' he shouts as he climbs in the van alone, 'see you on the other side.'

As he drives off, Haze says, 'Does he realise he's going to get there way earlier than us?'

'It's fine, he can start the unloading.'

With him gone and the job seemingly finished, all that remains is their empty home and the realisation that this is really it.

The three of them go inside and look around.

'It looks huge,' Haze says.

Jess is already in tears, the emotion hitting her like a ton of bricks she hadn't realised were hanging over her head all morning, all week even. She doesn't look at the height chart on the wall but runs her fingers down it as if trying to soak up the memories and take them with her.

Jacob makes a clicking noise with his tongue and Jess pulls him in for a hug.

The house looks kind of glum now that it's empty, and even with Mustafa's newly painted white walls everything seems tatty. Also, the job he did was so half-arsed, not bothering to paint behind the sofa or TV unit, that it's almost like there are shadows of where their life used to be.

Jess wipes her eyes. 'Okay, that's it then. I'm going upstairs to lock the windows.'

'I've done it already,' Haze says.

'Oh, then I'm going to double-check nothing's been left.'

'I've done it, Mum.'

Jess doesn't care, she heads up the stairs for what will

be the last ever time and feels a chill as she stands on the landing, seeing each of the rooms empty. She's never taken much notice of the mould in the bathroom, though without the cheeriness of their rainbow shower curtain, it's hard to ignore. Everything looks a little tired and sad, from the fittings to the windows to the carpets. It's definitely the right time to move on.

It's silent downstairs and she realises the children are sitting outside, already completely done with the house. Jess locks up and posts the keys back through the letterbox, then Mustafa's front door opens and Mustafa Junior, a softer version of his dad, comes over with his two little brothers in tow.

'Hi,' Jess says. 'Sorry, I thought you were all out for the day. I already posted the keys.'

'This is from my parents,' the oldest boy says, as he hands over two old ice-cream tubs filled with food. 'It's so you don't have to cook tonight.'

'Thank you,' she says, looking across at Mustafa's house with its perfect front garden and always too-bright white net curtains. She can't be mad at him for this, he was only doing what she and every other parent does. Putting their family's needs first.

As the last box gets into Pa's house, Jess hears her father shout something she had been suspecting about herself yet did not want to admit.

'Jessica Bakker, you're a hoarder.'

'No. You're getting us mixed up. You see, all this,' she waves her hand over the piles of stuff that now fill the hallway and living room, 'is from three people. Not one.'

He opens a box at random and pulls a pink knee-length stiletto boot from it. 'Jacob really does have great taste.'

Jacob climbs over, hopping from one place to another before bouncing onto the sofa. 'Told you they had lots of shoes. I hardly have any stuff at all.'

'That's not strictly true,' Jess says. 'Sure, you don't have lots of clothes, but you have computers, graphic novels, novelty hats,' she chucks the chicken hat at him. 'And Pa, you can't talk because this whole house is full of things you've not looked at in years, decades even. Yet, I'm the hoarder?' They're having a laugh with each other, but Pa really has made a lot of comments about the contents of the van.

'I am a keeper of the past, my things represent my full, well-lived life.' He shuffles over to the sideboard and has another sip of his beer. She can't be sure if it's the same bottle or a new one. He drinks slowly, raising it to her. 'To my daughter, the hoarder.'

Jess had paid for one storage unit to ensure they didn't bring more than they needed here. Yet the way Pa's going on you'd have thought he expected each of them to bring the one bag. The kids haven't picked up on it. But Jess will need to have a word with him later. If they're all to feel comfortable here, this isn't a good way of going about it.

'And you,' he says to Jacob, 'why so many computers?'

Jess bites her lip and watches her son's face.

'I feel like Nintendo brainwashed me,' he says, his voice filled with melancholy. 'I've been playing since I was a child and I don't know how to exist without one.'

'Let's remember this conversation at Christmas.' Jess sits on the arm of the sofa and picks some fluff from Jacob's hair. She wonders if he would entertain the idea of getting some sort of shape cut into it.

'Can I put these in Haze's room too?' he says, adding to a small pile of stuff by the door.

'More stuff,' Pa says, 'stuff, stuff everywhere.'

Jess nods, 'Sure, hun.'

She had been adding to the pile herself yet so far managed to avoid going into 'Haze's room'. As always, seeing it from the doorway was strange enough. How could it be that a room left vacant for so long still manages to feel like it belongs to someone? The walls have been repainted, the windows replaced, the carpet ripped up years ago and re-laid. Though it'll always be Dominic's room.

Jess receives a message from Ben.

Hope your move went okay.

He had of course offered to help again, but she thought it best to do things properly this time. Also, she wanted to prove to Haze, and herself, that she wasn't using him.

'*Liebling*,' Pa shouts from the hallway.

She takes a breath and calls back, 'What?'

'Can you help me find my cards? I want to teach this boy some real games.'

She replies to Ben:

Pa's already grating on me. Thought you said he cleaned up.

He sends back a laughing face. She can see he's typing then nothing. Again, typing, maybe he's finally going to bring up that dinner he promised her. Come on, Ben, she thinks, wandering over to the window and looking up at his flat. It's exciting to hear another message ping through. This really is like being a teenager again.

I left something in the fridge for you. Top shelf.

Haze is in the kitchen, at the sink. 'I'm rewashing everything,' she says. 'It's all a bit grubby.' They had agreed to start as they meant to go on, with no expensive convenience foods and everyone chipping in with the cooking and cleaning.

Haze's laptop and books sit open on the table, though it's already edging towards six p.m.

'You're going to study tonight?'

'I've got a few things to do before my tutorial tomorrow.'

'You never told me you had a tutorial tomorrow.'

'You never asked.'

Here it is again, Haze's mood, and the guilt she coats Jess in whenever she pleases. 'Do you want me to take over? I can do that if you need to study.'

'No,' she snaps, 'it's pretty much done now anyway.' She pulls off a glove to turn up the music.

Jess opens the fridge, her earlier excitement somewhat dampened. Then on the top shelf, at the back, is a mini bottle of sparkling rosé.

'What's funny?' Haze asks, not turning from the sink.

'Nothing.' Jess slides the bottle down by her side. What

is she going to do with it anyway? It's too small to share, plus she doesn't want to have to explain why Ben is buying her drink.

She goes upstairs, mini bottle in one hand and Jacob's basket of cables and consoles in the other. It's just a room, she thinks as she marches inside and dumps the box down on the floor. Just a room. The wardrobe is open and partly filled with Haze's clothes, slinky dresses and messy piles of colourful loungewear. Dominic used to be meticulous about his clothes. Jess had once gone upstairs to see his wardrobe doors open, everything hung neatly in colour order and all she wanted to do was muss it up.

'This is Haze's room now,' she tells herself. 'Dominic has gone. Dominic has gone forever.'

The night Dominic moved out, he had been in here with Pa for ages. The argument was loud and felt worse than usual, then it stopped and there was a thud. Jess ran upstairs to see Pa lying on the floor, slumped against the wardrobe with Dominic standing over him. They both looked at her then back at each other before Pa said to Dom, 'Get out.' At the time, Jess couldn't understand it, how Pa could order his own child onto the streets. Even having witnessed, as she did, the viciousness of Dom's words and the threat of his behaviour, he was still family. Yet Pa was chucking him out. Giving up on him. Jess had thought about it again after having her own children and was confused even more, because there was no scenario on earth where she would give up on either of them. It must have hurt Pa so badly. No wonder when Dom returned, years later, speaking of being a changed man, Pa welcomed him back with open arms.

Jess definitely needs a drink now, though the idea of drinking alone in her childhood bedroom is extremely depressing. She messages Ben.

I need an escape.

He's typing, then not typing. It's the same in real life too, like he's always on the verge of saying something but then pulls back. Again, she takes the reins:

What are you doing?

He replies:

Watching Gordon Ramsay cook a pig in a desert oven, while waiting for my microwavable lasagne. If you need a break, you're more than welcome to come over.

'How was it?' Ben calls over Harold's over-excited yapping.

Jess hopes her face conveys her exhaustion.

'That bad?' he laughs.

They stand opposite each other in the doorway and he puts an arm around her; it's comforting but also a bit more 'buddy' than she wants right now. She drops her head onto his chest. 'Remind me why I'm doing this?' she says into his T-shirt. They try to kiss but Harold keeps weaving between their legs, barking, and from the flat downstairs there's the sound of a man laughing loudly. Jess pulls away and Ben looks down at her, his eyes extra pale against his flushed skin.

'Have you been sunbathing?' she asks.

He taps his nose, 'No, I went out for twenty minutes *and* I had a hat on.'

Jess laughs, takes his hand and follows him through to the living room. 'This is terrible weather to move house in.'

Ben hands her a drink. 'Here, I can't drink that pink stuff.' He's actually got white wine in.

'Tonight, you are the pink stuff.'

He tuts and rubs some moisturiser into his face before joining her at the balcony.

'Odd that whoever designed these flats thought to put balcony doors yet no actual balcony.'

'It's a Juliette balcony.'

'Romantic,' she says, leaning over the rail.

Two ladies power-walking in saris stop and wave up at Ben. Harold yaps and Jess laughs. 'Friends of yours?'

'Of his,' he says, nodding down to Harold.

Her shoulders ache. Tomorrow her whole body will be in agony.

'What's with all the groaning?' Ben asks.

'Nothing. It's just a lot, you know. I left home when I was eighteen and I never looked back. Until now.'

'I'm sure it won't be this tough all the time. You probably need to get used to each other again.'

'It's more about being back in the house itself. It's weird. It wasn't always the happiest of places,' she sighs. 'Anyway, tell me something. It's not long till schools break up, how are you planning on keeping your little one entertained?'

'I've already booked everything. London Zoo, The Aquarium. Chessington.'

'I could have guessed you were one of those dads. You look like the type to spoil your kid rotten.'

'She's my little girl,' he says defensively, 'if little girls can't be spoilt by their dads, then . . .' he shrugs.

'Hmm, that's also my ex's approach to raising Haze. And we're all seeing how well that's working out.'

'Are you talking about your super-confident, high-achieving daughter? The one who's going to Oxford? The one who gave me a lecture on feminism within five minutes of meeting her?'

'Yeah, that's the one. Pain in the arse. She's hard work, Ben. Everything always has to be perfect with her, first place, first prize. She doesn't know how to cope when things don't go to plan. And of course, everything that goes wrong is always my fault. God, did I finish a glass that quickly?'

'I'll get you another. By the way, Jacob asked if he could walk Harold tomorrow.'

'When did you see him?'

'He was out the front earlier. He talked to me for half an hour. Mostly about dog breeds.'

She laughs. 'Sorry.' Though of course she's not, because this is one of the most charming things about her son, the way he obsesses about animals and expects everyone else to feel the same.

'Did you know there's a song by The Beatles with a sound that only dogs can hear?'

She laughs again and rests her head on the rail. 'Yes, he's told me that fact before.'

'He even wrote me out some notes on famous beagles throughout British history. I now have a reading list from your dad, homework on feminism from your daughter and notes on dogs from your son. What next?'

She turns to him. Despite the way his eyes wrinkle, there's something so completely boyish about Ben. 'Is this my cue to ask you for something?'

He blushes, actually goes red, and looks away. He's so shy. Yet maybe this is good thing and Jess needs to learn to slow down and take it as it comes. Rushing never got her anywhere with any of the other guys who've come and gone from her life over the last few years.

'How long do you think you'll stay at Wolf's?'

'Based on this afternoon? I think lasting till this time next week without putting a pillow over his face would be good going. Oh, I don't know. There's what, two weeks left of school, then we've got six weeks of holidays. Ideally, I don't still want to be there when the new school year starts, it's a big one for Haze. Though I'm not in the best state,' she pauses and looks at him cautiously, 'financially. The idea is to make sure I have a good job first and some savings, so I don't get into any more squeezes. The bug palace was beautiful but,' she stops again, 'even when I was working it would have been quite tight to pay the rent on it each month.'

'What about the council? You said you had a housing officer?'

'Oh yeah, he's absolutely useless. The first time I met him he basically suggested I become a squatter at Kenmure Street until Mustafa could get the courts to chuck me out. Then I called him last week and he advised me to move into a hostel. As if I'm going to take my kids to live amongst junkies and down-and-outs.'

'Hostels aren't like that. A lot of them are filled with families.'

'How would you know?'

'Because I used to work at some of them back in Essex.'

'Some of them? Why, how many are there?'

'They're everywhere, there's huge demand. There's one about fifteen minutes from here.'

The idea of families living in hostels seems like such an extreme thing. How can it be that hostels are *everywhere* and Jess didn't even know? 'I had no idea. No wonder the government isn't building more social housing. Why would it when it could just pile everyone into hostels?' Jess pours herself another wine, swearing to make it her last. She can imagine what Pa will say if she stumbles in drunk on her first night back home.

'I don't want to move into a hostel. I don't understand why it's even being presented as an option. The council can see I'm priced out, that I'm technically homeless. What would be the point of moving into a hostel, only to move back out when they find me something permanent? It makes no sense, and I don't want to put the kids through that.'

'Maybe if you saw a hostel, you would feel less anxious about it?'

'No. I hate this. I hate this whole situation. Would you live in one? With your little girl?'

'I'd live anywhere with Olivia,' he says immediately.

'Sorry.'

'It's okay.' He leans on the rail next to her, standing closer than before. 'You said your ex helped you move?'

'Yeah. Though I should have hired a professional. He broke most of my bowls. He went to St Margaret's too. In fact, he thinks he knows you.'

Ben's face changes, a kind of clouding over. 'I really didn't know anyone there.'

'Yes. I remember you saying that. Though I'm sure you weren't a complete recluse. His name's Steadman Glen. Tall, loud, brash, has a tendency to talk at everyone.'

Ben shakes his head.

'Come on, someone must have known you.'

'I don't stand out that much.'

Maybe he's right. Quiet as he is, he probably sailed through his years there with his head down. 'And you don't remember my brother, Dominic?'

His eyes drop away from hers, and not in the usual way she's come to notice him doing. No, this is something else, something she recognises from people she went to school with, her parents' friends, people from the area who knew what happened, who knew Dominic. What Ben did is what people always do the moment it clicks for them, when they put two and two together and realise who she is, who she's related to. 'I knew it.'

Ben puffs his chest up and opens his mouth, but all that comes out is, 'I, er,' then he stops.

This now makes sense, why it seems like he's into her, wants to spend time with her, yet keeps pulling away, holding himself back. It's nothing to do with him being hung up on his ex-wife, it's about *her* bloody past.

'I get it, Ben,' she says, her voice sharp. 'This isn't the first time someone's run a mile when they've found out there's a criminal in the family.' She downs the rest of the wine and backs away from the balcony.

'Jessica, why are you leaving?'

'What's the point in staying?'

'I hardly knew him.'

'Yeah, but you knew *of* him, didn't you? All this time, you've not said anything to me.'

'Yeah,' he says, looking down at his feet, 'and I'm sorry. I wanted to. But I didn't want to make a big deal out of it.'

She tries to replay Steadman's words from earlier, about if a man liked her enough, it wouldn't matter about her brother. 'I'm fed up of people looking at me differently because of things that happened in the past, things that had absolutely nothing to do with me.'

'I get that,' Ben says, standing in front of her. 'Do you want to talk about—'

'No,' she snaps. 'I absolutely don't want to talk about it. In fact, I'm sick to death of it and how it chases me. None of what happened with Dominic was anything to do with me. So why does it feel like it's always popping up to confront me? Getting in the way of my life?'

'It's okay,' he says, putting his hands on her shoulders, his face serious.

God, she's getting worked up. Too much stress, too much wine.

Ben presses his fingers into the tops of her arms and pulls her slightly closer. It's confusing.

'Does it bother you?' she asks. 'Knowing what he was like.'

He's taking too long to answer, his eyes flick marginally from side to side, as if quickly running through his ethics and where he stands on something like this. 'Ben?' There's a genuine nervousness, a holding of breath, and Jess realises she likes Ben way more than she set out to.

'It's all in the past,' he says, running his hands down her arms and taking her hands. 'And like you say, it had nothing to do with you.'

She nods and takes a step closer to him. 'Let's not talk about this again.'

'I agree,' he says.

Chapter Fourteen

Ben

Mum flicks through the rail of tiny synthetic dresses in the Disney Store and tuts. 'Remind me what I'm looking for?'

'Aurora,' Ben says. 'The pink one. Aged seven to eight.'

'It'll be massive.'

'Mum, she is massive.' Shanice had earlier sent him Olivia's height and Ben took the tape measure from his toolbox and held it against himself. What had Olivia been eating out there?

'Have you told her yet?' Mum asks.

'Told who what?' Though of course he knows full well what's coming.

'This girl you like. Have you told her?'

He doesn't want to talk about this, not now, maybe not ever. In fact, why did he even mention it to his mum in the first place? A further reason why men his age should have friends who didn't give birth to them.

'She knows I knew her brother. She doesn't need to hear any more than that. It doesn't matter.'

'For the record, I think the whole thing is a disaster waiting to happen. Though if you're insisting on stepping out with this Bakker girl you might want to mention that her brother made your life unbearable.'

'Mum. I'm not *stepping out* with her. Whatever that means.'

'You know what it means,' she says. 'I can tell from how red you've gone that you like her. For goodness' sakes, Ben, stop seeing her before things get complicated.'

Though after spending time with her last week, he can't imagine anything he'd want to do less than stop seeing Jessica.

'She lives across the road from me now,' Ben says, as if that justifies the heat in his face. 'With her dad. I'm going to end up seeing her often anyway.'

He hopes so. No, he hopes for way more than that.

'She lives with her dad?' Mum's face screws up. 'Doesn't she have a family of her own, kids and that?'

'Two kids. But she lost her job and lost her house.'

'Oh Ben, she sounds like a disaster. Two kids and can't even keep a roof over her head.'

'It sounds really bad when you say it like that. She's just someone who's had a lot of bad luck recently.'

Mum picks out an emerald-green belly top and shimmery trouser set, 'Who's this one?'

'Princess Jasmine. She's already got that.'

She dumps it back on the rail and Ben makes a point of putting it in the correct place before continuing with his search.

'I'd want to know,' Mum says. 'If I met a man who had run-ins with my family.'

He wants to tell Jessica everything, but what would be

the point? Also, she pretty much asked him outright if he was happy to pretend like Dominic never existed. It was the ultimate get-out clause.

'If you really like her—'

'Have you found Aurora yet?'

She grabs a tiny blue ball gown. 'This her?'

'No, that's Cinderella.'

'Who's Aurora anyway? There never used to be so many characters.'

'Sleeping Beauty. Here she is,' he says, holding up the right dress in the right size.

'Why are you wanting to get into another relationship so quickly anyway? Wouldn't you like to be single for a bit?'

'I've been single for over a year.' Though the truth is, he felt single while still with Shanice, a strange kind of loneliness that accompanied him on all those nights sleeping in the spare room.

'You don't need to put a time limit on it. You should be enjoying yourself. Getting out and playing the field a bit, like your sister did when she got divorced. She really made up for lost time,' Mum says with a suggestive laugh.

'I'm not like her. I'm not about to fly to Las Vegas and get my belly button pierced.' Ben had seen the Facebook posts and was almost impressed by his suburban sister acting so out of character.

Two small girls squish in front of him and coo over the display of dresses. One of them, who seems the closest in age to Olivia, gasps as she lifts up a pair of tiny silvery-blue high-heeled boots. Olivia would kill for a pair of high-heeled boots, but this is where Ben draws the line.

'Take it slowly, okay,' Mum says. Why is she still going on about this? 'You're only just back on your feet, there's no need to go rushing into another relationship.'

'I'm not rushing into anything.'

'I don't want to see you unwell again.'

'Unwell?' he scoffs. 'You can say it.'

'Okay, I don't want to see you fall apart again.'

Fall apart? It sounds so harsh, though the truth is, that's exactly what happened to him. As his life gradually collapsed, so did he.

When Shanice first said she was moving to Tenerife, Ben assumed Olivia would stay with him. It was like a punch in the gut when Shanice explained how she had already looked into schools, good schools, not like the failing primary nearest to their house, or the next closest, twenty minutes away, on a main road that made Olivia's asthma flair up. Tenerife was presented as some sort of utopia in which to raise their daughter, a place she would be able to play on the beach rather than in the sad local park where the hoodies hung out. A place where she would be integrated into a community of expats, sharing and looking out for each other, whereas in Essex all they had was each other and a social group Shanice seemed to have outgrown.

He lost his wife, then his daughter. And not only to another man, but to another country, a whole other life. Of course Ben fell apart.

Ben gets in the queue to pay, with Mum towing behind. He can feel she has more to say.

'I'm okay,' he says. 'I'm better.'

It's definitely not the first time he's tried to convince her of this, though it feels truer today than ever before. He's through it, he's building a new life for himself. And the best part is, Olivia will soon be part of it too. He steps forward in the queue and looks down at the dress over his arm.

'Anything else?' the too-smiley woman at the till asks.

Ben looks at the pile on the counter and doubts himself, maybe one dress is not enough. He pulls a glittery notepad and pen with a spinning princess from a tub and throws it on the counter. 'That should do it. Thanks.'

'Lucky girl,' Mum says. 'You sure you're not going to spoil her with all this?'

Ben slides his debit card from his wallet. 'What else am I meant to do?'

They step outside the shop, onto the bustling walkways of Westfield. It's busy now, with huge groups of teenage window-shoppers and people aggressively charging through with pushchairs. He stands opposite Mum, and for once he's going to be the one to cut short their time together. 'I have to get going now. Harold will need to be let out soon.' Though the truth is Jessica had texted him this morning suggesting that she pop over for another drink.

Mum stares at him and he braces himself for what she's about to say. 'Her brother made your life hell. Tell her that. Tell that old man how his darling son almost broke your jaw.'

'Mum, please. What can I do? I like her. She likes me too. I'm not going to give that up because her brother took a disliking to me over twenty years ago.'

'A disliking?' she almost shouts. 'He smashed your head against a wall. He stole from you. He terrorised you.'

Ben drops his head. 'He was young.' Is he really making excuses for Dominic Bakker? Knowing everything he does about what kind of person he was. How his evilness went far beyond bullying a peer.

'Is there more to the story, Ben?'

'What? No.'

'Cause I know young lads don't want to talk to their mums so I never pushed you at the time, but I've thought about it over the years and always wondered, was there more to it? Because it wasn't normal, how scared you were, the way you ran away to live with your dad, how you wanted so badly to escape . . . and even now, what am I missing? Why did you take all the abuse? And why do you still defend that bloody Dominic Bakker?'

Ben rubs the back of his head. She's got it wrong, she's got it so very wrong.

'Tell me, did he have something on you?'

'It was two decades ago. We were both teenagers. It doesn't matter. In fact, I'm going to tell Jessica the next time I see her, and she probably won't even care. No one will. Because it was so long ago.'

Mum recoils a little. 'Good. I hope you're right.'

'I am right. Now, let's not talk about it again.'

As he walks towards the flat, he sees the woman from downstairs coming towards him. Her ink-black hair is parted in the middle and Ben thinks she may be the only person paler than him. 'Oh, hi,' she says. 'I took in a delivery for you, let me walk back and get it.'

'You're on your way out, I can get it later.'

'No, no problem.' She gets out the keys to their shared front door. 'It's kind of taking up my whole hallway.'

Across the road, Wolf's curtains twitch, a window opens and he shouts across, 'Ben?'

'Is he house-bound?' she asks.

Ben laughs. 'You'd think so, wouldn't you? But no.'

She takes out the parcel, a huge sparkly lilac mermaid sleeping bag wrapped in plastic, and awkwardly hands it over. She then stares at Ben as if waiting for an explanation.

'It's for my daughter,' he says. 'She's coming to stay with me in the summer holidays.'

'Oh, right.' She widens her green eyes as if relieved that Ben's not a complete weirdo. 'I did wonder what a grown man would need with a life-sized stuffed mermaid.'

From upstairs he can hear Harold barking, his little paws scattering against the front door.

The woman smiles, a wide grin of perfect white teeth. They must have cost a fortune. 'Your dog?'

'Yeah, sorry. Does he make a lot of noise? Can you hear him down here?'

'No, not usually,' she locks her front door and then spins back to face Ben, 'Why, can you hear me?'

What is she worried about him hearing? His neck heats. 'No. I can't hear anything. You're very quiet. I'm Ben, by the way.'

Again, the striking smile. 'Great,' she says, 'enjoy your mermaid.'

'Uh, thank you.'

He jogs upstairs, where Harold is yapping at the door. 'Excited for a walk? What is it, Christmas?'

He dumps the shopping and mermaid in the hallway and grabs the lead. 'Come on, let's go.' Though typically Harold now only has eyes for the mermaid. 'Get off it.' Ben clips on the lead and they head out together, catching sight of Wolf, who is now outside, waving Ben over. 'Sonny Boy,' he calls, and there's so much hope in it, Ben can't walk by.

'What was that about?' Wolf asks, rubbing his hands together.

'Nothing. She took in a parcel for me.'

'A parcel, eh? Tell me everything. I've got the kettle on.'

'I need to walk Harold. He's been home alone all morning.'

Wolf's face falls. 'I hardly see you anymore. I feel like you're ghosting me.'

Of course, he's noticed how Ben has pretty much stopped dropping in on him. But how to explain it? And now, after what's happening with Jessica, things feel even more tricky. There's no way Ben will be able to act normal if she comes home right now.

'Sorry. Work has been busy. How's everything been this week with the eh . . .' Ben nods towards the inside of the house, unsure himself what he even means '. . . new housemates?'

Wolf puts the arm of his glasses in his mouth and ponders, 'It's been great. We've been playing cards, watching *The Philadelphia Story* and even doing a bit of TikToking.' He pops his shoulder forwards and does a shuffle.

Ben laughs on cue, though it's immediately followed by an awkward moment of silence where the real conversation settles between them. Surely Wolf knows Jessica told him about Dominic, that Ben now knows Wolf lied to him? Or maybe Jessica hasn't mentioned Ben at all. It's all a bit confusing.

'Are you coming in for a tea? They're all out, up at Ally Pally for Jacob's science thing.'

'Oh yeah, the Science Fair. You didn't want to go?'

Wolf shakes his head. He looks a little peaky today, tired. It must be taking a toll on him, having all those extra bodies in the house.

'Were you out drinking yesterday?'

'No. Had a bad night's sleep though. It was muggy and Jacob was up all night playing Mario Kart.'

'Mario Kart?'

Wolf smiles, pleased to have remembered something so relevant. There's a dark tint under his eyes, almost purple. He really doesn't look well.

'Stop staring at me, son. Come in and keep me company.'

Ben shrugs and follows him in.

'Oh, and I finally got a new doorbell. You can install it for me.'

Jessica's red jacket is on the coatrack, her spindly gold heels kicked under the bottom bookshelf. This is weird. Ben pauses by the living room, where a rolled-up duvet and pillows are piled on the flowery sofa. The old boxy TV is now on the floor, while another flatter one is on the stand next to it. There are clothes heaped up at the back of the room and suitcases in the bay window.

'Jacob's room,' Wolf says. 'I thought he would share with his sister but they both refused, so now I have no living room.

And the kitchen is a disaster. Hazel has spread out all sorts of books and computer things on my table. I don't want to mess anything up so I try to work around it.'

It's not only the things on the table that make the kitchen look smaller, there's also more stuff. The counters are loaded with wraps, rolls, bagels and loaves, while the cupboard tops are stacked with cereal boxes. Wolf's place has always felt cluttered but now it's teeming. The Hello Kitty stereo has gone and a Bluetooth speaker now sits above the sink instead.

'I have something for Olivia. I found some colours.' Wolf hands Ben a box of crayons, crusted over in white. 'They must have been Jess's.'

'Or yours?'

'Possibly, yes. Go and sit outside.' Wolf kicks at the back door, which creaks as it opens, and Ben makes a mental note to oil the hinges. Immediately Harold busies himself trying to catch a bumblebee in the overgrown tuft at the back while Ben loops the lead around the chair leg and sits on it. 'I've got to fix this fence,' he says to Wolf, 'I can't keep looking at it.'

Wolf hands Ben a plate with a slice of onion tart. 'Try this.' He doesn't take his eyes off Ben until he gets the reaction he's waiting for. 'This is amazing. It's like a packet of cheese and onion crisps in a pie.'

'It's gruyere and red onion. Count yourself lucky there's any left because those kids don't stop chomping away. Jacob ate a whole packet of halloumi the other night. In one sitting. Unbelievable. He didn't even offer me any. I'm going to have to start putting post-it notes on things.'

'Enjoying the company then?'

Wolf tips his head side to side. 'It's noisier than I imagined it would be.'

'Well, it's only the first week. I'm sure things will quieten down.'

'No, they won't. Jess has always been loud and messy.' Wolf grins.

'What?' Ben asks.

'You went the colour of a beetroot when I said her name.'

'I'm the colour of beetroot because it's thirty degrees out here,' he says, moving his chair further into the shade.

Wolf licks his lips and it's clear he's thinking up his next jibe. 'Has she been climbing out the window at night and sneaking over?'

Ben channels all his concentration into eating the pie and not thinking about Jessica *sneaking over*. Because he can't wait for that to happen again.

Wolf slathers a crust of bread with peanut butter and throws it over at Harold, 'Here, beautiful boy.'

'Ah, please don't feed him that.'

'It's good for him.'

'It's not.'

Wolf sits and meets Ben's eyes. 'I wanted to talk to you about something,' he looks at the back door, as if checking no one will unexpectantly pop out.

'I don't want to talk about Jessica with you,' Ben says quickly. 'You're her dad and it's really awkward.'

'No, not about that. You kids do what you like. I don't need to know. It's about Dominic.'

'Ah. Right.' Here it comes.

'I know Jess told you. I didn't mean to lie to you and I'm sorry. It's just that, well, I gradually stopped talking about him years ago. Now it's second nature that I don't bring him up.' Wolf stops and watches as a cat pops its head above a bush before seeing Harold and scattering away. 'I think about him often, but don't want to talk about him.'

'I guess part of me knew you were related in some way. There aren't too many Bakkers around.'

'I'm an old fool,' Wolf says. 'I've not seen him in eight years now. It's the longest he's been away. Of course, he spent most of his adult life in and out of jail. The last time I saw him, he was trying to get his life back on track. I really thought he had changed.' Wolf reaches out and pats Harold. 'How well did you know him at school?'

'I, um, well, I told Jessica that I knew *of* him.'

Wolf squints behind his glasses. 'But . . . ?'

'But, yeah, I don't think she gets that I actually *knew* him.' While saying this should feel like a weight being lifted, it feels more like a foot on the back of Ben's neck.

'You were friends?' Wolf asks, doubt in his voice.

Ben swallows. He doesn't know how to tell this story because he has *never* told this story.

'I know Dominic was a bully,' Wolf says, as if trying to help Ben out.

'Yeah. He definitely made things hard for me at school. In that last year, he, um, he—'

'He was a bully,' Wolf says again, more urgent this time.

'I guess so. Yeah.'

Wolf groans. 'Why did it start, was there a reason? He asked you to do something you didn't want to do?'

Harold catches sight of the cat and starts pacing the garden.

Ben thinks over Wolf's questions. A reason, yes, there was a huge reason it started, but saying this would only open another can of worms. Or perhaps, if Ben talks about what put him on Dominic's radar, Wolf might understand why it's a secret worth keeping. Ben takes a breath. 'It was,' he stops. 'Because—' the words get stuck. It's as if the story, so deeply buried, is refusing to come out.

'I can see it's painful,' Wolf says, clicking his fingers in an attempt to distract Harold.

Ben puts the plate on the grass and brings his hands together, squeezing them into a fist. Harold pads over to lick the plate then nuzzle Ben's hands.

'Was it to do with Dominic that you moved away?' Wolf asks. 'Why you ended up doing your exams at another school?'

Ben nods.

'And Jess, what does she know?'

'Nothing.' This is the problem. It's not that Ben has met Jessica at a point where both of their lives are a little less than perfect, it's that they have this shared thing.

'She's used to people judging her on what they know or have heard about her brother, even now. It's affected her whole life.' Wolf stands to collect the plates. 'Can I give you a piece of advice, son? If you really want to have a shot with her, make sure that, whatever it is, she doesn't find out about it.'

Chapter Fifteen

Jess

When Jess was growing up there used to be a homeless couple who would sit on the bench in the park. They were drinkers and possibly druggies. Though, to be honest, Jess never paid them enough attention to confirm either. In fact, they might not even have been homeless. Perhaps they spent their days drinking and arguing with each other on that park bench, watching the world go by and people avoid them, before making their way to their flat up the road.

But now, now it's different, because somewhere in the last decade the homeless have become a huge and very visible part of the area. And not just in the park either, they're outside Wilko's with their shopping trolleys full of carrier bags, under the car park in brightly coloured camping tents, and at night about a hundred of them make the old shopping centre their home. Jess has seen it herself more than once over the years, finishing work late and cutting through the centre to find people, mostly men, bedding down for the night in front of the iron curtains of clothes shops and cafes. Though during the light of day, like now, the only evidence of that is the odd person, like the woman dragging her feet over the marble floors to approach Jess. She stops dead in front, puts out her hand and says, 'Have you got any spare change?' Her face is dewy and ruddy as though it's been recently scrubbed though her neck is ringed with dirt.

'Oh. Yes. Hold on.' Jess takes a step back as she goes in her handbag, gripping her purse tightly in case the woman makes a grab for it. There's never any cash in there anyway, a few coppers and down the side the pound coin she keeps especially for supermarket trolleys.

'Here,' Jess says, handing over the coins. 'Sorry, it's all I've got.'

'Thanks.' The woman takes it in her rough hand and shuffles off into the crowd of shoppers.

Jess walks on and stops by a rack of reduced trainers outside Foot Locker to check if there's anything she can buy Jacob. She often hears people complaining about the rate their kids grow, how their sons burst through shoes two months after first wear and their wrists sprout from blazers before the end of term. Jess is lucky to have children who rarely seem to grow. Jacob has been wearing the same shoes for over a year now and, thank God, they've almost made it to the end of the school year without having to buy a bigger blazer.

She had noticed how little he owned when they packed up the house. How his things, which were mostly computers and books, fitted into a few boxes, while her and Haze's seemed to overflow into endless binbags and sacks – and this was after the clear-out.

The begging woman goes from person to person, and Jess notices how it's only other women she approaches. Very few acknowledge her, even fewer stop. It's brutal, but then Jess can't remember the last time she gave a homeless person money before today. Or rather, before she was classed as homeless herself.

'Mum?'

'Haze, hi, hun.'

Her daughter approaches, pulling off her headphones. 'What are you doing over here?'

'Shopping, because apparently that's what everyone does on a weekday. I mean, two p.m. on a Tuesday and look how busy it is here. What are you doing, slumming it over this side?'

'I needed some bits from Superdrug, and thought the queues would be less over here. They weren't. I can't believe so many people still shop here.'

Haze always said people fell into two distinct groups depending on whether they shopped at the 'old Stratford centre', with its large selection of useful pound shops, cafes and fruit and veg stalls or the glitzy Westfield mall. Jess enjoys both, but only really visits the latter when feeling flush.

Jess has on her *work clothes* and Haze makes a point of looking her up and down as if questioning the outfit. At The Anstey she always wore her own stuff, but when interviewing she makes a conscious effort to cram herself into a pastel-coloured shirt and pencil skirt in order to look professional.

'Your interview?' Haze finally clocks. 'How'd it go?'

'Fantastic,' Jess says, trying to drum up a suitable amount of enthusiasm for the events assistant role at Apple Hall. It was a great job on paper, though Jess had found the people who interviewed her terribly dry and the whole thing had gotten off to a bad start after she forgot to include her preferred pronouns on the sign-in sheet.

'They'll let me know if I get a second interview.'

'You've got to be interviewed twice for a temporary job at some art house no one cares about? That's ridiculous. And is this the job you said was like five grand less than what you earned before?'

'They're open to discussion. Let's stay positive.'

Haze's face remains blank. It's as if nothing makes her happy at the moment. Nothing impresses her.

Jess loops her arm through Haze's. 'While we're both here, you can come to the hair shop with me.'

Haze unthreads her arm and slips away.

'Please,' Jess tries, 'walk with me.'

Haze nods and they walk side by side up to the indoor market. It's a maze of repeating shops; hair, sexy dresses, glittery bedspreads, hair, sexy dresses, glittery bedspreads. Haze used to love it, in fact she used to badger Jess about it all the time. She loved to browse the toy stalls, get a Slush Puppie and have a ride in Postman Pat's tiny red van.

'It's unbelievable this place is still going,' Haze says now, her nose turned up.

'Everything changes so fast. Don't you think it's nice to have one thing that's stayed the same?'

'You mean stayed in the nineties? It's such an assault on the senses too.'

'Oh, stop moaning. What's your issue with the nineties anyway? The nineties were amazing.'

A small, almost half smile, appears briefly on Haze's face.

Jess still loves this place. She loves how the music, a different kind of which flows from every shop and stall, is always too loud. As are the smells: fried breakfast from the cafe filled with old-timers, popcorn from the machine by the mini arcade and dried fish from the Ghanaian food shop.

'Will you help me do my roots later?' Jess asks, hearing the slight desperation in her own voice.

'I'm studying, loads to do. I'm going to go to the library to see if I can work there.'

Jess pulls a coil of her hair taut; it's a hundred different shades of brown, blond, auburn and grey. It's definitely time to sort it out. Especially as Ben's asked to spend the day with her this Sunday. Their long-awaited date. She's not sure what he has planned, though he did mention the 'park' . . . again. It had bothered her a little but when she told Precious about their meet-ups in the parks and evenings drinking wine on his balcony, she cooed and reminded Jess of all her past relationship non-starters, which often began with dates in expensive restaurants. Ben was offering something different, something wholesome and real. He didn't have money to take her to fancy places and wasn't trying to hide it. Still, she wants to look nice for their date, wherever it is. She picks up a bottle two shades lighter than she usually goes.

'Isn't it time you went a bit darker?' Haze takes the bottle and puts it back on the shelf.

'Oh. You think?'

'Yeah. It's time for a more mature look.'

The girl on the packaging *is* very young. When did that happen? 'Okay, well, help me choose something new then. We can do it when we get home.'

'No, I told you. I'm going to the library for the rest of the day.'

'You're not coming home for dinner?'

'I might pop back for something,' Haze mumbles.

'Why can't you stay in and study at home? Jacob said the internet is really fast now.'

'It's too noisy. Opa constantly interrupts me and there's always someone popping by. You know he let the Hermes delivery guy in the house the other day to use the toilet?'

'You're kidding? I don't know how he's not been robbed yet. I'll have a word with him. And he shouldn't be interrupting you when you're studying. He knows how important the next few months are. Though you do seem to be working a lot at the moment. Don't burn out, hun. Are you taking the weekend off? Got any plans?'

'What, you mean after I spend half a day trying to find an outfit from one of the boxes?' Haze continues to grumble, walking slightly ahead of Jess.

'Slow down,' she calls, desperate to connect with Haze, to get in her head and reassure her things will be okay. 'I tell you what, let's go and get a coffee?'

'If we're going to break our no-eating-out rule, I don't think we should do it here.'

'I didn't say eating, but we could have a little something.' The seats outside the small bakery a few doors down are empty. 'Especially as Pa's making paella. It probably won't be ready till midnight.' The process had started at five a.m. with him crashing around the house, trying to wake up Jacob to go to Billingsgate Market with him. He then complained that Jacob wouldn't get up, despite showing interest earlier in the week. Pa forgets that Jacob has school and it's not like when Jess was younger and teachers were happy to have one less in the class. At the new St Margaret's, if you don't show up, your parents get a call before they've poured their second cup of coffee.

'How do you know this place?' Haze asks as they sit on the metal chairs.

'They do great coffee.'

The guy, who Jess always thinks is far too buff to work somewhere that sells pastry, comes over to take their order. He stares carefully at Haze then turns back to Jess, as if remembering his first love. 'This is your sister?'

'Oh, stop it,' Jess chuckles. 'I'm her mother.'

'No, you're too young. You are joking me?'

Haze rolls her eyes at the exchange.

'Such a charmer,' Jess laughs after he leaves the table.

'Is this why you come here?' Haze asks with a complete lack of humour.

'For a beautiful young man to flatter me while serving me cheese croissants? No, of course not.' She takes out her lip balm and puts some on, offering it across the table. 'So?'

'So?'

'Come on, hun, talk to me.'

'About what?'

'Anything. How's college going? Any exciting plans to celebrate the end of your first year?'

'No. Not really.'

'Give me something. You're making things really hard right now.'

Haze looks down at the table. 'It's a lot to deal with sometimes. I've got exams next year and work and now there's all this extra pressure around getting my UCAS application perfect. Like absolutely perfect. Do you have any idea how much I need to stand out to get offered an interview?'

'You always stand out.'

'Yeah, cause it doesn't take much to stand out around here,' Haze says as she flicks her eyes around the vicinity, almost as if trying to point out how beneath her she finds it all. 'This is different, this is Oxford.'

The coffees are put on the table, with an extra-large Danish to share.

'There's not a different kind of intelligence outside of East London,' Jess says. 'If you're smart here, you're smart everywhere. We all know you're going to get the grades and be offered an interview and dazzle everyone in it and—' Her phone buzzes mid-speech. 'Sorry, I'm waiting on the recruiter emailing something over . . . Oh, it's just junk mail. What was I saying?'

'There's this thing online where you can check the socioeconomic status of your area and see how it relates to your life chances.'

Jess puts her phone face down on the table. 'Okay?'

'Basically, if you're from a shithole area your life chances are obviously not great, but if you're from a shithole area and incredibly smart, unis want you so they can tick some diversity boxes.'

'Okaaay,' Jess says again, confused as to whether what Haze is telling her is a good or bad thing.

'I don't want to be the diversity tick, Mum.'

'Oh God. You won't be.'

'I will. The worst thing is, I'm starting to feel like it's the only thing that's going to make me stand out. That I'm from here and I'm a *person of colour*,' she says, bunny-earing the last part.

'Haze, stop. They're going to want you because you're smart. Because one day you're going to make a great solicitor.'

'My tutor asked me to include we're homeless in my personal statement.'

Jess sits back. This bloody tutor again. Where does he get off? 'We're not homeless.'

'Technically, we are. He thinks it will increase my chances. That it's another box ticked. It's really embarrassing.'

Is this what it comes down to? That Haze is embarrassed. It wouldn't be the first time. Haze gets openly uncomfortable whenever someone sees Jess for the first time, when it's clear they're trying to work out how young she was when she had a child. Perhaps Haze is ashamed. This bloody tutor is shaming her for a bunch of things she has no control over. This isn't Haze's fault, none of it is, it's Jess's.

'I'm sorry, you shouldn't have to deal with this. Also,

I think your tutor is out of line. There's no way any of this should be relevant or on your application.'

'It *is* relevant.'

'It's not.'

'It is. All this stuff has an effect.'

'All of it?' Jess asks, though she knows what Haze means, that she's pointing to the fact she's from a single-parent family, with a mum who had her young, and a dad whose only aspirations in life were to get a nice little council flat and part-time job.

They return to their coffees and Haze stares at her. 'I wish I could make things easier for us.'

A hole opens up in Jess's heart. 'That's not your job,' she says, her voice almost cracking. 'It's mine.'

'If there was something I could—'

'Stop it, Haze. You're eighteen. You're already doing everything you can.' Jess's phone rings and she flips it over hopefully. 'Ah, please be good news.' Because good news is exactly what she needs right now.

Haze's chair scrapes as she makes a move to get up. 'I've got to go.'

'Not yet,' Jess reaches out to grab Haze's hand. 'We're still talking, hang on.'

'No, I'll let you get your call.'

'No, stop.' Jess sends the call, from an unknown number, to voicemail and as she does she also notices a message from Ben. 'Haze, stop.' She pulls her back down to sitting. 'I need you to know, this *stuff* isn't you, it doesn't define you in any way.'

She nods. 'Fine. I don't want to talk about this anymore. It's really depressing.'

The waiter comes back out, espresso in hand as he leans on the doorframe. He stares at Haze and gives her a smile that she doesn't return.

'It's going to be okay,' Jess says.

Haze nods and picks at the crumbs on her plate. 'Course, Mum.'

'Now, is it okay if I quickly check in case they left a voice-mail?'

Haze nods and gets out her own phone.

There isn't a voicemail and Jess quickly reads the message from Ben, asking if she fancies bringing over some of her tinfoil chocolate bananas tonight. She laughs.

'It was him, wasn't it?' Haze asks.

'Who?'

'Man with Van.'

'He has a name. It's not like you've just met him either.' What's the issue? Haze has never reacted like this to any of the men Jess was seeing before. 'You don't like him?' she asks, confused, because Ben is the least unlikeable person you could meet.

'I don't have an opinion on him.'

'That's a little harsh. He's a nice guy.'

'I'm sure,' Haze scoffs.

'No. He is.'

'So, it is serious then?'

'No, it's . . .' Jess stops. 'Look, you were the one encouraging me to get out there and meet someone nice, someone different from all those other arseholes I've been with in the past.'

'Yeah, I was. But that was before. When we had a home and you had a job.'

'You're right. You're perfectly right.' Jess shouldn't be out galivanting with a new man when there's so much else to sort out, she knows that. She's already felt that guilt, yet it's nice being with Ben and having a break from all this crap. 'It's nothing serious,' Jess lies, 'we're friends. Anyway, what about you? Any boys on the scene?'

Haze scrunches her nose at the sudden change of topic. 'Are you seriously asking me that right now?'

Jess's phone buzzes again and she squeezes her eyes shut. 'Sorry. I should have switched it off.'

'You've never switched your phone off. Do you even know how to do that?'

'You say it like I'm on the thing all the time. Usually, the only people who ever contact me are you and Jacob. And of course, your dad, three calls this week.'

'Look at it then. You're not going to be able to relax until you do. Look.'

It's an email from Cat-Tie Tim. The subject line: Temporary hostel placement.

'What is it?' Haze asks. 'Is it about the job?'

'No, it's from the council.' Jess plasters on her smile. 'Cat-Tie Tim says there's a hostel place come up. He thinks we should go and have a look at it.'

'A hostel? I didn't think that was something we were considering.'

'No. It wasn't. Not at first, anyway. He suggested it last month, before we moved in with Pa. I was adamant we didn't need that sort of help. But things are moving slower than I thought they would, and this might help fast-track us to get a council place,' Jess explains confidently, pleased that she has a plan.

'Since when are you so set on a getting a council place? What's wrong with privately renting?'

'I can't afford it.'

Haze's face falls and Jess realises she's said the wrong thing again. 'I mean, once I start working, I'll be able to afford it, but you know, it would be nice to have a council place for the security of it. I don't really want to be at the mercy of private landlords anymore, of having to worry that every twelve months my rent is going to go up, or I'm going to have to move and do this all over again.'

'But a hostel?' Haze shifts forward in her seat, narrowing her eyes at Jess. 'We're not that desperate.'

'It's not about desperation,' she says as lightly as she can, 'it's about thinking long-term.'

Haze turns away and it looks as if she's about to cry. 'What if you get the events assistant job you went for? Will you wait a while longer? See if something comes up privately?'

'There's no point, Haze. I can't face looking anymore. There's nothing out there for us.'

'Oh, that's nice to hear. That you've got to the point where you believe there's nothing out there for us, so why bother trying.'

Jess sighs because yes, it does sound really bad when Haze says it that way.

'It's a bit of a different pitch than what you usually give.'

'I'm only talking about housing. I don't mean there's nothing out there for us in general. You've got the whole world at your feet.'

Haze raises a hand. 'Don't bother. I get it now. You've said it loud and clear.'

'You're taking this the wrong way.'

'How dare I assume you'll find a job you're qualified to do or that we aspire to live somewhere other than a hostel. How dare I—'

'Stop it,' Jess snaps. 'I'm trying. I'm trying my very best. You can't keep getting at me for every little thing, Haze.'

'I'm not.'

'You are. You're angry with me all the time. It's not my fault that rents are expensive or that your tutor's a judgemental arsehole. It's not my fault that all this is happening at the same time.'

'I've had enough. I'm going.'

'Haze?'

The table tips slightly in Jess's direction as Haze pushes the chair under it roughly. 'See you back at the house.'

Jess swears under her breath as she watches her daughter weave through the alleyways of shops until she disappears.

'Young girls,' the waiter says as he steps in to clear away the cups. 'Always giving headache. Best I stick with older ladies, yes? Less problems.'

*

Later that afternoon, Jess gets offered not just a second interview at Apple Hall, but the job itself. Apparently, there was
a lack of suitable candidates. She leans against the wall and
exhales. Relief, finally, something has gone the right way.
Sure, it's temporary and poorly paid, but it's with a growing
organisation, one that would, despite being a little more left-
wing than she was used to, present her with bigger opportunities, more space to grow, to develop. Maybe this is what was
meant to happen all along, that The Anstey closing could be
the catalyst for her to start focusing on her career for once,
something she could feel some self-worth from, rather than
the job she loved yet always had to fit around being a mum. It
gives her a little joy after the horrible falling-out with Haze,
which she hasn't stopped thinking about.

Inside the house, it's quiet. Oddly quiet. The living room
is empty and there's no music in the kitchen. Jacob is sitting
on the back doorstep which leads to the garden.

'Oh, you're there.'

'Hi, Mum.'

'What's that smell?' A mixture of fish and spice. Jess lifts
the lid on the big pan that sits on the hob. 'Ah, the paella.'

'I don't think we can eat that,' Jacob says. 'Because you
can't eat it cold and you can't microwave fish.'

She moves closer to him, noticing his mug is filled with
a milky liquid, dotted with orange bits. 'It's soup,' he says,
'a quick snack before I go to Cameron's. We're working on
our storyboard tonight.'

She wants to ask him what he means by storyboard, though

a part of her feels he's already told her about it. Perhaps while she was half listening and stressing about something else.

'Where's Opa?'

'I think he went upstairs.'

Jess hovers over the sink; there are two glasses in there. She picks one up to smell it. Pa's been drinking. Already. 'Was someone else here today?'

'Yeah, some lady was here when I got home. They were in the living room, watching *The African Queen.*'

'Again? How many times can he sit through it?'

'That's exactly why I came out here.' Jacob comes in and stands in front of Jess, he twists his mouth to the side. 'Do you want some soup as well?'

She's not hungry. Her mind is running too fast, exhilaration about the job mixed with anxiety about what's going on with Haze, and now why Pa is drinking whisky in the afternoon. 'No thanks. I've got a few bits to do around the house.'

Jess busies herself cleaning the bathroom, gathering laundry and even dusting, anything to take her mind off things. They should be celebrating this evening, not all hiding away separately. She considers telling Ben about her new job. She knows she won't have to sugar-coat the crappy pay to him because he's happy to hear any news from her. He makes her feel as if her every move is an achievement; it's such a change to have someone recognise her. That's what she likes about him. Well, it's one of the things she likes.

She returns to the kitchen to find Jacob back on the step. He looks so tiny sitting there. 'Mum?'

'Hmm?' She ensures the lid is fit snugly on the paella in an effort to stop the smell escaping.

'How much longer are we going to stay here? Like, will it be all through the summer holidays?'

Jess pauses. It's the first time Jacob's asked her anything outright like this about their situation. 'Um, it won't be forever.'

'I know that.' He crumbles a cracker into his second cup of soup. 'But do you know kind of, well, roughly how long?'

'Sorry. I don't.' She dries her hands on a tea towel and makes an effort to give him her full attention. Is this what she *hasn't* been doing with the kids? Giving them her full attention. 'I'm doing everything I can to speed things up. I know it's not ideal. It must be tough on you; you don't have much privacy in the living room. I'll talk to Pa again, tell him to be a bit more considerate. He doesn't mean to keep coming in, it's just his habit.'

Jacob puts the soup down on the side and says, 'It's not that.'

'No?'

'No. It's more because,' he looks down, 'my back hurts. I've been sleeping on the floor.'

'The floor? Why?'

'Because the sofa bed is broken. It leans to one side like this,' he says, holding his palm up lopsidedly. 'When I lie on it for too long, I roll off.'

'Why didn't you tell me?'

'Because I know we can't afford a new one.'

'When did this happen? How long have you been sleeping like this?'

'It's always been broken.'

A lump rises in her throat. 'You need to tell me these things.' She gets out her phone and pulls up the Argos website. At least this is a problem she can fix straight away. 'Why didn't you tell me?' She scrolls through the thousands of beds on offer. She'll order a new one for him right now and pay for it on credit. 'You can sleep on mine tonight. I don't mind the sofa, I don't mind at all,' her voice cracks. Jacob moves closer to her and puts his arm over her shoulder. 'Sorry,' she says, the screen blurring as her eyes fill with tears. 'I'm so sorry. I'm a terrible mum.'

'No, you're not.'

'I am. I'm not looking out for either of you, and I'm sorry.'

'Don't say that.'

And now she feels bad for upsetting Jacob. She's meant to shield him from all this, not throw it slap-bang in his face. 'Why didn't you tell me?' she repeats.

'Because you have loads of important stuff to sort out.'

'No. I don't. I have you. You're the most important thing. You need to tell me when you're not okay.' She stares at him till he nods back in agreement. 'I'm sorry,' she says, bringing her forehead to his. 'I'm so sorry.'

Chapter Sixteen

Ben

He parks up to take a call from work, something that could have waited until he was back on site. It's not until he hangs up that he realises where he is. The St Margaret's uniform is different now from what it used to be. Though to be fair, the kids look different too, they look more . . . well, more civilised. Everything's different, so different to how he remembered it. Though when he closes his eyes, the sound from the school gates is exactly the same. It throws him back to being sixteen. How much he hated the sound of class changeover. Less of a sound, more of a feeling.

He can sense it now, the vibration of fear as he moved through the halls, scanning faces and hoping to avoid Dominic Bakker. It went on for months and no one noticed. His parents had too much drama of their own, each living alone and trying to build their newly single lives, and the teachers at the school always seemed to be struggling to get through the day herding a bunch of kids who spent most of the time wanting to rip each other apart.

Ben rubs his face and watches the students, wondering if under the neater uniforms there's still the same horror, fear and unhappiness that defined not only his time at St Margaret's but the experiences of so many others from back then.

Then he spots Jacob walking with three other boys, all equally awkward and nerdy-looking. In the old days of St Margaret's a kid like Jacob, so weedy and different, would have been put through it, mostly by guys like Dominic Bakker. But Jacob looks happy, his face pulled into his small-eyed, goofy smile while his friends nudge him and laugh.

Ben needs to get over it. That's all there is to it. What happened to him here is in the past, long past. It shouldn't even be relevant to his life anymore.

Jacob and his friends pause at the end of the road. They lean into each other as a gaggle of girls in sunglasses pass, and one of them stops to throw Jacob a little wave. When the girls walk on, Jacob pops his collar and receives high-fives from his friends.

To get over things you need to confront them, that's one of the platitudes his therapist is always rolling out during their calls. Ben liked to refer to them as 'calls' rather than 'sessions'. It sounds truer. He finds having a therapist a lot like having a really one-sided friendship, one where he's encouraged to talk and talk, rather than what he usually does, which is ask all the questions and offer all the solutions. *Confront the things you fear.* That's what he's doing by being here, confronting it head on, and it's not as bad as he feared.

'I'm over it,' Ben says as he starts the van and drives off. 'I'm completely over it.'

That weekend, Ben puts on a nice shirt, something he thinks is suited for being seen in public with Jessica. She always looks so amazing no matter what she's wearing. It's annoying that he can still, sometimes, hear Shanice's voice in his head, criticising his shirt, the smell of his aftershave, his suggestion of going to yet another park rather than doing something fancier. It makes him doubt himself. He puts on sunblock, lots of it, checks himself in the mirror and walks across the bridge past the Olympic pool. A group of kids come out, the straps of their swim bags dragging along the floor, wet hair hanging over shoulders and of course that smell.

Jessica is on the grass, looking up at the faded Orbit sculpture, her hand shielding her eyes from the sun. She's got on a white dress, her hair down and the same red lipstick he's seen her wear in her Facebook photos. The phrase *out of his league* comes immediately to mind. 'Jessica?'

The fact she looks so happy to see him puts his nerves at ease and he steps forward to kiss her with confidence. She rubs his lips with her thumb, 'Sorry, lipstick. Are you okay?'

'Er, yeah. I've been inside most of the day. I didn't realise it was this hot.'

'It's amazing.'

'Hmm, yeah.' Ben tries to direct his attention away from the burning sensation on the back of his head. He should be wearing a hat really. Though hats make him look like a seven-year-old boy.

Her eyes pass over his shirt. It was a mistake. He puts a hand to his chest as if to cover it.

'I'm not used to seeing you out of your work clothes. Nice. I'm sure it'll cool down soon. Let me buy you an ice cream. What flavour do you want?'

'Vanilla?' he says, and her face falls, 'Oh no, you're one of those types.' One of those boring men, is that what she means? Maybe he *should* try something else. Shanice often refused to get vanilla so he would always end up having to try something revolting like tiramisu or strawberry cheesecake.

Jessica goes off and gets in the line while Ben backs into the shade of a signpost. He quickly reads a message from his mum.

Enjoy your date. Remember to tell the truth.

He promised her he would tell Jessica everything today, and he will. In good time.

'Here you go,' she says.

'You got me vanilla.'

'That's what you asked for, isn't it?'

'Yeah,' he smiles. 'Here's to your new job.' They knock their ice-cream cones together.

'Thanks. If you're very nice to me, I'll get you front-row tickets for our upcoming poetry exchange event.'

'That sounds great, we could do that if—'

She laughs and takes him by the arm.

'You're joking, aren't you?'

247

'Yes. Though it's good to know you'd sit through a poetry exchange for me.'

He'd sit through anything for her, but now's not the time to say it. They walk on through the park, the whole time Jessica commenting on how nice everything is, how clean and cultured. 'It's like a little wholesome bubble,' she says, watching as a group of teenagers practise a dance routine on a patch of grass. 'Why isn't our local park this classy?'

'Isn't it? I didn't notice.' Ben laughs, recalling how this morning he'd witnessed a member of the Fight Club pissing up the side of the sundial.

'Oh, I remember why,' Jessica says. 'It's because our park wasn't part of a nine-billion-pound regeneration. We live on the wrong side of Stratford.'

The water fountains are full of children stripped down to their underwear and adults with their trousers rolled up.

'You should bring Olivia here when she comes. Look at those kids, they love it.'

'Yeah. Good idea.'

'Where are we going, by the way? I want to sunbathe.'

'We didn't come here to sunbathe.'

'Are you serious? I'm trying to get a tan before it starts snowing again.'

'You said you wanted to go boating.' And that's exactly where he's led them, stopping at the top of the walkway where the swan-shaped pedaloes are.

Jessica makes a face. 'When did I say that? So cheesy.'

'Really,' he says, 'because it looks like you're dying to go on them.'

The last time they spoke Jessica had complained how men never wanted to do anything romantic anymore, and when Ben asked her to specify, going boating was one of things she'd said, along with going on a mini-break and dancing in the moonlight. Ben thought boating was the safest option.

They take a ride on the swans, though it's not as easy as it looks and they spend most of the time trying to steer themselves away from masses of reeds and other people. It's funny because all this time he wondered how hard he would have to work to impress Jessica, and now he's discovering she's not impressed by anything, she just wants to laugh, which she does often. He pedals the swan under a low-hanging tree, bumping it up against the side to keep it still. 'It's good to see you laughing,' he says.

She smiles back at him.

They float idly for a while and some of the romance drains away as Jessica gets that faraway look on her face again.

'So, Jessica, what's going on? You keep zoning out. Like something's on your mind.'

'It's the kids,' she says quietly, her mouth going to one side.

'What about the kids?'

'That's the thing: I don't know. I'm meant to. I used to. I definitely used to.'

Another swan veers towards them, a man and three small yapping children inside. They yell apologies before bumping off again. Jessica smiles at them. 'We all used to be so close. They used to tell me everything. And now, I don't have a clue what's going on. Haze is angry all the time and Jacob's taken on this role where he feels the need to protect me. That's not how it should be.'

Ben takes his feet off the pedals. He would love to move over to her side and put his arm around her, but the last thing he wants to do is capsize them. 'They're teenagers. Isn't it normal for them to start pushing away?'

'I guess so.'

'When you were their age, what was your relationship with your parents like?'

'My mum left when I was ten and,' she flicks her eyes up, 'you've met my dad.' She laughs. 'I could talk to him all I wanted, he never listened. He had other things to focus on.'

The boat begins to drift and Ben grabs onto the wall to keep it still.

'You're a great mum, Jessica. Your kids love you. Anyone can see that. They are teenagers, though.'

'Did you keep things from your parents?'

Ben scoffs.

'Tell me you weren't all good. There must have been stuff you got up to that you didn't run and tell your parents about.'

What does she want to hear? It's too uncomfortable. He looks away.

'I have *never* seen a person's face change so quickly. Now I really am intrigued. Were you a wild teen?'

'No,' he protests, 'far from it.'

'Oh yeah,' she raises her eyebrows. 'You just don't want me to know. I'll get to the bottom of it one day.'

'Your kids are great,' he says, desperate to get off the subject of himself. 'Don't worry about them. I'm sure they know that if they really needed to talk to you, you would be there for them.'

'Yeah. I hope you're right.' She gathers her dress in her hands and starts pedalling again. 'Let's get off this thing before I get a cramp.'

Afterwards, they walk on, looking for a shady spot to stop at, which is not that easy considering no tree in the park is older than a decade. Finally, they stop as Jessica finds a good spot to lie down in, closing her eyes to the intense sun.

'Remind me when your daughter's coming to stay?'

'In one week and one day. Finally. I feel like I've been waiting for ages.' He shuffles around until he's certain no sunrays are hitting him.

'I'm going to miss you.'

'Why? You don't have to stay away.'

She opens one eye and looks up at him. 'Nah, I'd feel a bit funny about creeping over in the night when she's with you.'

It had happened twice already this week, Jessica messaging him late at night, desperate for an escape from the house. Ben enjoyed it, of course, though found himself quickly wanting more than a few hours with her at night.

'You don't have to *sneak* over. You can come over anytime. For anything.'

'Hmm.'

'No. I didn't mean that. I meant like, come over for dinner. Come over to hang out. Even bring Jacob over.'

'I don't know.'

What is this? She's not even looking at him.

'I want you to meet Olivia.'

'Oh, Ben. I don't think so. It's a bit soon to start meeting your family.'

It gets his back up slightly, but he makes sure to keep his feelings from his voice. 'I've met your family. In fact, I see members of your family more than I see my own.'

'You already knew my pa before you knew me.'

'I see your kids. They know me. Hazel even said hi to me the other day.'

Jessica shifts on the grass, wriggling into a sunnier spot. 'That's more than I get at the moment. Remember, they know you through you being at Pa's; if us two had met elsewhere, they definitely wouldn't have met you yet.'

'What do you mean, met elsewhere? Like if we'd met at a bar—'

'A bar?' she asks, her eyes pinging open. 'When was the last time you went to a bar?'

'I can't believe you would have kept me hidden from your family.'

'There's no need for the kids to know who I'm seeing. It's none of their business.'

Ben shuffles over again to avoid the moving sunrays. This is not going how he planned at all. He thought Jessica liked him, that they liked each other. He had even allowed himself to see this as the start of something. Yet she's being so dismissive.

'Do you want to get out of the sun for a bit?' she asks.

'No. It's fine,' he snaps. She looks up at him and he adds softly, 'I love ultraviolet radiation.'

Jessica laughs in a way that makes him immediately thaw out.

'You're very red,' she says.

'I'm white. It's hot. I go red.'

'Have I annoyed you?'

'No.'

'I don't want to get in the way, Ben,' she says, reaching up and putting a hand his knee.

'In the way of what?'

'This is your first time having Olivia with you. I know how much you need it to go well. How do you think it'll go down with your ex-wife if Olivia starts talking about some lady who creeps over in the night?'

So this isn't about her keeping a distance from him and his life; she's trying to look out for him. 'You're right.'

'Of course I'm right. I've been through this, remember.' She sits up and faces him. 'Your ex is probably stressing that you're going to spoil Olivia so much she won't want to go home.'

'As if I'd spoil her.'

Jessica smiles and leans her head on Ben's shoulder. 'Can you tell me how much you've spent in the Disney Store recently?'

The girl at the till had recognised him when he went in the other day.

'Even now, Haze keeps going on about her moving in with Steadman while we wait for a new place and it's like, urgh,' Jessica mimes stabbing herself in the heart. 'I think it's because Steadman, for the first time, is able to offer her more than I can. He's a good dad though.' She considers this before shrugging and lying back down. 'I guess he deserves to be the favourite parent for once.'

'I can't get my head around this great relationship you have with your ex. My relationship with Shanice is—' Ben stops. 'I don't think I can talk about her and come off well.'

'Don't worry about it. I like how honest you are about what you've been through. I've been out with guys who've literally never once mentioned their kids and exes, almost denying them.'

He hadn't even considered doing that.

'At our age, it's pretty much impossible to meet someone without exes and kids and a past. So why pretend?' she says. 'They're a huge part of your life, don't apologise for talking about them.'

'It's not exactly great conversation. It's pretty horrendous, in fact.'

'It's honest. And that's what I'm looking for.'

A noisy group of young people carrying Sainsbury's bags, boxes of wine and a football walk close and settle down on blankets. Immediately two of them start whacking the ball back and forth.

'Lie down,' Jessica says, pulling the back of Ben's shirt. 'You're incapable of relaxing.'

'I know how to relax.'

'No, you don't. You're always busy doing something or looking for something to do. Lie down.'

'I'm not built for tanning,' he says while taking out his mini bottle of sunblock and moving into the dappled pools of shade on the grass. 'How can you comfortably close your eyes with that ball coming so close anyway?'

She lifts her head marginally. 'It's miles away. Besides, if the ball hits you, it hits you. Come on,' she says, patting the grass beside her, 'lie down with me.'

Lie down with me? Suddenly the ball really doesn't matter and Ben drops to the grass, his arm against hers and getting sweaty within seconds. 'You're so hot,' he says.

'I've heard that before. Are you relaxed?'

'I'm trying.' He closes his eyes and tries to concentrate on being still, on Jessica lying beside him, on the sound of the ball being kicked, on the sun searing his skin. This is a new kind of torture. He senses her move and when he opens his eyes, she's lying on her side facing him, her dress pulled tightly across her front, her cheeks flushed.

'I can't believe I've never been here before,' she says. 'It's nice to sit in a park without the fear of gang violence breaking out.'

Ben laughs. 'When I moved away it was still all factories and marshes round here.'

'It's nuts, isn't it? The way it changed so much. I can't even picture how it was before.'

'Because you're not meant to. Because they spent so much making it look like this instead.'

'Hmm,' she looks around and smiles again. 'I've lived here my whole life . . . though sometimes I feel I don't know it at all.'

'Do you ever see yourself moving away from East London?'

'No. I'm far too settled. Why would I? Still, the way things are going, I might have to. Can you imagine me living in the countryside? Wearing wellies and looking after chickens.'

'What about Wolf? Would he be up for leaving London?'

'Well, I wouldn't take him with me. I would call him once a month and see him on Christmas Day for an hour, like most sane people do with their parents. God, I can't imagine living anywhere else. That's so sad, isn't it?' She rolls back. 'Is it weird for you, being back here?'

A huge whack on the back of his head breaks the conversation.

Jessica screams, 'You fucking idiot, do you really need to play here?'

Someone calls back an apology and she gets onto her knees and rubs Ben's head. 'You okay?'

'Yeah. I'm good.' Though he's genuinely surprised his skull didn't explode, given the impact of the ball and his embarrassment. She keeps her hand on his head and brings it round to his cheek.

They spend the next hour kissing on the grass like teenagers, until her phone rings and she breaks away. 'Sorry, I know it's rude, but I'm waiting on a call back from the council.'

'No, course, get it.'

'Oh, it's Haze. Hi, hun.' Jessica's face contorts and she sits up. 'Why, what's happened? Is it Jacob?'

Ben mirrors her action. Something's happened.

'Is he still there now?'

There's a *him*, some ex-boyfriend come to win her back. Of course there is.

'I'm coming now.' She hangs up, then sinks back down to the grass.

'What? What's happened?'

'It's my brother,' she says, looking up. 'He's at the house.'

Chapter Seventeen

Jess

Jess struggles to find the correct key as she stands outside Pa's front door, the anxiety flooding her body and making her hands tremble. What does he want? Why is he here? And how can she get rid of him before Pa comes home from his afternoon pub session?

Dominic sits at the kitchen table with Haze. He turns when Jess enters and she's taken aback by how much he's aged since she last saw him eight years ago. His eyes look large and sunken, and neat lines of facial hair make his jawline harsher than normal. 'Hey, Sis,' he says, as if not a day's gone by.

'What are you doing here?'

He throws his hands up and looks at Haze in a way that tells Jess he already predicted her reaction.

'Mum?' Haze says. 'Dominic's come a long—'

'Can you go upstairs please?'

'Are you serious?' Haze's expression hovers between surprise and offence.

Jess holds eye contact and hopes this isn't one of those occasions where Haze will want to try and assert herself. Thankfully, she pushes out from the table and walks past, pausing at Dominic's side to say, 'I'll give you two some time to talk,' as if Jess and Dominic needed privacy for a heart-to-heart.

Once the sound of Haze's footsteps has faded, Jess dumps her bag on the table and leans against the worktop, facing Dom, though looking just above him. He still puts her on edge.

'You're not going to say anything?' he asks.

She looks down at him and he smiles, his lips pressed together. The same patronising, sneering smile he's always given her. 'What's your problem?' There's a familiar sharpness in his voice. He must know that he still intimidates her, that all those years of living with his unpredictability have had an effect.

'You shouldn't be here.' And it takes the sound of her own voice trembling to realise she's scared. 'Pa will be upset.'

Dominic clicks his head, left to right, wincing a little. There's a new tattoo on his neck, something dark and extensive that crawls from within his collar. 'How do you know he'll be upset? He might be ready to see me. It's been a long time.'

'Why have you shown up like this?'

'I've been trying to call him. He never answers. I knew I would get this kind of shitty reaction from you. So,' he shrugs one shoulder, 'here I am.'

She swallows and checks the time. Pa usually rolls in around now, drunk and merry, and Jacob said he would be home for dinner. He would struggle to remember his uncle, and Jess can't face watching them interact. It's bad enough knowing Haze has been in the house alone with him. And for how long? Anything could have been said in that time.

'I'm back to make amends,' Dominic says, again with the smile.

'Pa won't want to see you. Not after the last time.'

That too had started as *making amends*, though quickly turned into being about money, about him needing 'a little help' while he quit the warehouse job and looked for something else. It wasn't long before dodgy people started showing up at Pa's front door, asking for Dominic. One night, while Jess was there with the kids, Dominic had tumbled in, his face and knuckles bruised, that wild look in his eyes. 'I need money,' he shouted at Pa. 'Why won't you give it to me?'

Pa had held steady, claiming any money he had was to help out Jess.

'It's always about her,' Dominic complained bitterly. 'If she's big enough to have two kids, she should be big enough to look after them herself.'

He never had any time for her kids. She could see it in the way his eyes would pass over them, in his refusal to moderate his behaviour when they were close by. Especially with Jacob in those early years when his speech was still developing, and having any kind of relationship with him required way more effort than Dominic was willing to put in.

'I don't want him around my children,' she'd told Pa back then. 'So, while he's still around, we won't be.' It was the first time Jess had any control over the situation with Dom, that *she* got to make the rules. It was only after he left that she realised she wasn't only protecting her children but forcing Pa to choose between his two children.

There are footsteps above, perhaps Haze is coming back down. Jess should have sent her out of the house, far away from here, from him. 'You should leave.' Should. Why can't she be more assertive with him? She's not the little sister anymore.

He doesn't respond anyway, doesn't have to, because her words have never had any weight with him. 'Your girl says you live here,' he smirks. 'How did that happen?'

Jess closes her eyes. She's not felt a second of shame about the situation until now. It was the same when she fell pregnant, when Dominic looked her up and down and laughed, like it was so ridiculous she had a life of her own.

'Dom, you *need* to leave.' She sounds so pathetic, pleading with him like this.

His face changes and he bothers to look her in the eyes. 'Who are you to be telling me to leave?' He's not even annoyed, more slightly amused at her attempt to stand up to him. 'This ain't your house, Jess.'

'Pa has nothing,' she says, 'none of us do. If you're here for money, there is none.'

'You always think I'm back for money.'

'Aren't you?'

'It doesn't matter what I'm back for.'

'Pa has nothing,' she repeats. 'And as you can see,' she holds out her arms, 'neither do I.'

It's humiliating.

'That's what you said the last time too. There's no money, there's no money. There's always money, Jess. Pa's been saving his whole life. He didn't spend it on us growing up, or this place.' Dominic's eyes rove around the crowded kitchen, taking in the piles of washing-up on the countertops, the table cluttered with papers, books and jars. He drops his voice, 'The last time I came home, I was doing good. I had ideas, plans, a way to change my life. All I needed was a bit of help, a little leg-up for once.'

It makes her think of Haze. Of her preoccupation with being behind others, of being on the back foot due to her background. But no, Dominic is nothing like Haze, he's squandered every opportunity he's ever had.

'And you got the help, didn't you?' Jess says. 'I know Pa gave you money.' She never found out how much Pa had given Dominic the last time around. A few grand, probably. About the same amount as he's managed to save again.

'Yeah, a little bit. Then he sent me packing.'

'You would have left anyway. You didn't come back to make up with him, to rebuild your relationship. You came back for money, and you got it. It's not going to happen this time. Because there is no money. So please, just leave.'

Dominic leans back in the chair and looks her over again. 'Okay.' He stands up, coming close by her as he passes. 'Get Pa to call me. Your daughter has my number.'

The next morning Jess opens Pa's bedroom door. The curtains are drawn, but not quite properly, so a slant of light falls across one side of the room, illuminating the shoes and crumpled trousers lying by the bedside.

'Pa, we're going now.'

He grunts. He didn't get back till late last night. She was already in her room, biting her nails down to the quick and staring at the pink post-it pad Haze had given her with Dominic's number. When she approached Pa in the hallway and told him, he simply looked at the number, shook his head and walked off.

'Pa?' Jess tries again. 'I said we're going.'

He sits up half-heartedly. 'Where?'

'To see the place I told you about.'

His eyes look tiny and deep without his glasses. 'You're going to see a flat today?'

'No. It's a hostel. I told you.' What's the use? She's barely slept herself, up most of the night stressing about Dominic and this viewing. What a fool she had been yesterday, lying in the sun laughing and relaxing as if she didn't have a care in the world. How quickly her real life snatched her back.

'Please,' he croaks, 'bring me some ibuprofen.'

As a kid, Jess looked up to Pa like a hero, he seemed so strong and safe. Until he was frail and scared, cowering away from his own son mid-row. He's almost eighty now, there's no way he could fight off Dominic again, not physically or emotionally. Surely he knows that, surely he's not considering allowing Dominic back into their lives.

'Ibuprofen, please.'

'You're not allowed that anymore, remember?'

'A little bit won't hurt.'

Jess strops along to the cupboard at the top of the stairs and reaches for the shoebox where he keeps the household medication. Bottles of Calpol from decades ago, Bonjela, Tiger Balm, unidentified rash creams. So this is how it's going to be: he's going to pretend it's not happening, and all of them will have to live at the mercy of Dominic dropping by again.

'Mum?' Jacob calls up. 'I'm ready.'

'Coming.'

Haze emerges from the bathroom, dressed but without the flicks of eyeliner she never leaves home without.

'You're not ready.' It's not really a question, more of an accusation.

'I told you, I'm not going.'

'You need to see the place. It'll make you feel better about moving into it.'

'I'm *not* moving into it.' She pushes past Jess towards the bedroom.

'You need to come with us, you know that. We can't move without you.' Jess follows her in.

Haze stands in front of the mirror and rummages in her make-up bag before slowly beginning to tweeze her eyebrows. Is she serious? 'We don't have time for this, Haze. You should have been ready ten minutes ago.'

She reaches over to her phone and puts on *Hamilton*.

'Haze?' Jess switches it off.

'Why are you in here? I can never get any peace in this house.'

'The housing officer expects to see you there today. He's already unconvinced you'll be moving with us and if you don't turn up today—' she stops. Is that really the issue? Like Cat-Tie Tim has the time to dissect her family's dynamics and house them accordingly.

'When are you going to call him?' Haze asks.

Jess takes a deep breath, trying to buy time.

'Mum?'

'I told you, I'm not.'

'What about Pa? Why is he acting so weird about all this? He didn't say a thing last night.'

'He was drunk. I shouldn't have approached him about it then.'

'Is he really going to ignore his own son?'

Jess swallows and says, 'I hope so.'

Haze throws the tweezers back in the bag. 'Tell me the whole story.'

'You know what you need to know.' Why isn't it enough to know her uncle was someone they no longer had time for, that he was a waste of space?

'I know nothing. Except he made some mistakes when he was younger, like most boys round here. And didn't he spend years paying for it? Being locked up and rehabilitated? What does he have to do to move on from that?'

There's no moving on from what Dom did, and if Haze knew, she would understand. Yet, Jess doesn't want to tell Haze the full story because Dom's past is not relevant to her.

'Why are you so unforgiving?' Haze shouts.

'You don't know what you're talking about. You don't have a clue.'

'Because you won't tell me.'

'Jess?' Pa calls.

'Fuck.'

Jess feels as though she's leaving one fire to put out another.

'I can't swallow them dry,' Pa complains as she drops the

264

packet of pills on the bedspread. She runs downstairs, to where Jacob waits by the front door, a WWF panda baseball cap on, his wide earnest face watching her from under it. 'Give me a minute.' She fills a glass and runs back up to Pa's room. There she pushes open a window to allow the smell of sleep and alcohol to escape.

'Are you going now?' he asks.

'I've been trying to go for the last twenty minutes.'

Pa reaches up and grabs her by the wrist. 'I heard you, what you said to Haze.'

'I've told you where I stand, Pa,' she says. 'I don't want to see him again. I don't want him around me or the kids. He's no good. He never changes. He only comes back when he wants something.'

Pa squeezes her arm. 'If it was your kid, if it was Jacob, you would forgive him, wouldn't you?'

The lump rises fast in her throat. 'Jacob isn't Dom. He'll never be anything like Dom.'

'I know that. I'm not asking you if they're similar. I'm asking you to consider if you would give your own child forgiveness if they asked for it. No matter what they'd done in the past.'

'Dominic's not back for your forgiveness, he's back for your money.' Jess pulls her arm away. 'I've really got to go.' As she passes back along the hall, she stops at Haze's bedroom door for one last-ditch effort. 'Please. I need you to come today. This is about us getting a home. And when I say us, I mean *all* of us.' It's clear what Jess is doing; she's using Jacob as a way to guilt-trip Haze. It's the only thing always guaranteed to work.

Haze pulls in her bottom lip and starts to tie her hair. 'Okay. Give me two minutes.'

Ben was right, the hostel is a fifteen-minute walk, a small normal-looking block of flats Jess used to walk past on her way to work every day. Cat-Tie Tim meets them across the road, where he's sat at the bus stop, eating a salad covered in grated cheese. 'Sorry, just getting a late breakfast in. Been a busy morning.'

'No problem,' Jess says, sweaty from the heat and the rush to get here. Haze stands a few feet away with her arms folded and head down.

Inside the block there's a small reception area with a large palm plant, its leaves dry and brown on one side, yet lush and green on the other. A woman with a coffee in one hand, biscuit in another, calls over, 'All right, Tim. How you keeping?'

'Not too bad. Busy, busy, busy. Keys for number twelve, please.'

'Tell me about it,' the woman laughs with her mouth full as she searches in a wall cabinet for the key.

'No rest for the wicked,' he adds.

How often does he have to come here?

He takes the keys and turns back to Jess. 'This is where you sign in. You're meant to do it every time you come and go.' He looks behind her at Jacob and says, 'It's quite important. Will you make sure your son understands that too?'

'He *can* hear you,' Haze says.

'Sorry,' Cat-Tie Tim says.

Jacob smiles awkwardly and falls behind as they trudge up

the stairs. No one says anything apart from Tim, who rattles on about new windows and fire restrictions in the block.

'There are three other families on this floor. One I know, lovely mum and kids, not sure about the other. Here we go,' he says, unlocking number twelve.

Inside it's bright, that's the first thing Jess notices. It had been hard to picture in her head, though in her bleakest moments, at night as she lay in bed and her *everything's going to be all right* guard fell, she pictured somewhere dark and dingy. But this place has so much light, the whole long room is flooded with it. There's a set of bunk beds on one side and a single on the other, next to a wardrobe and chest of drawers. Down the far side of the room, fitted under a sloping roof, is a kitchen. Well, a worktop unit with a sink. She's not sure if there's a hob. An oven? A grill? Or if she would even want to cook in the same room they're all expected to sleep in. Jess wants to ask about these things, though is suddenly too overwhelmed by the reality of it.

'Oh, they left the microwave,' Tim says, walking deeper into the room. 'We'll have to remove that, I'm afraid. Health and safety. You can get your own and there'll be a fridge too. It usually goes here,' he says, marking out a little area with his hands. A fridge to store cold food, but where are they expected to store the rest of the stuff that usually goes in a kitchen? The tins and packets? The spices and saucepans?

The laminate flooring creaks as they walk across it. It's nice in this weather, though Jess imagines the place freezing in winter, especially being up in the roof, with the single-glazed windows. What does that matter? She won't be here in the winter anyway as the official guidance states they can't be placed here for longer than six weeks.

Jacob walks to the shortest part of the room and lifts his hands to touch the ceiling. He catches Jess staring and looks away when she smiles. He hates it. She can see it in the way he pulls strings from the bottom of his T-shirt and wraps them around his fingers. By comparison, Haze gives nothing away, other than pure attitude, standing close to the door, her eyes roving over everything, her top lip curling.

Tim stops talking and looks at Jess, as if picking up on the mood. 'Shall I show you the facilities?'

'Facilities?' Jess asks a little too brightly.

'Yes, the shared kitchen and bathroom.'

'Oh, of course.' Jess feels like an idiot, what did she expect? That he was about to show them the pool and spa room?

They don't step in the bathroom, just poke their heads in as Tim opens the door and closes it again; the same with the kitchen, which appears industrial yet spotless.

Back outside, they wave Tim off and Jess exhales loudly as if she's been holding her breath the whole time. Immediately she regrets it. It's her job here to set the tone. 'Quite all right. Don't you think?'

Jacob looks at Haze for clues on how to respond. Neither of them says anything.

'Bigger than I thought it would be,' Jess adds. 'And bright. Great light in there. Don't you think?' she asks them both, but really directs her question at Jacob, who has now twisted a thread of string around his finger so tightly that his fingertip bulges from it. Jess has to put her hands in her pockets to stop herself from grabbing it off him. Haze notices too. 'What time are you meeting Cameron?' she asks as she gently takes the string away.

He shrugs.

'Are you guys planning to film your masterpiece today?'

'Yeah.'

Jess marvels at how her daughter can do this, how with her words alone she can make Jacob's shoulders shrink back down, his fingers stop twiddling.

'It's all going to be okay, you know?' Jess says, pulling him in for a side hug. 'I promise.'

'I know,' he says, nodding at the ground. 'I'm going now. Bye.'

They watch him slouch away before turning to each other.

'Shall we go home and talk?' Jess asks, desperate to clear the air.

'I have work in like ninety minutes. I don't have time to go all the way to Pa's only to go back out again.'

'Okay. Well, I'll see you at home later.'

'Later? No.'

Jess scoffs. She isn't about to lay out all her dirty laundry here. No, this type of conversation requires more.

'Why are you acting so weird about your brother coming back?'

'I'm not.'

'You are. I tell you everything, Mum, all the time, I tell you everything and you don't even trust me with this.'

This used to be true. Before everything started going sour between them, Haze had always told Jess things: when she was happy, when she was stressed, when she liked a boy, even once when she thought she liked a girl. She had been open about everything, from her greatest achievements to her tiniest indiscretions. Though this doesn't mean that Jess has to reciprocate. They're mother and daughter, not BFFs.

'I don't want Dominic in our lives. He's a bad person, Haze.'

'A *bad person*? You're talking to me like I'm a child. Like I can't make my own choices.'

'There is no choice about this. We're not seeing him again, none of us are.'

'I'm fed up of your choices. You always think you're doing right by us, but look at the mess we're in, look at where your choices have gotten us,' she says, nodding back down the street to the hostel.

'Not this again. You guilt-tripping me for what's happened, as if I wanted any of this. You have no idea of the work I do. Of how hard I'm trying to give you and Jacob everything.'

A window slams shut on the street and they both look up to see an old woman shooing them before dropping her net curtain.

'It's always about you,' Haze says. 'You wanting credit all the time. You do it with Dad, with Opa. Dad can't sort his life out because he's lazy, and Opa is a mess because he drinks. When they mess up, it's unforgivable, but when you mess up it's because you're working so hard and your life is so unfair.'

This is it; this is how Haze sees things. She doesn't see Jess picking up all the slack because Jess always hides the fact that she does.

'And now you're doing the same thing with your own brother. He made mistakes when he was young and in your eyes that's completely unforgivable because you, oh you never make mistakes.'

'Stop it.'

'No. I'm fed up with everything being your call all the time. I'm moving in with Dad.'

'Did he suggest this?' Fucking Steadman. 'You're not moving in with your dad.'

'Who says I have to live with you at all? Maybe Jacob can come too and—'

The suggestion that Jacob, who struggles to sit through a lunch with his dad, would move in with him is ridiculous. But then Jess recalls the way he reluctantly told her about sleeping on the floor, how he felt he was doing the right thing by sucking it up and not telling her. 'Don't even suggest this to your brother,' Jess utters, suddenly fearful both her kids will move out, will leave her.

Haze looks defiant.

'I can't talk about this with you now, Haze. I just— I can't. Go to work, calm down and we'll speak later.' Jess starts to walk ahead.

'Tell me why you won't give your brother another chance.'

Jess stops and turns back.

'I'm old enough to know. By you not telling me, I'm left thinking the worst. What did he do? Why can't you forgive him?'

The worst? There's no way Haze could even imagine what kind of person Dom really is. How dark things got when he was in Jess's life. But this is what Haze wants to hear, what she thinks she's ready for. Jess shakes her head. No, she can't talk about this. She has the opportunity to protect her kids from knowing about Dom. Though there's the fear that, without knowing the full truth, Haze will gravitate towards him.

'Mum?'

'There are so many reasons,' Jess says.

Haze waits and Jess knows this is it, it's time to tell her. 'Burglary. GBH.'

Haze's face cracks and her lip wobbles in that way it always does when she's wrong about something. 'That was a long time ago, though. He didn't come across aggressive or anything when I met him, when I—'

'Stop,' Jess says, unable to hear her daughter defend Dom. She had hoped the first two would be enough. She had hoped Haze wouldn't need to hear the whole thing.

'He was also done for sexual assault – twice,' Jess says, her voice soft. 'I'm sorry, I never wanted you to find this out.'

'What?' Haze's eyes well up. 'I can't believe,' she looks away. 'Mum, I can't believe you kept this from me.'

Jess reaches out and holds one of Haze's hands. 'I'm sorry,' she repeats. What else is there to say? There's nowhere to go from here. Nothing else to explain.

'Why didn't you tell me?'

'You didn't need to know. I wanted to protect you.'

Jess's phone rings, causing Haze to pull away and fold her arms.

'Haze?' she tries, hoping her daughter will look at her,

will understand why she kept these things locked away. The phone continues and Jess rummages in her bag for it. 'Sorry.'

'Mum, are you seriously going to take a call?'

'No, I'll silence it.' Though when she looks at the screen, she sees it's her recruiter. 'Shit.'

'Just get it,' Haze says. 'Answer it.'

Jess tries to exhale her stress away before answering and putting on her chirpy phone voice.

'Jess, hi, it's Ellen from ArtHub Jobs. Are you on your way?'

'My way?'

'The people at Apple Hall called to say you didn't turn up. They were expecting you to start today.'

'No,' she says, 'it was Monday, 28th July.'

'Yes, and it is. Today's the 28th. Today's your starting date.'

Dread swims in her stomach. She got it wrong? No. Of course not. She pulls the phone away from her head and checks the date on the screen. She got it so wrong.

'Mum?' Haze says, her face contorted and hard.

Jess raises a finger while Ellen double-checks, though Jess knows the mistake is hers. Of course, the date was stuck in her head, along with the dates for all the other things she had to remember and didn't, all the other balls she's dropped over the last few months.

'Oh well, we all slip up sometimes,' Ellen says, though her voice sounds tight. 'Come by the agency and let's see what we can do.'

Chapter Eighteen

Ben

August

For the last week Ben has sent Jessica long text messages asking if she's okay, if there's anything he can do and offering his place to her if she needs an escape. So far, her response has been the odd message back, often a few words, 'Thanks hun' followed by a 'x'. Always a kiss. Though she doles these out to everyone, he's seen it for himself. Even once teasing her for putting them on emails to her estate agents.

Finally, she asks to come over and when she does, sulking through his front door, looking sad in a tracksuit and no make-up, Ben struggles because he can't think what to do to make it better. Also, because she's been very clear with him that she doesn't want a hero, some man galloping in, keen to sort her life out.

'Everything's fallen apart,' she cries. 'I really wanted that job. No, that's not true, it was a shit job. What I meant was,

I really *needed* that job. How could I get the dates wrong? What an idiot.'

'We all make mistakes.'

Harold climbs on the sofa between them, resting his hind legs on Ben and facing Jessica as if she's about to perform something for him.

'The recruitment agency tried, but the organisation thinks I'm an idiot. And it's true, I am. Why would they want to work with me now? I can't even turn up for my first day.'

'You're being too hard on yourself. Them too. It's out of order they didn't give you a second chance.'

'No. No, it's not. I get it. I need to be more focused. Everything is crashing down around me, and what am I doing? Flapping about on a pedalo in the park.'

He recoils a little and thankfully she feels it. 'Sorry, I didn't mean it like that. Because that's one of the few times recently I've felt happy, like I really enjoyed myself, but the fact is' – she wipes her nose with the back of her hand – 'I don't have time to be happy.'

He reaches over Harold to put a hand on Jessica's knee. 'That's a really depressing thought.'

'I'm meant to be the mum, the one who keeps everything ticking over and working. I'm not doing that at the moment.'

He wishes he could take it all away. 'You've had a lot of curveballs. It's not your fault.'

'It is. I should never have moved us into Pa's place only to start talking about moving us back out a few weeks later.'

'The hostel?'

'Yeah. I've looked into it properly and it's the only way

275

we're going to get a council place. The kids are both freaking out about it though. Especially Haze. She told me point-blank there's no way she's coming with us, that she'd rather move in with her dad. She's so angry with me. And then there's all this other stuff going on.'

'What stuff?'

'With my brother.'

Ben feels something inside himself sink down.

'Haze thinks I'm treating her like a child. That I don't respect her. All I was trying to do was protect her from knowing there's a person in her family who's like him. God, if I could have been spared from him growing up, I would have had a much happier childhood. This all sounds terrible, doesn't it?'

Ben swallows. 'No. I don't know what you went through.'

'Of course not. I forgot that Pa neglected to tell you he even had a son. It makes me angry when he does that, but then, I guess what I did was the same thing. I never told Haze much about Dom until she backed me into a corner, and I can't imagine telling Jacob.' She leans forward and sinks her head into her hands.

Ben taps Harold in an effort to move him, but it doesn't work because apparently Harold loves a woman in distress. He nuzzles at the side of Jessica's arm, causing her to raise her head and look at him. 'He's such a nice dog,' she says, putting her arm around him, which only encourages him to get closer. 'It's like he knows when you need a cuddle.'

There's a moment when they're both quiet and Ben's sure the floor is his, his for laying out what *he* knows. He turns away from her, leaning forward and squeezing his fists together, then makes a noise, a kind of heavy *humph*. 'Look, there's something I have to tell you. It's about Dominic.'

'Okay,' she says slowly.

When he turns back, her face is unreadable.

'At school, there was a period when I was on his radar. He thought I saw him do something at a party. And he wanted to make sure I didn't say anything to anyone.'

'Do something?' Jessica breaks eye contact, then when she looks back, she asks, 'It was something to do with a girl, wasn't it?'

'Yeah,' Ben answers, his voice barely audible.

'And did you . . . did you see him do something?'

Ben's aware of not taking too long to answer. 'Not exactly.'

'What does that mean?'

It was a supervised family party in a local hired hall. Aunties sat around the side, drinking box wine from plastic cups, children tore about squealing and Jim, whose sixteenth it was, wore a birthday badge. It was completely civilised.

Dominic was there with two friends who kept their distance from the others, standing outside in the small community garden that bordered the hall, watching everyone come and go. The only person to approach them was Jim's mum, who offered slices of cake and asked what they planned to do after GCSEs. It was strange to see these boys who everyone feared switch on their manners and make small talk with a parent.

Dominic caught Ben watching and beckoned him over.

Being acknowledged by Dominic was huge. 'Me?' Ben

asked, stepping away from the group of people he had been standing with, the group who had so far failed to include him in their conversations.

'Go in and get us a bottle,' Dominic said. It wasn't a request, it was a demand, and Ben felt himself fill with dread. 'How?'

'No one's gonna notice you get a bottle.'

Because to most people, Ben was invisible.

'Go on,' Dominic said, his friends laughing, 'get a bottle of spirits. Rum. Vodka. Something good.'

Dominic laughed too, and when he returned to looking at Ben his expression hardened. 'I'm not really asking, you know. Do it.'

Ben walked into the hall, which was at this point in the evening filled with women dancing to East 17 songs, and girls from school acting up, pretending to be tipsy from the small sips of cava Jim's mum had allowed them.

He walked around the edge of the dancefloor and stopped in front of the table at the far end. A bottle? How? The table was spread with plates of sausage rolls and bowls of crisps, a giant tub of lollipops and, along towards the end, the alcohol. A man sat on a chair close by, arms folded across a large belly, eyes partially shut in boredom. Ben made his way across, picking up a plate and piling it with whatever looked edible. As he got closer to the drinks, the man's eyes flicked open and he drew a one-sided smile at Ben. 'You boys don't stop eating,' he said. 'Plenty left, all gotta go.'

'Yeah,' Ben said, his heart beating. The crisps felt damp as he picked up a handful, and a little kid skipped up beside him and spent some time picking up, inspecting and then putting back down cocktail sausages, before running off. Ben wondered if he could do the same, run off, carefree, still innocent. Except what would happen back at school on Monday?

There were so many bottles, how was he meant to choose? He knew not wine, which was good because there was no way he'd be able to get out unnoticed with one of those boxes. Maybe beers would be a good bet. Though how many was he meant to take? He wasn't even sure what rum looked like, as his own parents didn't really drink, and when he finally spotted the slim bottle of rum, it was clear liquid rather than a dark one as he imagined. He put his hand on it and quickly slid it across the table towards himself. The old man, with his face turned up slightly and eyes shut again, didn't even flinch. Ben put the bottle under his T-shirt and tucked it slightly into the waistband of his jeans, pulling his waistcoat over it. Fearing the bottle slipping down his leg, he dumped the paper plate on the table and cautiously made his way back outside.

Dominic smiled at him. 'Victory?' he asked. The boys hooted as Ben pulled out the bottle. 'Nice, nice,' one of them said, and even though Ben knew what he did was completely wrong, he did feel victorious.

'You took an unopened bottle too,' Dominic exclaimed. 'I wasn't expecting you to get away with it.'

Ben had surpassed expectations. Surely this would be a turning point in his social standing. And then Dominic, the boy who'd never said a word to Ben before, invited him to share a drink.

They shuffled deeper into the community garden, ensuring

they were out of sight. Ben stood with them, drinking the spirit straight from the bottle and feeling not quite right. This wasn't who he was, and also he felt vulnerable down the side of the building, away from the eyes of others. Everyone had seen Dominic lose his temper over the years; his rage and aggression were notorious.

Dominic and his friends gradually turned their backs on Ben, and when some girls showed up to share the drink, Ben was fully pushed aside. He went back inside to find the friends he'd come with, the ones who hadn't even noticed his absence never mind gone looking for him. He persisted for another hour or so, attempting to drop in to the conversation that he had been outside drinking with Dominic, but the music was too loud to talk. Eventually, he made his way back outside, keen to head home. He took one last look down the side of the building. The group had gone and now it was only Dominic and one girl. The girl was sort of propped against the wall while he leaned over.

Dominic looked up and the fire was back in his eyes. 'What you doing?' he shouted at Ben. 'Piss off.'

The glow from a passing car threw some orange light onto them, yet Ben still couldn't really see the girl's face, who she was, what kind of state she was in. Though it looked like, if Dominic were to move, she would fall into a heap on the ground.

'Should I get someone for her?' Ben asked.

'Fuck off,' Dominic instructed, stepping back a little while keeping one hand on the girl's shoulder. 'I mean it, go.'

And Ben did as he was told.

The following Monday all anyone could talk about was the party, mostly tall tales of how drunk everyone was, who got off with who and who embarrassed themselves. It wasn't until a few weeks later that a rumour began to circulate about a girl from the year below them. She had been to the party, got drunk and separated from her friends. Everyone had their theories, though no one knew exactly what happened to her; she simply never came back to school.

It was around this time that Dominic started to make himself known to Ben. It was never discussed, though the message was clear. Keep quiet. You saw nothing.

'You lied to me,' Jessica says. 'You outright lied.'

All this time Ben's been stressing about Jessica discovering some version of himself she would find off-putting, like him being boring or a pushover, as if that was the worst thing she could find out. Yet, now he sees that the worst trait he could have ever showed to Jessica was that of being a liar.

'No. I didn't lie.'

'You did lie,' she says.

'At the start, when I met you, I didn't know you even had a brother. Then you told me and I pieced it together and Wolf said this thing about people always judging you, judging the family on what Dominic had done and—' He needs to explain things as quickly as possible so she doesn't get stuck with this horrible idea about him. But it's too late, he can see it.

'Does my dad know this too?' she asks.

This makes it worse, the idea that he and Wolf were complicit. 'Yeah, he knows some of it,' Ben answers, the air leaving his body as he sinks down with shame. 'He told me not to tell you.'

Her face reddens. 'And you listened to him? We've spent all this time together and you've never mentioned it.' Jessica gets up. Harold springs to his feet and totters out behind her into the hallway. Ben follows too. 'This whole time you've acted like you knew nothing about Dom.'

Ben hangs his head.

'I need someone I can trust,' she says, moving towards the door. 'Not someone who's going to keep things from me. Someone who can't stand up for themselves and, even worse, someone who turns a blind eye. You're not who I thought you were.'

'I was sixteen.' The way she's looking at him, it hurts. It's almost like she's disgusted. 'I was *sixteen*,' he tries again, because that's what it was, he was young and found himself in a situation he didn't know how to handle. 'I didn't get how serious it was. You think I'm not filled with guilt every time I think about it now? All these years—'

'Don't make it about you.'

Harold taps around their feet. He used to hate it when Shanice would shout, when she'd scream and wail at Ben.

'That girl knew no one would have backed up her story,' Jessica says. 'So she left the school. Left the area. No one gave a shit. And he got away with it. Then, three years later, guess what? He did it again.'

'Jessica, I'm . . .' But what can Ben say? That whole situation felt beyond what he was mature enough to deal with. And when the bullying started, he couldn't tell his parents the reason why Dominic was targeting him. So, just like the girl, he moved away too.

'This isn't going to work,' Jessica says, shaking her head and staring down. 'You and me. I should have known.'

No. She's wrong. They *were* working. They were becoming something. 'Jessica.' Though he doesn't know what to say next. He's broken her trust. Of course she doesn't want to be with him.

She glances at him then away, as if also unsure of what to say. Then she leans forward and hugs him tightly. He puts his arms around her back, making sure to angle his face away from her hair, knowing he's not strong enough to avoid burying his face in it. A familiar pain crawls into his heart and he wishes he'd never started any of this. When his feelings for Jessica began to emerge, he should have closed himself up and gone in another direction.

When they break away, she keeps her head down, though he can see the tears on her face. This upsets him even more, knowing that he's hurt this person who he cares about so much, this person who opened herself up to him.

She opens the door and takes off down the steps quickly and, as the front door slams shut, he knows there's nothing left to do other than move on again.

Chapter Nineteen

Jess

It takes less than a fortnight for Jess to feel she knows the routines of the other families in the hostel as well as her own. It's not just about when they use the bathroom or kitchen, there's also the panicked calls of 'I'm late' at around half seven each morning, the gasping and rhythmic thudding of someone doing exercises at lunchtime and every evening around seven, the sound of a mum singing 'You Are My Sunshine'. Though it's rare to see any of these people face to face. In fact, these days Jess feels as if she hardly sees anyone at all.

She has been keeping her distance from Pa, knowing that he has been communicating with Dom. Jess isn't sure what stage their 'reconciliation' is at, as she has refused to discuss it with him. She only knows that while Dominic is worming his way back into Pa's life and finances, she needs to steer clear.

Then, there is Jacob, who at first loved the novelty of eating takeaways on his lap but now prefers to eat at Cameron's house, which is a real house with a real kitchen and meals served on a real dining table. And Haze, well, she has moved in *unofficially* with Steadman, though she comes to the hostel three times a week. Her interactions with Jess during these times are minimal; she arrives late, sleeps and leaves early, making sure the staff see her. When Jess confronts her, Haze reiterates that she is only making an appearance in order to not mess up their housing claim.

Jess is lonely.

She has tried spending time with Precious, thinking cuddles with a baby would cheer her up. Instead there is something completely heartbreaking about watching a new mum rub noses with her baby daughter, while Jess can't even get her own daughter to look her in the eye.

And then there's the other absence in her life, Ben.

The break had been clean, no messages or calls and thankfully no run-ins with each other on the street that final week before she moved away. Her feelings towards him were far too complicated. She liked him, more than anyone she had liked before, and she had trusted him. Yet the whole time he'd had this secret, this horrible thing he'd done, or rather not done, which, for her, threw his character into doubt. It's such a harrowing image: a drunk girl propped against the wall. Why didn't Ben do something? He wouldn't have had to confront Dominic directly. He could have called someone else, alerted an adult. Just done something, anything. But he didn't, and because of his cowardice Dominic was able to get away with it. And do it again.

The last few months have been brutal, but Jess needs to stay positive. Tomorrow she'll start a new temporary role at a small museum over the other side of London. The commute is a nightmare, though the money is okay and it has prospects of growth, and that's what she needs right now. Growth. Change.

First the job – no, career. And then a home.

Jess goes into the kitchen to make herself some pasta. It's usually empty at this time of day so she's surprised to see one of the other residents. 'Sorry,' she says to the woman, who has thick black hair down past her shoulders. 'I didn't realise you were in here.'

'It's okay, I'm almost done.'

This woman leaves early each morning, stomping down to the bus stop with one baby in the pushchair and another on a little buggy board behind. She wears a uniform, a retail or service industry job, and doesn't get back till past six most days, the kids moaning and her looking exhausted.

'It's funny,' Jess says, 'we practically live with each other but this is the first time we've ever spoken.'

The woman puts a few slices of ginger into a mug and smiles, 'Yeah, well, I work long hours.'

'Me too,' Jess says quickly. 'I mean, usually I do. I start a new job tomorrow.' She doesn't want this woman judging her, thinking she's some layabout who's ended up in a hostel because she doesn't work.

'You have a boy, don't you? Likes to talk.' There's a slight Caribbean lilt to her accent, sing-songy, possibly Trinidadian.

'Oh, you've met Jacob. He never said. I've a girl too, she's eighteen, she's not spent much time here.' It hurts Jess to say this, to acknowledge out loud that her daughter would rather be somewhere else than with her. 'Crazy how they expect a teenage girl to live in the same room as her brother and mum,' she adds, hoping the woman will understand that it's the situation that has pushed Haze away. 'Still, it's not forever, is it?' She says this for herself as much as to keep the conversation moving.

'Hopefully not.' The woman spoons some honey into her mug. Catching Jess staring, she washes the spoon and adds, 'Though sometimes, it feels like it.'

'Do you know when you're moving on?'

'No idea. We've been here nine months now.'

'Nine months,' Jess repeats. 'Is that even legal?'

'We're waiting on a four-bed,' the woman says as if this explains it all perfectly. 'I also have two older children.'

'Still, why haven't they moved you somewhere else, some-where with its own kitchen and bathroom? You've really been living like this for so long?'

The woman shrugs. 'Those self-contained hostel spaces are really hard to come by. I don't know. I guess we've got used to it.' She shrugs and her smile veers more towards empathy than unkindness. 'They told you no more than six weeks, didn't they?'

Jess feels herself shrinking. Deep down she knew it was unlikely the council would be able to find her something within the six-week window Cat-Tie Tim had mentioned.

'They say that to everyone. But there's some loophole, you know, something about who owns and manages the hostel, which allows them to leave you here for as long as they want.'

'I'm so sorry. Isn't there anyone you can go to for advice?

Help? The council, they have a legal requirement to look after people. They can't leave you here for this long. They're surely breaking a law or something.'

'I know,' the woman says, picking up her mug. 'I should call the police on them, shouldn't I?'

Jess hangs her head.

'See you later.' The woman walks past Jess, down the corridor to the room she shares with her children.

Nine months and no end in sight. Jess can't get bogged down in thinking about this. Not right now anyway because she wants to be able to sleep tonight, to feel fully rested for tomorrow.

The bathroom has recently been used. The floor is damp, the shower screen striped with foamy lines where whoever came before tried to exercise courtesy and clean the screen after use. She gazes at the bath, which she suspects is only ever used by the woman's toddlers. Jess had once found a blue plastic boat on the floor, slick with soap. Jess misses baths, though can never imagine herself taking one here. Quick showers are the only way to go. The first few she took after moving in reminded her of the ones you take following swimming, where you rush through, trying to keep your bare feet off the floor and pulling on clothes before your body lotion is even absorbed.

After showering and washing her hair, she pads back to the room in her flip-flops and dressing gown. Jacob flinches and switches his screen off. 'The bathroom's free now, go and use it,' she says, wondering what he was looking at.

He's sitting on the floor with his back against the bed, looking glum. Poor kid. She felt sorry for him when they were at Pa's place, having a shared space as his bedroom, though sharing with your mum must be a million times worse.

'No thanks.'

'If you shower now you won't have to do it in the morning.'

Getting Jacob to shower daily has always been a problem. Here, it's even worse because he dislikes leaving the room without his external processor on. At home this was never a thing. He would sit with it off for long periods of time. The three of them in the living room, him immersed in a book, Haze typing on her laptop, Jess on her phone absently scrolling through the news. Occasionally one of them would want tea and, if it was his turn, Haze would throw a cushion across the room to get his attention, which he would always pretend to not notice. Jess misses this, she misses her family.

'You okay, hun?'

His face lights up as he switches back on the screen, and he looks startled, like he's about to confess something.

'What's going on?'

'Nothing.'

'Jacob?'

'Haze is here.'

Just then Haze's distinctive heavy footsteps can be heard outside. Jacob jumps up to open the door.

'I didn't know you were coming tonight.'

Haze takes a few steps into the room and slides her rucksack off her shoulder. 'You said three nights a week. Well, here I am.'

Jacob smiles up at her, his face glowing in a way Jess hasn't seen in a while.

'How's it going?' Haze asks. 'You want to go out?'

'Yeah,' he says.

'Oh, okay,' Jess says, pulling the towel off her hair. 'I'm just out of the shower. Let me put something on.'

'No, you're fine, Mum,' Haze says. 'We're only going to Maccy D's. We'll bring you a McFlurry back if you want.'

Oh, so the invite doesn't stretch to her. 'I've already eaten. Don't worry about me. And don't stay out too late.'

'I already said I'm staying tonight,' Haze snaps back. 'I don't need to spend the whole evening hanging out in this room too.'

'I meant more that the curfew is ten.'

Haze throws her rucksack on the bed. 'Fine. See you later.'

Once they've both left, Jess puts her hair in a fat plait and lies down on the bed to watch TV. A few minutes later she hears their voices. Are they coming back already? Maybe they want to invite her out with them after all? To ask her if she's excited about finally starting a new job tomorrow. Though as she mutes the TV, she realises their voices are coming through the window. They must be standing downstairs. Jess puts her hands on the frame, about to close the window, but stops when she hears Jacob say, 'I don't want to take sides.'

'It's not taking sides to visit your dad. I've not picked him over Mum,' Haze says.

'Yes, you have.'

There's a pause and Jess imagines Jacob fidgeting, shuffling, perhaps trying to find a way out of the conversation.

'It's nice to have some space,' Haze says. 'Dad is so relaxed about everything. You should come over and visit.'

A car goes past, taking a chunk of the conversation with it. Then Haze laughs and declares, 'Who says the kids stay with the mum anyway?'

'The world,' Jacob replies.

They stop talking and Jess knows she should stop listening, that she should move away from the window and turn the TV back up. It's an invasion of their privacy, something she's never done before. Because she never felt the need to.

Haze murmurs something Jess misses, then says, 'Don't get upset. Hey.'

Jess puts a hand over her mouth, she knows her son is crying. She's not seen him cry since the start of last year, when one of the ponies at the local farm passed away. It was so sad the way he came home, sat on the sofa and burst into tears. Jess didn't even like ponies but couldn't stop herself crying too, rendering herself too useless to offer comfort. At least Haze was there, ready to hand out the hugs and make them both laugh by showing them cat memes on her phone.

'I liked it when everything was normal,' Jacob says, his voice a little wobbly. 'When we lived in our own house and everyone was together.'

'Things change. You do know when I go to uni you'll see me even less than now. This is almost like good training.'

'No, it's not.'

There's some noise in the hallway outside, causing Jess to miss more of the conversation, then it moves on and she hears Jacob say, 'I liked Ben and Harold. Ever since we moved here, we don't see them anymore.'

Why is he bringing this up? While he's asked about Harold

and mentioned wanting to see him in the park, he's not said anything about Ben to her. No one has. Perhaps he wasn't around for long enough to make an impact on anyone. Except her.

She misses him the most in moments like this, when she feels so completely alone. When she's not sure what the right thing to do is. If Ben was here, he would encourage her, he would make her believe that whatever she decided would be the right thing.

Jess backs away from the window, sits on the bed furthest from it and unmutes the TV. It's now on another property programme. Why are there so many of them? All these people having their pick of what they want, moving into chateaux, building their dream homes from the ground up, casually rejecting places because of low ceilings or pokey kitchens.

Why can't she be one of them?

Her phone rings. It's Steadman. Steadman who at the moment is the effortlessly brilliant parent. Sometimes, when he calls to update her on Haze, it's almost like he's gloating. Like he enjoys telling Jess how much happier their daughter is living in his grubby little one-bedroom flat than waiting it out in the hostel with her and Jacob, which is where she should be.

'Hi, Steadman,' she says, accepting that it's better to answer him than be plagued with his long, rambling voicemails.

'I've worked it out,' he says.

'Hello, Jess,' she cracks. 'How are you? I'm fine, thanks for asking.'

'Yeah, sorry,' he says, 'hi and all that. Jess?'

'What?'

'I've worked it out. I've worked out who Braveheart is.'

'Oh God. Is this really what you're calling me for? It's almost eight p.m. I'm in bed.'

'Stop lying, you're not in bed at eight.'

She swings her legs under her covers and pulls the blanket up. 'I am. I start a new job tomorrow – not that it matters, not that anyone cares.' In this moment she's not sure who she feels sorry for anymore. 'The kids have gone to McDonald's to eat Big Macs without me.' She waits for some sympathy from him or a line of questioning that will allow her to offload, but it's as if he's not heard a word she's said.

'Now I've seen his face, I know who he is.'

'You're talking about Ben? How have you seen his face?' Every time Jess has caught sight of a white van, and there are a lot of white vans, she's held her breath, hoping it's him driving. A part of her feels if she can just see him again and look at him properly, there'll be a sign that she's got it wrong somewhere, that's he's not really one of those men who will keep things from her, that will protect bad people.

'You're Facebook friends,' Steadman says.

That was where it started. Ben had sent her a friend request. There wasn't much on his page, a cute photo of him and Harold and a wall with a couple of reposted memes, which Haze had glanced at and said, 'Stuff middle-aged people find funny.'

'Why were you on my Facebook page?'

'You put up some pretty racy photos, Jess. I often take a peek.'

'Do I even want to hear what you've got to say? Actually, no I don't, because I'm not seeing Ben anymore.'

'Already? How comes?'

'Long story. I'm surprised Haze didn't tell you. This was weeks ago.'

'Does it have something to do with school and your brother? Did you already find out?'

She sits up. 'Find out what?'

'The name, Jess: Braveheart. I told you I remembered that name. Then I see his face and boom. The last time I saw him, he had a black eye and a bust lip.'

'I don't think we're talking about the same person. And stop snooping on my Facebook. I'm going to unfriend you.'

'Wait, I'm trying to tell you something. Remember when Dominic beat someone up after school? It was a few weeks before he got expelled for good. That person got smashed up so badly he never came back. That was Ben Braveheart.'

Jess remembers this. Coming home to find Pa sitting on the stairs in the hallway. Elbows on his knees, chin in his hands. She had skipped PE that morning and was convinced he'd found out, that for once *she* was the one in trouble. Pa asked her where her brother was before suggesting she spend the evening at a friend's house.

'Jess?' Steadman asks. 'You remember what I'm talking about?'

'Yeah, I do.'

Jess was only in Year Eight then, but she recalls the murmurs and rumours, the way others gave her a wide berth, and of course how Dominic, so close to sitting the few GCSEs he was entered for, disappeared from school prematurely. He was moved to a behaviour unit, one that required him to leave the house before her to make the journey in. This lasted half a term and then he was back at home, all the time, completely out of the education system. And that's when things really fell apart.

'Crazy, right?' Steadman says. 'Dominic had already been laying into Ben for ages before that. Everyone who remembers says it was pretty brutal. There were always people your brother had it in for, though what I don't get is why Ben Braveheart? He wasn't exactly on anyone's radar. He was quiet. It doesn't make sense why Dominic made such a target out of him.'

Oh Ben. Jess wishes she had given him a chance to tell her the whole story properly.

'Oh God, I feel terrible,' she says.

'Why? It's not your fault. When you and Braveheart were doing whatever you were doing, did he ever say anything to you about this?'

'About my brother terrorising him? No,' she says, her voice cracking.

'Fair enough. I wouldn't have either. Still, I don't get why Dominic picked someone like Ben out. What am I missing here?'

Jess doesn't know what to say.

Chapter Twenty

Ben

'Daddy, feel this tooth.' Olivia pulls her lip down and points to one of her tiny front teeth.

'I don't think I need to feel it.' Ben's skin crawls as the tooth, which is partially hanging on, wobbles.

'Daddy, feel it,' she squeals.

'No. Seriously. I can't.'

'I think it's going to come out soon. I got ten euros last time.'

'Ten euros,' Mum shouts from the balcony doors. 'For a tooth?'

'Gerald says it's inflation.'

Oliva's changed so much, and not only in size. The colour of her skin has deepened, her face has thinned and her eyes have become more pronounced. Then there's all these other little things Ben couldn't have picked up on Skype calls, like how she flutters her arms when excited, gallops rather than walks, and hums when she's eating something she's enjoying.

She's growing up, becoming this tiny bilingual European who eats seafood and uses words like inflation.

Ben stands in the kitchenette and slices up an apple. He washes the plates from dinner and tries not to think about how after tomorrow's dinner he will have to drive her back to City Airport and say goodbye.

'Come here, Prime Minister,' Olivia says as she grabs Harold for an overly enthusiastic hug. 'Daddy, can we listen to music?'

Harold yelps.

'Squid, I think he's had enough hugs.'

'Can we hear "YMCA"?' she asks, making the signs above her head, not quite correctly.

'The Village People?'

'No, silly,' she laughs. 'It's by the Minions.'

'Er, hmm. I don't have their latest album.' Ben scrolls through his music library, trying to find something she might like. It used to be easy, he'd play stuff in the background and eventually she'd end up singing along, but he tried that this morning and she moaned, saying she didn't like Bob Marley because it was too slow and couldn't listen to Daft Punk because it was too 'headachy'. So far, his success rate in finding things Olivia likes is about 50 per cent. She's already turned her nose up at the Aurora dress, which was too 'babyish', as she now liked a French superhero who was part student, part ladybird, and the Olaf snow globe had been completely ignored in favour of Nanny's phone, which Olivia used to take seventy selfies with.

'Do you have the "Macarena" by Miss Piggy?' she asks while trying to balance a shoebox on Harold's head.

'The Europeans,' Mum says, 'they like that sort of music, don't they?'

'Mum, your smoke. Could you maybe take it outside?'

'I'm trying to do that but your balcony is impractical. Why didn't you get a place with a real balcony? Have you been over to your sister's new place yet? She's got a lovely big balcony.'

He sighs. 'I don't need a balcony. I have the park right outside. I said we were going out soon. Couldn't you have waited?'

'I've already been waiting an hour for this little madam to get her shoes on.'

'Olivia,' Ben calls, 'let's take Harold for his last walk, then we'll play some music when we come home. Go and get your shoes on.'

'Okay, I'm going for a poo first,' Olivia announces, dragging Harold by the collar. 'Come with me, Prime Minster.'

Ben tidies the pencils away and piles the colouring books neatly on the table. He feels Mum watch him. 'What?'

'Nice having her around, ain't it?'

He nods. 'Yeah, it is. It's been great.' He sinks down onto the sofa. The last three weeks of having her here have been amazing but also quite tense, with Ben finding himself constantly aware of the time and how it was slipping away at a speed faster than usual. 'You know, I've been thinking about moving,' he says. 'I don't know why I came back here.'

'No, there's nothing for you here, is there?' Mum says, suddenly offended.

'You don't need me, you've got plenty going on in your life.'

'Where would you go?'

'I thought maybe out to the coast. Next to Southend Airport. Then I could be on a flight and in Spain in three hours.'

'You said that about moving back here too, yet you've still not had an invite to fly out there. And is this the long-term plan, that you only get her in the summer holidays?'

'I'm not sure, but it needs to be worked out better than this. Moving back here looked like a really good idea on paper,' he laughs, recalling how everything had fallen so easily into place when he first moved six months ago.

Mum looks over at him and nods.

Ben jumps up and steps out into the hallway. Olivia is singing. He was bemused that while she had changed so many habits, the one of sitting on the toilet singing an unrecognisable song to herself for up to twenty minutes was still a thing.

'What about the Bakker girl?' Mum asks as he comes back in.

'What about her?'

'You're still not over her.'

'I haven't seen or spoken to her since the end of last month. So please stop bringing it up.'

'Not for want of trying though.'

There had been a few occasions recently where Ben had been out with Mum and Olivia, and perhaps he dawdled too long at the front door or looked a little too wistfully across at Wolf's place. Each time Mum caught him doing this she gave him a look of warning and said through a tight mouth, 'Don't do it. It's for the best.'

'I'm glad you're not seeing her. She sounded a right mess, moving house and job every time the wind changed. Though I did tell you: that family, trouble.' Olivia's high note penetrates through the flat. 'She's got your voice.' Mum blows the smoke directly into the room. 'And what would have happened if the brother came back? You'd be expected to get along with him. Pretend there was no backstory.'

'He's not around anymore.' Though Ben doesn't know this. He doesn't know if the family reconciled. If Dominic managed to get them all to forgive him. If he finally changed his ways.

'Families always find each other again,' Mum says. 'No matter what happens or who falls out with who, other people can't get in there and replace family.'

This is so far from Ben's experience of family, and it's not just based on what happened with Shanice. Even with Mum and his older sister, having a relationship with them has always felt like constant effort.

He can't believe how much he misses the Bakkers. Jacob's weird facts, Wolf's food and giving of random books, the warmth and mess of the house and of course Jessica. He had liked everything about her, and now he misses everything about her. How chaotic and beautiful she was. Her loud laugh and the way she'd put a hand on his arm and say, 'Do I look too old to wear this?' when she always looked amazing.

'You should never have got involved with any of them.'

'You know it wasn't my fault, what happened back in school.'

Mum stops and turns to him. 'I've never said it was. I've never blamed you for any of it.'

It's not true. She did blame him. She *still* blames him.

The toilet flushes and Olivia returns, lightening the mood. 'Good poop?' Ben asks.

She smiles and jumps up on the sofa. 'Nannnny, you're going to die from smoking.'

Mum laughs, stubs out her cigarette and chucks it over the rail. 'You're probably right, darling. I should give up.'

Ben rakes his fingers through Olivia's hair and imagines what kind of regular arrangement him and Shanice could come to if he were to move closer. At the moment it is all pipe dreams, though he has found a few good two-bedroom flats online for the same price as he is paying here. It would make such a difference if Olivia had her own room. It would make things more normal when she stayed and would encourage Shanice, so her and Gerald could go and do couples yoga or get matching henna tattoos, whatever it is they do.

'Right, are we ready?' he asks Olivia. 'Last walk of the day.'

While Harold doesn't look quite up for it, Ben knows it's a case of walk now or be woken up at five a.m. by whining.

Olivia excitedly pulls her coat on over her pyjamas and they all walk out to the park. A pair of community support officers share a packet of chewing gum by the gates and keep a close eye on the group of boys gathered around the benches. Mum notices too, so she pulls her doll's house-shaped bag closer and says, 'Why don't they just arrest them?'

'Because you can't arrest people for sitting on a bench,' Ben says.

'We all know what they're doing, Ben.'

'What *are* they doing?' Olivia asks as she makes goggles with her hands and stares at the group suspiciously.

'Thanks,' Ben mouths to Mum. 'Er, nothing. They're just hanging out with their friends.'

'No wonder you want to move,' Mum says. 'This park has always been rough.'

It is rough, that can't be denied, though Ben's come to like it here. He'd even go as far as to say he's made peace with the place itself, the place that ripped teenage him up. He likes the way he knows people's faces. How it's so big and anonymous, yet if you look around properly, you'll see it's always the same people doing the same thing, at the same time. The other dog walkers, the bored mums, the schoolboys having their overly sexual conversations and, of course, the power-walking ladies who now always stop to pat Harold and reiterate how much they want dogs of their own.

Harold sniffs around, then stops to eat some sunflower seeds off the floor by the sundial.

'Why's he still so savage?' Mum asks.

'He's not savage. He's a beagle.'

'Oh, he's giving me dirty looks now,' she says, checking the time. 'I've got to go soon, Ben, it's my girls' night. We've got Groupon vouchers for the Cocktail Club.'

Harold sinks down on top of the seeds and lays his head on the ground.

'Why's he doing that?' she asks.

Ben takes the lead from Olivia. 'Maybe he likes the feel of them or something. One loop and we'll head back.'

Harold stands up and follows Olivia, who walks backwards,

making faces in an attempt to make him move faster. A few steps later he stops again and stares out into the middle distance. It's like he sees something no one else can, his head tilts to one side and stays there.

Mum's still going on: 'Are you listening to me, Ben?'

Ben rubs the underside of Harold's chin.

'Oh, what's wrong with it now? I really need to get going.'

'Nothing. He's old. He's not been around a kid in half a year, I think it's tired him out.'

Olivia gets a branch and dangles it in front of Harold, singing a Spanish song Ben doesn't know.

'He's had enough, Squid, let's stop playing now.'

Ben feels relieved and exhausted when they part ways at the park gate. Originally, he had thought having Olivia around would soften Mum's constant insults and questioning; in reality, it makes her all the more draining.

Back home, he tucks Olivia into her mermaid bed and gets out *The Princess Diaries*, which he's managed to get her into again. She yawns twice before he's even got through a chapter. 'You're tired?'

'No,' she says, closing her eyes.

He switches off the light and leaves her. As he steps into the hallway, he's surprised to see Harold's not eaten his food, even though it's the beef and brown rice one, his favourite. He lies on his side by the bedroom door, as if guarding Olivia. 'You weird dog. She's knackered you out, hasn't she?' Ben says, patting Harold's head.

*

A noise jolts Ben from sleep. It's still dark and his first thought is Olivia. He gets off the sofa, where he had fallen asleep watching a poorly researched documentary about Isambard Brunel, and peeks through the crack of the bedroom door. Her head is surrounded by teddies, and the sound of her light snoring fills the room.

What woke him?

Then, a whimpering. It's Harold.

'Hey,' Ben whispers. 'What are you doing here?'

Harold is lying by the front door on the mat, which is damp at the edge. Ben touches his head but Harold doesn't lean into it like he usually does. His eyes half open then zip side to side before closing again.

Ben gets his phone and calls the vets, which of course at four a.m. is closed. So he looks for the emergency number and calls that, lists the symptoms and hears the word *stroke*. 'You need to bring him in straight away,' they tell Ben. As he hangs up, Olivia pads out, her hair stuck to her head. 'What's happening?'

'Nothing. Go back to bed.'

'Did Harold pee on the floor?' she asks.

'It's okay. Go to sleep. It's not morning yet.'

Harold looks up as Olivia puts her little hand on his head, then closes his eyes. Ben carries Olivia back into the bedroom, where she wriggles down into her mermaid. Her eyes remain wide, a touch frightened. 'Is Harold sick?'

'No. He's fine—' Ben stops. 'He just ate too much dinner and has a tummy ache.'

'Are you sure?'

From outside Harold whines in a way Ben has never heard before. 'Go back to sleep,' he says, squeezing his eyes shut as he leans in to kiss her on the forehead.

He shuts the door gently and says under his breath, 'No. No, no, no.'

He calls his mum's mobile, but it's switched off, and her house phone rings out. She's probably lying in bed with her eye mask and earplugs, sleeping off 2-for-1 cocktails with the girls.

Ben knew something was wrong the minute Harold started acting strangely in the park. Why hadn't he done something about it then, why did he wait till it was too late? And now this: Harold is hardly moving, his breath is shallow. He's dying.

Olivia's coat is hung up on the peg, her sparkly ballet flats by the door. All Ben needs to do is bundle her up and lay her in the van next to . . . next to Harold? Harold who is dying. He can't do this to her. He can't wake her up to have her watch this happen.

In a panic he calls the one person he knows always keeps their phone on at night. The one person he would trust to sit here with Olivia.

Jessica answers after two rings.

There's no traffic on the roads and within seven minutes he's parking up at the pet superstore where the emergency vet is. It's a dull morning and the lights are still on, illuminating the deserted retail car park. He had been here yesterday with Olivia, driving around for ages, trying to find a parking spot so they could go for an overpriced dessert at Creams.

Harold lies with his eyes open and mouth agape, and as Ben reaches across to pick him up, he pauses, as if suspended, because there's nothing in Harold's eyes anymore. He touches Harold's ear, his snout, his chin. Nothing. No flicker of the eyes, no warmth, no movement.

Chapter Twenty-One

Jess

The sound of a door shutting downstairs jerks her from sleep. The time on the oven clock says 6.45 a.m. Jess hadn't intended to fall asleep on Ben's sofa, she had planned on staying upright and awake, should the little girl get up and need an explanation of where her dad was. Where Harold was.

Ben comes up the stairs to the flat and in through the front door. Jess rubs her eyes, gets up and goes out to meet him. Olivia's bedroom door is cracked a little and Jess pulls it to. Olivia hasn't made a peep, but Jess feels her heart swell seeing signs of her all around Ben's flat: the colouring pencils and sparkly ballet flats, the lilac hair slides and browning slices of apple on a plastic plate. It makes Jess pine for Haze, for when she was still her sweet little girl who would leave a trail of herself around the house, her daughter who used to lean into her rather than push away.

Ben nods at her. He's holding some papers in his hand.

'She's sleeping,' Jess says quietly. 'She's not seen me.'

'Thanks so much, I don't know—'

'Stop,' she says, hearing how he's going through the motions, he's not even really here.

'It was a stroke. A big one. At his age, he didn't have a chance.' Ben looks down at the papers and folds them in half.

She steps forward to put her arms around him. The weight of his head sinks down onto her shoulder, though he keeps his arms by his side. 'I'm so sorry, Ben.'

When he pulls away, stands straight and looks past her, there's a split second where she wants to tell him she loves him. It's an insane thought. She bites the inside of her cheek and shakes the feeling away. 'Do you want me to stay? To do anything for you?'

He closes his eyes, 'No. You've done enough. Thanks.'

She swears he sways marginally towards the door, as if indicating for her to leave. Probably he wants to be alone, without her. Also, there's Olivia he needs to concentrate on now. At least he has a distraction.

'I need to get my head straight before she wakes up,' he says.

'Of course.'

'Thanks for helping me out.'

'No problem.'

Jess spends the whole day in a blur, recalling the sparkly shoes, the warmth of Ben's flat and his weight as he leaned on her when he returned home without Harold. By mid-afternoon she feels completely drained, tired and emotional. What can she do for him, how she can make it better? It's not even her place to anymore, they're not friends, they're nothing. The only reason he called her was complete desperation.

With Jacob out at Cameron's, Jess could get away with curling under her blankets and sleeping the rest of the day away, but she knows it will only make her feel worse later on.

Needing a distraction, she heads to Westfield and browses the packed shops. However, once there she feels nothing, no compulsion to spend on any of the things that would usually get her excited, the discounted satin court heels from Office or unnaturally blue-coloured roses from the florist counter on the ground floor. She's not even tempted by a £4.50 honeydew bubble tea. In a quiet corner of John Lewis, she browses bathware and fantasises about having her own bathroom again. It doesn't take long for her thoughts to circle back to Ben. Why can't she stop thinking about him?

Eventually, she gives in and sends him a message. What would be the harm in letting him know she's thinking about him?

> Not working today. If you need me for anything, to watch Olivia, or have a chat, I'm here.

Unusually for Ben, his reply comes instantly.

> Thanks.

Is he sitting with his phone? Maybe Olivia has left already. Perhaps the ex-wife came to collect her. Jess wishes that when

Ben had offered her the chance to meet his daughter and be part of their world she had said yes. She can't even recall what the reason was behind her shying away from being a bigger part of his life, especially when he had become such a big part of hers, eating cobbled-together lunches with Pa and walking with Harold and Jacob in the park.

It's almost five, so even though it wasn't her original reason for coming here, she decides to try and catch Haze at the end of her shift. Jess makes her way along the walkways, passing ladies holding champagne flutes at Searcy's and a stand-off between some overdressed teenagers, a girl from one group calling, 'My friend likes you,' across to the other. When this place opened, Jess couldn't believe how lucky she was, having a bougie shopping centre on her doorstep, but she now realises, if you're here with no money and no friends, it's a really depressing place.

As she arrives at Boost Juice, she spots Haze behind the counter, talking to a colleague while untying her apron. Jess has never seen her daughter at work before. It used to be one of their running jokes that when Haze said she was going to work, she was really just going to drink coffee and take selfies in the Zara fitting rooms, tying in with the fact that Haze, despite being so high-achieving, was openly quite lazy.

'Mum? What are you doing here?'

'I came to see you.'

While Haze had initially kept up with her three nights a week at the hostel, this quickly dwindled. Jess feels like she's hardly seen her daughter at all recently.

Haze stuffs her apron under the counter. 'Did you want a juice? My boss isn't here, so . . .'

'No, no. I was thinking more a coffee?' It sounds like a plea. It *is* a plea.

Haze looks away as if trying to think up an excuse.

'Come on, hun,' Jess tries, 'have one coffee with me.'

Jess gets a good table at the back of a coffee shop, away from the distractions of people-watching. Haze sits opposite and the awkwardness is heavy as she finishes up doing something on her phone then faces Jess expectantly. Her perfect eyebrows knot together. 'You look shattered.'

'I am,' Jess says, rubbing her face and wondering just how terrible she looks. 'Ben's dog had a stroke in the middle of the night and he asked me to go over, to watch his daughter.'

'A stroke?' Haze leans forward and Jess feels bad, as if she's using the tragedy as bait to engage her daughter. 'I didn't know dogs could have strokes. Is he okay?'

'No. He died.'

'Ah. That's horrible,' Haze says, her face softening. At first Haze had gone on about how dogs were smelly, noisy and required too much attention. Though while they were still all at Pa's it wasn't unusual for her to chuck a slimy ball Harold's way or get down on the floor to stroke his belly. 'Ben must be in pieces. He loved that dog.'

Jess nods, feeling as if she might cry. For Harold? No, she doesn't think so; it's Ben she's upset about. It's Ben she wishes she were comforting.

'Yes. He is. Anyway.' She pulls herself upright and distracts herself by taking a sip of the coffee, which is still too hot. 'Harold was quite old.'

'Still, doesn't make it any less sad.'

'No. Course not. I didn't mean that. Gosh, I feel so bad for him.'

'Me too.' Haze leans forward and shakes her head. 'It's so sad. Does Jacob know?'

'Nooo. I'll tell him when he gets home later. I didn't want to message him and ruin his day.'

Haze grimaces. 'And he's past the stage where Ben could just buy another dog and not tell him. Like you used to do with the gerbils.'

'No, I did not,' Jess lies.

For a split second Haze smiles, then looks down as if remembering they're still on bad terms.

'How are you doing, Haze? Did you get to enjoy the summer holidays or did you work here the whole month?'

'I've been lucky, I got a ton of shifts and I enjoy making money,' she says sharply. 'What about you? Are you seeing Ben again?'

'No,' Jess gasps, a little thrown by the question, by the suggestion that this is something even possible. 'I'm not seeing Ben. He called me to help because he had no one else. I was never seeing Ben anyway.'

'Yes, you were.'

'I wasn't. Not really.'

'Mum, you've never gone for a walk in your life and then you move in across from Ben and suddenly you're heading to the park every evening for fresh air. We all knew it.'

'I don't want to talk about this. I hardly see you. I want to talk about *you*.'

312

'I don't want to talk about me. You liked Ben. Jacob liked him too, and Jacob has never liked a single boyfriend of yours before.'

'Ben wasn't my boyfriend. I'm thirty-seven, I don't have boyfriends.' Jess puts her mug down and sits back.

'Poor Ben. I can't imagine him without Harold.'

'Why do you care so much?'

'Because it's sad and Ben's a nice guy.'

'Since when do you have an opinion on Ben?' Jess laughs, though she's slightly annoyed. 'You hardly gave him the time of day.'

Haze reaches in her bag and pulls out a Kit Kat, snapping it in two and passing half over to Jess. 'He wasn't *my* boyfriend, was he? But even I can't deny he's a nice guy. I liked him for you.' She bites the ends off the chocolate and sucks her coffee through it.

Jess shifts, a little uncomfortable with Haze's confession. 'You said Ben was boring.'

'He *is* boring. In a good, steady sort of way. Usually you date these men who are flashy and out to impress, talking about their cars and jobs.' Haze makes a gagging face. 'Now, *that's* boring. Ben was more like boring in his interests. You know he has Sky just for the History Channel? How many documentaries can one person watch about the Second World War anyway?'

Jess laughs. She had made fun of Ben about this, of how deep his interest in conflict, ancient civilisations and industrial revolutions ran.

'Did I make you feel guilty for seeing him?'

Surely Haze knows she did. Though Jess isn't about to tell her.

'I'm sorry,' Haze says. 'That was never about Ben, it was about the timing. There was all this chaos around us and I felt like you weren't that bothered because you were off with him.'

Is this how it looked from her side? That while the family was imploding, Jess was too busy with a man to sort things out? 'I'm sorry if that's how it appeared. I was struggling too. And I guess, on some level, Ben offered a kind of an escape from it all.' She thinks of how one evening, after bickering with Haze over wet towels on the bathroom floor, she had gone over to Ben's. He didn't ask her what was wrong but allowed her to fall asleep on his sofa while he watched a documentary about the Suez Canal crisis.

'You liked him, didn't you?'

'It doesn't matter.'

'It does, Mum. You being happy, it does matter.'

'I'm happy when *you're* happy. You and Jacob.'

Haze narrows her eyes as she dips her last piece of Kit Kat. 'That's such a typical mum thing to say.'

'It's true,' she smiles. 'I'm not perfect, Haze. I didn't grow up with a mum and, it's no excuse, but I'm kind of working things out as I go. I know I've messed up a lot over the last couple of months. I know I've let you down. That I've kept things from you when I shouldn't have. About the job and house and . . .' she trails off.

Haze pouts a little then opens her mouth to speak.

'You can ask me,' Jess says, pre-empting the inevitable.

314

Haze looks down at the table. 'I don't want to know any-thing more about your brother than what you've told me.'

Jess feels her shoulders sink. Thank God for that.

'But I still don't know *why* you kept it from me. Surely you knew I would find out one day?'

'I hoped you never would. I'm your mum, I'm programmed to try and protect you from the world.' Jess reaches across the table and puts a hand on Haze's. She squeezes it. 'I'm sorry. I should have told you about my brother sooner. I regret it.'

Haze shrugs.

They turn inwards, to their coffees, and watch a group of teenagers dressed in oversized nineties jeans and hockey shirts argue outside the E-Sports cafe.

'How's your dad?'

Haze rolls her eyes. 'Training. He reckons he's going to run a 10k this month.'

They both laugh at the same time.

'You like being at his, don't you?'

Haze nods. 'I know you want me to spend more time at the hostel, but it's good for me at Dad's. This past year at college was really intense and I have space at Dad's. I feel I can decompress, you know. There's less pressure.'

Jess smarts. Because to her this translates as Steadman not pushing Haze, not encouraging her to aim high. There's less pressure with Steadman because he's a man who never feels the need to do anything more than the bare essentials.

'So you're going to stay there once you go back to college?'

Haze nods. 'Yeah. Sorry, Mum.'

Jess plasters on a smile and says, 'Of course. I get it.'

They walk out of the shopping centre together and join the mass of people crossing over the advert-splattered walkway towards the bus station. Jess pauses by the screen showing bus arrival times and wonders what happens now. 'What bus do you take to your dad's from here?'

Haze looks down at the ground. 'I was thinking of coming home tonight.'

Home. When did that word start triggering so many emotions for Jess? 'I'd like that. Jacob would too.'

'Cool. Let's go then.' Haze threads her arm through Jess's and they walk on. 'Ah,' she says, 'when we get home, we can also talk about Opa's eightieth. Jacob and I have a plan.'

Chapter Twenty-Two

Ben

September

One of the things that had surprised Ben when he first moved back to East London was the provincial way people left piles of things they no longer wanted at the front of their houses for others to take. Boxes of books, video cassette tapes, casserole dishes, children's school shoes and uniforms. Most of the time the things would disappear within a few hours, though sometimes they would be left, rained on, and end up as more rubbish on the streets.

It took Ben weeks to get here, but when he finally puts Harold's silver feeding bowls and a bag of toys out the front he doesn't feel as wretched as he imagined he would. Maybe he should have done it sooner, perhaps having these things in the flat, bagged up and unused, was more painful in a way.

It's not necessary to leave a note, though he does. *Dog toys, please take.* It sounds a bit pleading. He wishes he'd gone for *Dog toys, help yourself* instead, though he's not going to change it now. He puts the bowls on top of the sign to stop it blowing away, then picks up the latest cluster of Budweiser bottles and laughing-gas canisters from the bottom of the tree.

'Benny Boy?' Wolf calls from across the street. The last time Ben talked with Wolf was brief. He had come over to offer his condolences on Harold, carrying half a banoffee pie. The whole thing with Jessica made everything awkward and Ben wasn't sure what she had told her dad about why they stopped seeing each other.

'How you doing, son?' Wolf calls, eager, and as much as Ben would prefer to wave and head back inside his flat, he feels he kind of owes Wolf a bit more, so he crosses over.

'I've been better,' Ben says.

'Looked better too. Have you not been sleeping?'

'Hmm. It's hard to sleep in this heat. How are *you*? Is the new medicine working out better?'

'Not really, it's making my arse swell up.'

Ben laughs, assured that Wolf is fine, of course he is, even though he's back to living alone.

'I thought you would have got yourself a puppy by now. When Jacob was little, he had these gerbils that used to die all the time. Jess swapped them out for new ones at least four times.'

'Wolf, come on.' He's trying to make light of it, but Ben isn't in the mood.

'Maybe getting a new pup—'

'No.' Why do people keep saying this to him? Like dogs are completely interchangeable. It's not even that Ben didn't see himself getting another dog one day and loving it just as much as he loved Harold. It's more the idea of replacing Harold that bugs him. Harold is irreplaceable. He was also, and this hurt the most, the last part of Ben's old life.

'What about a cat?' Wolf says. 'Personally, they creep me out, but you don't need to walk them.'

Ben sighs and shakes his head. 'I'm moving.'

'No,' Wolf backs away, his eyes wide. 'Why?'

'There's a break clause in my tenancy. I've found a few places in Southend that look good. I can be out by next month.'

Wolf's face falls as he considers this. 'What about your work?'

'I can work anywhere. I've already asked for a transfer.'

'Next month? So soon.'

'Yeah,' Ben says, suddenly panicked about how quickly this is all happening.

'I can't say this is the greatest news I've heard today, though I'm also not hugely surprised.'

Ben nods and wonders if now is a good time to make his excuses and leave before Wolf says something else about Harold, or moving, or Jessica.

An ice-cream van trundles past, playing a shrill version of 'I'm Forever Blowing Bubbles'. Nothing propels him back to his childhood more than this.

'Look at you, smiling,' Wolf says. 'Fancy a ninety-nine?'

'Maybe another time.'

'Am I allowed to ask you about Jess?'

Well, that didn't take long. 'There's nothing to say.'

'There must be. Because when you were having a crisis, it was her you called.'

'Yeah, cause I knew she slept with her phone on.'

'So do I. And I have a house phone.'

'Wolf, I don't have your number, I've never once seen you answer your phone, and Olivia would have been traumatised if she woke up and found you there.'

'Insulting,' Wolf scoffs. 'And?'

'There is no *and*.'

'What happened after? Between you and Jess? I'm happy you're speaking to each other again.'

Ben groans. 'There's nothing going on between us.'

'I don't understand what happened. It can't be because of Dominic?'

Ben looks away. So she *did* tell Wolf.

'The only reason Dominic continues to have an effect on Jess's life is because she lets him. What happened, Ben? The only boyfriend of hers I've ever met before was Steadman. And he was a prick. Then she meets you and she's laughing and smiling, and it all falls apart before it even begins and I'm not sure why.'

'Um, I don't want to talk about this. Especially with you. She's your daughter.'

'I know she liked you. I like you too. What's the issue?'

'You liking me isn't enough to hang a relationship with her on.'

The house phone rings behind Wolf.

'Your phone is ringing,' Ben says.

'Who would call me at this time of the afternoon?'

'Why don't you answer it and find out?'

'It's probably that woman from the bakery. Did I tell you

about her? She came over a few times to watch some films with me. Now she's constantly calling for phone sex.'

Is Wolf winding him up? Ben hangs his head and smiles.

'Ah, it grins. I forgot you had teeth. Do you want me to stop talking about Jess?'

'Yes. Yes please.'

'Is it making you uncomfortable?'

'She's your daughter, so yes, it's making me very uncomfortable.'

'I'm not asking about your sex life with her.'

Ben rubs his head. 'This isn't making you uncomfortable?'

'No. Because I'm not some tight-arse British person.' He knocks Ben on the shoulder and chuckles like he's enjoying himself. 'The kids are on their way over. They want to discuss plans for my birthday.'

'The big one, zero, zero?'

'I was planning on going to the Ministry of Sound,' Wolf says, doing a quick 'big box little box'. 'Are you up for it?'

'What happened to Hollywood?'

'Think I'll save that trip for my next lifetime.'

'That's a shame. You seemed pretty enthusiastic about it before.'

Wolf's face changes and his eyes momentarily squeeze shut. 'It was a lot of money. Money that was needed elsewhere.'

'Jessica?' Ben asks, though he knew she had started a new job. Surely things were beginning to fall back into place for her? When they were together, she had spoken about how adamant she was about not taking any money from Wolf, despite him offering repeatedly.

'Jess isn't my only kid,' he says with a resigned shake of the head. 'You must think I'm an old fool, and I probably am. But despite everything, Dominic is still my son and when he needs something, I give it to him. That's why he came back. He needed money. I had money.'

'Ah, Wolf. I'm—'

Wolf slaps his palms together as if signalling the end of the conversation. 'You sticking around? I'm sure Jacob would like to see you.'

Ben doesn't want to run into the kids. What would he say to them? Would he ask them how their mum is doing? Worse still, he can't bear to hear more condolences on Harold. Especially from Jacob; that would be tough. 'I need to go. I've got some stuff to do at home.'

'Of course you have,' Wolf says in a way that implies he knows Ben has absolutely nothing to do at home, never has. 'Good seeing you again.'

'You too.'

An hour later, just as Ben's getting dinner on, his buzzer goes. His buzzer never goes. He lifts the receiver, expecting a surprise package or, more likely, someone who wanted the downstairs flat. 'Hello?'

'Hello?' a familiar voice. It can't be. Why would it be? 'Hazel?' he asks.

'Benjamin?' she mocks.

'Everything okay?'

'You're going to make me talk out on the doorstep like

this?' There's rustling her end and then Jacob's voice. 'Hi, Ben. Can we come up?'

'Er, um, yeah. Okay.' He presses the entry button, then braces himself. Hazel stomps up, making far too much noise for someone so small, followed by Jacob, who gives Ben a really hard high-five as he passes into the flat.

'How long have you lived here?' Jacob asks as they all enter the living room.

'Six months,' Ben says.

Hazel's mouth drops open. 'Looks like you've literally just moved in. Did you paint the walls this colour on purpose?'

'The colour of these walls is actually the main talking point when people visit me.'

'I like the walls,' Jacob says, giving them a rub, 'they're textured, nice. I'd love a place like this. It's straight up bachelor-approved.'

Hazel's hardness breaks for a moment as a smile appears, then she sets it back to serious and says, 'I'm sorry about Harold.'

Ben nods. 'Thanks.'

Jacob rests his hand on Ben's arm and bows his head. 'I'm sorry too. He was the greatest dog I ever met in my life.' The kid is so earnest, Ben had forgotten how much he liked him.

'So, um, it's a surprise to see you both here.'

Hazel walks towards the balcony. 'This is nice. That you look right over the park. Do you stand here in the evenings and watch people shooting up?'

'Hmm. Do either of you want a coffee or . . .' he trails off, hoping Hazel will fill in the rest of the sentence with what it is they want.

'No thanks, cause you know Jacob is a child, he doesn't drink coffee.'

'I don't drink coffee because it's a drug. It gets everyone addicted and no one can do anything without it. Like you, before college, like this, *zzzz*,' he says, imitating a zombie. 'A hot chocolate works for me.'

Ben notices Hazel's eyes flick over to the Nespresso machine on the counter. 'Oh, you mean like a real coffee?'

'How else do you think I get up at five a.m. every morning?'

'In that case, yes please.'

'I had a lot of Weetabix earlier today,' Jacob announces. 'So I'm going to use your toilet.'

'Are you going to tell me why you're here?' Ben asks Hazel once Jacob has gone.

'Because we're neighbourly.'

He doesn't know how to communicate with someone like Hazel, so busies himself making her coffee and hopes she'll start speaking soon.

'I don't know what you know, but there's been a lot going on recently.'

'Yeah,' he nods. 'I can imagine the whole moving thing is really stressful, especially with your studies and—'

Hazel lifts a hand as if to stop him talking. 'I wasn't talking about me. I was talking about Mum.'

'Oh. Yeah. Of course.'

'The house, the job, Opa, us. This summer has been like

a wall of stress for her. And then, to top it all off, her estranged brother shows up.'

Ben grimaces and hopes she doesn't notice.

'My uncle, Dominic,' Hazel explains.

'Right, yeah. Jessica said he was back.'

'He was, for a little while. He's gone now. There was a lot of complicated family stuff, you know?' Hazel looks down at her fingers, and picks at her orange nail polish.

Ben feels bad for her because, behind all her sass and back-chat, she's still just a teenager who's gone through a ton of crap in a short space of time.

'Mum mentioned you knew him too?' she asks.

Ben nods. 'Kind of, yeah.'

'You know then?'

He almost wants to ask, know what? However, he stops himself. Hazel already looks out of sorts bringing this up, her usual brash confidence a little dimmed.

'I never gave it much thought before, why I have an uncle who no one ever sees or talks about. I guess I accepted that families don't always get along. Finding out the real reason was kind of a shock. It's hard to hear there's someone like that in your family. Someone who managed to do things and get away with them.'

'He went to prison.'

She stares him out. 'Only for the things he was caught doing.'

Ben rubs the back of his head. 'I guess.'

'Mum told me it was different back then. That when you

lot were at school, people got away with a lot of things they could never get away with now. Is that true?'

'It was a different time. Though, getting away with things . . . I don't know if I really agree with that. Because there's always some impact with whatever you do. Even if you think you got away with something and it didn't affect anyone, it can still have consequences, follow you around, come back to confront you at a later stage.' He's no longer talking about Dominic and knows he should stop.

Jacob comes out of the bathroom, smiling widely. 'I like that soap in your bathroom. Smell this.'

Hazel whacks his hand away. 'I don't want to smell your hands. Get off.'

'What were you two talking about?' he asks.

Hazel looks again at Ben, and as if snapping back into character says, 'We were talking about how Ben is the world's slowest barista.'

'Sorry,' he says, walking over and handing her the coffee and Jacob a hot chocolate.

'Look at this,' Jacob says, pointing to the mug, 'cream and everything. Living my best life here. Did you ask him yet?'

'Ask me what?' Ben says.

'Why did you and Mum split up?' Jacob asks the question so plainly that Ben feels it break the tension and he laughs.

'You didn't really come up here to ask me about this, did you?'

'Actually, we came to invite you to a party, but more about that later,' Jacob says in his game-show host voice.

'Come on, Ben,' Hazel teases. 'You can tell us. Because

it doesn't make sense. It's obvious you both like each other. Though men always like Mum, that's standard, but the way you like her, it's different. So why did you break up?'

He exhales loudly and thinks how much he would rather talk about the death of his dog than this.

'You should call her,' Hazel demands, and Jacob mimes holding a telephone receiver. 'You know she's pining for you.'

Pining. It gives Ben a little thrill, though he doesn't quite believe it.

'This coffee is amazing, by the way.' She then looks from Ben to Jacob and asks, 'Why is he just standing there? Why isn't he calling her?'

'Don't you find it tiring?' Ben asks. 'Being so bossy all the time.'

Her mouth drops open, cartoonlike. 'I can't believe you just called me bossy.'

'Yikes,' Jacob says, picking up the Olaf snow globe and shaking it.

'You have a daughter. You should be more careful with the language you use. If I was a boy, would you call me bossy? No, you would call me assertive. You would call me confident.'

'You are those things too. But mostly bossy. I'm not being sexist when I say that.'

'You know what, talk to me when your daughter's fourteen and grown men are shoving their numbers at her. When boys only text her to ask for sex pics.'

'That's an inappropriate thing to ask for,' Jacob says. 'Can I go out on your balcony?'

'It's not a real balcony,' Hazel snaps.

'I imagine boys your age are terrified of you,' Ben says.

Jacob laughs. 'Cameron once said Haze makes him forget how to speak English.'

'Cameron's a little pervert.'

Jacob pauses at the doors to the Juliette balcony. 'This balcony is ingenious.'

'Seriously though, what are you going to do about Mum?' Hazel asks again.

Ben wishes he'd never opened the door to them, that he'd switched the lights off and pretended he wasn't in. He doesn't want to be confronted with all this stuff by a pair of teenagers. 'What do you want me to say?'

'Mum's lonely,' Jacob says.

How could Jessica be lonely? She has everything. Her kids and Wolf. While Ben has nothing here. And even though he had felt that way when he first moved here, sitting in this sparsely filled flat, waiting for video calls, it wasn't until Harold died and he felt the absolute silence and absence of another living thing that he felt truly lonely.

'I've never heard so many Taylor Swift songs in my life,' Jacob says dramatically. 'She misses you.'

'I appreciate you trying to help and I'm, well, also really surprised. Still, your mum, she doesn't need another complication, and it's hard to understand—'

'Don't patronise me,' Hazel says. 'I know I'm young, which is exactly why you should listen to me. She likes you and maybe it's more than like.'

'Whoa,' Jacob says, 'you think so?'

She ignores him and says, 'You should go for it.'

'I already tried that. Remember, when I was hanging around pretending to fix taps and buying everyone noodles?'

'While those are fond memories, I was thinking more about when Mum was sneaking out to meet you, coming home smiling ear to ear.'

'It's too late anyway,' Ben says. 'I'm moving out of here next month.'

'What?' Jacob cries. 'Why would you leave this banging flat?'

'Where are you going?' Hazel asks.

'Southend. I've got friends there, work is easy to come by and I'll be close to the airport.'

'You're pretty close to the airport here as well. And you already have a job. As for friends, I'm sure we could work something out,' she says with a smile. Ben's never seen this side of her before, which, while still bossy and intimidating, is also a little bit funny.

'Are you really giving up on her because there's too much drama in our family?' she asks. 'Because if that's the case, I'll tone it down.'

'No, it's nothing to do with you, with either of you,' he says, taking Jacob in.

'Why then?'

'Because I messed up,' he admits. 'I wasn't honest about something from the past, because I didn't want it to change the way your mum saw me now.' He hopes they don't dig more. He's already said too much.

'So apologise and move on,' Hazel says. 'Or maybe you didn't like her as much as I thought you did?'

329

'That's not true. I do like her, a lot.'

Hazel and Jacob look at each other, their expressions completely unreadable. Maybe they're accepting that he isn't right for Jessica after all. It's sweet of them to come over here and push this agenda, but it's all too complicated and messy.

'What do you think, Jacob?' she asks. 'Do we revoke his invite to Opa's eightieth birthday party? Because it's going to be really awkward if him and Mum spend the whole time trying to avoid each other.'

'But that's the point of the party,' Jacob says, making a little heart sign with his hands. 'The party is a way to fix everything. A way to put everyone back together again.'

Chapter Twenty-Three

Jess

'Dad, no,' Haze moans as Steadman steps into the kitchen. 'Why didn't you make more of an effort?'

He's got on tiny blue shorts and a clingy neon-orange sports top marked with sweat. 'I've been running.' He pulls the top from his chest and allows it to bounce back.

'Didn't you understand the theme?' she says, stroking her hair, which is piled high on her head with a little tiara in the style of Audrey Hepburn. 'Even Jacob's made the effort. Can you go home and get changed?'

Jess is too busy blowing up a bag of gold balloons to get involved with this particular argument, but Haze is right. Steadman needs to sort his look out.

'I thought you were doing a little casual drink-up,' he says. 'Not some huge party. I'm embarrassed now.'

'As you should be. Let me look in Opa's wardrobe, maybe I can find you something less revealing,' she shouts as she storms off.

Jess ties a balloon as Steadman looks her up and down. 'You're looking sexy, Jess. All gold like an Oscar.'

'Don't even start. Here,' she throws him a bag of streamers and tinsel. 'Make yourself useful. Help Jacob decorate.'

Pa had insisted on buying tap shoes for the occasion and is getting his money's worth through frequent dance breaks on the wooden hallway floors. Jess checks in on the early arrivals, ensuring everyone has a drink in hand. Pa's friends have really made the effort with the old Hollywood theme. The women are in sparkly dresses and the men in tab-collared shirts, tweed jackets and one even sweating it out in a trench coat. Pa looks especially smart in his tuxedo, and he's had a haircut too, though she does wish he would give up the black dye, he's far too old for it to be convincing anymore.

Back in the kitchen she notices how Jacob and Steadman are working together to hang a garland of golden stars that spells out *Happy 80th*.

'How's school?' Steadman asks him.

'Cool,' Jacob replies, adjusting the battered old trilby he found at the local Sue Ryder shop.

'And you're getting on okay with your studies, finding somewhere quiet to do your homework? I can't imagine living in a room with your mum is very quiet,' he says, looking over at her and winking.

'I do my homework at school. Miss Begum lets me work in the form room.'

'And you're eating properly?'

'Ye-es,' Jacob says.

'Any nice girls on the scene?'

Jess steps closer to them, barging Steadman out the way to get to the fridge. 'Stop it,' she mouths.

Steadman clears his throat. 'These decorations look great, Jacob.'

'They do, don't they?' Jess says. 'Jacob pretty much organised this whole thing himself. Ordered the decorations. Sent out the invitations. Woke me up at six a.m. to go to Lidl.'

'My Young King,' Steadman says, gripping Jacob by the shoulder. 'So proud of you. Especially as you hate parties.'

Jacob stops dead. 'Who says I hate parties?'

The doorbell goes, blasting 'Rule Britannia' through the house. Steadman puts a finger in his ear and grimaces. 'I can't imagine how overwhelming this must be for you. All the sounds and noise and people.'

'I don't hate parties,' Jacob says.

'I remember when you were a kid, if too many people were over at the house, you'd cry. Don't worry though, if it gets too much tonight, I'll step out with you.'

'Are you listening to me?' Jacob snaps. 'I want you to listen to me. I *love* parties.'

'Do you? What about all the music though? And your cochlear? I thought if there was too much noise it would aggravate you or something.'

'If there's too much noise, I just take it off,' Jacob says, pulling off the external processor.

Steadman looks over at Jess for help, so she pretends to be deeply involved in arranging more of Pa's special recipe devilled eggs on a platter. It's not her place to keep getting involved in their relationship.

'There's not a party this year I haven't been to,' Jacob says, reattaching his processor. 'The deaf group barbecue last month was lit, as was the Science Fair after-party – that was crazy! And don't even get me started on Cameron's fourteenth birthday. Oh boy.'

'Oh, okay,' Steadman says. 'I didn't know this about you.'

'Well, you do now,' Jacob says.

The doorbell goes again and more voices fill the hallway. 'Jacob,' Jess says, 'exactly how many people did you invite to *this* party?'

Jacob and Cameron stay close to each other, looking around the busy kitchen with a mixture of horror and wonder on their faces.

'Let me ask you again,' Jess says as she stress-pours another tray of drinks. 'How many people did you invite?'

'A few,' Jacob answers.

'What's a few?'

'Cheese Louise,' Cameron says. 'These people drink more than my parents.'

'Stop staring,' Jess tries. 'Can you boys help me? Take through some of those samosas, check there's enough toilet roll, cut up some baguettes. Something. Is it just me or is it very hot in here?' She throws her arms up and checks the windows are opened. 'And where's your dad? Where's Haze?'

'Yeah, where is Hazel?' Cameron asks, taking an imaginary puff on the fake cigarette in the corner of his mouth.

'Why is no one helping me?' The last time Jess saw them, they were playing chess in the garden, Haze breaking into a twerk each time she outsmarted someone.

The old people are getting drunk. Or drunker. Pa can be heard through the walls, tap dancing and shouting lines from his favourite films in a terrible American accent before descending into a hacking laugh.

For the fifth time this evening, someone asks Jess about her housing situation, enquiring whether she's working or on benefits, if the council are helping or being useless. It's draining.

Steadman comes in, also drunk, and sweating through the white shirt Haze forced him to wear, which is slightly too short in the arms. He grabs Jacob and shouts, 'Come on, boy, show these people what your pops gave you.'

Jacob squirms away, 'You're not ready to see me dance.'

'What? The party animal doesn't dance?'

'No, I *do* dance, I just don't want to upstage everybody here.'

Jacob signs something to Cameron and they both burst out laughing before high-fiving each other.

'What was that about?' Steadman asks Jess, slightly wounded.

'I don't know,' she says. 'Just keep an eye on them, please. I've already had to confiscate gin from Cameron twice this evening.'

'Jess, will you come into the living room and dance with me?' He wiggles his hips in her direction.

'No. Seriously, no, because I just got groped by a seventy-five-year-old and I'm not in the mood.'

'Come on, Jess, remember when we used to go out back in the day, those all-night raves?'

'No. I don't.' She wants to be angry at Steadman for not helping, at Haze for disappearing on her and at Jacob for running away with this idea in the first place. But then, Jacob looks so happy she reasons that perhaps the house being trashed by a gang of drunk pensioners is a small price to pay for happiness after such a rough few months.

'Steadman, get off.' She bats him away till he finds two old ladies to dance with in a way that is both cute and terribly inappropriate.

A glass smashes in the hallway and Wolf yelps in delight. A bald man shakes his head. *'Betrunken,'* he laughs. 'Sorry, I said I think he's had enough.'

I know what you said, Jess snaps back in German.

Haze slides up next to her. 'How are they all this drunk already?'

'There you are. Where have you been all evening?'

'Schooling these OAPs at chess,' she says with a snap of her fingers. She's been drinking too then.

Jacob squints at his phone, then holds it in front of Haze's face.

'More guests? Tell them the party is over,' Jess says.

'It's Ben,' Jacob says.

'Ben? Why do you have Ben's number?'

'I send him clips,' Jacob answers.

'Clips?'

'Yeah, like funny dog videos and stuff.'

'That's why he's messaging you? About a dog video?'

'No. He wants to come over but . . .' Jacob stops and looks at Haze as if for back-up.

'You're on your own here,' she says. 'I already tried, remember.'

'What are you two talking about?' Jess feels paranoid, not knowing what's going on. She can't deal with any more surprises tonight.

Jacob wipes his nose and looks down at the floor. 'He wants to see Opa but he's trying to avoid you.'

'Oh, right then.' She turns back to the table, clearing away scrunched gold napkins and spent party poppers.

'Mum,' Haze says, putting her head on Jess's shoulder, the smell of wine on her breath. 'I think you need to give him another chance.'

'Hun, it's not about chances. It's about timing.' It reels off her tongue like an overused catchphrase. 'And maybe you should stop drinking as well. A glass of water, perhaps?'

'Ben's so nice,' Jacob says.

'Yeah,' Haze agrees, pouring herself another glass of white. 'Plus, he's moving away, did you know that?'

'Yes, I did. I heard.' Pa had told her the other day over lunch and she felt the way he watched her closely after saying it, as if trying to gauge her reaction. What was he expecting? That she'd run over there and beg Ben not to leave? It was bad enough that a tiny part of her was even considering doing it.

Haze and Jacob both look at her, staring until she feels completely ambushed. Never have her children expressed an opinion on a man like this, never have they even taken an interest in anyone she's dated before. 'I don't need a man right now,' she says defensively. 'I'm trying to cut down the amount of drama in my life.'

'Don't you want some joy as well?' Haze asks. 'Some fun. Literally the only time you've looked truly happy in the last few months was when Ben was hanging around, gazing up at you with his big blue eyes and agreeing with everything you said.'

Jess turns away to the sink to get Haze a glass of water. What is this she's feeling? Apart from hugely exposed. 'You're right,' she says when she turns back around. 'He is nice and that's why I think he should have someone else. Someone who's got the time for him, someone who's going to appreciate him. It's not me. Not right now anyway.'

Jacob's typing.

'Jacob, are you paying attention? You didn't invite him over, did you?'

Jacob raises his hands in surrender and takes a few cautious steps away.

'Text him back,' Jess says. 'Tell him the party's over.'

'Mum, he'll be able to hear this from across the road.'

What's the harm? She likes Ben, she really does. But this is so far from the right time to hook up with a guy, to feel what she felt when she was with him for those few short months. It's the kind of feeling that could grow and grow. Or perhaps it has already and it's too late. Her flight reflex kicks in and she knows there's no way she can stand across from him tonight and make small talk.

Haze starts a conversation about university in broken

German with some older ladies, who ooh and ahh at her despite the fact her tiara is now lopsided. Meanwhile Jacob and Cameron look shifty in the corner of the kitchen as they drink from their plastic cups and smirk. Ah, alcohol. Jess should intervene, but then there's the tune of the doorbell. Ben? She needs to get away and fast.

She runs upstairs and ducks into her old bedroom, which is packed with the things they couldn't store at the hostel. She squeezes herself onto the bed, falling between bin liners filled with towels and linens, and the vacuum-suction bags with their winter coats.

Jess isn't even sure what she would say to Ben if she saw him again. As much as she misses him, it still doesn't sit right with her that he kept that kind of secret. Especially when she never imagined he was that sort of man. From early on he had spilled so much of his life to her. Things that weren't exactly sexy to know either. He had spoken to her plainly about the falling apart of his marriage, how issues with his ex-wife had damaged his confidence, how he pretty much had a breakdown when it all happened. Jess can't think of a time a guy has been so open with her. In all those years with Steadman, they never really opened up and spoke like that.

There was something special about Ben, yet she'd pushed him away. Not so much because he made a mistake at sixteen, more because of his link to Dominic. For Jess, anything linked to Dominic was also linked to bad feelings, to trauma and uncertainty. The very last things she wanted to invite into her life.

Someone is coming up the stairs and Jess pulls herself off the bed and straightens out her dress, ready to go back out and face the party. The door handle turns and Pa falls in. '*Liebling*, why are you hiding up here?'

'Oh, just having a break. It's so hot down there.'

At some point Pa has undone his shirt, one button too many, making him look more dishevelled than usual.

'What are *you* doing up here?'

'I left a small bag of weed in here last week,' he says, sliding open the drawers and tossing things around.

'I didn't realise we were already at the getting-stoned stage of the party.'

Pa stops and leans on the wall, closing his eyes.

'Are you okay?'

'I'm wonderful. This is a wonderful party.' He widens his arms for her to step into them. 'Thank you.'

It's weirdly emotional, being in her old bedroom and getting a big bear hug from her drunken dad. 'I gave him the money,' he slurs. 'All of it. So you don't have to worry about him turning up again, you don't have to worry about the kids spending time here. He got what he came for.'

From downstairs, there's singing, hooting and again the patriotic doorbell.

Jess holds him tighter, the pair of them swaying a little.

'Oh dear,' she says, pulling away, not wanting the perfect eye make-up Haze did earlier to run. 'We should get back to the party.'

'I thought you would be relieved?' he says.

'I'm . . .' What is she? It's hard to know how to feel about

340

any of this. 'Dominic always gets what he wants in the end,' she says. 'Doesn't he?'

'You can as well.'

'Really?' she scoffs.

'Yes,' Pa says. He stops in the doorway, turns to Jess and says, 'Stop using him as an excuse for things not going your way.'

Chapter Twenty-Four

Ben

The living-room windows are cracked open and run with so much condensation that Ben can't make out a single face inside, just a blurring of laughing, colourful figures. The front door is ajar and he slips in unnoticed. The shelves in the hall have been cleared, more than half the books are gone, along with all of Wolf's little trinkets. Ben stalls at the photo of Jessica collecting her certificate. How young she looks there, how proud. Though when he had asked her about that day, she struggled to remember getting a prize at all. It was Wolf who had framed it and put it in a place the neighbours would see when they popped by for a chat. Possibly as something to show everyone that the Bakker family weren't all bad.

Ben sticks his head in the living room, where a group of old people sit on sofas and chairs arranged in a circle, drinking. A woman in an orange kaftan stands in the middle, swaying to the music, which is something Germanic, the kind

342

of schlager pub music Wolf once played to Ben, explaining how it was reserved for louts and a certain level of merriness.

'*Verrückt* party,' a lady shouts at him.

'Oh, no. Sorry, I don't understand.'

He should have come earlier but never thought a party full of the elderly would hit this level of messiness before nine p.m. He only planned on showing his face anyway, a quick in-and-out, reducing the possibility of bumping into anyone. Of seeing Jessica.

'You came,' Jacob calls as Ben walks into the kitchen. 'Yes!' he pumps his fist before turning back to Hazel. 'I told you he'd come.'

'Bit last-minute, aren't you?' Hazel says. 'Not like you had far to travel.'

'I didn't know what to wear.'

'I see you settled for the middle-aged dad at a festival look.'

'I'm James Dean,' he tries because, despite Hazel's face, Ben did spend a good half-hour considering what to wear.

'Good try,' Hazel says.

A man in a gold bow tie cuts between them at the door, nods to Ben and asks, '*Noch ein Bier?*'

'Why are people speaking German to you?' Jacob asks.

'I have no idea.'

Hazel laughs. 'I'm not surprised. I've always thought you had this Hitler's Youth look about you.'

It's almost as if now she's shown him her softer side, she's got to act even harder to compensate, to remind him they're not friends, nothing's changed. The three of them move towards the big table, which is pushed against the cupboards.

A boy about Jacob's age, and also wearing a cochlear implant, slurs hi through a mouthful of crisps.

Ben's surprised they got so many people to come so last minute. He himself only received Jacob's message last week and, as much as Ben hated parties, especially ones with the possibility of running into a woman who dumped him, it was hard to say no to Jacob, the world's most endearing teenage boy.

'Jacob, how many people did you invite to this party?'

'A few,' he answers. 'I didn't know this many of Opa's friends were still alive. They can really eat too,' he says, looking down at the empty plates, where there was nothing left except grease-smeared napkins and spilt chilli sauce.

Hazel dumps a bag of frozen chips on a tray and crawls under the table to reach the oven. When she comes back out, she says, 'I've got to do something to help them soak up the alcohol. They're not even using mixers.'

'Is this really all it's going to be?' Jacob asks his sister. 'They're just going to keep drinking and drinking till it's all gone?'

She rolls her eyes.

'They're old,' Ben says. 'What do you expect them to be doing? Getting up and flossing?'

The boys both laugh and Jacob's friend says, 'Yeah, flossing, cause it's 2018.'

'Rule Britannia' chimes through the house and a collective, good-natured boo rises from the crowd. Hazel tips her head back and huffs. 'How many more?'

'Opa, look who's here,' Jacob calls as Wolf staggers into

344

the kitchen, a bottle of something in each hand. He hugs Ben hard in the same way Ben's own dad used to when half-cut at parties, and Ben almost expects him to turn to the room and shout proudly, 'This is my son.' Though when he pulls away, he sees it's of course not his dad.

'How you been, Romeo?' Wolf asks.

'Good. You're looking very rakish this evening, Wolf. Happy birthday.'

'Thanking you, thanking you. I'm happy you're here.'

'Opa, let me relieve you of some of this alcohol,' Hazel says, taking the bottles from his hands and stacking them on the counter.

Wolf kicks at the back door and beckons Ben to join him. 'Come, I can't hear a thing in here.' Outside he pulls a bottle of beer from each pocket. 'Never underprepared,' he says, opening them against the table.

'You got the fence fixed.'

'I told you she'd do it. She couldn't resist the old charm, you see.'

Ben grabs the top of the fence. It's lower than he would have chosen and the paint job is pretty slapdash. 'There's a good paint sprayer at work. I could ask one of the guys to pop over and finish this off for you?'

Wolf shakes his head. 'Stop. Stop. Here you go, drink. This is a good idea. Fresh air will sober me up.'

'You really think there's enough air out here for that?'

'Oh, you're in comedian mode tonight?'

He's missed Wolf and looks over at the old man. 'You cut your hair.'

Wolf runs a hand over the short sides. It suits him. 'Yes, I've gone for a younger style.' He leans in towards Ben and says in an alcoholic whisper, 'Though the colour is still from a bottle.'

'I would never have guessed.'

Wolf laughs and mumbles, 'Arsehole. Though I wish you weren't leaving.'

'I have to. It was a terrible idea for me to move back here. And my mum, she doesn't need me. She's got her own thing going on. Her own life.'

Ben had been surprised by how much Mum protested at the idea of him leaving, claiming she was just getting used to having him around again. Yet it never felt like she wanted to spend that much time with him and, to be honest, he was starting to feel the same way. Mum was definitely easier to love at the end of the phone than in real life.

'Is there anything that could make you stay?' Wolf asks, a glint in his eye.

Ben shakes his head because there really isn't anything that could make him stay. He's done with being here.

'If only Jess would take that stick out of her arse—'

'It's too late. Anyway, I don't want to keep you out here, away from your party. I only came to briefly show my face and to say bye.' He puts the bottle on the table. It's not a big house, it won't be long before he runs into Jessica, and he'd really rather not. What would he even say to her?

'Come over tomorrow,' Wolf says as if sensing the unease. 'I'd much rather say goodbye to you without all these other pricks around. I'll make you breakfast one last time.'

'Breakfast? You really think you're going to be able to do that with the hangover coming your way?'

'Behave yourself. I've been in training for years, I don't get hangovers. I'll be up by dawn, as usual.'

The back door opens and a man and woman, who look even older than Wolf, stagger out, groping each other and laughing.

'Get a room,' Wolf says to the couple. 'Okay, son, I'll let you escape this sordid bacchanal.' He widens his arms and hugs Ben again. 'Don't forget: breakfast, bright and early.'

'I'll see you at noon,' Ben calls over his shoulder. As he walks through the house, he can't help but look inside the living room briefly. Jacob and Hazel are now sitting on the window ledge, pressed together, caught between laughter and deep embarrassment at the old people's behaviour. These two are so close, the whole family is. What made Ben think he could slide in and be part of it? He was never going to be anything more than one of Wolf's friends and, judging from the turnout of this party, there's more than enough of those.

There's not much to box up back at the flat. The furniture came with the place and he didn't buy as much as he thought he did. He puts the Aurora dress and Olaf snow globe in a bag for the charity shop, along with the tasselled cushions from Mum. The little plants look like they're close to death, though maybe someone smarter than him would know how to bring them back to life. He takes them downstairs to line up on the wall, the same way he did with Harold's things last month.

His neighbour walks up. 'Evening,' she says. She's wearing

a pink silky scarf and a long black mac, which reveals nothing, though Wolf is right, she would look sexy in a bin liner.

'Hi,' he replies.

'Ah, succulents. Are they yours?'

'Yeah. They were. I'm moving out on Tuesday. Having a clear-out.'

'That's a shame. You're the quietest neighbour I've ever had.'

'Really?' Though why is he surprised? He doesn't play loud music or have people over. He doesn't even have a pet anymore. His existence since he moved to this flat has been so minimal, it's amazing that his neighbour has even noticed him.

'They're not in the best state,' he says, pressing the damp soil of one. 'Not sure why though, I watered them loads—'

'Yeah, that's the problem, they're drowning,' she says curtly. 'You really don't want to keep them? Take them to your next place?'

'Nah. I give up. Do you want them?'

'Really? Yes please. Well, this is nice to come home to after a shitty night. I don't mean about you moving, I meant more about the plants.'

'Tough time at work?' he hazards.

'Yeah.'

'What is it you do anyway?'

'I'm a chiropractor.'

'Chiropractor?' he laughs. 'Oh, I never would have guessed. I thought you worked from home.'

'I do reiki at home for my private clients. Though most days I work out of a spa in Liverpool Street, and that's my bread and butter. Thanks for these.' She gathers up the pots and looks behind her, towards the noise from Wolf's place. 'I hope that doesn't go on too late. I've got an early start tomorrow. Anyway, goodnight, and if you ever need to de-stress, you know where I am.'

'Thanks. Goodnight.'

He laughs and wants to tell Wolf right away – it would make his night. Ben considers popping back across, but no, it can wait till tomorrow. Then the front door opens and Jessica steps out. She seems surprised to see him, standing out there on the other side of the road. She crosses slowly and Ben feels his heart beat so loudly he's embarrassed.

'You didn't stay long?' she says.

'No.'

So instead of doing this awkward kind of chat at the party, she's come over here to stand out in the cold and do it on the street.

'Why didn't you tell me?' she asks.

'Tell you what?' That he's crazy about her.

'That you're moving away.'

'Oh.' Yeah, that.

'Why? I thought you liked it here.'

'I do. Sort of. But I also have a break clause, and I found a great flat in Southend. I need two bedrooms.'

'You couldn't find a flat with two bedrooms in the whole of London?' She looks so pretty in her gold dress. He's not really seen her dressed up like this before. Getting dressed up for dates being one of the stages they missed out on. Why was that? Was it his fault because he never took her anywhere?

Or because there was so much else happening? Whatever the reason, he regrets it now.

She wraps her arms around herself. 'The kids said you couldn't stay at the party.'

'No. I, um, have packing to do, and I'll see Wolf another time. Lot of people there though, great atmosphere. Jacob did well to organise it.'

'Jacob, yes. I'm going to wait until tomorrow before I work out how to kill him.'

'Yeah, it's a lot of people in a small house.'

Jessica smiles. What is she doing? Why now? It's too late for this.

He's leaving.

'They're all so drunk,' she says.

'I noticed.'

'When I left, Pa was watching *Shanghai Express* and crying.'

They laugh a little. She looks so cold, she won't be able to stay out here for much longer. He wants her to turn away and go back into the house, but he also really wants to put his arms around her. 'Jessica, you should go back to your party.'

'I'm trying to apologise to you. To say I'm sorry for not getting the whole story. For being so harsh about something from so long ago.'

'No. You don't have to. I should have been honest about things as soon as I realised.'

They both nod and look away, anywhere except each other.

'It's cold,' she says. 'I can't stand out here.'

'I know. Go back.'

'No, I want to come up.'

What is she suggesting now? No strings attached? No way. He would only want more. 'I've got packing to do.'

'Why, have you suddenly accumulated a ton of stuff?'

He looks down, forcing his smile away.

'Ben, I'm trying to tell you that I really don't want you to move away, that I, more than anything else right now, wish you would stay. Stay here.'

'I can't. It's too late.' The transfer at work had gone through seamlessly, as had finding and signing a contract on a new place. It literally was too late. Even if it wasn't, what would be the point in staying?

'Ben, let's talk about it properly. Upstairs?'

Breaking eye contact with her is all he has, though it's not enough, he can still feel her gaze burning into him, making him question every quick decision he's made over the last few weeks.

'Please,' she tries, and there's something in her voice that forces him to look at her. 'Please, don't send me back to the Germans.'

Chapter Twenty-Five

Jess

October the following year

Whenever Haze comes *home*, she complains about the distance, the lack of online delivery options for food: 'Chinese and Indian only, what is this, the nineties?' To the fact that she needs to get a cab from the station. There's a perfectly good bus that Jess and Jacob get, yet Haze refuses, claiming she once waited an hour for it. A slight exaggeration, Jess thinks.

The walk from the station is only twenty minutes. It was fifteen minutes back in London. So why does it feel so different here? So much further? Is it because of how little you see as you make the journey? The lack of shops, people, life?

It was hard when they first moved. Jess found she had to slow down, quite literally. She never realised that she walked faster than others until the new friends she made at the women's Zumba class pointed it out. *You're such a Londoner*, they teased, as if Jess needed to be reformed.

There's community here, of course, but Jess has found she's

had to work at finding it. There are no friends she grew up with on the next street, no people she's known her whole life saying *morning* and no old school friends offering up their properties to her without a contract or deposit.

When Jess goes shopping on a Saturday, or into the town centre as they call it, she doesn't yet recognise all the streets or shops or drunks on the corner, because they have those here too. Nor does she share in her new friends' recollections of what once was there, *Remember where the Woolworths used to be?*

As soon as she left London, she found herself longing for things only her hometown could offer, like Oxford Street, the tube and the overpriced chips with pink mayo from her favourite food stall. She would occasionally wake up on a Friday morning and feel gutted that she lived almost two hours away from the Tate Modern even though in the last decade she'd probably only been there twice. Sometimes she saw a Leicester Square film premiere on the news and it put her in a bad mood because never again would she be out shopping and wander into crowds of screaming people and celebrities on a red carpet. Again, this wasn't something that happened often when she did live in London, but it at least felt like a possibility. Here, the most exciting thing to happen is a new branch of Greggs opening.

Admittedly, while she misses the variety, risk and unpredictability of London, she also enjoys the smugness that comes with being one of those who got away, who escaped the knife-crime capital with its headache-inducing crowds and huge prices of everything, from meals out and pints to council tax and haircuts.

'You know a cab here is cheaper than the bus?' Haze says. 'So ridiculous.'

Apart from buses, which *are* ridiculously expensive outside of the city.

'And the cab driver talked at me the whole way,' Haze adds. 'Did you really need to tell him I'm at Oxford?'

Jess pops a slice of cucumber in her mouth. 'I tell everyone you're at Oxford.'

Haze rolls her eyes, though she doesn't really mind. In fact, if they meet someone and Jess doesn't mention it, she feels Haze smart beside her, and begin looking for a way to wedge it into the conversation somehow.

Jess can complete the majority of theatre programming work from home, and when she does have to travel into London on Thursday and Friday evenings, she gets to see the city at its best. She loves getting to walk fast and tut at people standing on the wrong side of the escalators, but equally she's also come to love the way she can exhale as the train empties out, the stops get further apart and she finally reaches her station.

Home.

It felt like her life was the same for so long, her bobbing along in her lane, and then in a short space of time everything changed. It's only now, over a year on from that summer of complete freefall, that she feels things are beginning to settle down.

When the council first showed her this house she was in disbelief about how perfect it was. How much space there was for everyone and everything. Jacob loved that he would have his own room again and Haze loved the fact it had a separate bathroom, which she claimed would only be for her. Jess was overjoyed with all of it, especially the cupboard space for all her shoes and a kitchen with a strange amount of worktop space for Pa to pile all his crap. The only thing that wasn't perfect was the location.

'I don't want to leave London,' Jess had complained to Cat-Tie Tim. 'It's my home.' This was what she thought, until she realised that home could be anywhere and also, more pressingly, she didn't actually have a choice. She had no family left in East London, her friends had been scattered too, each of them moving further and further away as their families grew and they needed more space. Those at the mercy of local authority housing were split into two clear groups: a handful of lucky ones who had been able to cling onto council places in Stratford, and those who, like her, had allowed themselves to be moved away. 'Swept away to make way,' as Pa once put it during one of his outbursts.

But the truth was, it worked for their family. They were happier and there was less financial pressure.

Recently she'd gone back to Stratford. Taking a walk with Precious and the little one in the park, they'd passed Pa's house. It looked so different. Someone had restored the Victorian green tiles at the front door, as was the trend, and when Jess got closer, she noticed two doorbells. The house, which last year was occupied by Pa and a few hundred books, was now home to two sets of people.

Jacob pulls his hood up and shivers. 'This is the coldest autumn day on record. We're going to get hypothermia if we sit outside.'

Haze zips up her jacket, which is cropped and leaves some of her midriff exposed.

'Are you going to be warm enough in that?' Jess asks.

'You know me, Mum, I'm hot regardless.'

Jess takes the salad bowl and pushes the back door open.

'I hope that's not that cheap rubbish from Aldi,' Pa calls as they come out. 'Because I do still know how to make a salad. I am capable of such things. Ben, do you remember that anchovy salad I made the other week? They didn't like it, complained and called the Deliver Ooh people instead.'

At the end of the garden Ben disappears behind the trampoline. When he stands up again, his face is red.

'Ben?' Jess calls. 'We're going to eat now.'

He stomps over. 'Why is she still digging holes everywhere?'

'I don't know, hun. She's a puppy.'

Haze ducks and catches Benazir in her arms. The beagle flips herself tummy side up, her little paws pointing in the air.

Ben had warned Jess that beagles were a lot of work, he had warned everyone. Yet all she could remember was Harold lazing around, occasionally barking and sometimes having a sniff at the bins. But then Harold was a pensioner. Benazir is like having a baby, if that baby was completely mobile and marginally insane. At night, she leaps into their bed, burrowing her warm little body under the covers, her nails scratching Jess's legs while Ben moans, *I told you this would happen.*

'Hello, you little rebel,' Haze coos, 'you crazy little mutt, you naughty little dog.' Benazir whines and leans up to sniff Haze's face. 'Okay, you stink.' She lets her down again. 'Go play with Oli.'

Olivia sits shivering on a chair, unacclimated to alfresco eating in under twenty degrees, while Jacob fills her with Haribo.

This is the fourth time she's been over and Jess is feeling more comfortable in her own role this time around. She knows not to step in too much, as Ben has a particular way of raising his girl, which is remarkably similar to Steadman, in that Olivia rules. But then, as Pa says, Jess rules Ben. 'He's just that kind of man,' Pa explained. 'He's only happy when he's running around, helping everyone out.'

Jess recently saw a documentary about blended families; she didn't know it was a thing. These two people going on about how hard it was to bring their children together to combine rules and traditions. Though they hadn't tried doing it when one of the kids spent most of the year in another country and the woman had a fully dependent parent living with them.

Sometimes it all feels impossible. Still, they were managing. Taking things very slowly, each day as it came.

Jess puts the salad bowl down in front of Pa and adjusts his blanket.

'Yes,' Haze whoops. 'I got the speaker to work.'

Jacob and Wolf exchange a look and Pa crosses his chest. 'Again? Really?'

'Come on, even Ben's a fan now.'

Ben puts a finger on his lips as Jess laughs. He didn't want Haze to know that he fell asleep as soon as the curtains went up.

'I'll take my processor off if you play it one more time,' Jacob moans.

Jess shakes her head as Haze puts on *Hamilton*.

357

Acknowledgements

To my agent, Eve White, thank for you continuing to be such a positive presence and advisor. Also to Ludo Cinelli.

To the brilliant team at HQ, my editor Manpreet Grewal, as well as Claire Brett, Lucy Richardson, Melanie Hayes and Lisa Milton, thank you so much for all that you do.

Also thank you to Donna Hillyer and Anne O'Brien for additional editing, and Emma Rogers for another fantastic cover.

A huge thanks to Alex McMullan-Bell and the students in the ARP at Eastbury Community School for answering my questions. More widely, lots of love to everyone over in the primary school, thank you for supporting me as I bounced between teaching and writing. By the way, you all work too hard.

I'm lucky enough to know and be inspired by many amazing writers, so thank you to everyone at Gill's Salon and the HQ authors.

A special shout out to Matthias Mueller for checking my German and for also being an NHS superstar.

Thank you to all the book clubs, booksellers and

Bookstagrammers for their continued support and for making sure my TBR pile continues to be ridiculously undefeatable.

There's a reason why so much of *These Streets* happens within the confines of a postcode, and it's because most of it was written during the pandemic. For months at a time, home and the local park became my entire world. For making these times easier I must thank my family, friends and the bubble of my community, for all the doorstep visits, socially distanced chats in the park, videocalls, WhatsApps and walks, so many bloody walks.

Finally, to everyone who has shared their housing story with me, I thank you for your openness.

Turn the page for an exclusive extract from the heartfelt and compelling debut by Luan Goldie, longlisted for the Women's Prize for Fiction...

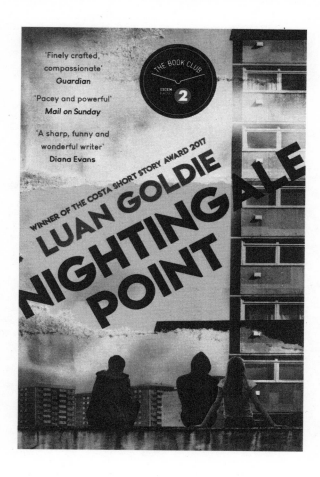

SATURDAY, 4 MAY 1996

The evacuation began this morning. No sooner had the bins been collected than the hundreds of residents from the three blocks that make up Morpeth Estate began streaming away in their droves.

Bob the caretaker sat in his cubbyhole on the ground floor, telling anyone who would listen that 'it's only a heatwave if it goes on ten days'. But no one listened, instead they asked when the intercom was getting fixed, if he knew the lifts were out and what he was planning on doing about the woman on the third floor who kept sticking a chair out on the landing. Moan, moan, moan.

Bob stubs out his cigarette and looks up at the grey face of Nightingale Point, smiling at the way the sun illuminates each balcony, every single one a little personal gallery, showcasing lines of washing, surplus furniture, bikes, scooters, and pushchairs. Towards the top a balcony glints with CDs held by pieces of string; a few of the residents have started doing it and Bob doesn't have a clue why. He must ask someone.

Mary is amazed at how well it works. Who would believe that hanging a few CDs on the balcony stops pigeons from shitting on your washing? She had seen the tip on *GMTV* and immediately rushed to the flat next door to ask Tristan for any old discs. His music was no good anyway, all that gangbanging West Coast, East Coast stuff.

Mary wraps a towel around her hair. Her husband could show up any minute and the least she can do for him, after being apart for over a year, is not smell of fried fish. She switches on the TV, but the picture bounces and fuzzes. She doesn't even try to understand technology these days, but heads next door to get Malachi.

Malachi sits behind a pile of overdue library books and tries to think of a thesis statement for his *Design and the Environment* essay that is due next Friday, but instead he thinks about Pamela. If only he could talk to her, explain, apologise, grab her by the hand and run away. No, it's over. He has to stop this.

Distraction, he needs a distraction.

On cue, Tristan walks over with *The Sun* and opens it to Emma, 22, from Bournemouth.

'Your type?' he asks, grinning.

But Malachi's not in the mood to see Bournemouth Emma, or talk to Tristan, or write a thesis. He only wants Pamela.

Tristan sulks back out to the balcony to read his newspaper cover to cover, just as any fifteen-year-old, with a keen interest in current affairs, would. After this he will continue with his mission to help Malachi get over Pamela, and the only way to do it is to get under someone else. Tristan once heard some sixth-former girls describe his brother as 'dark and brooding', which apparently doesn't just mean that he's black and grumpy, women actually find him *attractive*. So it shouldn't be that hard to get him laid.

There's a smashing sound from the foot of the block and Tristan looks over the balcony.

The jar of chocolate spread has smashed everywhere and Lina doesn't have a clue how to clean up such a thing, so she walks off and hopes no one saw her.

Inside the cool, tiled ground floor of Nightingale Point, the caretaker shakes his head at the mess. 'Don't worry, dear, I'll get that cleaned up. Don't you worry a bit.'

'Thanks,' Lina says. A small blessing in the sea of shit that is her day so far. She hits the call button for the lift but nothing. 'Please tell me they're working?'

The caretaker cups his ear at her. 'What's that, dear?'

'The lifts,' she says.

He fills his travel kettle and shrugs. 'I've logged a call but it's bank holiday, innit.'

Lina pushes on the heavy door to the stairwell and sighs as she looks at the first of ten flights of stairs. 'By the way,' she calls back at the caretaker, 'I think there's kids on the roof again.'

Pamela loves being on the roof, for the solitude, for the freedom, and for the small possibility that she might spot, walking across the field below, Malachi. She has to see him today and they have to talk. Today's the day; it has to be.

At the foot of the block the caretaker tips a kettle of water over a dark splodge on the floor and gets his mop out. Just another mess to clean up at Nightingale Point.

CHAPTER ONE

Elvis

Elvis hates to leave his flat, as it is so full of perfect things. Like the sparkly grey lino in the bathroom, the television, and the laminated pictures tacked up everywhere reminding him how to lock the door securely and use the grill.

'Elvis?' Lina calls. 'You want curried chicken or steak and kidney?'

Elvis does not answer; he is too busy hiding behind the sliding door that separates the kitchen and living room, watching Lina unpack the Weetabix, bread and strawberry jam. She unscrews the jar and puts one of her fingers inside, which is a bad thing to do because of germs, but Elvis understands because strawberry jam can be so tasty.

This is the nineteenth day of Lina being Elvis's nurse. He knows this as he marked her first day on the calendar with a big smiley face. There are fourteen smiley faces on the calendar and five sad faces because this is when Lina was late.

She puts the jar of jam in the cupboard and returns to the shopping bags, taking out a net of oranges. Elvis hates oranges; they are sticky and smelly. He had asked for tomatoes but Lina said that tomatoes are an ingredient not a snack and that oranges are full of the kind of vitamins Elvis needed to make his brain work better and stop him from being a pest.

Lina's face disappears behind a cupboard door and Elvis watches as her pink coloured nails rap on the outside. He likes Lina's shiny pink nails, especially when her hair is pink too.

'Elllviiiis?' she sings.

He puts a big hand over his mouth to muffle the laughter, but then sees Lina has removed the red tin from the shopping bag – the curried chicken pie. He gasps as he realises he wants steak and kidney.

'Bloody hell!' She jumps and raises the tinned pie above her head, as if ready to throw it. 'What the hell you doing? You spying on me?'

'No, no, no.'

'Elvis, why are you wearing a sweatshirt? It's too hot for that.' She slams the tin down on the counter.

'Steak and kidney pie,' he tells her. 'I want steak and kidney pie. It's the blue tin.'

'Yeah, all right, all right.'

'Can I have two?' he tries, knowing his food has been limited. He is unsure why.

'No, Elvis, that's greedy. Now go. Get changed. You're sweating.'

'Get changed into what?' he asks.

'A T-shirt, Elvis. It's bloody baking out; go put on a T-shirt.'

Elvis goes through to his bedroom and removes his sweatshirt. He stands for a moment and looks over his round belly in the mirror, moisture glistening among the curly ginger hairs

5

that cover his whole front. When he takes off his glasses his reflection looks watery, like one of his dreams. He then pulls on his favourite new T-shirt, which is bright blue and has a picture of the King on it. It also has the words *The King* in gold swirly writing. He smiles at himself before going to the living room to sit on his new squashy sofa.

Elvis listens carefully to the steps Lina takes to make the pie: the flick of the ignition, the slam of a pot on the gas ring. Then, the sound he likes best, the click of her pearly plastic nails on the worktops. He loves all the flavours the tinned pies come in and he likes the curried chicken pie most days, but today he really does want steak and kidney.

'Right, master, your pie is on the boil,' Lina says as she walks into the living room. 'Nice,' she says, acknowledging his T-shirt.

'Are we going to the bank holiday fair?' He had seen posters for it Sellotaped up on bus shelters and in the windows of off-licences: *Wilson and Sons Fairground on the Heath, 3–6 May. Helter Skelter, Dodgems, Ghost Train!* He really wants to go.

'Yeah, maybe when it cools down a bit.' Lina flops on the sofa next to him and picks up the phone. 'Go.' She waves him away. 'Why you sitting so close to me? I *am* entitled to a break.'

But Elvis is comfy on the sofa and he has already sorted the stickers from his *Merlin's Premier League* sticker book and watered his tomato plants on the windowsills. He has already carefully used his razor to remove the wispy orange hairs from his face as George, his care worker, had taught him, and rubbed the coconut suntan lotion into his skin as he knows to do on hot days. This morning Elvis has already done everything he was meant to and now he wants to eat his steak and kidney pie and go to the fair.

Lina has his new special phone in her hand. Elvis loves his phone; it is his favourite thing in his new living room, after the television. The phone is so special that you can only make a call when you put money inside and you can only get the money out with a special key that George looks after. Beside the phone sits a laminated sheet with all the numbers Elvis will ever need: a little drawing of a policeman – 999; a photograph of Elvis's mum wearing the purple hat she reserves for church and having her photograph taken – 018 566 1641; and a photograph of George behind his desk – 018 522 7573. Elvis is trying to learn all the numbers by heart but sometimes when he tries, he gets distracted by the fantastic noise the laminated sheet makes if you wave it in the air fast. Next to the phone is a ceramic dish shaped like a boat that says *Margate* on it. The dish is kept filled with change for when Elvis needs to make a call.

He watches carefully as Lina feeds the phone with his change and starts to dial, her lovely pink nails hitting the dial pad: 018 557.

'Go and sit somewhere else,' she snaps.

But there is nowhere else to sit apart from the perfect squashy sofa, so Elvis goes into the kitchen where he can watch and listen to Lina from behind the door. In secret.

'Hi . . . I'm at work. Elvis is driving me nuts today,' she says into the phone. 'He keeps bloody staring at me . . . Yeah I know . . . Tell me about it . . . Ha ha. Yeah, true true . . . ' She slides off her plimsolls and pulls the coffee table closer, putting her little feet up on it. 'But you know what my mum's like, always busting my arse over something: look after your baby, wash the dishes, get more shifts. I thought the whole point of having a baby was that you didn't have to go work no more . . . Exactly . . . Especially on a day like this. Bloody roasting out.'

Even from behind the door Elvis can see that the nails on Lina's toes are the same colour as those on her fingers, but shorter. The colour looks like the insides of the seashells Elvis collected at Margate last summer. He likes Lina's toes; this is the first time he has ever seen Lina's toes. He likes them but knows he is not allowed to touch them.

'Can I have a biscuit?' Elvis asks as he comes out from behind the door, now peckish and unable to wait for the pie to boil.

'Hang on. What?' Lina rests the phone under her chin like one of the office girls at the Waterside Centre, the place where Elvis used to live before he was clever enough to live by himself in Nightingale Point.

'Can I have a biscuit?' he asks again.

'I'm on the phone, leave me in peace.' She tuts then returns to her call. 'But look, yeah, I'm coming to the fair later. Soon as I'm done with the dumb giant here I'll be down . . . I'll get it; pay me later.' Lina slides the rest of the money from the ceramic boat into her pocket.

Elvis pictures the laminated sheet of Golden Rules that hangs in his bedroom. Rule Number One: Do not let strangers into your flat. Rule Number Two: Do not let anybody touch your private swimming costume parts. Rule Number Three: Do not let anyone take your things. Lina is breaking one of the Golden Rules. Elvis must call George and report her immediately.

Lina picks up the laminated sheet of phone numbers and uses it to fan herself. It makes her pink fringe flap up and down, and Elvis wants to watch it but he also knows that he must report her rule break. George once told him that if he could not get to the house phone and it was an emergency, he could go outside to the phone box to make a call. The phone box, on the other side of the little field in front of the estate, is the second emergency phone. Elvis must now go there. He leaves the living room and slips on his sandals at the door. *Jesus sandals*, Lina calls them, but Elvis does not think Jesus would have worn such stylish footwear in the olden days. He opens the front door gently, quietly enough that Lina will not hear. Then, and only because he knows he is allowed to leave the flat to use the second phone for when he cannot use the first phone, Elvis steps out of flat thirty-seven and heads into the hallway of the tenth floor.

Make sure you don't miss this breathtaking novel from Luan Goldie...

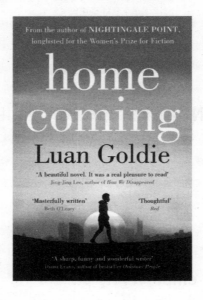

From the author of NIGHTINGALE POINT, longlisted for the Women's Prize for Fiction

home coming
Luan Goldie

'A beautiful novel. It was a real pleasure to read'
Jing-Jing Lee, author of *How We Disappeared*

'Masterfully written'
Beth O'Leary

'Thoughtful'
Red

'A sharp, funny and wonderful writer'
Diana Evans, author of bestseller *Ordinary People*

For years **Yvonne** has tried to keep her demons buried and focus on moving forward. But her guilt is always with her and weighs heavily on her heart.

Kiama has had to grow up without a mother, and while there is so much he remembers about her, there is still plenty he doesn't know. And there's only one person who can fill in the gaps.

Lewis wants nothing more than to keep Kiama, his son, safe, but the thought of Kiama dredging up the past worries Lewis deeply. And Lewis doesn't know if he's ready to let the only woman he's ever loved back into his life.

When Kiama seeks Yvonne out and asks her to come with him to Kenya, the place that holds the answers to his questions, she knows she can't refuse. And this one act sets in motion an unravelling of the past that no one is ready for.

ONE PLACE. MANY STORIES

Bold, innovative and
empowering publishing.

FOLLOW US ON:

@HQStories